Tom

When finally she co

edge of his cloak, he … her bonnet even straighter as though she was in church, the silence that followed was in no way oppressive.

It was he who broke it.

'I was dismayed to hear you had lost the inn, Miss Grimshaw. Indeed I had the idea I might call and . . .'

'Yes, Captain Cooper?' Her voice held a warning note since Sally Grimshaw required no man's sympathy . . .

'I suppose last January . . . well, you were kind to me.' He grinned, not looking at her. 'Kind in that no nonsense way you have and I felt . . . perhaps . . . I could . . .'

'Yes, Captain?' Her chin lifted even higher . . .

He looked up, 'Do you know, Miss Grimshaw, it is the very devil trying to persuade you to allow a kindness.'

More Coronet paperbacks by Audrey Howard

The Mallow Years
Shining Threads
A Day Will Come
All the Dear Faces
There Is No Parting
Echo of Another Time
The Woman from Browhead
The Silence of Strangers
A World of Difference
Promises Lost
The Shadowed Hills
Strand of Dreams

About the author

Audrey Howard was born in Liverpool in 1929 and it is from that once-great seaport that many of the ideas for her books come. Before she began to write she had a variety of jobs, among them hairdresser, model, shop assistant, cleaner and civil servant. In 1981, out of work and living in Australia, she wrote the first of her novels. She was fifty-two. Her fourth novel, *The Juniper Bush*, won the Romantic Novel of the Year Award in 1988. She now lives in her childhood home, St Anne's on Sea, Lancashire.

Tomorrow's Memories

Audrey Howard

CORONET BOOKS
Hodder and Stoughton

First published in Great Britain in 1997
by Hodder and Stoughton
A division of Hodder Headline PLC
First published in paperback in 1998 by Hodder and Stoughton
A Coronet Paperback

8

British Library Cataloguing in Publication Data

Howard, Audrey
Tomorrow's Memories
1. English fiction – 20th century
I.Title
823.9'14 [F]

ISBN 978 0 340 66607 4

Typeset by Hewer Text Ltd, Edinburgh
Printed and bound in Great Britain by
CPI Mackays, Chatham ME5 8TD

Hodder and Stoughton
A division of Hodder Headline PLC
338 Euston Road
London NW1 3BH

I would like to dedicate this book
with my thanks for their help and patience
to all the staff at St Anne's Public Lending Library.

Today we make tomorrow's memories.

~ 1

Sally Grimshaw was twenty-four and a virgin, though neither of these factors was uppermost in her mind as she breathed heavily on the already gleaming brass, gave it another vigorous buffing then stepped back to study her handiwork. She narrowed her eyes, sighed and shook her head as though not at all satisfied.

She was polishing the handles of the pumps, engrossed in her work, going at it with her customary furious determination, and when the soldier hesitated in the taproom doorway she failed to notice him. She was giving the brass handles "what for", as Freddy jokingly called it, just as she did everything, from the mud traipsed across the taproom floor to the ordering of the maidservants in her employ, throwing the whole weight of her slight body into her work. Freddy, who was a bit of a wag in his own opinion and was never short of a word on any subject, said she gave the impression that a puff of wind would have her over. Not a "pick" on her, he said, but not unkindly since there was not an unkind bone in Freddy's body, but as she had proved since she was eight years old and their ma died, her appearance was deceptive. She had heard herself described as dainty, fragile as gossamer, whatever that meant, slender as a willow, but she had a strong spirit and a natural confidence which overcame these, what you might call handicaps, and had put them to good use. She could do more work in half the time and with double the efficiency of Bridie and Jane put together and they were considered to be good workers. They should be. She'd chosen and trained them. But she liked things done properly and she'd found that the only way to achieve this was to do it herself. Obviously this was not possible in an inn the size of the Grimshaw Arms so she did the next best thing which was to keep a keen eye on everything the two servants did.

She was humming to herself as she worked the duster round the pump handles. She had her own way of doing it. You folded the duster lengthwise a couple of times, then, taking an end in each hand, you worked it backwards and forwards round the handles, your arms moving to a swift rhythm. You got a lovely shine on them but you had to go at it a bit, so she was unaware of the figure who wavered in the doorway. She was also unaware that the enthusiasm with which she applied her duster moved almost every part of her body. Her silver-streaked tawny hair, silken and curly when loose, tumbled and bobbed, floating tendrils wisping down across her face. At intervals she blew them impatiently upwards but they drifted down again. Her shoulders jerked with the action of her arms and her nicely rounded breasts jiggled in two separate movements beneath the immaculate white cotton of her pin-tucked bodice. Her sleeves were rolled up to allow her to work more freely, and to protect her cuffs, and the creamy skin of her arms glowed in the sunshine which flooded in through the two deep bay windows.

She was just leaning forward to check that she could see her own reflection in the gleaming brass when she suddenly became aware that she was no longer alone. She pivoted sharply, beginning to frown when she saw the silent, motionless figure in the doorway. The door, which led from the taproom in to Prescot Lane, stood wide open to let out some of last night's pipe smoke, which created an impenetrable fug at times, and the clear January light was at his back, outlining his tall frame. It startled her and when Sally Grimshaw was startled or upset she went on the attack at once. She'd get herself into a pickle over it one of these days, Freddy warned her good-naturedly, but she couldn't help it.

"Saints preserve us, don't you know better than to lurk in a doorway like that?" she snapped, putting her hand and the duster in it to her breast. "You gave me an awful fright. What are you doing?" And when there was no answer, "What d'you want? Are you to come in or go out? Make up your mind because I've no time to stand about passing the time of day," as though the man was doing his best to engage her in conversation. "We open in half an hour and this floor's still to be scrubbed."

Not that Sally Grimshaw was to scrub it. Bridie or Jane would get down on their knees and do that, for Sally was the publican's sister and did not concern herself with heavy or menial work, except the eagle-eyed overseeing of it.

She paused, again blowing upwards a gleaming strand of pale hair which had drifted across her lips, then, as though becoming unexpectedly aware of her dishevelled state, she smoothed her two hands over the wayward, sliding mane of it. In a moment she had it captured and disciplined, severely scraped back from her forehead into some invisible fastening at the nape of her neck, though a few short and endearingly wayward tendrils still managed to escape over her ears. With a couple of fluid movements, neither of them wasted since Sally Grimshaw was not one for waste of any sort, she rolled down her sleeves, whisked off her apron, then lifted an imperious head, satisfied that she presented the orderly and businesslike appearance she and her customers were used to. She tapped her foot and tightened her lips which, moments before, had been parted and rosy.

"Well?" she challenged, waiting for the man in the doorway to answer but he continued to hover there, swaying slightly, she thought, and at once her suspicious mind jumped to the conclusion that this was not the first inn he had visited today.

"Didn't you hear me? We're not open yet," she went on sharply, "so if it's a drink you're after you'd best wait outside. There's a bench if you want to sit down," which, it seemed to her, might be wise in his present state though it was not exactly the weather for hanging about. A thick hoar frost was spread like icing sugar across the fields opposite the inn, the sunlight turning every blade of grass, every tree and hedgerow to a silver and white tracery against the paleness of the winter blue sky. They sparkled with frost crystals, dazzling like tiny diamonds but it was not the kind of daydreaming Sally Grimshaw had time for, not with a bar to open, dinners for God alone knew how many travellers to be got ready, Freddy to flush out from wherever he hid himself whenever there was work to be done, the cellarman to supervise and the maids to chivvy into the kind of activity which the busy inn demanded.

But though Sally had been born in, had lived and worked in an inn for the whole of her life there was nothing she abhorred more than drunkenness and if she was not mistaken, and she very seldom was, this chap was in the far stages of it and it wasn't even midday yet!

Her lips thinned into an even grimmer line and she scowled, treating the pump handle to another vigorous slap with her duster. Now that she had given the brass "what for" and the length of her tongue to the man leaning in the doorway, she was ready to turn away towards the kitchen and the steak and kidney pies she had put in the oven twenty minutes ago and which would be ready to come out. She'd need to get behind Bridie and Jane if the taproom, the bar parlour, the snug and the coffee-room were to open on time. Fortunately the last overnight guest had gone, dashing off in the direction of Liverpool in a hackney cab after eating one of Sally's splendid breakfasts, on urgent business, he had told her, as he settled his bill.

The soldier did not move except to take off his cap and put a hand to the door frame to steady himself. Sally clicked her tongue impatiently.

"I'm sorry, sir" – doing her best to be polite since this was an inn and all men were customers – "but I'm afraid I must ask you to wait outside." Her voice was firm. She was not unduly concerned that he might turn nasty, for any woman who could deal with Abe Cartwright after he'd drunk his usual dozen or so pints of ale or stout on a Saturday night could certainly handle this chap, whoever he was. Freddy said it was like watching a kitten square up to a tiger and well worth the losing of Abe's custom as he turned tail and fled into the night, which was the sort of daft thing Freddy was always saying. Besides, in the unlikely event that Sally Grimshaw could not manage, she knew Job was within calling distance.

The soldier appeared not to hear her or if he did was not prepared to do as he was told. What was the matter with the man? Didn't he speak the Queen's English, or was he deaf? Surely he could see the place was not yet open for business? Well, she would soon see him off her doorstep with a flea in his ear – she must get Bridie to give the step another wipe-over – since she'd neither the time nor the inclination to be arguing with him. Really, some folk thought they could just ignore the rules by which others lived and worked, marching high-handedly wherever they chose and demanding service as though it was their due. Anyway, even if she was persuaded to let him stay, which she wasn't, she couldn't have him sprawling at his ease by her fireside, legs stretched out to the flames as Bridie did her best to scrub round him.

Stepping out from behind the bar counter, her chin raised in a manner many of her customers would have instantly recognised and quailed from, Sally walked purposefully across the taproom towards the soldier, ready to throw him out into the lane herself if necessary, noticing for the first time that he was an officer. He wore a long, medium grey coat, double-breasted, which ended about twelve inches from the floor, with brass buttons which half of her mind registered needed a good polish. What she could see of his trousers were dark blue, narrow, with a red stripe down the outside of each leg.

"Madam," he said at last, his voice somewhat slurred, confirming her opinion that he was already drunk as a fiddler's bitch, which was one of Freddy's more colourful phrases. As he spoke he bowed politely but instead of straightening up again he continued a downward journey in a fall as slow and graceful as a tree which has just been felled. Even with the light behind him she could see every vestige of colour drain from his face. His eyes rolled up and he hit the floor with a thump Sally felt through the soles of her well-polished boots. His sword, which hung from a belt at his waist, made a horrible clatter as it hit the floor.

"Dear heavens, what next?" Sally fretted, just as though

the soldier had fallen with the sole purpose of annoying her. Even yet she still believed he was the worse for drink, though you didn't often find a gentleman, an officer, in such a condition at this time of day, and alone. Sometimes the young squirearchy, those from what were known as "good" families, or "old" families, came carousing on their fine thoroughbreds, clattering into the yard, invading the taproom and the bar parlour, loud, arrogant, thinking it a "hell of a joke" to drink with the common man. Four or five of them at a time, taking it as their right to make free with her two pretty barmaids who didn't mind a bit but she did, and said so.

But they were like children in a nursery who had been reprimanded by Nanny when Miss Grimshaw had done with them. Good as gold and quiet as mice, almost apologising, which made the regulars smile, for they knew that so long as no one offended the publican's sister by swearing, spitting, or taking liberties with her or her barmaids, their money was as good as anybody's at the Grimshaw Arms. Mind, it'd be a brave man who tried to take liberties with sharp-tongued Sally Grimshaw!

But this was and always had been a country inn, plain and unpretentious, which attracted the villagers from Old Swan, Knotty Ash and the surrounding district. Farm labourers, men from the Liverpool Crown Glass Works, the nurseries at Oak Vale, the Rope Works in Eden Lane, gardeners, grooms, underfootmen from some of the big houses in the area, but certainly not an officer who, though Sally did not know his rank since she was not familiar with the insignia on his overcoat, appeared to be from a Liverpool regiment.

She leaned over him gingerly but could detect no smell of ale or even brandy on his breath, brandy being the most likely drink a man of his class would take. So what was wrong with him? Now that he was no longer blocking the doorway the pale sunlight fell across him, touching his hair which was a dull grey mixed with pure silver. It was thick, uncut, a shaggy tumble of rough curls which fell over his ears and the high collar of his overcoat. His cheek was pressed to the stone flags, his face in profile. It was as grey as his hair and dewed with sweat.

Sally knelt down, her full, serge skirt, which was held out by half a dozen starched white petticoats, billowing out around her. The skirt was dark grey, plain, well made and eminently suitable for the mistress of a plain household, which Sally considered herself to be. Round her slender waist was a broad belt from which hung a beautifully crafted filigree housekeeper's châtelaine. From it hung a dozen keys, a small pair of silver scissors in an embossed sheath, a watch, a thimble, a tiny scent bottle with a silver top, scent being Sally's one weakness in her total disregard for female embellishment, each article with its own silver chain linked with swivel catches to the silver-embossed plate which was attached to her belt. It was an exquisite thing which she had seen in the window of Thomas Dismore, a silversmith in Dale Street and which, in an unusually impulsive gesture, she had fallen in love with and purchased.

She put out a tentative hand to the soldier's hair, for some odd reason feeling a strong urge to smooth it back from his brow. It was rough, unbrushed and sweated on his scalp. His face was gaunt, sunken so that the bony sockets of his eyes and the high, flat bones of his cheeks seemed about to pierce his flesh. The flesh itself was hot, damp and pale.

He lay as one dead as her fingers gently rested on the line of his jaw which was prickly to her touch as though he had not shaved recently, the whiskers gleaming a dull silver in the shaft of sunlight which fell across him.

There was a crash from the kitchen and voices were raised and it was this that brought her back to the realisation of not only where she was but what time of day it was. A frantic glance at the clock on the wall told her she had less than half an hour before customers would be hammering on the door to be let in.

"Freddy," she called out. "Freddy, where are you? Get yourself out here and fetch Job with you. And don't be all day about it, either."

"Sal, Elly's just dropped the soup pan and I'm—"

"Never mind the soup pan, Freddy, Elly can see to that. Get out here right away."

"But, Sal, I'm—"

Before the aggrieved voice could enlarge on the crisis in the kitchen, Sally raised hers, not loudly but with that tone which told her brother that he'd best look lively or there'd be trouble.

"Never mind that, Freddy Grimshaw. Go and find Job and then come back here, both of you, and quickly, please."

"Aah, Sally . . ."

"Freddy!"

The soldier looked so dreadful and so uncomfortable with his cheek pressed to the floor that without thinking Sally moved from a kneeling position, lowering herself beside him until she could turn him a little and lift his head into her lap. She was shocked by the drawn lines of suffering about his mouth and the deep smudges beneath his eyes. He had strong, pronounced eyebrows, dark against his putty-coloured flesh, a wide mouth which, even in his present sorry state, curled at the corners as though he were about to smile and the longest, thickest eyelashes she had ever seen on a man.

They began to flutter as she bent over him and a sound which might have been a groan emerged from between his pale, parted lips.

"Freddy, where the dickens are you?" she called out through gritted teeth, since Sally Grimshaw was not known for her patience and, as though her voice had reached down into the dark cavern where he had toppled, the soldier opened his eyes. They were blank, unfocused and yet even in their emptiness were the striking colour of the "dolly blue" Sally's ma and then Sally herself put into the dolly tub to whiten the white of Freddy's shirts and the linen from the beds. Against the grey of his skin and hair they were startling.

Consciousness was returning to him, showing itself in a frown as though he were wondering what the devil he was doing with his head in the lap of a woman he did not recognise.

He stared up at her, then blinked, his almost black lashes falling and rising slowly a couple of times as his eyes became properly focused. Something that might have been a smile flickered across his face.

"Well, lad," he said, as though to himself, "if you're going to faint you might as well do it into the arms of an attractive woman."

"Sir?"

"Madam, I do beg your pardon." He was doing his best to sit up and his voice was as weak as his efforts. "I cannot think what came over me. Have I been here . . . long?" He put one trembling hand to his head and with Sally's help managed to sit up, supporting himself on the stone-flagged floor with the other.

Sally scrambled to her feet. She smoothed down her skirt, then lifted a hand to her hair, briskly brushing back several wayward tendrils.

"No, sir, not long. I think you must have fainted but my brother has gone to fetch the cellarman to give you a hand up."

"That's extremely good of them and perhaps . . . if you have a stable lad. My horse is at the front."

"You've ridden here on a horse?" He might have admitted to flying in on the wings of a bird she was so astounded. Her tone was biting, telling him he should have had more sense in his condition.

"Yes, I'm afraid I did. A cab would have been more prudent, I know." He smiled ruefully to reveal excellent teeth.

"Indeed it would," she answered crisply, giving her full skirt a vigorous twitch to reinforce her disapproval.

"It's just that I've been cooped up for weeks on that bloody ship . . . oh, do forgive me. I have been so long in the company of men my manners have been forgotten. I am so sorry."

"That's all right, sir," she heard herself saying, incredibly, since she did not allow "language" in *her* taproom. "But don't try to get up," as he began an attempt to get to his feet "I don't know where Freddy's got to but he won't be long and then he and Job will give you a hand. Or perhaps I could . . ."

He looked up at her and smiled weakly. She was no bigger than two pennorth o' copper, as his old nanny used to say, slender as a wand with a tiny waist and fine-boned wrists, though he did notice that her bosom was pleasingly rounded. He must be feeling better, he told himself, or was it that it was so long since he had seen a woman who was not swathed in a voluminous nurse's apron he could not help but be aware of this one's shape? It was not that she was even very pretty though she did smell quite delightful. Some light fragrance that was not sweet but sharp and pleasant, like the sandalwood which came from the vast continent in which he had fought so many battles, not all of them as a soldier.

'I'm heavier than you think, madam, despite a lack of what might be called a decent meal for many months. And then the voyage . . .' He sighed pensively then shook his head as though his thoughts were getting away from him. He fell silent and Sally wondered what he had been about to say.

There was a clatter of hobnailed boots as heavy feet climbed the stone steps from the cellar and two men emerged from behind the bar counter, one big and burly and unsmiling, the other tall, long-boned, slender and as fair as the woman. The relationship between them was very evident. He was smiling cheerfully.

"What's up, Sal?" he enquired, then, catching sight of the soldier who, despite his own efforts, was still sprawled at Sally's feet, his smile deepened and a knowing look appeared on his face. Before he could say what was obviously on his mind, Sally spoke tartly.

"This gentleman is not well, Freddy, and we'd be obliged" – unconsciously linking herself to the fallen man – "if you and Job would get him to his feet and into the chair by the fire."

"Right, Sal." Freddy's grin deepened even further and to Sally's mortification he winked at Job. Job seemed not to notice.

If it was possible, the soldier's face became even whiter as the two men lifted him and a small moan escaped from between his lips, the bottom one of which he caught in his teeth.

"Be careful, the pair of you," Sally admonished sharply.

There was a sturdy rocking-chair before the fire with a rush seat and, urged by his sister, Freddy and the cellarman placed the soldier carefully in it.

"There you are, sir, how's that?" Freddy asked affably, again turning to wink at Job.

They had gone off to their respective tasks, obedient as children to Sally's orders and she was about to suggest, if he was capable of it, that she and her patient might move to her private sitting-room when there was another interruption.

"We've done bedrooms an' upstairs landin', Miss Grimshaw," a voice piped from the back regions of the room and the head of a young woman popped over the bar counter. The head was neatly encased in a snowy white cap so that not a scrap of her hair showed and her face was scrubbed to the colour and polish of a rosy red apple. "Me an' Bridie was wonderin' . . ."

The woman's jaw dropped and her eyes widened dramatically as they ran over the scene in the taproom and again Sally tutted and frowned. Her brows dipped over her eyes which turned in a fraction of a second from a warm, golden glow to a flat brown.

"Never mind wondering, Jane. You know what has to be done as well as I do but before you start go and tell Tim-Pat there's a horse at the front needs seeing to."

"A horse?" Jane gasped.

"Yes, you know what a horse is, I believe."

"Yes, mum, but . . ."

"And when you've done that you and Bridie can scrub this floor." Sally glanced at the man who was slumped in the rocking-chair as though every tiny movement of the rockers was agony to him, and then back at the clock. "You have ten minutes."

"Nay, we'll never manage it in ten minutes, Miss Grimshaw." Jane was clearly appalled.

"Of course you will, but first bring me a brandy."

"A brandy, mum?" It was plain the maid was becoming seriously confused.

"Please, and on your way close the front door. It's getting cold in here."

"Yes, mum."

"And before you bring your bucket just check that Elly's taken the pies out of the oven."

"I don't know if I can remember all that, mum," the maid wailed plaintively, dithering from foot to foot as though not sure which direction to take first and Sally sighed.

"Never mind, I'll get the brandy." Leaving her charge for a moment she whisked behind the bar, uncorked a bottle which stood on a dresser at the back, poured brandy into a glass and on her way back closed the front door with a graceful kick of her booted foot. Sinking to her knees before the soldier, she put the glass to his lips with the resolute air of someone who would not be argued with.

"Drink," she commanded him. "Slowly."

He drank.

"I'm sorry to be so much trouble," he managed to say between sips, but already a wisp of colour was returning to his face.

"Rubbish. It's no trouble. Now drink."

The soldier sipped his brandy, holding the glass himself now, a small smile lifting the corners of his mouth.

"I hope you won't be offended if I say you remind me of a drill sergeant I knew in India. Are you always this autocratic?"

"I have to be," she answered crisply, "else they'd all be at sixes and sevens and nothing done."

"Yes, I can see that. It's the same in the army. Someone has to take command. Does your family own the inn?" He was recovering now but Sally continued to kneel at his feet, much to the amazement of the two maids who had brought in their buckets and brushes and were preparing to attack the mixed red and blue flagstones at the far end of the room.

"Move that chair, Bridie, you can't scrub round it," her mistress told her testily then turned back to the man in the chair. "I'm sorry, you were saying? And drink all that brandy, if you please." Sally's voice was firm.

"Oh, I will, I daren't do otherwise. I was asking if your family own the inn."

"Yes, my brother's the publican."

"But you're the master."

Her mouth dropped open in surprise and she sat back on her heels.

"I beg your pardon?"

He smiled and shrugged. "You've just admitted it. It's your voice they listen to."

And his now, Sally noticed, as the two maids moved steadily across the floor towards them, ears cocked so as not to miss a word.

"Do you feel well enough to walk through to my private sitting-room, sir?" she asked briskly. "Only the customers will be in in a moment and it can get very noisy. You'd be more comfortable there. And from what you tell me it seems you are in need of a proper meal. I'm a good cook," she told him with a hint of pride in her voice. A touch of pink flushed her cheeks and she smiled, a wide smile which altered her whole face, lighting it from within so that her creamy skin was like porcelain with a candle held behind it.

And her smile was crooked! It was in every way different to the polite, professional smile she bestowed on her customers and, in the past fifteen minutes, on him. One corner of her mouth lifted higher than the other, giving her an elfin look, almost mischievous. Her eyes were golden, like the sun trapped in honey and the soldier marvelled at the change in her.

"There's a steak and kidney pie with good brown gravy and a decent crust, cabbage mashed with pepper and butter, and potatoes, the vegetables home-grown. And I make a nice custard which I think you might like . . ." you being under the weather, her incredible eyes told him. He was clearly startled, watching her with new interest. "Then, when you're feeling better we'll see about getting you home. Do you live nearby?"

He indicated that he did and she nodded her head in a satisfied way.

"Tim-Pat's taken your animal round to the stables and I think it would be best if you took a cab home. Tim-Pat will ride your animal back for you. That was a nasty fall and . . ."

He smiled wryly and held up one hand as though to ward off a persistent may-fly, careful not to spill the brandy. "Miss Grimshaw . . . it is Miss Grimshaw, is it not? We could have done with your talent for command and organisational skill at Scutari, indeed we could."

"Scutari?"

"It's in the Crimea, Miss Grimshaw."

"Yes, I know where it is. You were in the Crimea, sir?"

"Yes, I was wounded at Inkerman. They nursed me – I caught a fever – then it was decided that as many of the sick and wounded as possible should be sent home. Two hundred and forty-three rank and file. I was one of four officers who, being useless as fighting men, were put in charge of the arrangements. The steamship *Cambria* arrived in the Mersey yesterday and after seeing that the sick and wounded were comfortably housed in a building adjoining the workhouse I commandeered one of the horses and since my house is close by . . . well, I rather foolishly imagined I could ride there and . . . you know the rest."

He shrugged, sipping the brandy which slid down in a comforting stream to his stomach where it rested in warm and soothing peace. Perhaps he would have some of Miss Grimshaw's steak and kidney pie before he set off for home, for it was a long time since there had been anything on his plate which tasted or smelled of anything resembling food. If he could get to his feet with the help of this young woman he might remove his greatcoat. His damned arm was aching like the devil, the pressure of the heavy material rubbing on the half-healed wound which ran from the back of his neck to his elbow.

He sighed and took another sip of brandy. The young woman, Miss Grimshaw, was still at his feet and now that she had lost that ferocious air of a sheepdog herding a flock of reluctant sheep was quite pleasing to look at. Her eyes were the exact shade of the brandy he was drinking and her hair, dragged back from her forehead into an enormous chignon, was a mixture of gold, silver and pale streaked amber, its obvious inclination to curl totally annihilated by a stiff brush and a ruthless hand. It was very pleasant to sit here, relaxed, warm, comfortable and relatively free from pain for the first time in months.

There was a deep silence. The two maids exchanged glances, grimacing since they had never seen their mistress look so . . . so . . . well, in their shared opinion, so witless! She was just kneeling there looking up at the gentleman who was nothing to write home about when all was said and done. He was old, with grey hair and a face on him like a suet dumpling. No, not a dumpling. That implied he was fat and he wasn't. In fact the army greatcoat he wore looked as though it had been made for someone else and when, at last, he stood up with Miss Grimshaw's arm to help him, the sword at his belt seemed to drag him lopsided.

Their mistress suddenly became aware that not only were the maids waiting patiently to scrub the bit of floor she and the soldier were standing on but that several fists were hammering at the outside door.

"Good Lord, what are you two doing hanging about with your buckets in your hand when there are customers at the door? And where are Edie and Flo? Go and find them at once. I don't know, I only have to take my eyes off you for a moment and chaos reigns."

Bridie, who happened to glance at the soldier as her mistress was speaking, was disconcerted, then reduced to a fit of the giggles when he winked at her.

"And I can see nothing funny in that, Bridie."

"No, mum, sorry, mum. Shall we let them in?"

Sally turned to the patient figure of the soldier whose manner implied he was waiting for his orders.

"Now then, sir . . ."

"My name is Cooper, Miss Grimshaw. Adam Cooper of Coopers Edge. Late captain of the Lancashire Fusiliers." He tried for a formal bow, wincing as he did so.

"Cooper? Of Coopers Edge, you said." Her voice had an almost accusing note in it as though he had deliberately withheld some vital information from her.

"Indeed, you know of my family?"

"Of course, who doesn't round these parts?"

Even as she spoke she knew she had put her foot in it. His face closed up and his clear eyes froze to chips of blue ice. The words had popped out before she could stop them and she could have bitten her tongue. She had deeply offended him, she could see that, but the irony of it was she had not meant what he obviously thought she did. Certainly his history was well known and a provoking one it was too, with everyone for miles around in a positive ferment of excited fascination when it had happened. At the time she had felt as sorry for him as the rest of the community. She had been a girl of no more than fifteen or so but even then she had had none of the other females' inclination to gossip.

But it was not the scandal she had referred to when she spoke out, simply that the Coopers were an old Liverpool family of impeccable breeding and were well known, as the Hemingways or the Osbornes were, to them all. From the rigidly clamped line of his mouth and the set of his proud head that was not what *he* believed.

"Of course." His voice was hard and he drew himself up, dragging his arm from her supporting hand. "Now, if I may avail myself of your offer to wait in your sitting-room until a cab is called. Thank you, no, please, do not concern yourself about me any further. Go about your duties as though I weren't here. I will not detain you any further."

"Will you not have something to eat, Captain Cooper?" she asked him, lifting her own regal head, not caring for his extremely polite but barely concealed arrogance. It was as though he was telling her she was no more than a servant after all and he was sorry he had allowed himself to be involved with her.

"Thank you, no."

"Very well."

She turned, her eyes as dark as those of an eagle he had once seen while deer-stalking in the Highlands of Scotland.

"Go about your business," she snapped at the two maids and they hastily edged away from her.

"Madam, the room, if you please." He could not wait to be out of her company, it seemed.

"Bridie, show this gentleman to my sitting-room."

"Yes, mum."

"Thank you, Miss Grimshaw, I'm obliged."

"Not at all, Captain Cooper. I hope you are soon recovered."

She nodded coolly and, lifting her grey skirt an inch or so from the still wet floor, swept from the taproom with the hauteur of a duchess.

2

The Grimshaw Arms had been in the hands of the Grimshaw family for forty years. Sally's grandfather, Ned Grimshaw, having had enough of farming, he told his patient wife, sold his farm and bought himself an inn on the road between Old Swan and Knotty Ash so that, on a fine evening, he could sit in his own bar parlour, drinking the pint of ale he himself had pulled and look out over the land for which he had got a good price, but it had stolen enough of his youth and even his middle years and he fancied taking it easy from now on. He'd earned it. Since he was a lad of six he'd got up at the crack of dawn in all weathers to sow seeds, milk cows, feed hens, plough fields, weed and harrow and harvest and then, at the right season, begin all over again.

And she'd no need to look at him like that, he added petulantly, which was rich really since Alice Grimshaw, once Jordan, knew better than to show anything but blind obedience in the face of what her husband considered to be his rights.

The farm had belonged to old Tom Jordan, Alice's father, who had become Ned's father-in-law and it was not until Ned and Alice were wed and the old man six feet under, Alice being his only child, that the farm finally fell into Ned's eager hands.

"We'll call it the Grimshaw Arms, Ma," he told Sally's grandmother – he could not bring himself to call her by her given name since he had despised her for years – stamping his feet in huge delight, for it would give him great satisfaction to hear his own name on every man's lips. The Grimshaw Arms, of course, had no actual arms and everyone who patronised the inn knew it, but Ned Grimshaw didn't give a fig for that. It was customary to name an inn after a local landowner, but Ned didn't care about that either. This was his place and he'd call it what he damn well liked.

He and his wife had one surviving child, Sally's father, Ted, the rest of them succumbing to one or other of the many diseases which afflict children in their early years, even well-fed, country children. Edward, they christened him, as all the eldest boys in Ned Grimshaw's family had been christened since time began and if Edward objected, at the age of twenty, to being torn up from his farming roots and planted in the unfamiliar soil of innkeeping, he did not say so since it did no good with a man as strong-willed as his father.

"Learn to be an innkeeper or go and work on some other man's farm," Ned had told him and though Ted Grimshaw had been appalled at the thought of living and working cheek by jowl with his domineering father all day and every day, he chose the inn. It would be his one day, after all, and if this was the only way to get his rightful inheritance he must accept it.

He was always to take the path of least resistance, and his son was the same.

Old Ned had enjoyed his new venture for no more than five years when, his body bloated almost beyond recognition by a life of doing nothing but sitting on his bum and drinking the ale his son pulled for him, fell down dead in his own taproom, at which his son danced a little jig, thanked the good Lord and took himself a wife.

Mary Grimshaw, a doughty woman from a farm up in the wilds of the North Riding of Yorkshire, was plain and quiet but with a talent for cooking and an instinct for home-making, which more than made up for her lack of looks, and in five years she had turned the Grimshaw Arms into a thriving concern famous in the county for its hospitality. Coaches stopped there every day, coming from Manchester, Sheffield, York and from the south, debouching men who were to do business in Liverpool but who preferred the warmth, the comfort, the cleanliness, the good wines and superb food, the welcome to be had at the Grimshaw Arms to the hotels that were available to them in Liverpool. There was a decent hackney service from Old Swan to the stand in Castle Street and in the opinion of many it was well worth the slight inconvenience and the couple of bob it cost for the cab to spend the night at the Grimshaw Arms.

In those days there had been a great hustle and bustle about the place with the stamping of horses' hooves on the cobbles in the yard, ostlers calling to one another as they thrust baggage into the boot of the coach, the coachman's cursing, the slamming of doors and clamouring of bugles. The coaches had splendid names like Truth, Daylight and the Lancashire Express, famous coaches which travelled the land at incredible speeds bringing, along with passengers, such sad news as the death of King George IV and the heart-stirring description of the coronation of King William IV. That was how news got about then, messages carried on coaches to every part of the land and everything going into Liverpool was often first heard at the Grimshaw Arms.

The coming of the railway had stopped all that but

the inn, having gained its reputation as the best within a thirty-mile radius, though it did not do the business it once had, continued to prosper. Old Grandma Grimshaw died of pneumonia just before Sally was born, joining her husband in whatever place he had gone to. A year later came Violet, Ted and Mary's second child to survive, and a year after that Freddy who was the last and, thankfully, a son. In the graveyard at Old Swan was a row of tiny graves containing Edward and Sophie, another Edward, Lucy and Emma, born before Sally, each of whom had lived a few sickly months and it was not until Sally had come into the world, even then lustily yelling her displeasure at something she didn't seem to care for, that Ted and Mary started their family.

From the first Sally Grimshaw was a little madam, everyone agreed on that and had she been a boy would have grown into her grandfather all over again. She had the belief from an early age that there was only one way of doing a thing and that was hers. Since both her parents were easy-going and good-natured, they allowed it, a little in awe of this prodigious infant of theirs who, from the age of five or six liked nothing better than to give the place a good "bottoming". She could bake a pie, of any sort, sweet or savoury, the pastry melting on the tongue, turn out bread light and crusty, roast a superb game bird or a shoulder of lamb, prepare and cook a full breakfast of bacon, eggs, sausage, mushrooms and kidneys for a dozen travellers without so much as becoming flushed, and her mother, who had taught her all she herself knew, was heard to remark, laughingly, that there'd soon be no need of *her*!

It was said in jest but in 1839, when Sally was eight years old, Mary Grimshaw died of a cancer in her breast and Sally took her place. She still attended school, of course, since she meant to have a good grasp of all that was needed to take over the running of the inn when it was passed on to her since she was the eldest.

Several years later she was incensed when her pa confessed to her, somewhat apologetically, that the inn and all it contained would go, as was only right, to his son, her brother Freddy.

"But Freddy can't run this place, Pa," she declared fiercely. "You know what he's like. If there's any way he can get out of work he'll find it. Set him to a task and walk away and when you look in on him half an hour later he's vanished, though he's always got some good excuse. Him and Jacky Norton get up to more mischief than a barrow-load of monkeys and how you can contemplate handing over a thriving business to such a profligate is beyond me."

That's how she talked, even at fifteen, using words like "contemplate" and "profligate" which half the men who were regulars in his taproom wouldn't know the meaning of anyway.

It was time, Ted Grimshaw told himself, that he started to look around for a likely husband for her, there was no question of it, since it was obvious she was ready for marriage. She'd make a good wife and mother, a good manager, since she could make one penny do the work of two and it was really only fair to Freddy, and Freddy's wife when he had one, that Sally should by then be settled in her own home with a family to order about.

For three years, until his death, Ted Grimshaw did everything but offer a dowry to any suitable lad who would take his self-willed daughter off his hands. Without her being aware of it he put her on display, since she wasn't a bad-looking lass if she'd relax a bit, asking her to take over in the bar as often as he could without arousing her suspicion. He'd had a couple of nice-looking barmaids in those days, one for the taproom and one for the bar parlour, attending himself to the "snug" which was frequented by the older men and was therefore more peaceful.

They liked to play dominoes in there and Ted played with them, telling Bert or Fred or Tom to help themselves to a pint since they could pull one as well as he could.

Mind you, if Sally found out there'd be fireworks but Sally, in the evenings, was often busy with those who were dining, with the supervision of hot water and clean towels for those who were staying overnight, with the accounts, the menus – she did all the cooking – and apart from her "rounds" which she was foolish enough to do regularly on the hour, scarcely showed her face – unless asked – in the public bars.

It was that tongue of hers that put them off, for what man could contemplate living the rest of his life with a woman who would be at him all day long to take off his shoes, to watch where he put his pint of ale, to give over dropping crumbs on her freshly swept floor and to mind his language?

It made no difference anyway since she showed not a scrap of interest in any of them, the men who were customers at the Grimshaw Arms and in a way Ted could understand it, since she was too clever by half. Violet, his younger daughter, was as good-natured and pliable as his Mary had been. Pretty too, in a pale sort of way and when Arthur Atkinson, who was a clerk at a shipbuilder's in Birkenhead and had happened to drop into the Grimshaw Arms on his way back from visiting his ma in Prescot, had begun to court her, Ted had despaired. Not because Violet was to marry Arthur but because Sally wasn't! Why couldn't Arthur have taken a shine to his older girl? Ted asked himself when Sally, her eyes narrowed, her straight-backed, fine-boned body stiff with outraged resentment, told him she had no intention of allowing her brother to try out any of his knuckle-headed, crack-brained ideas on a business which had prospered due to the practices her mother had begun twenty-odd years ago. Innkeeping was an art. Innkeeping was of vast importance to the travelling public even if the railways had taken some of their trade. An English country inn such as the Grimshaw Arms was not merely a place to sell the traveller, and indeed any customer, on a strictly commercial basis, of course, certain services in life. The Grimshaw Arms and its landlord had an individuality which must be respected. That's how passionately she felt about it. That's how she talked about it. The Grimshaw Arms was home-like, making its visitors feel at home, its host, or in her case its hostess, welcoming them as any mistress of a well-run household should.

It was not long after this conversation with her father that he died, taking a chill which attacked his chest and turned to pneumonia just as it had with his mother. That was in 1850, five years ago. Since then Sally, with Freddy's cheerful but unreliable help, had run the Grimshaw Arms, proud of her talent, her skill, her shrewd business sense which ensured that the inn continued as a successful, profit-making concern.

The strange encounter with the soldier might never have happened as far as Sally Grimshaw was concerned and Bridie nearly had her head snapped off, she said resentfully to Jane, when she mentioned him the following day. She'd only wondered out loud how the poor gentleman was, she complained, and Miss Grimshaw had turned on her as though she had said something nasty.

She was not to know, none of them was, that Sally Grimshaw had spent several hours during the night asking herself the same question. Was he recovered? she wondered.

Had he arrived home to warmth and care and a well-cooked, nourishing dinner like the one she had prepared and which he had icily refused? Had they warmed his bed, dressed his wound, put him in a hot bath before a good fire which was what he needed?

Dear God, what was the matter with her? she asked herself, staring wide-eyed at the window. Why should she concern herself with a man who, before yesterday, she had known of only through the scandal which had set the neighbourhood alight eight years ago. Though Coopers Edge was not far away, being situated halfway along Ash Lane which lay just beyond the Grimshaw Arms, in her ramblings about the lanes and meadows she had never once come face to face with him.

Of course, being a soldier, he had been abroad for a good deal of those eight years and besides, was years older than her and even before she was born had gone away to be educated at one of those famous public schools the gentry favoured for their sons. And from there he had gone into the army. India, rumour had it, and what had happened in between, leading up to the scandal several years later, had held little interest for her. Sally Grimshaw had been too busy learning her trade at that time, and, when her pa died, putting what she had learned to good use, to concern herself with what was none of her business and in which, to be truthful, she was not greatly interested.

She fell asleep at last but even then the soldier with the streaked grey hair and gaunt face followed her into her dreams. His incredible blue eyes beseeched her for something and she didn't know what it was. Nor did she care, she told herself brusquely when she awoke to the sound of the cock crowing at the back of the inn. He had servants by the score up at Coopers Edge to care for him, surely, though it was well known that a house without a mistress soon fell into sloppy ways. Again that was of no interest or concern to her. It was unlikely they would meet again and even if they did his affairs, his health and welfare were nothing to do with Sally Grimshaw.

The heavy frost continued and though trade was slow in the days that followed, Sally found that Captain Cooper's vivid blue eyes occupied less and less of her thoughts. She read in the newspaper that two of the wounded soldiers brought back from the Crimea on the *Cambria* had died and that there was to be a special funeral for them which she supposed the captain would attend but she gave it no more thought than that. She had plenty to keep her busy, taking the opportunity to put her girls to a spot of spring cleaning, ignoring the sidelong look Bridie and Jane gave to one another. It was only January, those looks said. Hardly *spring*, was it? Nevertheless under her sharp-eyed supervision they hefted bedroom furniture from here to there and back again, polishing and scouring until you could have eaten your dinner off the floorboards, even behind the wardrobes, Bridie muttered.

It was the same in the bars and the coffee-room where Edie and Flo were set to similar tasks. The beer engine was a simple, manually operated pump which drew liquor directly from the cellar below to the pump taps. There were two on the counter in the taproom and one each in the bar parlour and the snug. Sally had each one taken to pieces, thoroughly cleaned and put back together again, ignoring Freddy's grumbles that it had only been done just before Christmas. He recognised that his sister was a skilled publican who knew how to keep her beer looking and tasting good but sometimes, in his opinion, which no one took heed of, she went too bloody far.

He was not to know that the soldier who had collapsed on the taproom floor a few days ago was to blame for it all.

The Grimshaw Arms, though Sally still preferred to call it an inn – much to the hidden amusement of her customers – was in actual fact what was now known as a public house. Alehouse was a term she did not care for since it seemed to bring to mind the beer-houses which had sprung up all over the country, eight hundred in Liverpool alone, twenty-five years ago when the Beer Act had been passed. The Act had freed the trade in the sale of beer which was a good thing, some said, though Sally was none too sure, since it meant a licence was no longer required to brew and sell it, a licence which hitherto had been controlled by the magistrates. Now anyone who paid rates and had the two guineas for the excise licence could brew beer and sell it even in their own dwelling homes. The Grimshaw Arms was very much above such low-class trading. It had a licence to sell spirits, for one thing and had its liquor delivered by whichever brewer Sally – let there be no doubt about it – chose to give her custom to. Her brother was an independent publican, owning the Grimshaw Arms outright and in her clever way Sally Grimshaw, even while her pa was still alive, played off the suppliers against one another in order to obtain the best beer at the lowest prices. Despite the loss of much of its "inn" trade, the Grimshaw Arms had, over the past five years, never once dropped below its annual turnover of one thousand pounds, making a profit of three hundred pounds a year. There were taxes to pay, of course, licence fees, fuel, lamp oil, overheads such as wages, allowances for bad debts and breakages, but Sally Grimshaw's head for business plus Freddy Grimshaw's talent as an easy-going, affable landlord made for a good partnership. The inn had been and still was a family business. Freddy, as the publican, decked out in his short, fancy apron, white as the driven snow, naturally, and wearing a single-breasted, bob-tailed coat, could not afford to be over-sensitive – and wasn't – as he mingled with the customers. He was brash, jolly, ready to crack a joke which often made Sally wince from her position behind the bar counter but she was realistic enough to understand that, within reason, she must allow it. Freddy made sure every man was drinking and was ready to call for Job to help extinguish any dispute which might get out of hand, while Sally, as its landlady, since she was Freddy's sister, played hostess. She kept a careful eye on the girls who worked in the bars, filling and collecting mugs, and on the board where drinks were marked up to the customers' "score". She dealt with men who argued when their credit ran out, allowing none of them another drink after the end of the week if their debt was not paid. They never got the better of her, for there was not one who cared seriously to take on Sally Grimshaw when her curiously golden eyes turned to the muddy brown of wet soil and her rosy lips became two thin white lines. She really didn't need to speak. A look was enough.

Freddy, as publican, as well as being the inn's "front" man, was supposed to deal with the brewer when his stock was running low, to check the quality and quantity of the drink when it was delivered and it was up to him to see that his liquor was in a good condition. Hot weather could spoil a cask, or dirty equipment turn the liquor mouldy, but it was taken for granted by the servants that the responsibility for such tasks was in the steady, capable hands of Miss Grimshaw. She was a skilled publican in all but name and it was rarely they turned to the man who employed them when they were in need.

In Grandfather Ned's day there had been prize fights, dog

fights and cock fights at the back of the Grimshaw Arms, but Ted Grimshaw, under pressure from his daughter, it must be said, had reluctantly done away with such fiendish practices even though it lost him some trade.

"Fights bring men from miles around, Sal," he said in his mild way, "and these men'll drink in the taproom and the bar parlour, before the fight and afterwards. Fetch a bit o' cash in, that would."

"I don't care, Pa, it's barbaric and I won't have it. If it loses custom, though I don't believe it will, not with our good name, then it's just too bad. I like to think the Grimshaw Arms is in a class above the alehouses in which such things flourish. The Bull in Knotty Ash attracts a very rough crowd . . . yes, yes, I am aware that many of the young sparks from the gentry frequent such sport but they are not a very large part of our custom and we'd hardly miss them if they stay away. Fighting, whether it's between men or animals, is a filthy business and I'll not have it."

And though Ted Grimshaw was publican and his daughter no more than eighteen at the time, he had concurred and there were no more bare knuckle prize fights in which one man did his best to maul and maim another; no more dog fights in which savage bull terriers tried and often succeeded in tearing one another to pieces; no more cock fights in which blood flowed to the vicious chants of the men who gambled on them.

It was just two weeks later as January gave way to February that Sally put on her sensible winter bonnet and coat and set off to visit her sister over the water. She liked to check up – Freddy's words, not hers – on Vi and her family, making sure that all was well with them and that no knotty problems might have arisen in the Atkinson household requiring her practical help. Vi was not a good manager, let it be said, at least Sally said it, and Sally's sound financial common sense could often find small ways in which a shilling or two might be saved. She had guided Vi ever since their mother died, and even before if the truth were told and though Freddy seemed to imply she was interfering she could not simply let her younger sister get into difficulties, of any sort, if she, Sally, could help to avoid it.

Sally Grimshaw was neither obsessed with fashion nor was she oblivious to it. She somehow fell between, choosing good-quality, hard-working materials of a neutral shade and having them made up for her by a seamstress in the village. Often, when she was being fitted, Miss Riley would gently try to tempt Sally to something a shade more frivolous than a plain skirt or bodice in a stark gunmetal grey or a sombre chocolate brown, urging her perhaps to a lighter colour, to a frill or a bow, nothing ostentatious or showy, of course. A touch of white muslin at cuff or collar maybe, or a ruching of pale chiffon beneath the brim of her shallow bonnet, but she would not allow it. She was not pretty, she knew it – Freddy had all the looks in their family – and felt that to titivate herself up as though she were did her no credit, particularly in her work where she came into close contact with so many men. Let her be neat and clean was all she asked.

It was said in the fashion magazines that the speedy influx of fashion and the abundance of cheap, tawdry finery gave a maidservant an opportunity to dress up as grandly as her mistress which, being so, made it almost impossible to recognise working girls when they were in their Sunday best. Gauze bonnets they decked themselves out with, marabou feathers, lace scarves and silk gowns which could now be bought cheaply, while lace-fringed kerchiefs were flourished by those whose parents scarce knew what a pocket handkerchief was.

Today she wore her chocolate brown, a severe day dress of Bedford cord, well fitted to her breast and waist where it was held out in a wide but flexible bell by half a dozen starched white petticoats. She had refused absolutely to wear the new crinoline since it was difficult enough already to accommodate three women behind the bar counter. She moved from crowded taproom to equally crowded bar parlour and snug and coffee-room, not to mention the kitchen and the hazard of manoeuvring the vast, cage-like expanse of a crinoline skirt in such cramped conditions was just not practical.

Her brown three-quarter-length waisted overcoat had pleats at the back and sides from the waist down and was edged with a decent bit of brown fur which was snug about her neck. Her brown bonnet was devoid of all ornament but beneath its brim her glossy hair shone like pale silk.

The cold put pink flags in her cheeks and her eyes glowed in anticipation as she stepped out of the front door and set off up Prescot Lane in the direction of the horse-drawn omnibus stand in Old Swan which ran the length of Liverpool Street, Kensington Road and on to the White Hart in Dale Street.

It was Candlemas Day, 2 February, and Sally smiled as she remembered the old country rhyme her ma used to recite to her.

> If Candlemas be fair and bright
> Winter will have another flight.
> But if Candlemas be clouds and rain
> Winter is gone and will not come again.

If it was true then the icy frosts they had known in January were to return, for today it was brilliantly sunny and even mild, the sky an arch of azure blue stretching from horizon to horizon without even the faintest wisp of cloud. Unseasonal gnats danced above the hedgerows and so high she couldn't see it, a lark sang. Under the hedges violet roots were sending up little green trumpets of new leaves and Sally felt a lift to her spirits, though she couldn't for the life of her think why. Spring was coming but that had never excited her interest before other than the extra custom the arrival of better weather brought.

It was not often she had an outing so perhaps that was it, though a visit to Vi's in Birkenhead could hardly be described as such since it was a duty Sally felt obliged to perform. Still, she did enjoy the trip across the river on the ferry and there was something always going on along the streets of Liverpool the nearer you got to the docks. Street musicians would be tootling their penny whistles, banging their drums and tuning their fiddles. Organ-grinders would be rollicking forth their cheerful songs, the gleaming black eyes of the scarlet-jacketed monkey which balanced on the organ-grinder's shoulder causing her some distress though she didn't know why. Lumbering bears up on their hind legs, pathetic in their lost dignity, and little dogs with ruffs round their necks jumping through hoops.

Gaiety and music, the cries of street vendors, the crash of horses' hooves on cobbles as the great Clydesdales drew the brewer's dray – Bass, it was, which Sally served in her bar – and the refined clip-clip of sleek horses pulling the carriages of the wealthy. A kaleidoscope of colourful sound and movement which never failed to please something in her though she could not have explained what it might be. This was her city, this great, bustling, prosperous seaport and these were her people. Well, some of them, since she would not like to ally herself with the barefooted, filthy urchins who begged on every street corner, nor the sozzled men and women who stumbled out of the beer-houses and gin-shops to fall in the horse droppings in the gutter.

The steam ferry sailed from George's Pier to Birkenhead every half-hour but though she had just missed one she didn't mind since the day was so glorious. While she waited for the next she walked along the Marine Parade, feeling the sharp slap of the breeze coming up the estuary in her face.

The parade, with the sliding pewter water on one side and the busy docks on the other, was alive with people as though the brave sunshine and soft air had drawn folk from their winter nests to sample it. Ladies dressed in fashionable bodices adorned with short basques, or a jacket with a waistcoat front attached and the widespread splendour of outrageous crinolines. They wore bonnets and hats, the latest "round hat", mushroom-shaped, trimmed with ribbon round the crown with floating ends at the back, the hat kept on with ribbons attached under the brim and tied beneath the chin. Shallow bonnets worn at the back of the head like her own, and small dome-shaped parasols of every conceivable shade. They were made from lace and silk and organdy, fringed in black with sticks of ivory or coral, lovely delicate things to protect a lady's complexion from the damaging rays of the sun but which Sally scorned as frivolous.

In sharp contrast was the motley crowd disembarking from an Irish immigrant boat which had just beaten its way across the channel, up the Mersey and was tied by the dock. It carried a sombre procession of human debris carelessly flung into what they prayed would be a new and better life than the one they had left behind, men, women and children huddled together as though for comfort. Several began to wander this way and that, not at all sure which way to go. Some lucky ones had relatives to meet them and Sally watched as a baby and an old, bewildered grandmother, along with bags and boxes and paper-wrapped packages, were piled into a wheelbarrow and trundled away. A fearful confusion of starving people with nothing behind them but destitution and nothing ahead but an uncertain future which might be worse.

It was a scene of great variety with hundreds of sailing ships moored along the docks, bobbing and curtseying on the tide as though they were moving to some music only they heard. The miles of rigging sang in accompaniment as the breeze plucked at them, like fingers on the strings of a harp. Men whistled and shouted to each other, shifting great boxes and crates as though they were children's toys, tossing them here and there with careless ease. Dogs barked and slatterns touted for business quite openly as sailors disembarked from ships which had come from every corner of the globe. Sally could smell tar and coffee beans, timber and Indian tea, citrus fruits, camphor and nutmeg. All the aromas which titillate the nostrils – for the most part unnoticed – of the vast multitude of people who lived and worked beside this great stretch of water which led to the sea.

She had gone as far as St Nicholas churchyard, ready to turn back by the flight of steps which led to the parade, when she saw him. His tall figure was almost a foot in height above other men, moving stiffly as though the wound he had received in the Crimea still pained him, and he held his shoulder at an awkward angle.

He had not seen her and for a dreadful moment she panicked. She didn't even know why. She just felt an urgent desire to turn and run, for God's sake, she, Sally Grimshaw who was afraid of no one and nothing. She almost *did* turn and run but that fierce knot of resolution with which she had been born and which had developed inside her since she took over from her ma kept her rooted to the bit of ground she stood on by the marine wall.

He looked better, his awful pallor of two weeks ago almost gone. He was still thin to the point of emaciation, she noted absently, and his good clothes, obviously tailored for him in earlier days, hung on him. He was dressed in an expensive and well-made jacket and tight trousers in a shade of pewter grey and under the jacket he wore a waistcoat of pale lemon. His overcoat, in a shade of grey which was almost black, was unbuttoned and he wore no hat, though it was considered ill-mannered not to do so. His hair, which had been washed, naturally, since last she saw him, gleamed a pure silvery grey in the sunlight.

Walking one on either side of him were two of the prettiest young girls Sally had ever seen.

He stopped, surprised for a moment and the young girls stopped with him, looking up politely into his face as though wondering why he had done so. He did not smile.

"Good-day to you, Captain Cooper," Sally said calmly, though her heart for some bewildering reason was banging like a drum.

Still he did not smile but then neither did she.

"Good-day, Miss Grimshaw."

"It seems spring is come," she went on, amazed by her own ability to speak so impassively.

"Indeed."

They looked one another in the eye for several seconds, which seemed like hours and hours to Sally, neither of them quite knowing what to do next, both remembering the coldness at the end of their last meeting. Then, recalling the manners which had been bred in him, he drew forward the two young girls.

"May I present my daughters, Leila and Aisha?" he asked her coolly. "Girls, this is Miss Grimshaw." His voice was curt.

They both curtseyed prettily and inclined their small bonnets.

"Miss Grimshaw," they piped in unison.

If Miss Grimshaw was diverted by the strangeness of his daughters' names she did not allow it to show.

Believing that was all that was needed he made as though to move on but Sally Grimshaw was not the kind of woman who allowed herself to be brushed aside like a troublesome midge.

She bowed graciously to the girls. "Good-day to you both and may I ask after your health, Captain Cooper?"

"You may and it is improved, thank you."

He had had enough of her, it appeared, and his manner said so. Bowing just as graciously but with a frigidity which unnerved her, he took each of his lovely young daughters by the arm in a way that seemed to bewilder them and drew them away along the parade.

When she boarded the ferry for Birkenhead she was surprised to find that the brightness had gone from the day though the sun still shone from a cloudless sky.

3

Vi had put on her usual tea-time spread, the sort she imagined a lady who *was* a lady would put on, determined to show her sister that she also knew a thing or two about playing the hostess. It made Sally smile inwardly, for whenever she went to visit Vi's small but trim villa which lay just far enough away from the dock area to be described as being "in the suburbs", Vi went out of her way to display the refinement being the wife of a clerk had brought her.

It was six years since she and Arthur were married, Vi only seventeen at the time, and in those six years Arthur had become head clerk at the small shipbuilding firm of Brooks Brothers and she had borne and reared four children. Her success as wife of the man she considered to be a professional gentleman, as hostess to the small circle of lower middle-class shipping clerks and bank clerks and the like with whom she and Arthur mixed, and as a mother, had put her, in her own eyes at least, in a position slightly above that of her elder sister who was that pathetic creature, a spinster. A woman who relied on a male relative, their brother Freddy, for a roof over her head, the clothes on her back and every mouthful of food she ate. She took no account of the fact that Sally earned her own living just as efficiently as Arthur did; that she ran the Grimshaw Arms single-handedly, since Freddy could hardly be described as a "partner"; that she had a head on her shoulders that not only equalled Arthur's but could have easily managed and made more prosperous the firm for which he worked, given the chance. In Violet Atkinson's opinion a woman's true vocation was to be a wife and mother, as she was, and because Sally had been unable, or unwilling, to become either she was a failure, to be pitied and held, though Vi would not have admitted it, in some scorn.

Violet had been seven years old when their ma died, a year younger than Sally in age but no more than a toddling infant where grit, grasp and gumption were concerned. Sally, in effect, became Violet's ma, taking Mary Grimshaw's place, fitting the cloak of Mary Grimshaw's authority about her own thin, childish shoulders. She led them all, though they, and she, were not aware of it, through her pa's grieving, through Freddy and Vi's bewilderment and on to a place which was as safe and calm as it had been before their ma's passing. There had been barely a hiccup between the funeral and Sally's appropriation of the place her ma had occupied; in fact, hadn't Sally been occupying it, with her ma's help, naturally, through Ma's last days? It had all been so easy, so effortless, that Violet and Freddy, and even Pa had scarcely recognised the strength of character, the courage, the sheer bloody-minded need to succeed which had guided Sally from a child of eight years old with her own grief to deal with to become what she had.

As they grew Violet had always felt sorry for Sally. Well, she was as plain as a pikestaff with a sharp tongue on her which could cut bread and soon saw off any chap who took the slightest interest in her, not that many had as far as Vi knew. She was clever, give her her due, but men didn't want someone clever. They liked a woman who looked up to them, who agreed with whatever they might say, because weren't they always right? They liked a submissive wife who warmed their slippers and their beds and didn't look down her nose and smile contemptuously when they aired their masculine opinions as Vi had seen Sally do a hundred times. Sally could cook and clean as well as, if not better than, Violet – who had a skivvy in her kitchen now to do the heavy work anyway – and would have made a decent wife if she'd shaped, but when Vi said so Sally only laughed.

"Why should I spend my days taking orders from a man whose brain is not even half as clever as mine, Vi? I do exactly as I like now, you know that. I run the inn and without me Freddy would let the place go to the devil. If I were to marry, and so far no one has had the courage to ask me" – smiling that whimsical crooked smile which even Vi admitted changed her whole appearance – "I would do just what I'm doing now but at the behest of some man who thinks, because I'm a woman, my mind has not the capacity to reason or make decisions as his does."

"But you would be married, Sal. You would have a husband and a family of your own," Vi declared solemnly as though what other state could any woman aspire to?

"Oh, Vi, can you see me dancing attendance on someone like Arthur?"

"What's wrong with Arthur?" Vi bristled.

"Nothing, I suppose. He's a good job and is kind to you and the children, which is what he thinks *you* are but I couldn't spend my days like you fiddling about with social activities, Church bazaars and afternoon tea and . . . well, whatever you and your friends do with your time. I like being valued for my ability to—"

"So you think I'm not valued, do you?" Violet raised her chin.

"Of course you are." Sally's voice was impatient. "But in an entirely different way. I'm only telling you that what suits you and thousands upon thousands of other women wouldn't do for me. I like my independence too much."

"You're no more independent than I am, Sally Grimshaw. You live under Freddy's roof."

"I do all the work under Freddy's roof and if it wasn't for me there would *be* no Freddy's roof. And it's been the same ever since old Grandfather Ned bought the place."

"What d'you mean?"

"Who did all the work, Vi, tell me that? It certainly wasn't him from what I can gather. He just sat about and enjoyed what Grandma's hard work brought in and then, when they'd gone, Ma took over. Oh, I know Pa worked but it was Ma who made the inn what it is and it's me who's carrying it on, not Freddy."

"Oh, give over."

"No, it's true and you know it."

"Eeh, Sal, you won't see it, will you?"

"See what?"

"That you and me are in exactly the same boat only you're dependent on your brother instead of a husband."

"Never!"

"Suit yourself," and because they were sisters and had a fondness for one another they would move to another subject, one less thorny. They were at total ends of the spectrum as women, or so Sally would have it, since she saw absolutely no likeness in her busy, fulfilling life to the tedious one Violet lived.

They drank tea that afternoon which Vi's skivvy, on this occasion called a "parlourmaid", brought in to them. She was a dumb mountain of a girl dressed up incongruously in a frilled cap and apron and answering to the name of

Lizzie. They ate seed cake and coconut macaroons while three of Violet's well-scrubbed children, Benjamin, Margaret and Amelia, brought down especially for their Aunty Sal's inspection, sat in a fidgeting row on their mother's red plush sofa in the minute parlour. In a room above, which Violet grandly called the "nursery", twelve-month-old Florence slept, one hoped, the peaceful sleep of an infant.

The parlour was so cluttered there was scarcely room to move and Sally watched Lizzie with her heart in her mouth lest the ox-like creature, more at home with a scrub bucket than a tea tray, should trip over one of the many footstools or pouffes that were scattered about. The room had a wooden floor, the centre of it covered by a square, brightly patterned carpet. There was a picture rail from which hung Violet's innocent taste in "pretty" pictures, some made from shells or dried flowers or needlework, at least two dozen of them and hardly visible behind them was a heavily flocked dark red wallpaper. There was a cast-iron grate in which a small fire burned, for though the day was cold Arthur required Vi to be careful with his money which was why she had so often to resort – reluctantly – to accepting the help and advice Sally could give her in the sorting out of her domestic financial affairs. The grate was guarded by a brass fender and above it was an elaborate mantelshelf along which was fastened a frill of red plush to match the heavy curtains at the window. A vast domed clock, all curlicues and scrollwork, painted figures and colourful birds, ticked sonorously in the centre of it.

The chairs, the tables, the sofa and sideboard were all solid, dark and carved, good stuff, for Arthur liked value for money. Arranged on every small table and indeed on every available surface in the room were glass vases and "fancy goods". A massive glass dome covered an intricate floral arrangement and another a stuffed bird, with boxes of all sizes trimmed with shells or tassels taking up any space remaining. There were pot ornaments, many of them with royal connections. Prince Albert and Queen Victoria and their charmingly grouped children, for example, with many heroic figures in uniform astride horses, though who they were Violet could not say.

It was a veritable minefield for even the neatest, most dextrous parlourmaid and how the lumbering Lizzie coped with it all was a mystery to Sally. She had two of the best maidservants in Liverpool, picked and trained by herself, but even she would hesitate before letting them loose in her sister's parlour.

Vi was dressed in what she believed was the height of fashion, a day dress with a dozen flounces down the wide skirt and a tight-sleeved bodice in which strained her plump breasts. It was a vivid green moiré silk trimmed with purple, since bright contrasts in colour were in fashion. She had put on a lot of weight since her marriage and the birth of her four children but her hair, a darker blonde than her brother and sister, was prettily arranged with a centre parting and side ringlets frothing over her ears. It was a style only for the young but then, despite her married state and four children Violet Atkinson was only twenty-three. She had a twist of purple ribbon in her curls, for she had read in the fashion magazines that the "day cap" was no longer the thing among young married women.

"Would you care for another macaroon?" his mother asked five-year-old Benjamin, showing off her gentility and her son's well-rehearsed manners to this sister of hers who had chosen to live in what Violet called – privately, of course – a public house.

"Yes, please," lisped the child and it was then that the

restrained atmosphere became too much for three-year-old Amelia who flung herself off the sofa and made a play for Prince Albert who stood enticingly on a low occasional table beside the sofa. Lizzie, who had scarcely let out her breath since entering the room lest the movement of her vast bosom disturb something, froze against the sideboard and four-year-old Margaret, who, or so Violet said, was sensitive, began to howl. Benjamin scoffed the macaroon and under cover of the pandemonium whisked two more off the fancy cake plate and tried to cram them into his mouth. Amelia squealed, sounding just like the piglets at the back of the Grimshaw Arms, then clutched at Sally's skirt, pulling herself to her feet.

"Oh, dear," Violet said.

"I want anovver cakey, Mama," Margaret announced petulantly between shrieks. "Benjie's got anovver cakey and I want one." And Amelia, who still clung to Sally's good skirt, Prince Albert clutched to her smocked chest, fell down again and vanished into the folds of the tablecloth.

"Oh, dear," Violet said again, while Lizzie backed even further against the sideboard as though terrified she was to be blamed for the whole thing.

Sally tutted. "Lord, Vi, can't you control these children any better than this?" she said tartly. "I don't know why you drag them in here when you've got visitors. Couldn't that . . . that girl see to them?" nodding in the direction of Lizzie.

"Strange as it may seem, Sally, I thought that you, as their aunt, might like to spend half an hour with them. Forgive me if I was wrong." Violet was seriously affronted.

Sally sighed. "I do," she lied, "but now that I have I'm sure we could serve ourselves. They are very young and would be happier in a more . . . relaxed environment." She knew full well Vi had only fetched Lizzie out of the kitchen to impress herself, which was a bit of a laugh when you pictured the spotless order which reigned in her own household.

"It's not as easy as that, Sally. Children . . ."

". . . are children, Vi, and should not be allowed to stir up this . . . this chaos. They are far too young" – and badly brought up, she longed to add – "to be expected to sit through afternoon tea, but if they are you should keep them in their place."

"It's easy for you to say, Sal. You've none of your own and haven't the faintest idea how difficult it is to—"

"I know this much, even if I have none of my own. I know naughtiness when I see it."

"Really, I sometimes wonder . . ."

Sally shook her head in exasperation and without raising her voice turned to Benjamin who had the fingers of both hands in his mouth as though to help in the mastication of the half-chewed macaroons.

"You are an ill-mannered and greedy little boy and if you don't behave and do exactly as your mother says you will be sent to your room at once. With no tea," she added.

The boy stared at her, his eyes enormous in his face, not even daring to chew any more. It was not what she had said, since his mother often threatened him with the same punishment, it was the absolute belief that, unlike his mother, his Aunty Sal meant every word.

Violet watched in stony-faced silence, her heaving bosom displaying her annoyance at what she saw as a blatant disregard for her authority in her own home.

"And you, Margaret." Sally turned her cold eye on her elder niece. "Stop that caterwauling and sit up straight or you will suffer the same fate. Close your mouth, if you please, and not another word."

"Really, Sally, there is no need to speak to them as though they were ruffians."

"There is every need, Vi, and you must learn to apply it if there is to be discipline in your house."

She reached down and plucked Prince Albert from Amelia's flaccid grasp then lifted the little girl to stand before her.

"Don't let me see you touch your mother's things again, d'you hear me?"

The open-mouthed child nodded.

"Now go and sit down on that stool by your mother and if you all three behave you may have another macaroon."

The child meekly did as she was told.

Lizzie let out her breath on a long-drawn-out sigh of relief though she was well aware there would be ructions when Miss Grimshaw had gone. Her mistress didn't like it, you could see that, even if her children were now sitting like little angels gazing at their Aunty Sal with wide-eyed respect.

"Really, Sal, I can manage my own children you know, without your interference."

"Interference! Dear God, they'd wreck the place if you let them. Children need a firm hand and it seems to me—"

"Oh, give over . . ."

"No, I won't give over. With four young children—"

"Sally, really . . . please."

Violet stopped speaking abruptly, putting her hands to her flushed cheeks, her expression one of deep resentment and at the same time something that looked like embarrassment.

Sally leaned forward, placing her cup and saucer on the table, watched nervously by the three children. She narrowed her eyes in which the firelight had placed a glint of topaz, her gaze concentrating on her sister's face as though she sensed her formidable organising abilities were about to be put into action in the disorganised muddle of her sister's life.

"What is it?"

"Well . . ."

"What is it, Vi?"

Violet's glance moved uneasily to Lizzie and she grimaced in what purported to be a smile.

"Take the children into the kitchen, Lizzie and . . . well . . . find something for them to do."

"Yes, mum." It was plain from the expression on the girl's face that she couldn't for the life of her think what that "something" might be. Violet and Arthur Atkinson's "villa" was no more than a semi-detached box with a tiny square of garden to the front and the same at the rear. There was a parlour, behind which was a dining-room and behind that a kitchen and scullery all reached by a narrow hallway. Upstairs were three bedrooms, one behind the other and an attic room where poor Lizzie slept the sleep of the overworked. There was simply nowhere for the children to play, though thankfully Benjamin was to go to school in the near future.

"Well?" Lizzie's mistress asked her sharply.

"Er, wharra they ter do, like?"

"Oh, for goodness sake, Lizzie, you come from a large family. Surely you know how to play with children. What do your brothers and sister do?"

"Well, mum." Lizzie was not sure she knew how to tell Mrs Atkinson that her brothers and sisters, of whom as Mrs Atkinson said so rightly there were a vast number, spent their time making matchboxes in her mam's cluttered and none too clean kitchen for which they might earn a few pence a week though it was terrible hard on the hands. The three oldest girls, who were not yet ten, worked in a local factory licking adhesive labels to be stuck on tins, sometimes until they were actually sick. Play! They didn't know the meaning of the word.

Lizzie stared agonisingly at the irritated face of her mistress.

"Have you any flour, Lizzie?" Miss Grimshaw interrupted and Lizzie transferred her anguished gaze from Mrs Atkinson to her sister.

"Flour, mum?"

"Yes, flour."

"Well . . ."

"Mix some with water as though you were to make pastry . . . you know how to do that?"

"Yes, mum," since flour and water baked in the oven was a regular meal, when times were bad, for Lizzie and her family.

"Then let the children play with that."

"Sally! They will get filthy." Vi was clearly appalled.

"They can be washed, Vi," Sally answered mildly, "and it will keep them occupied while you and I chat."

"Well, I don't know."

"Go along, Lizzie, and take the children with you," Sally ordered calmly, just as though this were her house and her servant, Violet thought resentfully, but when they had all gone and the sisters sipped another cup of tea in the delightful peace which fell about the room – though a crash from the kitchen made Vi wince – she had to admit it was very pleasant.

"So, Violet, you have something to tell me?" Sally said at last. She sat in what was Arthur's chair, deep and comfortable as behoved the master of the house, though her back was as straight as an arrow and did not touch the plump, velvet cushions. For once her hair was all in place, dragged achingly back from her smooth white forehead with not an escaped curl to be seen and Violet thought she looked exactly what she was: a dried-up old spinster.

She straightened her own back defensively. "I couldn't say anything in front of Lizzie though she'll know soon enough, I suppose, and I only hope she doesn't take it into her daft head to leave, though with all those brothers and sisters I can't see her giving up a good job like this."

Sally raised an amused eyebrow but didn't say anything and Vi didn't appear to notice.

"What is it, Vi? Don't tell me you're pregnant again."

Violet gasped. "Really, Sally, need you be so crude? But . . . well . . . yes, I'm in the family way and if you say a word about it I shall scream. I can't help it, can I, when Arthur" – she blushed furiously – "well, being unmarried you will not know . . ."

"Vi, I know exactly what you mean, even if I am a dried-up old spinster." Sally grinned her lopsided grin as Vi looked up guiltily. It seemed her sister had read her mind. "But I'm surprised at you and Arthur, really I am. Florence only twelve months old and already you're what . . .?"

"Three months." Vi hung her head as though in shame. She had known Sally would have something to say on the matter, for when would Sally Grimshaw, who really knew nothing about men and their frequent demands, learn how to mind her own business? She knew she was often glad of the sound advice Sally gave her on how to spin out the housekeeping Arthur handed over each week but she did wish she would learn that, apart from that, she had no right to interfere, or even speak about, what went on between a man and his wife.

Sally shook her head and sighed. She just could not understand why it proved so difficult for folk like her sister, and indeed all the other women who were overburdened with children, to arrange their lives into some semblance of order. Five children in six years was not only foolhardy but careless and if Arthur had been her husband which, thank God, he was not, she'd soon have put him right when he came sniffing round her. There was, as far as she knew since she was ignorant about such matters, no way to prevent the conceiving of a child except one, which was abstinence, and surely any considerate husband would agree to it. Vi, of course, was lucky in so much as she had a man bringing in a comparatively decent wage. She had a small but comfortable house, even a strong girl to do the heavy cleaning but there were thousands upon thousands of women who, being pregnant for most part of every twelve months, either about to deliver a child or getting over a birth, who simply slid into squalid indifference, overwhelmed to the point where it was easier to give in than to fight.

Sally Grimshaw would not have been one of those if she had married. She would never have allowed herself to be dragged down to the status of a breeding animal subject to the whims and fancies of some man and depending on his ability to be a good provider. Not clever, quick-thinking, hard-working Sally Grimshaw. Not the woman who ran the best inn in Lancashire and was famous for her clean cellar, the immaculacy of her well-aired beds, the succulence of her steak and kidney pie and the good value she guaranteed a customer who spent his money in her establishment.

She proceeded to tell her sister where she had gone wrong, even if her sister didn't want to know, and to advise her on what she was to do in the future if she was to put it right and, when she rose to leave, satisfied that her course was sound and if followed would soon have Vi's household affairs in good order, she failed entirely to realise that Vi was perfectly content with what she had. It was not what Sally Grimshaw would have wanted nor put up with and she was convinced Vi must feel the same. The din from the kitchen was quite horrific and from upstairs the fretful wail of the baby drifted down the narrow staircase.

Violet shrugged her plump shoulders almost apologetically, reduced from the fashionable, socially committed young wife of a go-ahead businessman she had been before her sister arrived to the ineffectual figure Sally always seemed to make of her. She would take no notice, of course, since the vague muddle of her own household suited her perfectly as did Arthur's affectionate embrace in their bed. Yes, he was demanding in that area of their marriage but that meant he loved her as a man loves a woman, which was more than could be said for her sister who had known no man's attentions, in or out of bed.

It was almost dark when Sally arrived home, entering through the taproom. The lamps had been lit ready for when the place opened and a cheerful light in the bar window shed a bright ray across the road and even illuminated the hedge on the far side. From the window nearest the fireplace came a flickering orange and red glow which told her that one of the girls had made up the enormous fire Sally liked to keep and she sighed in deep contentment. The inn would be open in half an hour and the first customer arriving, but hardly before she had her bonnet off, Bridie grumbled in an aside to Jane, she was at them with that tongue of hers. Had Bridie cleaned and polished all the windows with vinegar as her mistress had instructed and why weren't the tables laid in the coffee-room? Those pump handles in the bar parlour weren't as bright as she liked them to be and the fire in the snug, which was leaping warmly halfway up the chimney, was nearly out! Why was Elly sitting about drinking tea, she asked menacingly, when there was a distinct smell of burning coming from one of the ovens? And if the pies she herself had prepared this morning before she left, with orders to put them in the oven on the stroke of four, had even a singe on them, there'd be trouble.

They all sighed. They really enjoyed the relaxed atmosphere which prevailed when Miss Grimshaw took it into her head to visit her sister over the water, though no doubt the poor woman had been on the receiving end of what was their daily diet seven days a week. "My way is best" would be carved on Miss Grimshaw's tombstone, they told one another, though they all agreed that she did run a splendid public house. Sometimes when they heard her giving "what for" to some customer who had offended, they wondered why these men drank there at all. The Bull at Knotty Ash was just as close and free and easy, it was said, but then the publican there had a name for sharp practices and watered beer. At the Grimshaw Arms there was good ale at a fair price, superbly cooked food to be had from a freshly made four-course luncheon or dinner in the coffee-room, to pickled eggs and onions, cheese and home-baked bread, pork pies, pease pudding and faggots for the working man to eat at the bar counter or at one of the well-scrubbed deal tables in the taproom. A game of darts or dominoes was always available and Miss Grimshaw did not object to a farm labourer bringing in his dog, providing the animal was clean, quiet and well behaved. Rather like themselves, in fact.

The solid walls of the public rooms were painted a gleaming white, given a new coat every six months or so and the floors were flagged in glowing squares of stone in shades of blue and red, ochre and rose. There were deep cushioned chairs to sit in and benches pulled up to the tables. Stools of elmwood stood against one wall but not along the bar counter, for Miss Grimshaw understood some men need to stand to drink their ale. The lamplight gleamed on well-polished copper and brass and before the gigantic log fire stood a settle carved in yew with a rocking-chair beside it. It was a grand room, Miss Grimshaw's taproom, but not overwhelming. Homely and bright and something in the order of their own farm kitchens. There was laughter and sometimes a song or two if the words were respectable and the regulars were all used to Miss Grimshaw and her strict ways by now, not appearing to object to them, no doubt because of the value for money they received from her.

'This 'ere cask needs changin', Miss Grimshaw," Job told her an hour after opening time. His badly mauled face was quite without expression just as though the beatings he had taken as a bare knuckle prize fighter had smashed away his capacity to rearrange it, either to frown or smile. His eyebrows were virtually non-existent they had been split so many times, but when he spoke he revealed a mouthful of surprisingly good white teeth. One ear was scarcely more than a twisted nub and the other not much better. It was impossible to guess his age. Even Job didn't know it himself but his hair was greying and there were deep grooves running down beside his mouth. He might once have been a handsome man and folk who cared to look closely – and there were not many of those – might have been startled by the soft colour and kindliness in his pale grey eyes.

He was the best cellarman Sally had ever had, quiet, respectful, enormously strong and a great asset on the rare occasion when there was trouble in the bar. Sally had found him one day in the yard at the back of the inn chopping wood for the bowl of soup Elly had promised him.

Though he was plainly exhausted and thin as a rake, since a man on the tramp does not eat well, he would not accept the soup until he had chopped and stacked a pile of wood so high it would last a week.

"Give him some bread and cheese as well, Elly, and a piece of that fruit cake I made this morning," Sally told the kitchen maid, nodding pleasantly at the man in the yard, for she did admire a good worker, but Job would not accept the extra food until he had chopped some extra wood.

They might have gone on all day, neither Job nor Sally satisfied that a balance had been reached and Job's debt, or hers, had been paid in full. He was the most stubborn but unrelentingly honest man she had ever known, she told him when finally he had decided he had earned the food she pressed on him.

That had been four years ago and still he was here, working for proper wages now, which he took reluctantly, believing that the good food in his belly, the warm bed he slept in over the stables more than enough in payment for what he did. He rarely spoke, not even to Freddy as they loaded or unloaded casks of beer, changed barrels or hefted crates of liquor up and down the cellar steps.

He kept his worship of, and devotion to, Sally Grimshaw, who had given him a life when he had none, to himself.

"Well, get Freddy to give you a hand, Job," Sally told him over her shoulder as she handed a plate of pease pudding and faggots across the counter to Arnie Thwaites, surprised that Job was even telling her since he knew very well that it was his and Freddy's job. Besides which it should have been attended to before opening time.

Job stood stolidly at the top of the cellar steps, clenching and unclenching his large fists and flexing the bunched muscles of his great shoulders which, in the four years he had lived at the Grimshaw Arms, had returned to him. On his face was what on any other man would have been an anguished expression, for, try as he might and strong as he was, he just could not lift a full cask to change it over by himself.

"Well?" Miss Grimshaw said sharply. "What are you standing there for?" Her frown of disapproval cut him to the quick.

He opened and closed his mouth a couple of times and Arnie Thwaites, his plate of pease pudding and faggots in his hard, labouring fist, waited with interest, for a "to-do-ment" between Miss Grimshaw and one of her staff, or even one of her customers, was vastly entertaining.

"Come along, Job, I haven't all day." Miss Grimshaw was plainly becoming annoyed as her hands on her hips and the tapping of her foot indicated.

"'Tis . . . cask . . ."

"Yes?"

"It be . . . too 'eavy." He was mortified to admit, not only before this woman but one of her customers that he was not strong enough to heave the cask by himself, a cask which was almost too much for two men, let alone one.

"Too heavy! What on earth d'you mean? You've managed it up to now."

"Not . . . not on me own, miss."

"On your own! Dear Lord, Job, we're not asking you to . . ."

Suddenly, as though Job's anguished eyes and the crestfallen slump to his shoulders conveyed some message to her, she turned back to Arnie Thwaites who was still hovering by the counter.

"Thank you, Mr Thwaites," she said briskly, "that will be all," dismissing him as though he were a bloody lad, he told his missis later. "Now, if you'll excuse me I must have a word with my cellarman."

She was always polite, was Miss Grimshaw, even when she was being rude.

4

"I'll not have it, Freddy, and there's an end to it and if I'd known what you were up to it would never have gone this far. I suppose it's that Jacky Norton who put you up to it."

"Now hold on, Sal. I know I went with Jacky since he's a member and I wouldn't have been admitted otherwise but he didn't twist my arm, you know. It was only meant as a bit of fun, that's all. You can't blame a chap for wanting a bit of fun, surely? It just got a . . . well . . . a bit out of hand, but a fellow has to have some excitement in his life, doesn't he?"

Freddy's voice was aggrieved and he clapped down the glass of brandy he was holding with such force on to the counter top, most of the contents spilled. Freddy Grimshaw didn't like the way his sister, who was, after all, only two years older than him, was implying that he was no more than a callow youth who had been led into mischief by a person of ill-repute. He and Jacky had gone to school together, fought back-to-back against other lads, and against each other, roamed the countryside as boys do in search of frogspawn, birds' nests and apples from the orchards of local farmers. They had grown up together, got up to all the tricks growing lads get up to and had shared their first sexual experience with the obliging dairymaid from Daisy Wood Farm who had, for the price of sixpence apiece, let each fifteen-year-old boy fondle her bounteous breasts, lift her skirts and "do" her while the other watched. Freddy had been second, having lost the toss, and had nearly "come" before Jacky had finished, he had got so excited, and for several months he and Jacky had spent every penny they earned on the delights of the buxom and cheerfully willing maid.

"I don't care how it happened, it will not happen again. All I want to know is how many times you've been to this club and how much money you've lost?"

Sally's voice was deceptively mild but Freddy, who knew her well, was aware that beneath the surface of her calm was an explosion of outrage which would surely blow him to smithereens should it escape.

It was almost two o'clock in the morning and the inn was as silent as the grave, with every servant in bed. A haze of blue-grey smoke from dozens of clay pipes still hung about the ceiling like fog on the Mersey. The only light for miles around shone from the taproom window, lying in a golden beam across the cobbles and the lane at the front of the inn, beyond which was the impenetrable darkness of the countryside at night. Not a glimmer showed anywhere, for those who begin work at dawn are early in their beds at night. Faintly from some room above their heads Sally could hear someone snoring and from beyond the bolted front door came the creak of the sign which proclaimed the name of the inn.

"I don't know if that's any of your business," Freddy answered sullenly, turning his back on her to refill his glass. The lamp lit his mop of fair curls to pure gold. "I'm twenty-two, Sal, and not some bloody lad you can order about. I own this inn and if I want to spend some of the profits, which *I* helped to earn, on a bit of harmless gambling then that's my right." His voice, though defiant, had a strange tremble in it.

"Is that so?"

"Yes, that is so," and as though to demonstrate his freedom to run his own life as he pleased, Freddy raised his glass to his lips and drank deeply. His face was already flushed and his eyes were over-bright. Sally thought how handsome he was, wondering idly why, though they were so alike, it was he who had all the looks. She was not surprised by the rumours which said that every lass in the district was in love with him. He was not only good-looking but good-humoured and if he had only been a shade more reliable and a mite less easily led would make some woman a kind husband. A good catch was Freddy Grimshaw, what with his bonny face and his bonny inheritance, if he would just settle to his responsibilities. He was weak, she knew that, always had been, but then he had always had her to carry the burdens and assume leadership so there had been no need for him to shape himself as any other man would have had to do. Perhaps it was her fault for taking on so much of what were really his duties, for allowing him to slip away on some jaunt or other with Jacky Norton – whose own father, a farmer up beyond Knotty Ash, was indulgent with him – knowing that she was there to see to the smooth running of the inn.

But if she had sat back and left it to him there was nothing more certain than that there would have been no trade, no business, no inn for him to run! Still, this could not go on. Apparently he had been sneaking out after the inn closed, when she had thought him to be in his bed, meeting Jacky Norton and riding hell for leather on their horses to this club, which, it seemed, remained open as long as there were men who wished to gamble. The Royal Club House, it was called, in Bold Street. God alone knew what went on there but whatever it was Freddy had had his last crack at it, she meant to make that quite clear.

She pulled her fleecy white shawl more closely about her shoulders. It was large, square, with a point at the back which fell to the hem of her plain, high-necked nightgown. Her hair, which she had loosened from its knot and brushed vigorously as she did every night, was thick and curling, hanging down her back to her waist in a vibrant curtain of silk, the light from the lamp on the bar counter setting it on fire with streaks of tawny gold. A narrow blue velvet ribbon held it back from her face, a ribbon so frivolous and unlike anything he had ever seen on his sister, Freddy wondered where she has come by it. She looked like a child, no more than twelve or fourteen, small and defenceless, without the dignity and maturity her usual dragged-back, high-piled chignon gave her and Freddy was quite startled by the change in her appearance.

"I asked you a question, Freddy, and I'd like an answer, if you please," she declared in that tone of voice they all knew well.

Freddy had had more than a few brandies during this night. "What question was that?" he asked truculently, his eyes shifting about the room, resting on this and that, anywhere but on Sally. It was very evident he was rattled by something.

"First, how many times have you frequented this . . . this place?"

"I can't remember. Half a dozen I suppose, perhaps . . ."

"Perhaps more?"

"Well . . ." He turned away from her impatiently.

"And the money you lost?"

"Who said I lost?" His voice rose on what could have been fear.

"Did you win, Freddy?"

He shifted from foot to foot, a small boy caught with his hand in the biscuit barrel, his face pulled into mutinous lines.

"No."

"How much did you lose then?" She was infinitely patient with him since her naïve mind dealt with a guinea or two, perhaps twenty, since he had no more. She paid him a wage, for a man must have money in his pocket, but he left everything to her, even the settling of his tailor's bill which was sometimes excessive, she thought, but what he had put by could not have been much.

"Well, it depends on what you call losing." He shifted uneasily, unwilling to meet her gaze.

"Freddy, I wish you would give me a straight answer to a simple question. Either you lost money or you won. Surely that is easy enough to understand? Now let's get this sorted out and then we can get to our beds. It's nearly three o'clock and I'd like to get an hour or two's sleep before the servants stir, so, how much did you lose?"

"Not a lot of . . . money, Sal." His eyes still refused to meet hers.

"Well, that's something to be grateful for, I suppose. You will just have to pay it back week by week from your own wages."

Sally felt the tension ease in her, suddenly aware of how tired she was. She was used to being on her feet for the best part of eighteen hours a day but somehow today had been unusually draining. For a second a face flashed across her vision. A thin, drawn face with no warmth in it, no smile to light the crystal depths of blue eyes. A face set in hostile lines, a face that said the man had not forgotten, nor would forgive the affront to his pride she had offered him with what he had thought to be a curt rejoinder regarding the scandal in his family's past.

Why should she think of him at this precise moment, she mused, unless it could be that it was he who was the compelling reason for the weariness which bore her down? She had forced him from her mind since that day in the taproom even though he had made a curious impression on her at the time. His life did not impinge on hers and so she had put the memory of that day from her. She had been enjoying her walk on the parade, looking forward to her sail on the ferry, and the sight of him and his two lovely, unusually named children had badly upset her for some inexplicable reason.

She had carried that strangeness home with her, longing to have the evening over and be in her bed, and now this bombshell had exploded about her. Job had not wanted to tell her that Freddy was missing and if he could have tackled the cask on his own, or even with Tim-Pat's help, which would have been no help at all since Tim-Pat had once been a jockey and was as small and thin as a cat's elbow, he would have done it. Job's eyes had bored into hers in that way he had, with such a look of pain in them she had been surprised, for why should Job care if Freddy was up to some trick or other, and it was only when she had threatened him with the sack if he didn't tell her the whole of it that he had given Freddy's secret away. Even then his eyes had seemed to beg for forgiveness as though the whole thing were his fault. Of course, she was well aware of his loyalty, both to Freddy and herself, who had taken him in when his life as a pugilist was at an end, forcing him to the life of an itinerant in his search for work, and of course she wouldn't have sacked him, but she did wish he'd told her of this sooner, she added brusquely, before it had got out of hand.

They had both been mortified when Job was forced to accept the offer of smirking Arnie Thwaites's help in the changing of the cask for which Arnie was delighted to receive a couple of free pints of Miss Grimshaw's best bitter and should they need any more assistance they'd only to ask, he had added, winking at the customers who had overheard the exchange.

"Well?" she asked her brother now, shivering as she pulled her shawl more closely about her. The fire was almost out and the room was cold.

"Look, Sal, if you'd just give me a bit more time I'm sure I could raise the money to . . . to repay what I owe."

"Repay what you owe! What does that mean?"

"Well, Jacky's not dunning me, of course, since it's not a large amount he lent me and he knows he'll get it back as soon as I've got it but . . ."

He had begun to look about him in a speculative way which Sally, though she didn't know what it meant, did not care for. It was as though he was assessing the value of the big clock on the wall, the one that had ticked there for the past forty years, the carved yew settle Grandfather Ned had sprawled on, so it was said, the rocking-chair, the copper pans on the wall and all the other good solid stuff which furnished the room.

It was at that precise moment that a tiny frisson of ice trickled through Sally's veins. She couldn't have said why, for she had no idea what sort of a pickle Freddy had got himself into over the past three months. In fact since last November, though she was not aware of it, when Jacky, whose father had a bob or two and allowed his son a more than decent allowance, had announced to his friend that he had just become a member of the Royal Club House. Come and have a flutter, he'd invited Freddy, that is if you can get away from that sister of yours for an hour or two, he'd added with a touch of amused spite and it had been enough for Freddy.

"Freddy." Sally made a great effort to control the fierceness in her that wanted to get hold of her brother and shake out of him whatever predicament he had got himself into. Why would he not just come out with it like she did and tell her so that she, who had always kept the family, the inn, the servants and indeed everything else in her control, running in that smooth, well-ordered way she liked, could put it to rights? He was a good lad at heart and had never caused her any serious anxieties and she would be prepared to overlook this one lapse if he would only own up to it and promise never to do it again.

"Freddy, tell me exactly what it is you have done and then we can set it right." She smiled encouragingly though she would dearly have liked to reach up and smack his face.

He sighed, then sagged against the bar, the fight, the truculence, the defiance gone out of him.

"I'm . . . I'm in the hands of a moneylender, Sal."

It had begun with his own money which had been little enough and soon gone on the roulette table where the wheels click and dazzle and whirling colours had mesmerised him. Lend me a guinea or two, he had begged Jacky when his own had gone and Jack had obliged and within an hour the pile of gaming chips beside him had doubled and tripled and a crowd had begun to gather about him. Freddy had known nothing like it in his life before, not even the thrill he had experienced up the dairymaid's skirt. The numbers seemed to go his way with every spin of the wheel and Freddy had become intoxicated with it. His eyes glittered and his fingers feverishly clicked the chips together and when the number he called let him down he could not believe it. For an hour he had felt like a god with everything he called for falling like the brilliance of the stars above into his lap and now, suddenly, she had turned away from him, that elusive creature known as Lady Luck.

For the rest of that evening and on all the others he and Jacky had visited the club it had been the same. Up and down and round and round the roulette wheel, for nothing else interested him but that dancing, whirling spin of chance until, two weeks ago, when having lost every penny he owned and with Jacky refusing to oblige him just once more, he had found someone who would.

"I signed an IOU and I lost, Sal." Freddy's voice was the merest whisper in the room but Sally felt as though it were as loud as the bells which rang in St Nicholas Church beside the quay. They drowned her, deafened her, filled her head with a roar like the waves which had been known to pound over the walls of the Marine Parade and she felt herself going under in what would have been the first faint of her life.

She swallowed frantically, trying to keep down the surge of nausea which seemed determined to flood her throat. Her hands were white-knuckled where they clutched at her shawl and her eyes were golden pools of shocked horror in her colourless, stricken face. Even her open rosy mouth lost its flush as she did her best to get the question from between her lips.

"How . . . how . . . much?"

She did hit him when he told her, letting the shawl slip to the floor as her hands clawed at his face, which he did his best to protect with his arms. Her fingernails found the flesh of his cheeks, drawing eight lines of flowing blood, four to each side, and she screamed again and again, for he had just taken from her the only thing in her life she valued. He'd stolen her life, in fact, and for the first time, and the last, Sally Grimshaw lost control and gave way to despair, to hatred, to a bitterness she couldn't manage. When strong arms pulled her into their protective circle and a broad chest presented itself for her to lean on, she did not resist, not even aware of who it was who was proving such a comfort to her.

"There, there, miss, don't tekk on so," a soft voice told her, while gentle hands smoothed her hair. The hold on her was respectful and infinitely comforting and she clung to it gratefully lest she float away somewhere and never set her feet on firm ground again. She was conscious of shadowy figures about her and the sound of someone moaning, then a hand shoved a glass of brandy into hers; at least she thought it was brandy, for the sharp smell of it and the hot flare of it down to her stomach made her gasp and her eyes watered. It made her feel better though. Warmed her ice-encased body and steadied the deep trembling which had begun somewhere inside her, moving outwards and threatening to have her off her feet.

"I'll tekk 'er," she heard someone say. She thought it might be Bridie but the arms about her tightened and she was glad. She felt safe for the moment. Safe from the nightmare which had sucked her into its centre and was doing its best to whirl her round and round like one of those hurricanes in foreign parts she had read about.

"She's all right where she is, poor little maid," a deep voice rumbled and she heard it come at her from the chest against which she lay.

"Nay, she's not, lad," Bridie seemed to be telling whoever it was who soothed her. "She'd be best wi' one of us.

Wharrever's up wi' 'er, d'yer reckon? Eeh, I've never sin mistress like this, 'ave you, Jane?" Jane agreed she hadn't. "She's always so steady, like. What's ter do, d'yer think, an' will yer look at master. 'Oo give 'im them scratches? Surely not 'er."

Bridie sounded deeply shocked and yet at the same time excited by this drama which had boiled over while they had all been fast asleep in their beds. They'd awakened, her and Jane with whom she shared a room, to the most awful screams and for a moment she swore her hair stood on end until she realised it was a human voice and not a supernatural one that had awoken her. Even then she'd been scared witless and she and Jane had collided with one another again and again as they blundered about the bedroom in search of a candle and then, when they got out on to the landing, crashing into Elly and Flo who were cowering in the doorway of the bedroom they shared. Like ghosts they all were in their flowing white nightgowns, frightening one another to death, the echo of those ghastly screams still drifting along the landing.

They were even more startled when they stumbled down the narrow staircase which led into the coffee-room and from there to the taproom to find their mistress clasped against the burly chest of her own cellarman. It gave her a nasty turn, Bridie was to say later, for apart from the embarrassment of it, what woman would like to find his ugly mug in her face and his brawny arms holding her close? Them ears of his were enough to put you off men for life and how he'd the nerve to put his hands on their immaculate and totally unapproachable mistress was one of life's mysteries. It was not right and best if he handed her over to one of them, she told him again, which would give them, the women, a chance to find out what it was all about. Get her in the kitchen, stoke up the fire, put the kettle on and while she was still mazed with whatever it was that had mazed her, have the whole story laid out for them.

She was raising her eyebrows to Jane, signalling with a nod of her head to the woman with whom she worked side by side for most of the day and to whom she was the closest, to give her a hand.

With a suddenness which took them by surprise, Miss Grimshaw stood away from Job. Bridie would have liked to think she tore herself, with a gasp of disgust, from his arms, but she didn't. Miss Grimshaw actually gave him a grateful smile and patted his bare, hairy and well-muscled forearm before turning on them.

"What's going on here?" she snapped, just as though the four of them had been caught behind the bar upending a bottle of her best brandy. They exchanged stupefied glances, for had she really expected them to lie in their beds as though nothing had happened with her screaming the bloody place down? Loud enough to raise the dead, it had been and you'd have thought she would at least feel indebted to them that they'd run down to help her in whatever it was that had upset her, but no. Not her. Not Miss High and Mighty Grimshaw.

"Well . . ." Bridie began to stammer.

"There's nothing here that concerns you so get back to your beds. You've to be up at six so look sharp."

"But Miss Grimshaw . . . them screams . . . we was . . ."

"It's nothing to do with you but I thank you for your concern. Now, back to your beds at once."

They had no choice but to go, edging away behind Bridie's candle into the pitch dark of the coffee-room and the staircase, their flapping white nightdresses gleaming in a huddle as they moved, sidling so close together they kept bumping into one another. They glanced back a dozen times, their wondering gaze dwelling on the quiet, enormous bulk of the cellarman who seemed to them to be hovering protectively over the slight figure of their mistress. The master was slumped with his back to them over the bar counter, a white square of handkerchief held to his face, a bottle of brandy at his elbow, a shudder running through him in a regular pattern. Miss Grimshaw, in nothing but her unfrilled, untucked nightgown, her hair falling about her face like a silver waterfall, her soft shawl in a pool at her feet, was completely motionless, waiting for something perhaps, though God alone knew what it might be.

Sally sat down slowly, feeling her way into the rocking-chair where, two weeks ago, Freddy and Job had sat Adam Cooper in his extremity and now it was her turn. She felt quite numb with nothing in her head to get a grip on and think about. No sense of what she should do next, but at the same time conscious of the swirl of disorientated thoughts – no, they were not even firm enough to be called thoughts – which flew round and round in her head like a flock of starlings. She knew she was deep in shock, the enormity of Freddy's folly – what a ludicrous word to describe the chaos he had caused – scarcely grasped yet. Maybe tomorrow when she had recovered somewhat from the grievous blow he had struck her she might be able to pull her thoughts together and find some answer. Dear God in heaven, she felt like laughing hysterically at the very idea of there *being* an answer. Some way out of this monstrous dilemma, if you could call it that, but in the meanwhile all she wanted was to drag herself, or preferably be carried, up to her bed, and sink into oblivion. She couldn't do it, of course. She couldn't just snuggle down beneath her warm quilt and drift off to sleep as she had done thousands of times under the roof of this inn which, she realised now, she loved more than life itself. It was her life. She had given it life. Her mother had begun it, taught her the complexities of good management, good housekeeping, for that was all it was. The keeping of a house and doing it well. Providing for its guests, making them welcome. Ma had passed on her skills in cooking and Sally had taken them, and all the other talents needed to be a successful publican, and she had become the best.

Now, in a few short, self-indulgent weeks her brother had taken it from her. They could never hope to repay the money Freddy had "borrowed from a man". That was how he had put it in his vague, unimaginitive way. "A man" at the club who seemed to know him and trust him and was quite willing to take his IOU providing he could put something up as collateral.

He had put up the Grimshaw Arms!

The big man waited patiently in the shadow of the room, his grey eyes alert and never shifting from the huddled figure of the woman in the chair. He had handed her her shawl and had even tucked it about her since she was shivering, and it had not seemed odd to either of them. He had coaxed the fire back to life with hands that were huge but amazingly dextrous, then, when it was blazing warmly, stood back and waited.

"When is he coming, this man?" her harsh voice said at last. She did not turn round to face her brother.

"Look, Sal, don't worry about it. I can arrange something to get us over this." Even now Freddy was unable to grasp the enormity of what he had brought on them. He'd always managed to extricate himself, or been extricated by his pa, or Sally, and he seemed to see no reason why it couldn't be done again. Sally had uncharacteristically, but justifiably, flown off the handle when he had told her the amount he owed but there would be bound to be a way out, wouldn't there? Sally was clever and she would find it, if he couldn't.

"We can perhaps borrow the cash and pay him off," he went on. "That way we can keep the inn . . . Perhaps Jacky's pa . . ."

"Stop it, Freddy."

"I was only—"

"You were only doing what you're best at," she cut in bitterly, "playing the fool." Her voice was weary but his words had stirred a bit of hope in her heart. Perhaps they *could* borrow the money, from the bank, say, using the inn as collateral, if it was legal to do so now that it appeared to be in the hands of "the man". That way at least she would still be who she was. Who she had been for the past five years ever since her pa died. She would still be Sally Grimshaw, publican, if only in name, of the Grimshaw Arms.

The big man continued to stand in the shadows between the taproom and the dark kitchen. There was a tiny flicker of flame in the fire behind him which touched the white walls to the palest apricot and put a dull gleam in the well-scrubbed copper pans which hung in rows above the big, blackleaded range. It outlined his powerful frame which blocked the doorway where he stood, his arms crossed on his chest.

For five minutes nobody spoke. The only sound was that made by Freddy as he splashed brandy into his glass and the cheerful crackle of the fire in the fireplace.

At last Sally stirred and the big man straightened slowly, waiting, or so it seemed, for her to tell him what he was to do next, what she wanted him to do next, what she needed of him, for whatever it was he would do it. Give her brother the thrashing of his life, perhaps, since he deserved it, or even murder him, for though Job had the patient, mindless look of a dumb animal, his brain was keen despite the fifteen years of battering it had received in the prize fighting ring. He knew exactly what the young bastard had done to his mistress. Words like collateral and interest were unfamiliar to him since never in his life had he had to deal with either but he knew what an IOU was and what it threatened Miss Grimshaw. He, of them all, was totally aware of what the loss of the Grimshaw Arms would do to her, for it was husband, lover, friend, child to her and how was she to live her life without it? Who would look after her? Certainly not that pathetic specimen of a brother of hers. You'd only to look at him blubbering in his brandy, sorry to have caused all this aggravation, as he kept on telling the emptying bottle, but totally unconcerned about who was to put it right. Not him, that was for sure, since even now he was completely insensible as to how it was to be done or who was to do it.

"I can't . . . can't think just now," Sally said to no one in particular, swaying to her feet. "My brain's gone numb . . ." Her voice trailed off uncertainly and Job moved round the bar counter with the speed and agility he had once shown in the boxing ring, not touching her but ready to catch her should she fall.

"I'm going to bed . . . perhaps . . . tomorrow . . ."

Aye, tomorrow she would rise from her bed, put up her hair and dress herself in the neat, respectable garments she considered suitable for a woman in business to wear. She would carry on as she always did, stubborn, hardworking, conscientious, sharp-tongued, with that passionate spirit which no one but Job seemed ever to have recognised. When "the man", whoever he was, came to call in his IOU she would deal with it, displaying the challenging courage he had loved in her from the moment she had told Elly to give him bread and cheese to go with his soup, and a slice of the fruit cake she had just made.

5

The man rode into the yard a week later, got down from his fine bay and, as Tim-Pat skedaddled round from the back of the stable block, threw him the reins. He looked about him keenly, strolling to the front of the inn as though he owned the place, which he did!

His name was Richard Keene, he told Sally genially, looking down at her from a great height since he was exceptionally tall and thin.

It had been a bitter week and if Richard Keene had offered her Freddy's IOU in exchange for the five hundred guineas he wanted for it she couldn't have given it to him. The amount she had tried to borrow at the Royal Union Bank in Castle Street was more than the property was worth, the bank manager had told her, clearly astonished by her request and wondering what she was to do with such a large sum. He had begged her to tell him until he remembered the account, held by herself and her brother and into which all profits from the inn were put, and which, during the past three months, had been systematically emptied. When Miss Grimshaw drove down to the bank on her regular visit to deposit the week's takings she had not enquired as to the balance since, in her usual methodical way, she had her own records. She knew to the last farthing how much there was in the account on which both she and her brother could draw, a mistake in Mr Moore's opinion, and since, as far as she was aware, nothing had been taken out except what she needed for the inn's expenses, the entry she had in her record was a true and accurate one.

She had not seemed surprised when he had told her that it was not.

"Are you in financial trouble, Miss Grimshaw?" he had asked her tentatively.

"You might say that, Mr Moore."

Miss Grimshaw leaned back tiredly in her chair, exuding the tension which Mr Moore recognised having seen a hundred times in the gentlemen who sat where she sat now and who were strapped for cash. They did their best to hide it, as Miss Grimshaw was doing, but Mr Moore had been a banker for many years and knew what it was immediately. Miss Grimshaw, and her brother, of course, though one was prone to overlook him in the matter of business, had a small but thriving concern in their public house the Grimshaw Arms and he could not imagine what had gone so wrong that the publican – he could only call her that – needed this extraordinary amount of money. The inn was not mortgaged and the profits earned each week were more than satisfactory for a public house of its size. He had been most disturbed, even mortified, since he should have been told of it, to find that as fast as Miss Grimshaw was depositing that profit, for the past three months her brother had been drawing it out.

"I could arrange a loan up to the value of your property and business, Miss Grimshaw, but that would be only half of what you're asking, I'm afraid. You see there would be a great deal of interest to pay on such a loan, beside the repayment of the loan, and from your accounts, which I have here before me, I cannot see how you can possibly repay it. Five hundred guineas is a lot of money."

Though he knew he had struck her a body blow there was still an air of determination about her which manifested itself in the set of her small chin and the firmness of her lips. A determination which told him that she was not beaten though God alone knew how she was to win through.

"I see I must try elsewhere then, Mr Moore," she said, leaning forward again and smiling in a way he had never seen her do before. She was a plain young woman, plainly dressed with her hair dragged back uncompromisingly into her close bonnet, with nothing about her to attract a male eye and yet when she smiled it changed her in some way, even putting colour in her cheeks, her smiling lips and the sudden tawny glow of her slanting eyes. He was quite fascinated for a moment but then, as quickly as it had come, it disappeared and she was as he had always known her.

She stood up and straightened her back and he could have sworn she winced as though she ached in every bone of her body but her prim bonnet lifted and so did her chin.

Mr Moore leaped to his feet as she held out her hand. "Oh, please, Miss Grimshaw, I beg of you, don't do that since I suppose you mean a moneylender?" His face was almost comical in its woe.

"What else can I do, Mr Moore?"

"But surely there must be something?"

"Believe me, I have racked my brains and there is nothing."

The moneylender's office, as though it knew its purpose was unsavoury, was off a street which led to another and then another, going deeper and deeper until she reached a squalid back alley which stank of cats. She had almost turned back, since who knew what loathsome creature might lurk in a dark doorway, ready to steal her purse, her cloak, her boots, her virginity.

She might as well have saved herself the trouble. The moneylender was quite willing to extend such a loan, he said, after he had thumbed through her account books, his shifty eyes running over her neat and respectable figure like rats in a sewer, beady and assessing. Oh, yes, no trouble at all, my dear, mentioning the sum she must pay him each week and the penalty if she failed to do so and even she, desperate as she was, knew it was out of the question.

It seemed that Freddy had not told her the full story which, when it was dragged from him, was as loathsome and plain stupid as he was himself. "The man" had been one of those who had stood admiringly at Freddy Grimshaw's back on one of his runs of luck at the roulette wheel, clapping him enthusiastically on the shoulder as the chips piled up beside him, commiserating with him when they dwindled away to nothing.

"You seem to like a game of chance, Mr Grimshaw," he had said affably to Freddy. "What say we play poker which is a particular favourite of mine. I'm sure it would be enjoyable for us both and if you won, and you have as good a chance as I, you would recoup your losses and pay off . . . I do beg your pardon but I could not help but overhear your conversation with a certain person who shall be nameless but who is a well-known moneylender in Liverpool. You could settle your account with him, and with anyone else whom you are in debt to and even have a bit over to get back into the game," nodding at the roulette wheel which was still spinning hypnotically.

"Does five hundred guineas sound tempting, Mr Grimshaw?"

A week later Richard Keene folded his long frame into the chair Sally offered him, stretching out his legs to the good fire which burned in the hearth of her private sitting-room which was just off the kitchen to the rear of the snug. It was small and comfortable, used only by herself since her ma died, a woman's room, her pa and Freddy called it. There were two red velvet wing chairs, one on either side of the fireplace, and a round table covered with a red chenille cloth. There was a dresser, come from the farm in which her grandmother had grown up and on its shelves were bits and pieces of ornaments, nothing grand, mostly Staffordshire. A sailor in a broad-brimmed hat and baggy trousers, two figures, a man and a woman kissing beneath a parasol; figures in rural settings, farm animals and "comforter" dogs. The principal colour used to paint the figures was a deep blue and they glowed, at least a dozen of them, against the pale pine of the dresser. There was a rag rug before the fire and the languorous ticking and sonorous chiming of a long-case clock which stood against the wall. It was said to be over a hundred and fifty years old and had never, the story went, stopped ticking in all those years. The carcass was of oak, covered with delicate and intricate marquetry and Sally allowed no one but herself to touch it.

"Fine clock," Mr Keene said amiably enough, though Sally did not care for the speculative narrowing of his colourless, close-set eyes as they roamed about the room.

"Yes, it belonged to my great-grandmother." She sat stiffly on the edge of her chair without the slightest indication that she was waiting, as those in France must have waited, for the blade of the guillotine to fall. Not to chop off her head but to cut her life into small and unmendable pieces.

"Indeed."

Freddy, since it was he, after all, who had been owner of the inn and the one who had, on the turn of a card, given it into the hands of the man who sat opposite Sally, perched himself on a chair which had been dragged in from the kitchen.

"Worth a bit," he said incautiously, then, catching Sally's eye, clamped his lips tightly together as though to reassure her that he meant to leave the talking to her, as she had instructed him.

"You keep a good fire, Miss Grimshaw," Mr Keene remarked, nodding at the leaping flames and glowing embers in the grate, "and in a room that one would suppose is scarcely used."

Sally looked surprised. What was her fire to do with him? she thought, then, biting her lip, reminded herself of why he was here. Perhaps he thought that, having acquired the Grimshaw Arms he was entitled to describe all that was in it, even the coal in the cellar, as his. Well, he could just think again, the smarmy-faced bastard. She tilted her chin and her eyes flashed dangerously. Her lips thinned and her voice sounded like crystals of ice tinkling in a breeze.

'It's a cold day, Mr Keene, and may I remind you that the coal was paid for with money *I* earned."

"Of course, Miss Grimshaw, of course." He inclined his head sardonically in her direction and she had the uneasy feeling that if it came to it, things would be very different under his supervision.

"Now then, Mr Keene," she pronounced firmly, doing her best to smile, for she had not yet given up hope that some deal might be struck with this man who reminded her strongly of a fox. Pointed nose and pointed ears with a thin mouth and absolutely no expression nor warmth in his face. He was sipping the brandy he had asked for with evident relish and his hand toyed with the handsome gold watch chain across his waistcoat.

"Yes, Miss Grimshaw?"

"Freddy . . . my brother and I were wondering if perhaps we might come to some arrangement regarding the IOU he gave you." She spoke in the clipped voice of someone who has a toothache and is in great pain and her eyes glowed a deep molten gold, for Sally Grimshaw was not accustomed to begging. At that moment, if she had not held herself on the tightest of reins, she felt as though she might reach down for the brass poker and set about her brother's head with it. She hated Freddy fiercely for what he had done to her and even if everything worked out as she hoped it would, she would never forgive him. But there was nothing else she could do but bite her tongue, for this was *her* living she was pleading for, not his. The inn belonged to him, and Sally Grimshaw, as his unmarried, dependent sister had no part in this . . . this . . . could she call it a transaction? But how could she leave it to Freddy? It was his stupidity that had got them into this mess. His greed, his childish inability to deny himself the thrill of "a bit of a gamble", and unless she could do a deal with this foxy-faced man who sat opposite her, they would all be out on the streets, including the servants, she supposed.

"What had you in mind, Miss Grimshaw?" he asked smoothly. He placed the brandy glass on the table beside him then put his hands together as though in prayer, tapping the ends of his fingers against his lips. Sally felt hope surge in her breast.

"I could . . . we could raise half the money that . . . Freddy . . . that we owe right away . . ." Oh, how bitter those words tasted on her tongue, since Sally Grimshaw had never owed a penny to a soul in her life. "And then . . . we would have to put in place the strictest economies, of course, but we would be prepared to pay you back a certain sum each month until the debt is repaid. There would be interest to pay, I know but . . ."

Freddy sat forward eagerly. "My sister is a good manager, Mr Keene, and it'd be paid off before you know it."

They both, Sally and Mr Keene, gave him a withering look.

"And how long is 'before I know it', Mr Grimshaw?" Mr Keene asked pleasantly.

"Aah, well, you'd best ask Sal that." Freddy grimaced and raised his fair eyebrows ruefully as though Mr Keene should know by now that Freddy really had no head for figures.

Mr Keene turned back to Sally.

"Miss Grimshaw?"

"It would depend on the interest you charged us."

"Of course, and after a casual glance at your records I would put that at about five years and I'm afraid I can't wait that long for a return on my . . . er . . . investment. No, I'm afraid I have no choice but to sell the inn, as the IOU your brother signed entitles me to. I think I could make a decent profit."

Her heart, so sorely tried, lurched in her chest then fell sickeningly and she felt the dead cold of hope lost turn her body to ice. The bile rose to her mouth. She longed to leap to her feet and smash her fists into this man's smiling face and then when she'd bloodied it to her own satisfaction, to start on Freddy. If only she could shrug her shoulders, get to her feet and leave the room, indicating that as there was no more to say on the matter she was off to pack her bags, but how could she do that? How could she? They all knew in the kitchen what had happened and though they did not have as much to lose as Sally Grimshaw since they would find jobs somewhere, particularly on her recommendation, they were anxious to stay where they were well fed, comfortably housed and fairly paid, even if Miss Grimshaw was a martinet.

"Please, Mr Keene, won't you allow us a . . . a few more weeks?"

Her face was like paper and her eyes copper coals of loathing in it. Self-loathing that she must humble herself to this arrogantly lounging man, loathing for the man himself who was enjoying this enormously and loathing for her brother who had put her in this indefensible position.

"To do what, Miss Grimshaw? You have already told me you can only raise half the money, which is no good to me, so what purpose will a few more weeks serve?"

"We could . . ."

"Yes, Miss Grimshaw?"

"Well . . ."

"Exactly, there is nothing to be done."

Sally leaned forward, her face, which had softened in its pleading, becoming hard again. She could not seem to formulate her thoughts coherently since there were so many feelings and images crowding her mind. There must be something she could do, or say, to stop this insolently smiling bastard from taking what she loved most in the world, but the confused working of her usually uncluttered mind could not think what it might be. She was frightened, terrified, she admitted it, for where were they to go, she and Freddy? To Vi's over the water? Squash in with her and Arthur and four children, with another on the way? Dear Lord . . . oh, dear God in heaven, help me to find the words to persuade this man . . .

"What do you want this place for, Mr Keene?" were the words that actually came out of her mouth, surprising not only her but Mr Keene as well, while Freddy, who lolled on his chair with every appearance of someone not involved, was seen to yawn! "You say you are to sell it and if so, as you have told us and as others have said" – not wishing to mention Mr Moore – "it is valued at only half the amount you were prepared to wager."

"Yes, you're right." He paused reflectively. "The Grimshaw Arms is a very profitable business and perhaps, under certain conditions, I might be persuaded to . . . hang on to it."

"What conditions are those, Mr Keene?"

"It seems to me that you are the one who has made it as profitable as it is, Miss Grimshaw. Even your brother says you are a good manager. If you were to remain and with some of those strict economies you spoke of, and one or two other practices I mean to implement, the inn could make an even bigger margin of profit for me. What d'you say, Miss Grimshaw, can I interest you in the post of manager of the Grimshaw Arms?"

She stared at him as though transfixed, her face emptying of every expression and turning even whiter, if that were possible. There was nothing in her head now, nothing but buzzing and bird twitterings and a kind of numbness that would not allow her brain to send messages to her hands which wanted to hit something, or her feet which wanted to kick out, or to her mouth which wanted to speak words of such obscenity she shrank from them. She was totally frozen and speechless.

Not so Freddy. He sprang to his feet, his face splitting into a delighted grin, his eyes alight with satisfaction, his well-booted feet ready to do a jig on the rag rug.

"There, you see, Sal, I said it would all come right in the end," he chortled, laying a congratulatory hand on her rigid shoulder. "I know we shall be working for Mr Keene who I'm sure will reward us with wages in accordance with our abilities and hard work, won't you, sir?" beginning, it seemed, as he meant to go on. "We shall be doing exactly what we have always done, won't we, Mr Keene, and really, Sal, you'll scarcely notice the difference."

Sally turned to look at him and even Richard Keene felt compelled to stare in what seemed to be amusement. Her face flamed in the firelight with an anger that was ready to consume her and her eyes flashed tawny sparks which boded ill for Freddy Grimshaw, but before she could speak Mr Keene rose to his feet. There was not a great deal of space on the rug and Freddy was forced to step back a pace towards the closed door.

"Oh, no," Mr Keene said softly, his eyes like granite in his pallid foxy face though his mouth still smiled. "Oh, no, Mr Grimshaw, the offer of work does not extend to you. I have no intention of employing a man who could throw away a thriving business on the turn of a card. No, you will pack your bags and be out of my inn by nightfall and your sister with you, if she's a mind. But if she wants it, the job is hers. The sale, or not, of the Grimshaw Arms depends entirely on her. Now, I'll just have a look over the place, speak to the servants, decide who is to go and who to stay, then I'll be off. Let me know, Miss Grimshaw. I'm at the Adelphi."

There was a hollow, echoing silence after he had gone, as though the words he had just spoken were still swirling round and round the room like autumn leaves in a high wind. Brother and sister remained in the frozen postures into which Richard Keene's statement had flung them, not looking at one another, overtaken at last by the true horror of their situation. The clock ticked and the fire spat as a piece of coal fell and they each waited for the other to speak. In his wildest dreams, or nightmares, if he had had the imagination to have them, not once had it occurred to Freddy Grimshaw that "old Sal" would not have the predicament sorted out in no time and running to the well-ordered plans she would dictate in the future. They'd be short of a bob or two for a long time, a long, long time, even he realised that, but he was prepared to make sacrifices since the fault, he readily admitted it, was his. No more racketing off with Jacky to the gaming club, naturally, and he'd have to forgo that new velvet jacket he'd promised himself. A few economies in the bars, of what sort he wasn't awfully sure but Sal would know. Tighten their belts a bit, though again he was not exactly certain what that meant but Sal, who had the cleverest brain he'd ever known in a woman, would get them through it.

Now, with a few words, smilingly delivered, the new owner had cut through Freddy Grimshaw's complacency like a hot knife through butter and Freddy didn't know what to do next. He did what he had always done in the past.

"Sal?" he asked quaveringly. "He didn't mean it, did he, Sal? He can't just turn us out like that, can he? We've been here . . . the family . . . for forty years and we can't just be turned out without so much as a . . . as a . . ." His voice tapered off uncertainly.

Sally raised her hands in a gesture Freddy had seen her make a thousand times, smoothing back her already smooth hair. She adjusted the shining coil at the back of her head, then, with a movement which typified her fierce will to overcome, she squared her slender shoulders in readiness for the heavy burden which was to be placed on them.

"You should have thought of that when you chucked away my hard-earned cash in that club, Freddy." Sally's voice was without expression, and so was her bone-white face. "And yes, it seems he can. This inn belongs to him now, and all the fixtures and fittings as well, Mr Moore's lawyer tells me. We can take Great-grandmother's clock and . . . personal things but everything to do with the inn belongs to him."

Her voice was dream-like, giving the impression that she was in some vague, slightly unreal world of hopeless and despairing resignation and yet behind her blank face her mind was skittering and slithering like a duck on a frozen pond, propelled by its own need to make some sort of sense out of all this. Richard Keene had told her that she might stay on and work for him, which meant exactly what? she asked herself. Was he implying that she was to carry on just as she had done all these years, mistress and publican in name only, which, she had to acknowledge, was what she had always been. The profits made would go into his pocket, not hers and she was only too well aware that those profits would be much more substantial than what she had made. A dishonest publican could cheat his customers as easily as falling off a log, particularly when they'd had a few pints of ale and the meals, for which Sally had always used the best quality ingredients, could easily be tampered with. And what was that he'd said about the servants? Which were to go and which to stay? Was she to take it that the inn was to be run just as it had always been run but with only half the staff? His remark about the fire now made sense and if what she was thinking was correct, coal, and indeed everything that made the Grimshaw Arms the comfortable, welcoming, well-thought-of hostelry it had always been was to be in short supply.

"I'm sorry, Sal," Freddy said defensively. "I've been a fool, I know, and if I could go back and make it right, I would. I just never thought, when it began, that it would get such a bloody hold on me. You know I'd never hurt you on purpose, don't you? It was just . . . well, a bit of fun but . . . it got out of hand."

"*A bit of fun*! *Out of hand*? Dear God in heaven, Freddy, you've just destroyed my life, taken away everything that meant anything to me and you talk as though you'd lost a few bob that can be easily replaced. Have you any idea what this means to me, have you?"

Sally's voice rose to a pitch which she recognised as close to hysteria and she fought to control it. It didn't matter now, about Freddy, or the gambling, the "bit of fun" he had got up to, since it was too late for recriminations. Too late for anything really. She had to pull herself together and force her poor aching brain into some semblance of coherence. She had decisions to make, a life – her own – to decide on and Freddy's whining was getting badly on her overstretched nerves. Even yet she could see he was waiting for her to tell him where they were to go, what they were to do, for it did not seem to have occurred to him that from now on he must fend for himself.

She stood up blindly, reaching with a trembling hand to summon one of the maids and when Bridie appeared, badly flustered since "that man" had been "poking about", as she put it, where, in her opinion, he had no right to be, Sally ordered a tray of tea.

"'E's bin in't cellar an' pantry, Miss Grimshaw, askin' Elly ter open this an' that, an' even down in't cellar."

"He has a right to go there, Bridie," Sally said patiently. "Now fetch that tea, there's a good girl."

"Job were proper purrout, Miss Grimshaw, an' we thought there might be a right terdo, like. 'Course, Job'd've made mincemeat out of 'im, an' that chap knew it burrit didn't make any difference. Down't cellar steps 'e went, askin' Job about casks an' such."

"Cheeky devil," Freddy said indignantly.

"Right sir, that's what we thought, an' 'e keeps on about a new 'ray jeem', wharrever tharris when it's at 'ome."

"The tea, Bridie."

The situation, in the servants' uncomprehending minds, was exactly as it had been in Freddy's. They had no idea of the havoc which was almost upon them. In their vague and uncertain way they had grasped that the inn now belonged to the insolent fellow who was peeping into Miss Grimshaw's jars of pickled onions, the plums and damsons and peaches from the old orchard at the back of the inn, which their mistress had "put up" last back end; her store of cheeses, of tea and coffee and sugar, but they had not yet grasped the fact that all these things no longer belonged to Miss Grimshaw. That he was, in fact, taking an inventory of the inn's assets. They didn't think it was right and they were surprised at Miss Grimshaw, who could be a real termagant if she wanted to be, for letting him do it.

"'E were off ter look at bedrooms, 'e said, mum, an' there were no need fer Jane ter show 'im't way. 'E'd find 'em 'imself 'e said. Bold as brass off 'e went up back stairs, shoutin' over 'is shoulder 'e'd 'ave a look at stables next. Eeh, what's it come to when . . ."

Bridie shook her head in total disbelief, her immaculate cap bobbing over her forehead with the force of her displeasure. Bridie had been in service for a long time, nearly thirty years, in fact, ever since she was ten years old and she'd seen a few things in her time but nothing like the cheek of this fellow who was at this very minute, as far as she knew, pawing through Bridie's clean undergarments in the chest of drawers she shared with Jane.

She left the room still muttering and Freddy sighed. He

shoved his hands deep in his trouser pockets, strolling over to the small window which looked out across the stable yard. He lounged there in brooding silence, waiting for Sally to say something, to come up with some idea for their future.

The tea came, Bridie still deliberating on the "nerve" of that chap who was even now counting bottles of brandy and whisky and rum in the bar parlour, making notes on a little pad, she said, along with all the others he'd jotted down in the past hour. If she was surprised that her mistress, whose existence was a positive and articulate presence in the lives of the servants, had nothing to say on the subject, she did not voice it, at least not to her, grumbling on the way in, grumbling on the way out, though when she returned to the kitchen she did remark to Jane and Elly that the mistress looked right peaky.

Freddy refused a cup of tea, saying he thought he might have a brandy, casually strolling out into the taproom to pour himself a glass. When he returned he took up his stance again by the window, sipping reflectively while he waited for "old Sal" to come up with some idea that would get them out of this hole they were in.

It began to grow dark. Richard Keene had ridden away on his splendid mount, giving Freddy a cheery wave as he went. Freddy had waved back!

Sally placed her cup and saucer carefully on the tea tray, then stood up. She smoothed her hair and then the sombre grey worsted of her skirt.

"Well, Freddy," she said equably, "I suppose we'd best be getting on. There's an inn to open and I don't suppose Flo and Edie will notice the time. And hadn't you better be getting on with your packing? Mr Keene did say you were to be off the premises by nightfall."

Freddy, who had turned to watch her, let his mouth fall

open in consternation, then, in sudden relief, he began to smile.

"Now then, Sal, you shouldn't joke about such a serious matter."

She shook her head wonderingly. Her face was a hard white mask and her eyes even harder, a dark and depthless brown.

"Believe me, Freddy, I'm not joking."

"But you can't . . ."

"I can, Freddy. I have made up my mind to stay, since I have nowhere else to go and know of no other way to earn my living. You see, I cannot rely on you to support me, can I, so I must do the best I can with what I have. The only thing I know is innkeeping so I have decided to accept Mr Keene's offer."

6

She thought it was without doubt the worst day of her life, even worse than that of three weeks ago when Freddy had told her he'd thrown their home, their livelihood and her life away on the turn of a card.

Richard Keene had asked her to see that the servants, all of them, were lined up in the kitchen as he wished to speak to them. A matter of planning the new régime, he told her smoothly and the sooner it began the better.

They stood in anxious silence, their eyes swivelling to follow his progress as he sauntered down the line, stopping before each one in turn, eyeing them up and down, his hands pressed together as if in prayer, tapping his teeth and shaking his head as though a sorrier bunch he'd never come across. Edie, who lived out with her elderly mother who had a small cottage in Old Swan a quarter of a mile down the road, had been the last to arrive. She flung off her coat and bonnet in great haste since "the man" looked none too pleased to be kept waiting, even for thirty seconds.

"What's your name?" he asked her, smiling, which he did a lot of and which should have eased her apprehension but somehow didn't.

"Edie, sir."

"Edie . . .?"

She looked at him blankly. Edie was a good barmaid.

Older than Flo who shared her duties, perhaps thirty-two or -three. What was known as the "carriage trade", since the gentlemen arrived mounted on horses, drank in the bar parlour where spirits were served and they liked Edie. She was handsome in a stately kind of way, pleasant and comfortable, not the sort of barmaid a man would flirt with but a good steady worker who knew her trade. She could neither read nor write but put some coins in her hand and she knew to the farthing how much was there. The prices of the different spirits were as familiar to her as her mam's face and she had never "wrong-changed" a customer in the ten years she had been at the Grimshaw Arms.

But set her in a situation such as this one where she didn't know what was expected of her and she gave the impression of being dull-witted. Her good-natured equanimity deserted her and she began to stammer.

"Wha' . . .?"

"Your name, woman, I'm asking you your name."

"Edie, sir."

Sally, who stood in line with the other servants, for that was what she was now, interrupted tartly.

"Edie Cotton . . . sir. Edie is barmaid and a good one."

Richard Keene turned his smiling countenance on her and she had time to wonder how a man could smile as much as he did and yet be so completely without humour. His eyes ran over her with an insolence she had never, in all her years of working among some of the roughest labourers in the area, met before. His close-set eyes lingered for a moment at her breast. Her mouth tightened ominously and from behind her, where the enormous bulk of Job loomed, there came the hiss of an indrawn breath.

Job had been, during the period since Freddy had revealed the terrible loss of the Grimshaw Arms, always close at hand, unusually so. It had never interfered with his work, which during the past few days had been doubled without Freddy, but whatever she was doing, wherever she happened to be, Sally would sense his eyes on her, his presence protective and welcome as though some curious link had been forged between them when he had held her in his strong, benign arms on that night. It gave her a feeling of calm in a world which had gone mad, without being in the least threatening, to realise that he was there should circumstances arise in which she might need him, though God alone knew what those circumstances could be, she thought wryly.

She found she had begun to talk to him, even to confide her fears to him which was quite incredible when one considered the difference in their status, their background, their gender, even their education, for Job had none. Like Edie, he could neither read nor write but his quiet air of patience and his willingness to listen to and understand what she told him were infinitely soothing.

When she had revealed to him, before she said anything to the others, that Freddy had left and could he manage, perhaps with Tim-Pat's help, he had shaken his head, not in refusal as she had first thought but as though in wonderment that she needed to ask. His ugly bruiser's face had broken into that curiously attractive, white-toothed smile and creases had appeared at the corner of each eye.

"Don't you fret none, Miss Sally. I'll manage."

Neither of them appeared to notice, or if they did were not concerned, when he began to use her christian name, with the respectful "miss" before it, naturally.

"It's just that things are going to be awkward. No, that's the wrong word, Job, they're going to be difficult, damnably difficult for all of us."

"I understand, Miss Sally." And he did, for they would

all be serving under a man none of them knew, a man who had no scruples, it appeared, in taking what was not morally his. It would be doubly difficult for the little maid – that's how he always thought of her – since she must now take orders instead of giving them. "But yer've not ter be afeared," he finished.

Sally sighed, leaning against the enormous cask he had just physically manhandled down the outside steps to the cellar.

"I try not to be, Job, but the outlook is not propitious."

Job didn't know what "propitious" meant but he could tell by her face and manner that it was not good.

"I know, Miss Sally, but yer've not ter be afeared," he said again and his words, amazingly, had given her some small comfort.

Later, and with some ingenuity, he had devised a curious set of wheels with two sturdy handles and a kind of step, all of the pieces come from the junk yard at the back of the ironworks in Wavertree. With a bit of guidance and a word of cheerful Irish whimsy from Tim-Pat, they were managing, he and the stable lad, doing what he and Freddy had once done. It was as though, knowing she needed it and there was no one else but himself to supply her need, his great strength had doubled, become almost superhuman, enabling him to perform tasks which would previously have been beyond him.

"Now then," Mr Keene was saying genially, perching his lean buttocks on the huge, well-scoured table in the centre of the kitchen. On the table stood two dozen meat and potato pies, just come from the oven, crisp and golden brown with deliciously fragrant steam whispering from the leaf-shape cut-out in the centre of each pie. There was an enormous cooked ham, lean and pink and succulent, a saddle of beef "resting" before it was sliced ready for the noon trade; a bowl of polished red apples from the storeroom, several cheeses, Lancashire, of course, with Cheshire and a Stilton of great age. There were jars of pickled eggs and onions and a row of crusty white loaves, their humble aroma as good as any found in the fancy restaurant at the Adelphi where French food of the gourmet kind was served.

A good fire leaped behind the blackleaded bars of the grate, throwing dancing lights on the copper pots and pans which hung on hooks on the chimney breast. From the enormous oak beams which divided the ceiling hung onions, dried herbs, a couple of smoked hams, mushrooms in a net and half a dozen game birds which were not yet "high" enough for the table. It all spoke of superb housekeeping, a passion for cleanliness and a talent for cooking which could be surpassed by none.

"Now then," Mr Keene repeated, his eye falling directly on Sally. "I think it would be best to speak of economy right away. Miss Grimshaw has done well in the past with this public house but I intend to do even better and the only way to achieve this is to economise. Wastage is a sin." He paused to let this sink in. "I have noticed a certain indiscriminate use of coal, and improvidence where commodities in the kitchen are concerned and it must stop immediately. I shall have a private word with Miss Grimshaw who, as you know, is to be my manager here and in fact will do and be just as she was before the Grimshaw Arms came into my hands. She will pass on my orders and complaints."

Sally kept her eyes averted. She was afraid to look into the face of the tall, thin man who was now her master lest he should see the expression of contempt and loathing there. In her mind, though she was not certain why she thought so, there was no doubt that should she displease him he could make her pay for it. He knew full well, as the man who had taken his livelihood away from him, that Freddy Grimshaw was incapable of looking after himself, let alone his sister, and that fact ensured that Sally had no option but to remain here. She could probably earn a living as Edie and Flo did, behind the bar counter of some alehouse but she would be in no better circumstances than she would be here. He had gambled on that fact since the success of the inn depended on her. He had her fast, his narrowed eyes told her, and she'd best dance to his tune from now on even if hers was more acceptable to her. Though he had said nothing yet beyond the need to be careful with the coal and . . . well, she was not certain how he imagined they could save on the staples that were used in the kitchen but she was aware that there would be worse to come. The saving of a couple of scuttles of coal a day, or a few logs of wood, a tablespoon or two of flour or sugar, tea or coffee would make little difference to the profit margin. He was frightening the others, she could see that, which was what he meant to do with his talk of cutting down. She knew perfectly well that though they were bewildered as to the reason for it, in fact scarcely understood the words he was using, he was telling *her* that, despite cuts, the customer would be charged exactly the same.

And he would expect them to increase the number of hours they worked, he said, since their wages were, in his opinion, excessively high.

"That is, of course, those of you who are to remain in my employ for it seems to me that this house is vastly overstaffed. Dead wood, and I mean to remove it, for it is unprofitable."

There was a long, painful silence as the drooping row of servants did their best to get to grips with this last ominous sentence. They had no idea what he meant, of course. They wished to God he would speak plain English so that they could all understand it. It was written on their mystified faces, their total incomprehension, but Sally knew, and so did Job.

Richard Keene turned his head in a leisurely fashion and in his cold eyes something unpleasant stirred. His face was quite without expression and that smile which he had clothed them with was gone. Sally recognised that behind the smooth blankness of his face, his shrewd brain, that which had enticed her brother into a game of poker and with it taken this profitable business from Freddy's weak grasp, was adding up the money he was saving here. Money which would go into his pocket.

The servants, still silent, not quite sure what was happening, or was about to happen, waited like beasts in a pen at the abattoir for the knife to fall. Keene continued to stare enquiringly at Sally as though he knew full well he would not go unchallenged. He was looking forward to it, his expression said. He had spoken of who was to stay and who to go and now it seemed the time had come to let them know into which category each was to fall.

"You . . . you at the back there, the big chap, step forward, yes, you," as Job hesitated. Not that he was afraid. Job Hawthorne was afraid of no man. He had always been a big lad, tearing his way out of his mother's womb over thirty years ago, his birth killing her and leaving the boy with his brothers and sisters, those who had survived infancy, to an uncertain future in the hands of a father who neither cared whether they lived or died.

Despite a poor diet which seemed to consist of nothing but oats and potatoes, Job had thrived, working, from the age of three, in the fields about the village where he was born, stone picking, rook-scaring and indeed anything that put food in his constantly hungry belly. His brothers and sisters did the same but where, as they grew, his brothers drifted away to a life of crime and his sisters to prostitution, Job found that, because of his size and strength, he could earn his living, and a good living, in prize-fighting rings across the north of England. He'd been a good-looking lad then, no more than twelve or thirteen but fully grown, well over six feet tall and weighing fifteen stone of hard muscle and bone. Quick on his feet, graceful as a panther, he'd had fifteen good years, living well with the pick of the women, some of them ladies, who came to watch him fight and, sometimes with the blood of his opponents still on him, drew him into their bed.

But his great strength, his agility, his eyesight could not last for ever and the fights, at fairgrounds and circuses, behind inns and out on the moors beyond Oldham, became fewer and fewer and those he had were with men who were much younger and fitter than he was. Time took its toll and so did those contemptuous younger men who found no glory in fighting an old-timer like himself.

He had taken to the road. He had no home, nobody who gave a damn if Job Hawthorne lived or died and so, for several years, he had drifted here and there, working at whatever came to hand, growing older, finding no place to put down roots, knowing he might not survive another harsh winter, until, one day, a little bit of a girl with sunshine in her hair and eyes had told her kitchen maid to "give him some bread and cheese to go with that soup, and a piece of my fruit cake," smiling, but casual, with no awareness of what she had wakened in his heart.

That moment, the moment when he had held her in his arms and she had wept despairingly against his chest, had been for him the most glorious in his life. He did not expect to repeat it, with her or any woman, but if she asked him he would lay down his life for her.

And now she needed him, his protection, his friendship even. His instinct, his urgent desire, was to smash this bad bugger's face in, force him to his knees and twist his arms up behind his back until he apologised to the little maid, but he kept his face blank and stepped forward.

"What's your name?" the man asked.

"Job, sir."

"Dear God in heaven, has no one a surname in this bloody place?"

The servants gasped, all turning to stare in stunned consternation at Miss Grimshaw who allowed no one to swear in her bars, but she simply gazed ahead of her, her eyes devoid of all expression.

Job scratched his head wonderingly and Sally bent her head to hide her smile.

"Sir?"

"Oh, for God's sake, never mind. You'll be the cellarman, I take it?"

"Aye, sir."

Job nodded his head obligingly and touched his forelock in a parody of an underling kow-towing to his feudal lord, but Richard Keene, who had been born lacking humour, saw nothing in the gesture but the respect he thought was owed him.

"And you earn?"

Job turned hesitantly to Sally, the picture of the dim-witted simpleton, all brawn and no brain, the simpleton he wished Mr Keene to believe he was. He didn't know why. It was just some instinct that warned him that one day it might come in handy if Mr Keene believed, as they said in

Liverpool, that Job Hawthorne didn't "have all his oars in the water".

"Fifteen pounds a year and his board," Sally said crisply, daring Keene to argue.

"Very well, that seems reasonable enough, providing he will also take on the duties of the man you now have in the stables. An indolent good-for-nothing if ever I saw one who I believe was having a quiet smoke behind the stable block when I rode into the yard this morning. Typical of the Irish, of course, who come over here expecting to live off the gentry as they do back in Ireland. He can go at once, Miss Grimshaw. Pay him up to last night, if you please."

Tim-Pat, who was lurking somewhere to the rear of the women, looked as though a trapdoor had opened at his feet where he had expected firm ground. His face blanched and his mouth, in which several of his teeth were missing and the rest decayed, fell open and he began to mouth a denial. No . . . no . . . no, it said, though no sound emerged. Tim-Pat had a wife and eleven children in the tiny cottage which was adjacent to the stables. His sweet-faced and patient wife worked at a tub at the laundry in Banastre Street in town, walking the three miles there and back each day with the youngest, a girl not yet weaned, on her back where the docile infant remained all day. Two of his girls, eleven and twelve years old, scrubbed at the Vauxhall Dispensary in Vauxhall Road and his sons, three of them, worked in the fields at any casual labour that was available to them. The other five, all under ten, fended for themselves, coming home at night to sleep in a sprawl in one of the cottage's two bedrooms and somehow they managed. And would again, he supposed, but the double loss of the cottage and the job which gave it to him was a catastrophe.

"But sur, sure an' how's the missis an' meself an' eleven childer ter manage? Holy Mother o' God, 'tis hard enough . . ."

"I'm afraid that's your problem," Mr Keene said distastefully. "That will be all. Go along and see to the packing and removal of your things from the cottage. I intend to let it."

"Mr Keene, you can't do this."

Sally felt that familiar prickle inside her which would lead to the surge of white-hot rage which, before she had learned to control it, had got her into trouble in the past. They had lost a couple of customers over it, before her pa died, when, having been offended over something said, and having been refused an apology, she had given whoever it was the length of her tongue. The heedless, maddened words had poured from her then and were in grave danger of doing so now. Not only was Job to do his own job and Freddy's, but Tim-Pat's as well, which was surely beyond the strength and resolution of his powerful frame, and he was to do it for the same wage! And on top of that, Tim-Pat, who Sally had to agree was inclined towards laziness but was good-tempered about it, was to be chucked out on the street with his family. They would be forced into one of those squalid basements in the tall and crumbling houses which made up the tenements about the dockland. Their whole, teetering way of life, which somehow they had managed to juggle safely through each week, would tumble and be smashed. It was not right, not just, not necessary and she would say so.

"You cannot propose simply to throw a family of young children into the street, Mr Keene. Where will they go? You just cannot do it."

"I can and I have, Miss Grimshaw, and where they go

is their own concern. The cottage is mine, like the inn, to dispose of as I wish."

"Like these people, you mean?" Her eyes narrowed to golden slits of outrage and at her back Job clenched his fists and got ready to spring at the man who had caused it.

Mr Keene smiled and fingered his freshly shaved chin, his eyes glinting in what might have been admiration. Sally was not to know that the force of her argument had brought a flush to the petal smoothness of her skin. Her hair, which she had scraped back and plastered to her skull as though it were painted there, was working into its natural waves, as it did at the slightest provocation, escaping in an engaging froth of curls about her neck and ears, and her breasts, which were surprisingly full and rounded on one so slender, were heaving in the most delightful way. Mr Keene was enjoying it immensely.

'I am merely asserting my right, as the owner, to do as I please in my own establishment, Miss Grimshaw." He smiled amiably.

"No matter who it hurts, even young children?"

"Apart from the children who are surely the responsibility of their parents" – giving Tim-Pat a withering look – "they are able-bodied men and women who are capable of finding other employment."

'They are needed here. They have worked for me, sometimes far beyond their capabilities, and should not be treated like this. They are, all of them, good workers and as honest as the day is long."

The women, who were still not awfully sure what was happening, preened a little, for it was not often Miss Grimshaw handed out praise.

"You cannot do this, Mr Keene," she repeated, desperation in her voice, but it did no good. With a speed and brutal coldness which left them with no room for argument he disposed of Bridie, who was getting on a bit, he told her, and not as active as he would have liked, of Edie, who was the same, and of Elly since, as he put it, there was no need for two cooks in one kitchen.

With a few words, a smile and the appearance of enjoying every moment of it he reduced the staff of the Grimshaw Arms from seven to three. If they were not agreeable, those he had chosen to stay, he told them, then they were at perfect liberty to look elsewhere.

But Sally was not finished and her eyes glittered, again giving Richard Keene what seemed to be a great deal of pleasure.

"I can see you have something else to say, Miss Grimshaw. You really are the champion of the underdog, aren't you? Well, let's have it since I have to be in town shortly."

"Yes, I have. These . . . these underdogs, as you so contemptuously call them, have worked well and faithfully for me and my father and—"

"Can these folk whom you so hotly defend not speak for themselves, Miss Grimshaw?"

Sally looked along the line of frightened, bewildered servants. They were bewildered because they were not awfully sure what had happened to them. They had risen from their beds this morning knowing they were to be employed by the new owner of the inn but Miss Grimshaw, who they all agreed was a fair employer if you worked yourself to a standstill for her, would still be in charge of them. There would be little difference in their circumstances. Mr Keene was a businessman, not an innkeeper, Miss Grimshaw had told them, the sort of businessman who had a finger in many, many pies and who travelled up and down the country making sure no one else put theirs in what was his. They'd see little of him, they were led to believe, and they had believed it.

Now, somehow, catastrophe had overtaken them and the worst thing was they must grin and bear it or, when they went, the bugger wouldn't give them a character reference. To be turned off without a reference was something they all feared since it led to unemployment and the workhouse and that was worse than death.

They stared at one another with eyes like saucers in their white faces and said nothing, for what was there to say? Even Miss Grimshaw had shut up. They were not allowed to move, even those who had just been fired, listening apathetically as Mr Keene unfolded his plans, which would turn the public house into the most efficient and well run in the north of England, which they had thought it was already, but which Sally knew meant, by any means he could, the most profitable. She knew exactly what he intended. He was not interested in a long-term investment. He was not concerned with retaining the good name of the Grimshaw Arms, with what her mother, her father and then herself had built up. The goodwill, the reputation for honesty and fair dealing which had been a source of great pride in the Grimshaw family meant nothing to this man. He was of the breed who saw an opportunity to make a quick killing, buying, or, if he could manage it, cheating the owners out of thriving businesses. Businesses which were reputable, whose customers trusted those who ran them. They would continue to frequent the Grimshaw Arms because she was still behind the counter, scarcely noticing the "little economies", for Mr Keene would require her to be clever at it. There would be practices which, or so she had heard, other publicans got up to, to increase the bulk of whatever it was they were selling. Brick dust in coffee, sand in sugar, chalk in flour. There had been stories of brewers who had added green vitriol or sulphate of iron to put a good "head" on their beer. Water added to the beer itself, and to milk. China tea doctored with verdigris, Indian with black lead, all these contrivances lining the pockets of unscrupulous tradesmen.

He meant to reintroduce one or two of the little entertainments that had once taken place at the Grimshaw Arms, he told them, not saying what they were to be. But Sally knew. Cock fights and dog fights that would attract a certain kind of gambling man, the rougher element of the neighbourhood which had been forced to go elsewhere when Ted Grimshaw had put a stop to it years ago.

And when that happened Sally Grimshaw would be off to look for something else, no matter how menial, or ill-paid!

At last he dismissed them with a peremptory nod, summoning her with a wave of his hand to follow him, strolling through the doorway which led into the low, smoke-blackened bar parlour, taking one of the best chairs by the hearth.

"I think I've time for a brandy before I go. I've a spot of business to see to in Castle Street but I'll be back later to discuss the . . . aah . . . measures which I shall require you to undertake while I'm away. I'm to go up north. I've a concern which needs my attention, but it should take no longer than a few days, perhaps a week . . . or two."

He smiled lazily, letting her know without exactly saying the words that she'd no need to imagine she could relax, revert to the ways that had been hers when she was mistress of this place. He would count every bag of sugar, every sack of flour, every commodity in her store cupboard and pantry, *his* store cupboard and pantry, every cask and barrel and bottle in her bars, even, she suspected, every lump of coal in her coal cellar. If there had been apples on the trees in the orchard he would be prepared to go out there and count those too. He would expect to see an increase in takings, a drop in expenditure, he told her, and woe betide her if she could not show him at least twice the profit she herself had made. He would not tell her when, precisely, she might find him looking over her shoulder, implying that it would probably be when she was least expecting it.

"See that Paddy and his tribe are gone by nightfall, and the rest of them as well and I'm relying on you to keep those who remain—"

"You mean all three of us?" Her voice was cutting and the hectic flush of her clamped-down rage still washed beneath the fine skin of her face. "I hope that I can find the time, sir, since it seems I shall need to labour twenty-four hours out of every twenty-four to keep up with my own duties. The cleaning alone—"

"Get that barmaid to help you," he interrupted, just as cuttingly. "She'll have nothing to do when the inn is closed."

"If she stays. She's not afraid of hard work but this is beyond any woman's capability. Three bars need three women."

"That big chap can give you a hand."

"In between seeing to the horses, taking care of the cellar and—"

"Miss Grimshaw, you have only to say the word and you may leave with the rest. No one is forcing you to work for me, are they?" His smile deepened and he swirled the brandy, which a flustered Flo had brought him, round and round in his glass.

"No."

"So there you are then. We can take it you are here of your own free will?"

"Yes."

Sally stared bleakly out of the side window which gave on to a view of the stable yard. Tim-Pat stood in the centre of it, his bony shoulders drooping in a line of sheer despair. He did nothing, merely stared hopelessly at nothing which, she suspected, was what his future held now.

But Richard Keene was speaking and for ten incredulous seconds what he said made no sense to her and when it did she was too dumbfounded to answer.

"You know you and I could be . . . friends if you go about it the right way, Miss Grimshaw. You'd not find me ungenerous. With your hair loosened like that and your face so prettily flushed you make quite an attractive woman. Why don't you leave it like that when you're working in the bar? It might increase the takings."

7

To make it more bearable, though God knew how she found the time, she said to herself ruefully, she took to walking, sometimes for hours on end, sometimes in sheets of rain or in the teeth of a howling gale, in the meadowland and fields which lay beyond Old Swan and Knotty Ash.

It was nearly four months since Richard Keene had come into her life and in that time she and Job and Flo had worked harder than the slaves in the cotton states of Southern America who were, Sally had heard, treated no better than beasts of the field.

At first she had been determined to keep up the high standards she and her customers were used to. She had risen at five every morning, conscious of Job's huge, silent figure working beside her, scrubbing and polishing and scouring passages and stairs and bedrooms, the flagged floors in the three bars, turning out the coffee-room where she still served the tasty meals she cooked to passing travellers. She cleaned out grates, carried coals – when Job's back was turned – lit fires, washed and dried glasses and tankards, cleaned windows, attended to the washtub and the ironing and all before she began her cooking duties in the kitchen.

From nine until twelve she baked pies and bread, both containing the inferior ingredients her employer insisted upon, though she refused absolutely to add the bulk-enhancing products he would have liked her to add. She scrubbed and peeled vegetables, stirred soups and broth, roasted cheap cuts of meat, producing dishes which only her talent and ingenuity could disguise so that the quality seemed the same and her customers would not notice the difference. The whole time she was at it she felt the need to look constantly over her shoulder as though the man who employed her might have come stealthily upon her when her back was turned.

Which he did. There was no pattern to his visits and he gave no explanation as to why he had "dropped in" as he put it, smiling his stoat's smile. Sometimes there were only a few days between visits, sometimes as long as two weeks. He would brood over the incomings and outgoings, the cash in the box which was kept locked in a safe he had provided, the provisions in the pantry and storeroom, the cellar where the beer was kept, even the coal which Sally swore to Job he counted piece by piece.

So far he had not put into operation the "entertainments" he had planned for the Grimshaw Arms, or rather for the enclosed yard and barn at the back of the stable block. He told Sally that the moment he had found the right man to arrange them, meaning the dog fights and cock fights he had in mind, one he could trust, for the games had been illegal for some twenty years now, then she was to start spreading the word, discreetly, of course, that there was a bit of "sport" to be had for those who were of a mind.

"When that happens, Mr Keene, you can find yourself another manager," she had told him icily, but he had only laughed in that insulting way he had, saying there would be something in it for her if she was a good girl and if she didn't like it she had only to look the other way.

Without Job she could not have managed. Flo was a

good steady worker, willing and conscientious, flitting like a demented mayfly from bar to bar wherever there was a customer who needed serving. Sally had placed a bell on each bar counter so that her patrons – who were flabbergasted by the new arrangements – could summon service when they were ready for another pint or a plate of pease pudding and faggots and either she or Flo, or Job when they were rushed off their feet on pay day, ran to attend to them. She knew the customers, who liked an attractive barmaid to see to their needs, did not care for Job's battered, expressionless face and his non-committal answers to what they considered a bit of witty banter, but there was nothing she could do about that and she meant to tell Richard Keene so when next they met. It was just a physical impossibility for her and Flo to tend to three bars, especially when Sally had her duties in the kitchen and coffee-room to see to at the same time.

She lost weight and though she didn't notice it since she'd no time to be inspecting herself before the mirror except to ensure she was clean and tidy, her face wore an expression of haunted foreboding, a drooping of her features which put ten years on her age. The customers were dismayed by it. She'd been a tartar before she lost the inn but at least she'd been lively, ready to tick them off for the slightest thing but they had become used to that. Now she was short, sparing of words and appeared to them to be totally uninterested in anything they had to say which was not a good trait in a barmaid.

She found she was constantly bone tired and once, after a particularly hectic evening when, it being pay day, a horde of navvies who were working on a branch line of the North Western Railway descended on her like a swarm of locusts, ready to strip her hostelry clean, she had actually fallen on her bed still fully clothed and lost consciousness for nine solid hours.

She had been appalled when she clattered frantically down the stairs the next morning at gone nine o'clock at the thought of the work she must catch up on before the inn opened but Job had been patiently getting on, performing not only his chores but hers.

"I couldn't manage them pies though, Miss Sally," was all he said, a curl of humour at the corner of his mouth.

Flo did her share, of course, more than her share, for as she had pointed out tartly she was a barmaid, with a barmaid's talents and did not expect to do skivvying. She was nearly twenty, and attractive, saucy when it was required but a respectable girl none the less. Sally was only waiting for the day, which would surely come soon, when Flo would hand in her notice since she could easily find work in another public house. If it had not been for the fact that she was "walking out" with one of the young gamekeepers from Knowsley Park and whom she expected to wed as soon as there was an estate cottage available for them, she would have been long gone. It was no more than two miles from the park, an easy walk for her intended when he had finished his duties of an evening, so for the moment Flo was willing to put up with the extra burden of work which had been loaded on to her young shoulders.

Sally had been thinking about Freddy on that day. He had called in a week ago to bring her the news that he was to marry the plain, but well-dowered sister of his friend, Jacky Norton.

Sally was not surprised. Freddy had a talent for falling on his feet. Since the night he had left he had been staying with his old chum, helping out on the farm, or so he said, in repayment for Mrs Norton's kindness in having him. Like

Jacky, who would one day inherit his father's land and farm and who, in consequence, was trained for nothing but that, he went out each day under the pretext of work, roaming about the farm and surrounding fields, looking terribly busy with a pitchfork or a plough if Farmer Norton should come along, terribly grateful for the accommodation Jacky's family had offered him. Just until he found his feet, he always said winningly, which wouldn't be long for he had several ideas for the future in his old noddle, which was a lie, of course.

But it had become increasingly clear, even to the amiably thoughtless Freddy Grimshaw, that his host and hostess were wondering how long they were to have beneath their roof this engaging but feckless friend of their son. They were fond of him, who could help but not be, since his manners were flawless, his humour always unruffled and his boyish eagerness to please endearing. He had been in and out of their home, as their Jacky had been in and out of his, since they were little lads and they would not dream of turning him out, they told Jacky privately, but it could not go on for ever.

With that instinct for self-preservation that Freddy Grimshaw had always possessed in abundance, he had turned his vast charm on Dorothy Norton, a year older than he was and beginning to look as though she might be consigned to that sorry plight of spinster sister in what would one day be her brother's home.

It had taken no more than an hour among the drifts of snow-white May blossom in the orchard to convince her that he had secretly harboured a deepening love for her, and if her parents were dismayed that they were to gain a son-in-law who was not only penniless but without prospects they gave in, since Freddy was very presentable, biddable and would be good to their girl.

They were to be married in June.

"So you are to be a farmer, just like Grandfather Ned," Sally had said to him, the bitterness on her tongue as acid-tasting as an unripe lemon. That was how she was now, increasingly bitter, increasingly sharp and contemptuous of all men with the exception of Job, the soul inside her corroding in the belief that there was not one among them who would not stab her in the back for the boots on her feet. She suffered such exhaustion, and such fear too, for she could not continue for ever in this life Freddy had forced on her. She had become brittle, feeling as if she would break at the slightest touch, lightheaded sometimes, caught in a trap she must escape, or go mad. Her whole, overstrung body ached, her head and her back jarred at each step she took as the evening wore on and yet she must do her best to be bright, polite at least, behind the bar.

"Oh, hardly that, Sal. Jacky is delighted since it will mean, when the old man's gone, that he will have me to help out."

"God help him."

"There's no need to be like that, old girl. I only came to tell you the news. I didn't want you to worry about me."

If she had not been so heavy-hearted she might have laughed. "Freddy, you really are the bloody limit." Her voice cracked and Freddy looked startled. "Do you seriously believe I have given you a thought, let alone worried about you since you left?" which was true. "You could be at the bottom of the Mersey for all I care, in fact, I wish you were, or had been six months ago and then I would not be working nineteen, twenty bone-breaking hours a day for a man who treats me as though I were no better than a drab on the dockside. I sometimes believe I would be better off in the workhouse, or breaking rocks like a convict than working for Keene."

"Then why don't you leave, for God's sake? I'm sure Mrs Norton would—"

"Oh, grow up, lad. We aren't all so short of backbone we have to go crawling for charity as you've done. Some of us like to stick at what we have determined on and can you just imagine Mrs Norton's face if you went back dragging me at your coat tails?"

"I'm sorry, Sal." He brightened. "When I marry Dorothy I promise I'll find room for you in our home."

"Freddy, just shut up, will you?"

"Why don't you try for barmaid at the Bull? Jacky and I were in there the other night and there was talk of them being short-handed."

"Would they take Job?"

"Job?" Freddy looked bewildered. "Why Job?"

"I'd go nowhere without Job."

"Sally, surely you don't mean . . .?" Freddy's face had blanched.

"Oh, for heaven's sake, Freddy, will you get out of my sight. I've things to do and it's nearly opening time."

She had gone for a walk later. It was a pleasantly warm day and she stopped on the gentle slope of the hill which ran down to Farmer Norton's land. She leaned her back against the broad trunk of a solitary oak tree and gazed down at the soft landscape spread out before her. She had followed the path up from the outskirts of Knotty Ash, an overgrown path which, as the summer advanced, was slowly becoming blocked with the wild flowers growing along its verge. They crept towards its centre, coltsfoot and cowberry brushing the hem of her skirt, vivid against its sombre grey. Yellow vetch was bright in the green wavering grasses which stretched down the slope, already beginning to blossom in the warming air. At the bottom of the slope was a narrow, slow-moving stream, curling back on itself like a snake and along its banks trees grew thickly, new leaf hazing the branches, buds opening wide to the sun. Over the top of the trees she could see Farmer Norton's fields, lush and green and filled with well-fed cattle standing knee-deep in clover, hedges trimmed neatly, even symmetrically as though some earlier farmer had carefully measured the distance between each one before planting them.

When she turned round, the village of Knotty Ash was clustered below her, sheltered in a wide, shallow fold from the fierce winds which blew, not only from the estuary but from across the Pennines in the east. Old cottages with roofs of red and pink and brown and grey, some slated to withstand the weather, others still thatched but in decent repair.

She sighed, then in a slow awkward movement slithered her back down the tree trunk until she was crouched among the deep-set roots. It was like being in an armchair, her arms along the rough bark, her feet resting on the rich deposit of mosses which grew about it like a fat cushion. There were midges dancing frantically in the hazed sunshine and, disturbed by something, two magpies lifted, their black and white plumage flashing against the sun. What was it they said, one for sorrow, two for joy? Well, thank God for that, she could do with a helping of joy! The leaves above her head stirred in a vagrant breeze and, as she did so easily these days whenever she sat down for a moment, she felt her eyelids droop and her breathing slow.

Perhaps it was his shadow falling across her, or that instinct within us all that warns, even in sleep, when danger is near. It woke her, bringing her suddenly from a nightmare world in which, these days, she seemed constantly to dwell. Her chin, which had dropped to her chest, shot up. She was blinded for a second or two, seeing only the large, menacing shadow of what looked like an enormous bat hovering over her. She lifted both hands, palms outwards as though to ward it off, shrinking back among the tree's roots, beginning to moan deep in her throat, for really she did not think she could stand any more suffering in her already afflicted life. To be raped, or robbed, or even spoken to roughly by some passing tinker would be the last straw to break Sally Grimshaw's sadly fragile back.

"I'm sorry. Dear God in heaven . . . I do beg your pardon, Miss Grimshaw. I did not mean to startle you like that. I thought you were ill. You were moaning . . . do forgive me for frightening you. Really, I cannot forgive myself and after all that has happened to you. You were so pale, you see . . ."

"And so would you be if you woke to find a vampire hanging over you," she snapped.

"A vampire?"

"It must have been that cloak of yours. Really, Captain Cooper, I might have suffered an apoplexy. Have you no more sense than to go about frightening folk?"

"You spoke those same words, or very like them, the first time we met, Miss Grimshaw. I don't think I have ever met a female more easily put out when she is not even threatened."

"Threatened! I feel . . . or felt very threatened. How was I to know you were not some . . . some brigand with . . . with . . ."

"With designs upon your person, Miss Grimshaw?"

"Exactly, so I'd be obliged if you'd get out of my way and allow me to get to my feet."

"Let me help you, please."

She waved away the hand he held out to her. "I can manage perfectly well on my own, thank you."

"You make it very hard for a gentleman to help a lady, Miss Grimshaw."

"I am not a lady, Captain Cooper, but a hardworking woman who was merely having a . . . a rest so if you'd stand aside I'd be grateful."

He straightened up and so did she, stamping some feeling back into her legs which seemed to have gone to sleep when she did. She straightened her bonnet, which had come comically askew as she slept, brushed some loose bark from her skirt and moved away from him before speaking again. This time her voice was softer, apologetic even.

"I'm sorry. I didn't mean to snap at you. I was . . . startled."

At once his grim, offended face relaxed into a faint smile. "Of course you were. I should have realised. I would have passed you by," indicating the fine chestnut mare which cropped peacefully a few yards away. "You were tucked in the roots of the tree, barely discernible and had you not been making such a . . . well, you appeared to be having . . ." He shrugged and raised his dark eyebrows. "You seemed to be having a nightmare if one can have such a thing in the daytime. Anyway, something of that nature so . . ."

"I probably was, Captain Cooper," she answered without thinking.

He frowned and she began to notice how much better he looked since the last time they met on the Marine Parade. He was evidently spending much of his time out of doors, for his face was tinted brown by the sun where then it had been pallid and gaunt. His cheeks had filled out. What had been grey hollows had smoothed into flat planes with the high, level cheekbones of a Norseman. His wide, soft mouth was curled up at the corners as though on the verge of a smile. His greying hair had been cut, lying in loose curling waves about his head, gleaming with pure white strands in the sun and his vivid blue eyes were clear and alert. He was still too thin for his height, which was over six feet, but he stood easily, gracefully, no longer in pain.

"Your wound is healed, Captain Cooper?" she asked quickly, doing her best to distract him from the words which had come thoughtlessly to her lips.

He was not easily distracted. "Thank you, yes, Miss Grimshaw, but may I ask what you meant by that last remark?"

"About your wound? Surely that is obvious?"

"Don't prevaricate with me, Miss Grimshaw. You are too intelligent for that." He scowled, shifting from one booted foot to the other, slapping his riding crop against his leg.

"Or what? You will flog me with that whip you have in your hand?"

For a moment he was startled then his face broke into a reluctant grin and he shook his head in amusement. She could not help but smile back at him, that curiously attractive lop-sided smile which lit her eyes to the colour and brilliance of amber in crystal. Her lips, which in repose were a full rosy pink, parted over her even teeth and a flush of rose touched the soft curve of her cheek. He had been pondering on her plainness, her lack of colour, even her fragility which seemed to border on emaciation. He had not really noticed it on the two occasions they had met, and he wondered if she was ill perhaps, but now, with a smile, it seemed to disperse, lighting her from the inside like a taper put to a lamp.

"I doubt any man would try that, Miss Grimshaw, not if he wished to keep his health."

He looked about him for somewhere they might sit. He had heard of her misfortune, as who had not in the vicinity of Old Swan and Knotty Ash and had been sorry, for though he did not frequent public houses, or at least not now, he had known that the Grimshaw Arms had a reputation for honest dealing, good food and good ale. For the warm welcome it extended to its customers, for decency and cleanliness and certainly the latter had been much in evidence, even to him, when he had been there in January. It was her brother who had lost it all, it was said, gambling away what had been in the family for three generations and now this young woman, having no one to provide for her, had been forced to take up employment in the business she, or rather her brother, had owned. There were rumours too of a falling-off of standards, nothing much to speak of and not considered desperate enough yet by her customers to send them elsewhere. They were men who had been attracted by the cheerfulness, the light, the warmth offered there, the congenial company and the freedom, for a little while, from the pressure of domestic worries and daily care. This woman had given them that. She had a clever, nimble brain which had encouraged the inn to prosper. She had a passion for cleanliness, an obsession if you like, to run a decent place, a hatred of drunkenness and obscenity, a tigress, they said of her, in her resolution to keep the best inn in the north-west of England, but underneath was a heart which knew how to make them feel at home, and they had.

Now would you look at her. Pale and harassed, her sudden bloom gone and so worn out she had fallen asleep in broad daylight on the edge of a public pathway along which any knave might have passed and found her. Four short months, careworn beyond belief and yet neither her spirit nor her humour were broken, even if her back was heading that way.

"Sit down, Miss Grimshaw," he commanded, settling down himself and patting the cloak he had spread out on the grass. "Here in the sunshine, and tell me why you have nightmares."

She bristled and drew her three-quarter-length coat more closely about her.

"Indeed I will do no such thing, Captain Cooper, and I'll thank you not to order me about as though I were one of the infantrymen under your command. Besides, I must get back."

"No, you must not." His voice was patient, his eyes, such a deep and determined blue a moment ago, soft with kindness.

"I must. I have an inn to run, servants to direct and . . . well, I only stepped out for half an hour to get some air and—"

"How many servants do you have?"

"Really, sir. I do wish you would not keep interrupting me." She lifted her head, imperious as a duchess and for some reason he felt a soft melting gather inside him. She was so prickly, so bloody ruthless in her determination to have no man pry into what she saw as her business and yet there was a vulnerability about her which seemed to speak of approaching despair.

"I'm sorry, but please, sit down for five minutes and tell me about . . . what happened."

"What happened has nothing to do with you."

"Just as . . . my concerns are nothing to do with you." His voice was very soft.

"What?" She was visibly startled.

"On the occasion of our first meeting you informed me that the whole district knew, and apparently discussed, matters that are private to my family. I took offence and I'm sorry and if you like I will tell you exactly what happened eight years ago."

She began to back away, her face distressed, putting out a hand as if to ward off an attack though he was still sitting on the ground. "Oh, no . . . no, Captain Cooper, please, it's nothing to do with me. When I said that in January I did not mean . . . Dear Lord, I hate gossip and when it happened, though I wasn't very old, I gave the maids the rounds of the kitchen for . . . well . . ."

"Oh, Miss Grimshaw, do sit down. We shall speak of nothing but what a pleasant day it is and how sweetly the blackbirds are singing and . . . well, whatever you want, or we shall sit silently. It is your choice." He smiled so amiably she felt herself relax.

"Well . . ." She glanced about her as though expecting curious villagers to be dallying along the path, villagers who would be wondering what Captain Adam Cooper, who had already provided them with plenty to gossip about, and Sally Grimshaw from the Grimshaw Arms might be doing in one another's company. If they were seen together there would be more fuel for tittle-tattle. He was, to all intents and purposes, the local squire and she was no longer the sister of a reputable and prosperous innkeeper but merely a barmaid. Poles apart, in class, status, background, even education and yet, when finally she consented to sit primly on the very edge of his cloak, her back straight, her bonnet even straighter as though she were in church, the silence that followed was in no way oppressive.

It was he who broke it.

"I was dismayed to hear you had . . . lost the inn, Miss Grimshaw. Indeed I had the idea I might call and . . ."

"Yes, Captain?" Her voice held a warning note since Sally Grimshaw required no man's sympathy.

"I honestly don't know." He bent his head, watching his own slim brown hand pluck at a blade of grass. Sally found she was watching it too but when he put the grass between his lips, biting the sweetness with his strong white teeth, she hastily looked away.

"I suppose last January . . . well, you were kind to me." He grinned, not looking at her. "Kind in that no-nonsense way you have and I felt . . . perhaps . . . I could . . ."

"Yes, Captain?" Her chin lifted even higher and the gold of her eyes darkened, the pupils a deep sable in their centre.

He looked up. "Do you know, Miss Grimshaw, it is the very devil trying to persuade you to allow a kindness, a word of . . . of . . ."

"Sympathy? Is that what you were going to say? Well, I want none. I manage very well and shall continue to do so."

He sighed resignedly. "Yes, I imagine you will, though you . . ."

"Yes?"

"You don't look well."

"I'm sure my appearance is no concern of yours, Captain Cooper. I admit I work hard."

"I can see you do, Miss Grimshaw, something in the order of twenty-four hours a day I'd say and if—"

"Captain, you said a moment ago that we might talk of the weather, the scenery, whatever I chose but since then you have done nothing but question me and make comments a gentleman, or so I have been led to believe, particularly on such short acquaintance, should not make to a lady. I am fit and well and managing my life quite . . . quite admirably, so can we speak of something else?"

"Of course, Miss Grimshaw, you are right. What you do with your life is your own business but if ever—"

"Captain!"

He ducked his head almost shyly, then lifted it, pushing his hand through his silvery grey-streaked hair. He smiled. His eyes crinkled at the corners and she found herself wondering what shade of blue they really were. It was an incredible colour . . . was it hyacinth, perhaps . . . or cornflower . . . the colour of a summer sky? No, none of these and yet all three colours were there since they seemed to change and merge with his mood, or was it the light?

He was looking at her questioningly, nothing in his expression but kindness and sympathy and she hastily dragged her gaze away.

"How are your daughters, Captain Cooper?" she heard herself babble, for she did not care to acquaint herself with the sudden lurching inside her chest.

"They are well, Miss Grimshaw, but sadly in need of a woman's . . . supervision."

"Of course."

Again there was silence since again they were treading on awkward ground.

"Do you happen to know what that bird might be?" she went on, pointing to a perfectly ordinary thrush which flashed its yellow, spotted chest in the branches of a tree.

'A thrush, I believe, Miss Grimshaw. Listen to its song."

And they did in a companionable silence which gradually calmed her to a tranquillity she had not known for four months.

Afterwards she was to wonder what they talked about in

the next half-hour but whatever it was it eased the strain in her, put a spring in her step as she strode out along Prescot Lane in the direction of the inn. It lifted her bruised spirit and gave her a feeling there might be a chance it could heal.

The strange unease that had affected her over the question of Captain Cooper's eyes was pushed firmly to the back of her mind.

8

"I think I might avail myself of one of your splendid rooms for a night or two, Miss Grimshaw, if you have one available, that is. I have several engagements in Liverpool, business and social, over the next few days and it seems foolish and a waste of good money to pay for a room at the Adelphi when I can stay here. It will also give me an opportunity to check on the standard of the hospitality you offer. You have a room, I take it? A decent room."

Richard Keene smiled and his pointed fox's teeth gleamed wetly in the sunlight which streamed in through the open front door. He seemed to find nothing even the slightest bit insulting in his choice of words. It was as though Sally's ability and reputation as an innkeeper was in some doubt and must be spied upon, despite what she had achieved in the past. As though his standards were higher than hers.

Sally kept her face completely expressionless, for she knew he liked nothing better than to "get a rise out of her" as she thought of it. To goad her into protesting, or arguing over something, something she could really do nothing about since he made it quite clear he was now the master of the Grimshaw Arms. Instead she put her mind to which of the two vacant rooms where the servants had once slept she might put Job while Keene was under her roof. She didn't know why really, since he had offered her no threat but something in her would feel easier, she thought, if she was not alone in the building with him after dark.

"Of course," was all she said. "We have no guests at the moment."

"I thought as much. I wonder why that is, Miss Grimshaw?"

That's easily answered, she almost said out loud. Because no matter how imaginatively she disguised what she cooked and no matter how well she cooked it, the ingredients were second-rate. Cheap cuts of meat, however they are done up, are not the saddle of beef, the rack of lamb, the succulent pork chops, the pheasant and grouse – in season – which had once been served in Sally Grimshaw's coffee-room and which those who dined there had come to expect. They did not care to be served with the inferior bottles of wine Miss Grimshaw had to offer and though the comfort and cleanliness of her rooms were as they had always been, she was a trifle sparing with her coals and the constant jugs of hot water they had been used to. The port, the claret, the spirits which were served in the bar parlour were no longer of the best quality and, as Sally had known it would, that side of her trade was beginning to fall off. The taproom and snug, where an informal midday meal might be had, were just as busy since it was easier to hide the economies from the working man who ate and drank there. Tripe and onions were tripe and onions, after all, needing only someone who knew how to cook them. The same with cow-heel, pigs' trotters, pease pudding and faggots, the rough, crusty loaves with cheese and pickles she served over the counter, all simple and filling and cheap. These men were not accustomed to brandy or port, neither were they much acquainted with pheasant, and though now and again Abe Cartwright or Arnie Thwaites might complain that their first pint of ale tasted a bit peculiar, by the third, the seventh, the tenth they no longer noticed.

"I couldn't say, Mr Keene," she answered now, her voice icy, turning to watch as Mary, their new barmaid, lumbered off with the speed of an oxen pulling a plough to answer the bell in the snug. Mary had been with them, them being her and Job, ever since Flo had gone off to be the wife of the young gamekeeper at Knowsley Park. Mary had been willing, she said, to help out in the kitchen as well as her barmaid duties but she was not Flo and never would be. She was what Sally had described to Captain Cooper whom she met now and then on her walks during the summer, as *stately*! She could not be hurried no matter how urgently the bell was rung in one of the other bars.

"I've only one pair of hands," she would shout, but whatever she settled to, whether it be cleaning the windows or scrubbing the front steps at her own purposeful speed, she did it thoroughly. Sally had been glad to employ her, for she was the only applicant who had agreed to do the "bit of cleaning", which Sally was ashamed to admit was how she described the endless scrubbing and scouring and polishing which had to be got through each day at the Grimshaw Arms.

When Flo left Sally had begged Keene to allow her to bring Bridie back, if she would come, that is, for everyone knew by now the sad state of affairs at the inn but he would not have it, saying Bridie was too old and had no experience as a barmaid.

She can learn, Sally had pleaded to no avail, wondering somewhere deep inside her where hope and trust had once lain, what had happened to that plain-spoken, enduring, uncompromising woman, the *real* Sally Grimshaw. Seven, eight months ago she would have told this presumptuous, cold-eyed bastard to go to the devil if he had looked at her and spoken to her as he was now doing, but *she* had been the "master" here then, with the right to dispose of any man who offended her.

The bar parlour where she and Keene sat was a pleasant room with benches about the walls and a settle to the side of the empty fireplace in which Sally had placed a big copper jug of dried wild flowers. There were round tables here and there with wrought-iron legs on which empty tankards still stood and Sally knew she should get up and clear them away. Though the company might be better, she thought sardonically, it was very enjoyable just to sit here in the band of warm sunlight in which dust motes quivered, and relax her tired body which never, never got enough rest. She studied, her eyes narrowed against the light, the fox's head above the fireplace, pondering on how like Richard Keene it looked, even to the slightly raised muzzle and long teeth and it was his sharp voice which roused her from the state of somnolence into which she had fallen.

"Miss Grimshaw, I do believe I am keeping you from your bed," he drawled, smiling in a way she did not like. "I have the impression you were about to fall asleep."

She was horrified at being caught in such a vulnerable and embarrassing position. Immediately she stretched her back to its usual rigid inflexibility, then stood up and began to move about the room, gathering tankards, reaching for the clean damp cloth which was kept at the back of the bar, going over every surface with such vigour one or two of the seated gentlemen looked alarmed. They drew their glasses to their chests, leaning back in their chairs as though afraid they might get the same treatment, exchanging glances, for it was a while since Miss Grimshaw had shown such spirit.

Dear God in heaven but I hate him, she thought, her teeth clenched in case the actual words should slip out of their own accord. There was something nasty in the way, as she turned in his direction, she found he was watching her. She knew she was not attractive to men, particularly these last months when the weight had fallen from her, stripping even what had been – she thought – a quite pleasing fullness to her breasts. Mind you, she didn't care about that. She had enough to contend with without trying to avoid the often lustful hands of the men who drank here, as Flo had had to do, and even Mary, despite her matronly bulk. She, Sally, had nothing to draw a man's eyes to her since she kept her own hooded, her hair twisted back into a knot that sometimes hurt the flesh of her forehead and wore a respectable, white, high-necked bodice and a modest grey or black skirt to conceal what claim she might have to a female figure. They didn't see her really. She was just a hand that passed a tankard of ale to them or a voice wishing them "good evening".

But this man, whenever he came, which was too often for her liking, had the ability with just one look to make her feel slightly dirty, as though there was something foul sticking to the sole of her boot or as if she had put her hand in some nasty substance which had spilled on one of her clean tables. His eyes seemed to narrow speculatively when they looked at her, or rather ran over her and the look was always accompanied by that smile. He often ran his tongue round his lips and his hands in his pockets moved in some strange way which suggested all manner of dreadful things. She loathed him and she would never forgive Freddy for putting her in the frightful position where she was forced to consider Keene's every word and to be polite about it.

She was often tempted just to up and leave, find a job,

however menial, where she could at least do an honest day's work for a fair wage, with none of these niggling restrictions he imposed on her and which she was forced to practise in his greed for profit. Better the devil you know, the saying went and so – for now – she stuck it out, for perhaps, who knew, it might be a case of out of the frying pan and into the fire.

And then there was Job. Without Job she could not do what she did. He had been the rock to which, figuratively speaking, she had clung, the anchor which kept her steady and without him to talk to, to pour out all her frustrations and sheer bloody resentment to, she would have gone under months ago. She couldn't leave him to drift off on the road again, as he had done before he worked for her, since she was sure, if only to spite her, that if she left, Richard Keene would turn Job off without a reference.

She had attended Freddy's wedding in June though she still could hardly bring herself to speak to him. Despite her reluctance she felt she must accept the invitation and she had found it to be a pleasant break in the monotonous round of hard grind she suffered every day. She did not admit, even later to herself in the seclusion of her own room, that her enjoyment had been heightened because Adam Cooper had been there.

She had worn her apple green silk, the dress made for her over six years ago for Violet's wedding to Arthur Atkinson. She herself had been only eighteen then, more frivolous than she was now and the gown was pretty. The huge skirt was held out by six flounced petticoats, each one edged in the finest Honiton lace. The three-quarter-length sleeves were wide and had white lace undersleeves which fell about her fine-boned wrists and her pale face was framed by a small apple green bonnet of silk. The underside of the brim was ruched in fine white chiffon, the crown of the bonnet frothing with white silk lily of the valley.

When she and the captain came face to face after the ceremony she did not notice the startled expression on his face and had she done so would not have connected it with her own emergence from chrysalis to butterfly. Only a common or garden small tortoiseshell to be sure, nothing showy like a Purple Emperor but vastly different to the sombrely dressed Miss Grimshaw of the Grimshaw Arms.

Violet and Arthur were with her, their five children, including the latest, named Leopold after the dear queen's youngest son who had been born on the same date as Vi's only two years earlier, all at home in the frantic hands of poor Lizzie. Vi was plumper than ever, her ornate bulk in direct contrast to the dainty, elfin figure of her older sister. She wore a matronly purple trimmed with emerald green, and Arthur, as befitted his job as head clerk at Brooks Brothers, was in a well-cut frock coat and trousers, his shirt front and cravat immaculate, his expression revealing his eagerness to be introduced to the "gentry", for such an acquaintance might be of great value in his career.

"Miss Grimshaw, how pleasant to see you and how well you look," the captain was saying, his admiration apparent to Sally's sister and brother-in-law, if not to her.

"Captain Cooper, Freddy did not tell me you were to be a guest."

"Oh dear, if you had known would it have made a difference to your own acceptance, Miss Grimshaw?"

He smiled whimsically and so did Sally. He often said things like that when they met up at the back of Knotty Ash where he had told her his own house stood. They would lean on a wall or sit if the weather was fine and the grass dry and speak of this and that, pleasantly relaxed with one another as a man and woman who are not sexually attracted can often be. They discussed the war in the Crimea and the marvels being performed by Miss Nightingale at Scutari. Sally's eyes glowed deep and golden with the depth of her regard for Miss Nightingale. She was just the sort of woman Sally most admired. She had a fine brain, was not only a gentle, caring nurse but a resolute organiser who knew exactly what she wanted to do and had been determined to do it. When cholera had broken out among the British troops she had taken a ship to Scutari where she and thirty-eight of her ladies had transformed a vast, dilapidated, filthy set of barracks into a hospital and if, at the time, Sally could have been spared, she'd have gone with her, she told the captain. She'd have soon whipped them all into shape, like Miss Nightingale had, meeting the challenge and revelling in it. The exalted lift of her head said so and Adam Cooper smiled down into her ardent face, marvelling at the change in her when she forgot the dragging misery of her present circumstances.

She was interested in so many things, matters which did not commonly concern other women. The riots among the starving poorer classes who plundered the bread shops in search of the food they could not afford to buy. They discussed education, since it seemed she approved of the bill introduced by Lord Russell – which was not, unfortunately, accepted – giving towns of more than five thousand inhabitants power to levy an education rate. There needed to be a department of education, she told him sternly, as though it was he who was preventing it, for all children must have schooling if they were eventually to better their lot. They talked of poetry and literature, discovering they both had a great admiration for Tennyson and Browning. Their conversation often bordered on argument since they did not always agree and, as he had quickly learned, Sally was not afraid to state her opinion and since neither was he, it was often lively.

Arthur cleared his throat conspicuously and Violet fidgeted with the flounce at her waist and Sally turned to them with reluctance, since she was aware of her brother-in-law's determination to "get on".

"This is my sister and her husband, Mr and Mrs Arthur Atkinson, Captain Cooper. Violet, Arthur, this is Captain Cooper."

If Arthur and Vi were astonished that Vi's plain and plain-spoken sister was acquainted with the tall, splendidly dressed and obviously wealthy – not his own wealth, but wealthy just the same – member of one of Liverpool's oldest and most prestigious families they did their best not to let it show. Arthur shook his hand enthusiastically and Vi almost dropped a curtsey.

Sally sighed with deep irritation and attempted to move them on, for they were blocking the pathway from the church porch to the lych-gate. Guests were forced to step off the path and sidle round the lurching headstones, throwing furious glances at the group, especially the ladies, for the grass was damp. Freddy and Dorothy were being borne away in a carriage done up with white satin and pulled by four perfectly matched greys to the enthusiastic cheers of Jacky Norton and his wild friends. He'd done well for himself, had Freddy Grimshaw, when you considered what had happened to him earlier in the year, they were saying, for the well-dowered daughter of a wealthy yeoman farmer was not to be sneezed at. Dorothy, who was small and square and plain, was most unsuitably dressed in a wedding gown of white satin with a vast skirt covered with lace frills, bows and lover's knots, a beautiful dress, they said at least the ladies, but was Dorothy tall and slender enough to carry it off?

That had been in June and now it was almost September and already Dorothy was pregnant, Freddy told Sally triumphantly, his place in the Norton dynasty safely assured. A villa – to Dorothy and her mother's specifications – was already being built on Amos Norton's land to house his daughter, her husband and, more importantly, Amos's grandchild. No doubt one day Jack would marry and have children of his own but in the meanwhile the old gentleman meant to have the supervising of this one close to hand, since he was not prepared to leave it in his son-in-law's feckless if charming control.

The matter of Sally moving, as Freddy had promised, into his marital home was not touched on.

There had been a man, as big as Job and with the same beaten-up face of a pugilist but hard and menacing, who had come last time with Keene. They had gone round the back of the stable block, poking about in the barn and standing in a ruminating kind of way in the yard as though something of great importance was being discussed. He had been introduced to her as Frank O'Connell, Keene's "sporting" manager and she had been told to expect Mr O'Connell to be a frequent visitor to the Grimshaw Arms.

"With what in mind, Mr Keene?" she had asked bluntly and both Keene and O'Connell had smiled. She had wondered at the time if that smile was mandatory among Keene's employees or was it just a coincidence that O'Connell's leer was an exact replica of his master's? A thin, sneering smile curved about thin, sneering lips, which made her heart pound with dread, since it seemed the time which Keene had promised had come.

"Nothing to concern yourself with, Miss Grimshaw. I told

you that when . . . aah . . . certain sporting fixtures were put on in the barn you merely had to get on with your duties in the bar. There is no need for you even to think about it."

"There is every need, Mr Keene, because, quite simply, I will not put up with it."

"You have no choice, Miss Grimshaw."

"Indeed I have and if I see that man" – nodding contemptuously at O'Connell— "hanging about these premises I shall have him turned out."

"Then you will be looking for other employment, Miss Grimshaw."

"There is not the slightest doubt of it, Mr Keene."

Later that evening when the inn had closed and with the memory of this conversation still fresh in her mind, she turned in the direction of the stairs which led to the second floor.

"I'll bid you goodnight, then, Mr Keene," she said to the man who sat before the empty fireplace nursing a glass of brandy. "Your room is ready . . . hot water and towels and . . . well, goodnight . . ."

Her voice trailed off and she wondered why it was this man had the power to render her into a state she could only call witless. It was that smiling stare that did it, she decided, that cold air of watchfulness that made her uneasy though she couldn't have said precisely why. He was polite enough, she supposed, and as long as his profits were to his liking he had nothing to say on her running of the inn. And it was not as though he lived permanently at the Grimshaw Arms. For most of the time she was free to do as she pleased providing she put money in his pocket. It could be worse.

She was about to put her foot on the bottom tread of the stair when he made it so.

"Oh, Miss Grimshaw," his voice called after her, "will you see to it that there is plenty of rum and brandy in the cellar. There is to be an . . . event tomorrow night and I should not like it if our customers did not have what they wanted to drink. The winners will be longing to celebrate and those who have lost will wish to drown their sorrows. See to it, will you, Miss Grimshaw."

"I shall not be here, Mr Keene," and she continued up the stairs as though she had just told him she was to have the evening off. She went directly to her room and closed the door behind her, leaning her back against it. She stood for several minutes, her mind quite numbed, then, lifting her head, she moved to the wardrobe, took down a small portmanteau and began to pack it.

She could not sleep. It was hot and though her bedroom window was open there was not a breath of air moving the flowered curtains which hung there limply. She had plaited the thick, springing mass of her hair after she had brushed it as she always did, her mind calm and empty and yet still concerned with routine. Her nightdress was damp with perspiration before she got into bed and it clung to her as, for what seemed hours, she tossed feverishly in the tangled sheets. She must get to sleep soon, for she must be up early tomorrow if she and Job were to be on the road towards whatever the future held in store for them. She knew, of course, that Job would go with her to wherever it was to be but for the life of her she just couldn't seem to be able to make any plans. It had come on her more quickly than she had expected, though she should have been prepared since Keene had made no secret of his plans to introduce the fights which he hoped would draw gambling men not only from the immediate area but from towns within travelling distance of the Grimshaw Arms. She was amazed at her own lack of feeling, of fear as she stared sightlessly towards the half-drawn curtains and beyond to the darkness, and imprinted on it was the image of Adam Cooper whom she had met only two days ago.

He had been walking. He had removed his jacket in the heat and had slung it over his shoulder and his arms were brown and well muscled, covered with a fine down of dark hair to his wrist. Not hairy, by any means, she had noted idiotically but proving a kind of male virility which disturbed her. His cravat had been stuffed in his pocket and his shirt was undone at the neck, revealing a firm brown throat. His sun-darkened face was strong, almost aggressively so and she wondered what he did out of doors that had turned his skin to the pleasing amber it had acquired in the seven or so months since he had come home. He was completely restored to health, that was obvious, and strangely pleased to see her, it seemed.

She had removed her bonnet and run her hand over her loosened hair, at ease with him, her usual stiff and challenging need to be neat and immaculate gone for the moment.

They had chatted in a desultory manner for half an hour then, unaccountably and vulgarly, she had fallen asleep, her back against the broad trunk of the oak tree where she had first met him. This time they had settled themselves in its shade. He had been lying on his back, his head on his rolled-up jacket, his voice soft and deep as he told her something about his life in India and when she came to with a start she was appalled to find he was leaning on one elbow watching her, an unusual expression on his calm face. She couldn't guess what it might be and didn't care really, for to fall asleep in the company of a man who was practically a stranger, in the company of *any* man, was surely unforgivable.

She sprang to her feet, babbling foolishly of how sorry she was and he must not think she had been bored or anything like that. It had been absorbing what he had told her of his travels and what must he think of her and really she must get home and all the while he had leaned on his elbow, saying nothing, watching her with that quiet air of seriousness which made her distinctly uneasy.

"How old are you, Miss Grimshaw?" he interrupted her, cutting off the coursing flow of words which were pouring unchecked and quite ridiculously, she knew that, from between her lips.

It stopped her like a slap in the face.

"I beg your pardon?" Her voice had turned to an icicle.

"Why is it when you ask a lady her age she is most offended?" He sighed.

"Because it's no one's business but hers, Captain Cooper, that's why."

"It's nothing to be ashamed of."

"Is it not? Well, whether it is or it isn't I have no intention of telling you." She jammed her bonnet on her head and pulled at the ribbons with such force one of them broke away.

"So it seems. I was only wondering if . . ."

"You can just stop wondering then because your curiosity is not to be satisfied."

"It is not idle curiosity, Miss Grimshaw. I have a—"

"Good-day to you, sir. I must go." And with that, despite his voice begging her to let him explain, dammit, she was off down the path towards Knotty Ash.

Now she wondered what it was he had been about to say. He was, despite his good humour which was evident in his face and eyes and the curl of his mouth, a serious man. He had suffered in the past, not just from his wounds in the Crimean War but in his personal life and it showed in the shadow which sometimes fell about him, the brooding look of contemplation she had disturbed in one of their quiet moments on the hill. He never spoke of the past, nor of his children and, taking her cue from him, neither did she. She asked after their health now and again and he answered courteously that they were well, but he made it plain that he did not wish to discuss them, nor their mother. She did not understand really why he seemed to seek her out, to enjoy her company, to find her sharp, acerbic humour amusing, but she did not question it since she knew, along with Job's patient strength and protection, Adam Cooper gave her life an hour's content now and again.

Some sound was bothering her, one which was familiar and yet not usual at this time of the night and she lifted her head from her pillow to listen but it was not repeated.

She punched her pillow vigorously, dragged her thick rope of hair from about her neck, then turned on to her stomach, her mind still cradled in that curiously calm state into which it had fallen when she had come up the stairs. She couldn't understand it since she had no idea what tomorrow or the next day were to bring but it seemed now that she had made up her mind to leave, or had it made up for her, she was glad about it. After all, she was fit and healthy, a hard worker and so was Job and surely they would find something to suit them?

She turned again, this time on to her side so that she was facing the door. She felt herself begin to slip away into that pleasant euphoria which comes just before much needed sleep. You can feel it approaching and want to hold on to it for a moment since it is so satisfying before you drift off. Her eyelids drooped, then opened, then drooped again and as her lashes meshed and her body melted into the damp tangle of the sheets, she was ferociously dragged back to wakefulness by an explosion of sounds and shapes and frantic movement which appeared to be taking place just inside the door of her room. It was dark and yet there must have been a source of light from somewhere since she could see what seemed to be one of those sea monsters which live on the ocean bed and which she had seen in her school book as a child. All arms and legs but no head, heaving and grunting in the doorway, crashing against the frame of the door with such force she distinctly heard the rending of protesting wood as some part of it tore loose.

Dear God above, what was it? Was that the noise she had heard? This . . . this *thing* creeping along the hallway, pausing at her door. What *was* it, for the love of God . . . and how had it got into the inn, whatever it was and from where? And . . . and what designs had it on her?

The thing spoke, or rather hissed venomously and with a shock of returning senses she realised that the voice was Job's.

"Yer filthy bastard . . . yer scum . . . I'll kill yer fer this, yer rotton piece o' shite. Think yer can do . . . as yer bloody well please. I know your sort . . . I'll tear yer bloody prick off . . ."

The gasping words were interspersed with the sounds of flesh striking flesh and of flesh striking a solid object: of a burbling moan which rose and fell, of panting, quick and jerky, and with a thrill of horror Sally became aware that there were *two* creatures on the threshold of her room and that one was murdering the other. It took but a moment to realise who they were.

"Job . . . Job!" The scream was torn from her mouth and she knew her eyes were bulging in her face as they did their best to pick out what stage the murder had reached. Was he dead yet, the victim, or had she still a chance to stop it?

From upstairs she was vaguely aware of Mary's voice babbling and there was a crash as though, in her terror, she had knocked something over but Sally had no time to be concerned with it.

Like a greyhound from the trap she sprang from her bed, cursing as the damp sheet did its best to tie her up in it. Her nightdress, which she had rearranged tidily below her knees only minutes before, was in a swirl of hampering folds about her legs as she flung herself towards the door.

Some freak of chance got her there just as Job's broad back presented itself to her and like a monkey she leaped on it, legs about his waist, arms about his throat. An instinct, from where she didn't know, told her to hurt him as painfully as she could, since it was the only way she might fetch him from his murderous rage and with a snap of her jaws she sank her strong teeth into his good ear, hanging on for dear life like a fighting terrier, tasting his blood, hearing his grunt of pain.

His hand rose to swot away whatever it was that had attacked him, an automatic gesture of self-defence which, for a brief moment, released the terrible stranglehold he had on Richard Keene.

"Job . . . Job . . . stop it," she screamed directly into his ear and she felt him jerk as though a needle had been plunged into it. Her mouth was full of his blood and she knew she couldn't hold on much longer without choking on it.

In fact she was convinced she had the lobe of his ear, or at least some fleshy part of it which had parted from the rest, halfway down her throat.

Slowly, as the madness ebbed away, as the awareness of what he was about, though he was not sorry for it, filtered into Job's inflamed brain he relaxed his grip on the figure of Richard Keene who flopped to the floor like a landed fish, his nightgown settling about him like a shroud.

Even then Sally continued to cling to him, like a child playing piggy-back with an adult. She had released his ear, sinking her bloodied face to the back of his neck and, after a moment, he reached up to her and gently lifted her from him, setting her violently trembling figure to the floor. He held her arm to steady her as she leaned against him.

No one spoke. The man on the floor coughed and heaved and when Sally moved to help him to his feet, glad of the noise he made since it meant he was not dead, he shook her off viciously. He did not look at either her or Job as he struggled hand over hand up the wall, to his feet. They were still deep in shock with nothing to say to one another, or to him, though it was very evident from Job's curling fists and the fighter's stance he was still in what he would like to do to the man he had found fumbling at Sally Grimshaw's door. Had she not stopped him he would have killed him, swung for it, and gladly.

Richard Keene reached his door and turned. They could hardly see him in the gloom and his voice was hoarse in his strangled throat so that they could barely make out the words.

"Be . . . out . . . of . . . here . . . in . . . the . . . hour, both of . . . you . . . and don't . . . think you've . . . heard the . . . the last . . . of this."

9

Adam Cooper was at breakfast when his butler, who was overseeing the serving of the meal, was hurriedly summoned from the room by a footman.

While he studied *The Times* Adam continued to pick over the indifferently cooked bacon and eggs on his plate, wondering idly why the woman who worked in his kitchen and called herself his cook could not fry an egg without breaking the yolk. He was not a particularly demanding eater since he had, in his army career, been forced to feed himself on whatever his orderly could contrive when out on patrol and, more recently, during the Crimean hostilities, but really this was hardly better. There were mushrooms, sausages, kidneys and all manner of things nestling in a skim of congealing fat beneath the massively embossed silver of the serving dishes on the sideboard. Newton, the head parlourmaid, stood to attention over the dishes which were barely a quarter full, the food inside quickly losing their heat. He supposed he should have a word with Mrs Chidlow, his housekeeper, but somehow he couldn't seem to get up the enthusiasm to take the trouble.

He turned the page of the newspaper, glancing up as the door opened again, smiling as his daughters glided, graceful as swans on a lake, into the breakfast-room. They were immaculately turned out, as always, in matching dresses of soft pink grenadine, the slightly full skirts which came to halfway down their childish calves revealing the slip of white lace on their petticoats. Their narrow waists were tied about with broad sashes of deeper pink velvet and in their dark red glossy curls were ribbons of the same colour. They were both quite breathtaking in their young loveliness, with velvet grey eyes and a fine ivory and rose complexion. Slender and dainty and unruffled, which was how they always looked, as though they had just been gone over with a chamois leather, without a curl out of place or a flounce out of line, but then, he thought sadly, what could you expect of two little girls who had, for the past eight years, been brought up by servants?

"Good morning, ladies," he said, smiling encouragingly, hoping for some childish response to his whimsical humour. A warm and answering smile, perhaps a kiss or some show of affection, a readiness to run or hop or skip, to be as children are but their nanny, Nanny Mottram who had come with his wife when they married, had had them far too long and their training was complete. And of course Miss Digby, whom Nanny Mottram had engaged as their governess while he was still in India, and was of the same opinion on the matter of the upbringing of a child as Nanny, had carried on that training.

"Good morning, Papa," they chorused dutifully, their eyes cast down, long dark lashes brushing a crescent of shadow on their soft pink cheeks. They were eleven and ten years old respectively.

"Don't eat the eggs," he whispered to them conspiratorially, winking as their startled eyes lifted to his. They were plainly mystified, not only by his words but by his wink.

They exchanged glances, then, as her training demanded,

Leila, who was the elder of the two, asked politely, "Why not, Papa?"

Adam looked at her, his smile slipping, then at Aisha. He shrugged a little, opened his mouth and shut it again, at a loss for words. He didn't know what he had expected. Perhaps a giggle, an exchange of something that might simply be called *fun*, an understanding that he had just made a small joke which he and his daughters might share.

They continued to look at him enquiringly, their faces innocent and serious, as they had been brought up to be. It was eight months since he had come home and in that time he had become no closer to them despite his strained efforts to get to know them.

At first he had taken them about with him on an excursion or two. A visit to the Zoological Gardens in West Derby to gaze at the caged wild beasts which roared there. A walk on the Marine Parade to view the lovely, graceful sailing ships and, when this had failed to excite their interest, to the Royal Institution in Colquitt Street where a splendid exhibition of paintings, or so it was said to be, was on display.

They had been polite, well behaved, straight-backed miniature ladies, in fact, who, because he had commanded it and he was their papa and therefore to be obeyed, had accompanied him on these outings he seemed to favour. He was a stranger to them. They had scarcely seen him since they had been brought back from India by him when they were barely more than infants. Their memories still held clouded pictures of dark skins, of vivid colours, heat and smells, exotic flowers, but since then they had known nothing but the comfortable protection of their nursery, the discipline of the schoolroom and the undemonstrative affection of the two women who ruled there. They had not been unhappy. The routine of childhood had given them a sense of security and though they knew their papa meant to be kind, they did not understand him. They ate breakfast with him at eight thirty every morning. He insisted on that at least, but apart from ten minutes in his study before bedtime when he awkwardly asked them about their day and they just as awkwardly answered him, their lives went on just as they had done for the past eight years.

They were delicately spooning porridge into their soft pink mouths when the door reopened and the portly, self-important figure of Henton, the butler, entered the room. Closing the door behind him, as carefully and quietly as though he were entering a funeral parlour in which a deceased person lay in a coffin, he began a stately tread across the flowered carpet until he reached his master's chair.

"I beg your pardon, sir." His eyes looked into the distance somewhere over Adam's head.

"Yes, Henton, what is it?"

"I'm sorry to disturb you at breakfast, sir . . ."

"Yes, yes . . .?"

"There is a person to see you . . . at the kitchen door."

"The kitchen door?"

"Yes, sir."

"Who is it, Henton?"

"I'm sure I couldn't say, sir, only that . . . the . . . er . . . person was most insistent on seeing you at once. I said that—"

"At the *kitchen* door, you say?"

"Yes, sir."

The two girls, as though something had at last happened to fracture their absolute composure, something they sensed was unusual, stopped eating, watching their papa's face with what could have been childish interest.

"Well, show this person into my study, Henton, and say I'll be there directly."

"Oh, hardly, sir. If you could see the state of . . . well, sir, it would not be fitting."

Adam looked surprised and his eyebrows lifted enquiringly. He dabbed at his mouth with his napkin then threw it to the table. Pushing back his chair he rose to his feet.

"What the devil d'you mean, man?" he snapped, beginning to show signs of the intense irritation the butler often roused in him. The man was so bloody pompous and high-flown you could be forgiven for thinking he was the master of this house. He was chilling in his belief that, even if he didn't own it, the house was run to his principles and for his convenience. Often Adam had a strong desire to hit him on the end of his imperious nose and tell him to go to the devil but it was like the matter of the cook, simply that to leave things as they were was the easiest course for Adam Cooper to take. It was just too much bloody trouble to find someone to replace them.

"Am I to believe that you wish me to speak to this person on the kitchen doorstep, Henton?" he asked ominously.

Henton didn't want his master to speak to the caller at all. He himself was not in the habit of addressing people at the back door – it was beneath his dignity – and he was hoping he might have the pleasure of ordering the intruder off the premises with a sharp word and a disdainful sneer, both of which he was good at.

"Sir, that is for you to decide, but with the young ladies about . . . well . . ." He shrugged as though to say who knew what might happen but if anything should, Charles Henton could not be blamed for it since he had warned his master. If his master wished to ignore that warning then on his own head be it. "I am only informing you that you would not, in any circumstances, invite this—"

"Oh, for God's sake, Henton, do stop drivelling on. In my study, man, and at once."

Henton would never forgive him, he made that perfectly clear as he majestically showed in the unkempt and exhausted man whom Adam had last seen in the well-scrubbed taproom of the Grimshaw Arms. Even so he might have failed to recognise him had it not been for his size. He looked to have lost a couple of stones in weight. His hair was dusty with what appeared to be wisps of hay in it. His clothes, a shabby jacket and corded breeches, looked as though they had not been off his back for a week and one of his ears was torn and seemed to be badly infected. He had dirty grey stubble about his chin and cheeks and Adam was not surprised that Henton had shown a great reluctance to let him into the house.

"Sit down, man," he said, for the cellarman swayed quite dramatically on his feet.

"Nay, sir, I've not time. I must get back, yer see." His haunted eyes were sunk in the pallid grey of his face. They searched about the comfortable room as though there might be some dreadful danger, though at whom it might be directed was not clear.

"Get back? D'you mean to the inn?"

"Aye, but not the one you're thinkin' on. We're not theer any more, the little maid an' me . . ."

"The little maid?"

"Miss Sally. He chucked us out a week or two back. We were goin' anyway, like, Miss Sally said, on account o't fights . . ."

"Fights?" Adam said in a faint voice.

"Aye, but when I found 'im . . . well . . ." The hot, menacing colour flooded the man's face and as though his rage were weakening him he put out a hand to a chair back to steady himself.

"For Christ's sake, sit down, man, you're all in. Here, I'll pour you a brandy."

"Nay, sir, theer's no time."

"Sit down and drink this brandy," Adam Cooper said in the voice he had used as an officer in Her Majesty's army. "Then you can tell me about it. When did you last eat?"

"Eat? I dunno, sir." Job looked vaguely irritated as though the matter of food and when he last had any was of no importance to anyone, particularly himself.

Adam rang the bell at the side of the fireplace and scarcely before his hand had left it a maidservant was knocking on the door, giving the impression that she had been hanging about in the hall waiting on his call. The servants were all agog, naturally, longing to know what the uncouth fellow who had had the temerity to tell Mr Henton to "look lively" and who had trampled mud across Cook's clean floor, since it was a wet day, had to say to the master.

Within five minutes there was a tray of food – a meat pie, ham sandwiches, cheese and a hunk of bread – on a small table beside Job Hawthorne's chair. He demolished the lot in the precise manner of a man stoking an engine as he talked. The brandy had strengthened him and now, eating in a way that surprised Adam since it was so mannerly even though the man was obviously starving, he recounted the story of what had befallen Sally Grimshaw in the last ten days.

"He were at 'er bedroom door when I come across 'im, Captain. Well, I didn't exactly come across 'im" – he grinned wolfishly – "I'd seen way 'e looked at 'er, the sod, an' I knew what he were after . . ."

For the space of five seconds Adam Cooper's eye carried

the image of prim little Sally Grimshaw as he had always seen her, except perhaps on the day of her brother's wedding when, he recalled, she had worn something light and pretty. And on the occasion of their first meeting. Then she had had a kind of rumpled look about her. Bare arms, her breasts bouncing joyfully as she polished something on the bar, her hair coming down in wisping curls, her rose pink lips parted. She had soon pulled it all together when she had become aware of him, so quickly he had barely had time to register it and from then, whenever they had met, she had been neat, trim, soberly dressed, as respectable and virtuous as a spinster aunt. The novel idea that some man had indecent intentions towards the stiffly upright, tightly buttoned, firmly bonneted little woman was almost comical, had it not been so . . . so bloody outrageous. He surprised himself with his own sense of outrage.

"An' I were ready fer 'im, sir. Waited on the landin', I did, hidden like. I'd 'ave killed 'im if it hadn't bin fer't little maid. She did this ter me," touching his ear and wincing. "Jumped on me an' near bit me bloody ear off . . . pardon me language, sir . . . burr I get that mad when . . ."

The man's in love with her, was Adam's next incredulous thought.

"That bugger" – Job's face twisted in a snarl – "he told us ter be out within the 'our. I were all fer beggin' 'im ter keep 'er on, then I thought about what 'e'd bin up to an' I knew she weren't safe. She's bin good ter me, Captain," he added simply.

"I know." Adam's voice was soft.

"So, 'er an' me we set off. 'We'll soon find work, Job,' she ses. You know 'ow determined she can be."

"Yes."

"I begged 'er ter go to 'er brother's . . . he's livin' at Norton's Farm until . . . well, she wouldn't an' when I said what about 'er over the water . . . she's a sister in Birkenhead, no, that didn't suit neither. 'Five children, they 'ave,' she ses, 'an' no room fer me an' you', an' I realised then it were me she were bothered about. 'There'll be inns where they'll want a barmaid an' cellarman, you'll see,' she ses, but there weren't, sir. One or t'other, not both of us an' I wouldn't leave 'er an' she wouldn't leave me so there we were, pair of us, sleepin' rough. Can yer imagine it, 'er, what's used ter clean sheets an' . . ."

Job shook his head in disbelief but somehow Adam wasn't surprised. That's just how she would be. Sharp-tongued, grim-faced, downright ungracious at times but with a loyal heart so big and brave she would not abandon this enormous and yet strangely gentle giant of a man who, or so she believed, without her would finish up in the workhouse.

"Any road" – Job shook his head as though to clear it – "last night the landlord at Plough, t'other side o' Prescot, said she could start theer . . . well, we was desperate by then. 'I'll 'ave ter tekk it, Job,' she ses, 'or we'll both starve. You keep outa sight an' I'll fetch yer some food when I can.' Well . . ." Job shook his head again and on his face was an expression of such absolute devotion Adam felt the need to look away. It was like spying on some private thing, some precious secret belonging to this man alone.

"I couldn't let 'er, Captain. Little bit of a thing she be, workin' 'er fingers ter't bone all 'ours God sends. She's a lady, sir. Theer's all sorts goes on at Plough – cock fightin' an' badger baitin' an' yer'll know what kind that attracts. So, this mornin' I legged it over 'ere. I told 'er I'd 'eard of a job towards Everton. She were glad fer me, she said, but she 'ad this sorta stricken look an' I knew she were frightened to be on 'er own an' I knew you were a friend to 'er. Well, I'll be 'onest wi' yer, sir. I followed 'er a time or two when she went off on 'er walks, just ter mekk sure yer weren't . . . well, yer'll know wharr I mean, sir."

It was plain to Adam Cooper that Job Hawthorne believed there was not a man living who would not see, and want, what he himself saw in Sally Grimshaw.

"The Plough, you say."

"Aye, sir. She'll not come away fer me, Captain."

Adam Cooper rose to his feet. "She will for me," he said quietly.

The noon trade at the Plough on the main road just beyond Prescot was surprised when the glossy, maroon-coloured carriage pulled by two sleek, black horses drew up outside the front door and a well-dressed gentleman who was evidently gentry climbed down from it. They were not used to gentlemen and carriages at the Plough. It was a simple alehouse where labourers and farm hands, and more often than not a very rough element from about the area, liked to drink and gamble, and they gawped in astonishment at the unusual sight.

"I shan't be long, Alec," those who stood near the open door of the taproom heard him say to the smartly dressed coachman.

"Very well, Captain," the coachman answered respectfully.

The man, tall, grey-haired and with what seemed to be a soldier's bearing, strode into the taproom and looked about him. He was dressed as though he were off to the city, these country lads thought, though many of them had never been beyond the perimeter of Prescot, let alone to the city. He wore a morning coat, unbuttoned at the front, single-breasted, waisted with small pockets and which reached to just above his knees. It was in a rich blue merino. His trousers were tight in the leg, pale grey with straps beneath the foot and his waistcoat was striped in shades of blue and grey. His cravat, tied in a flat bow beneath his chin, was the same colour as his coat. He was immaculately turned out, though his pin-tucked shirt was woefully laundered and ironed. His wide-awake hat, which he held in his hand, was black. He was a real toff and no mistake and the men drew back respectfully, wondering what the hell he was doing in their humble alehouse.

They were soon to find out.

"Is there a Miss Grimshaw here?" he asked, his breeding revealed by the arrogant turn of his head and his authoritative voice which would brook no argument. He had no need to raise it since the hubbub of noise which normally fills a public bar had died away as he entered.

They looked at one another in bewilderment. What the devil was he up to? The sort of female he would consort with, whether a lady or not, would not be found in a place like the Plough.

"Who wants to know?" the landlord asked truculently. The new girl, known by the name of Sally, had given him her full name, which he had immediately forgotten, when he had taken her on, much against his better judgment he might add, for she hadn't a "pick" on her and certainly didn't look the sort who would please his customers with what he liked to call a bit of "barmaid's sauce"! But he had been pushed, his second barmaid having fainted dead away behind the bar yesterday dinner-time, her condition revealed as she lay flat on her back on the cold stone flags. Mind you, the new one could work, he'd give her that, once they'd fed her. She'd eaten enough to fill a good-sized man, he had thought, wondering where she was putting it. After that she'd never stopped, giving the floors a scrubbing they'd not known for years, running about from bar to bar with an unflagging energy which had amazed him. When the public house closed, she'd fallen like one dead, or so Rosie, who was kitchen maid, said, into the bed they were to share. He had been pleased with her and didn't want to lose her, especially with Agnes six months gone and no longer any use to him, so best find out what this swell wanted before revealing her presence.

"I do." The man's attitude was overbearing, like all the bloody gentry, his eyes hard and implacable and though he had stared down many a troublemaker in his time the landlord's eyes dropped.

"Is she here?" the man continued ominously.

"Nay, never 'eard of 'er."

"I take it you will have no objection to my . . ."

It was at that precise moment that Sally's head popped up over the bar counter, just as neat, her hair just as disciplined as it always was and Adam was constrained to wonder how she had managed to get herself so clean and respectable-looking in a place like this after, from what Job had told him, she had been on the tramp for over a week. Her face was thin though her golden eyes still blazed their defiance at him.

"Yes, Captain, can I serve you?" she asked him challengingly.

"No, you bloody well can't, Sally Grimshaw," he snapped. "You can get yourself out from behind that bar, collect what things you have and climb into that carriage out there."

"On whose orders, Captain?" She tossed her head and the crowd was hushed, waiting for what was to come next.

"On mine, dammit."

"And where do you mean to take me, if you don't mind my asking?"

"Home, of course." His voice was irritable. He should have known that she would not come easily. He wanted to shake her and tell her not to be such a bloody nuisance. To get her out of this low-down place and back to Coopers Edge where she should have been in the first place. He should have been more firm with her weeks ago, up on the hill behind Knotty Ash but she was so damned infuriating with her absolute refusal to listen to any voice but her own and her determination to go no one's way but the one she chose. Since that day he had been up to the hill several times in the hope of seeing her and had just begun to think he had no choice but to ride over to the Grimshaw Arms and accost her there when this brouhaha had started. He was seriously affronted by the whole damned thing, wondering why she could not have come to him when it happened and he meant to put the question to her at the first opportunity, damned obstinate woman.

But first he must get her away from here. These men were thoroughly enjoying the spectacle of a barmaid, one they had not seen until last night, and had scarcely noticed since, for she was not the usual sort to serve them, but a barmaid just the same, bandying words with one of the upper class and they hardly dared raise their tankards to their lips for fear they might miss something.

"Home is it? And whose home might that be, Captain, since I no longer have one?"

"Miss Grimshaw, will you stop this bloody—"

"I'd be obliged if you would be less free with your 'bloodies' in my presence, Captain Cooper. If you think because I am working here it gives you the right to address me as though I were . . . were . . ."

"Yes, Miss Grimshaw, you need say no more. I apologise. Now, will you do as you're told?"

"No, I will not. No man tells me what to do unless he employs me. Mr Jenkinson here" – bowing graciously in the direction of the open-mouthed landlord – "pays my wages and has the right to give me orders. Now, if you'll excuse me I have customers who need serving."

She turned and bestowed her brilliant, crooked smile on the astounded man nearest to her, taking his empty glass from his flaccid hand. "A pint, is it, sir?" she asked him and he nodded his head, though in fact he had just been about to leave when the excitement had started. His old woman would be expecting him home and if he was late for his dinner there would be hell to pay, but this was worth a rollicking and besides, wouldn't he have something to ginger up the normal monotonous conversation at the kitchen table!

"Miss Grimshaw, must you be so stubborn? Look about you and then convince me that this is the kind of place you wish to work in."

"Now listen 'ere . . ." the landlord began, suddenly realising his hostelry was being insulted.

Adam ignored him. His voice was quiet and it told Sally Grimshaw he was in deadly earnest. It was so quiet those at the edge of the crowd pressed forward, begging those who were nearer to tell them what he was saying.

"This is not for you, Miss Grimshaw. I know what happened at the Grimshaw Arms. Job came to . . ."

"I was just about to ask you how you came to find me, Captain Cooper, and I should have known. So it was Job, who else? The tale about a job in Everton was merely a ploy. He came to beg you to . . . Dear sweet God, why is it men think they can have the ordering of any woman they choose? Why do they always imagine they know best?"

The man who was waiting for his pint nodded sagely, whether in agreement with her remark, or with her, it was not clear.

"He shall be fired at once," she went on, her face a furious pink. "I'll have no man working for me who . . ."

"Miss Grimshaw, he is already fired. He no longer works for you. He is . . . not as strong as you. Oh yes, physically, but not . . . inside him and if he is left alone he will go under. I admit he'd fight any man, or woman probably, who said so, but he needs to work. I have work to give him but he won't come without you. He'll continue to hang about here, protecting you, as he thinks, but unmanned by his need for work and his inability to find it. Unmanned by his dependence on you for handouts, the very woman he wants to see secure. I know that bloody independence of yours would keep you here, or in a place like it, until you dropped down dead from overwork but will you not consider what you are doing to others?"

"What others . . . besides Job?"

"Dear God, woman, I don't know," and he didn't, though something strange fluttered in his chest. "Just do as you're told for once without arguing."

"Captain, I can't walk out of a decent job unless I know what I am to have in its place. I must have work and really, you cannot just expect me to—"

"Miss Grimshaw, I am warning you, if you won't accompany me of your own free will then I shall come round that bar and drag you out."

"'Ere, hold on," the landlord began to bluster, not caring tuppence for the argument between these two but suddenly afraid he was going to have to serve this crowd alone, except for one indolent barmaid, or so she seemed next to the energetic drive of the new girl.

"You mind your own business, Mr Jenkinson. This is nothing to do with you," his new barmaid had the nerve to tell him. "This gentleman and I have something to settle before he leaves."

The fascinated hush continued as the customers hung on to every word, swearing later they had not been so entertained since Bertie Cockcroft brought his prize pig into the bar and gave it a pint of the landlord's best stout. Well, it *had* just taken first prize at the annual fair!

"Miss Grimshaw. My patience is coming to an end. I mean what I say." Adam Cooper took a step towards the bar. He had put on his hat as though he might need two hands for the task of dragging, or carrying the scrawny, half-fed kitten who was Sally Grimshaw out of the alehouse and into his carriage.

Sally watched him. Her heart was doing handstands in her chest and she was afraid those about her might see the movement of it under the cotton of her bodice. She wanted, beyond anything, to go with him since he represented a promise of decency, security, respectability, a release from the gnawing fear and uncertainty of the past eight months. She didn't know what he had in mind for her and she was rapidly approaching the state of mind when she didn't really care. But she trusted him, she suddenly realised and whatever it was it could not degrade her any more than she had been degraded for the past eight months. She was tired. Aching with weariness and yet strangely unable to sleep. She had spent night after night staring wide-eyed into the dark, these past few without even a roof over her head! She had tried, God how she'd tried, to clutch back to her that sweet independent security she had known before Freddy had wandered like some irresponsible child into that gaming house in Liverpool and thrown away what was hers on a game of chance. He might just as well have taken all that they owned and chucked it into the shining waters of the Mersey.

Now, somehow, in what way she didn't know, this man seemed to be offering her an escape from it all. From the humiliation, the hunger . . . aye, hunger now, for Sally Grimshaw, who had eaten nothing but the best all her life, had known what it was this last week almost to starve. Adam Cooper had got into his fine carriage and come looking for her, like a friend would, holding out a hand, as a friend would, to get her over a bad patch, smiling inwardly at the description – a bad patch – of the horror of the last months.

"What are you offering me, Captain Cooper?" she said, like a young queen in her dignity.

He didn't know yet. He was acting on impulse, making it up as he went along. He had one compulsion and that was to get her out of this place and away to somewhere safe, clean, decent, somewhere she could apply her particular and unique talents to whatever she was to do with the rest of her life, he supposed.

But his thoughts were scarcely rational, he was aware of that, and he must assemble them into some order, for she would require it.

"Miss Grimshaw, does it matter for the moment?" he asked her.

"It does to me."

"Yes, I suppose it would."

"You know the saying, from the frying pan into the fire."

He began to laugh, looking about him at this particular "frying pan" with comic disbelief.

"Miss Grimshaw, surely nothing could be worse than this? I have no intention of selling you into the white slave traffic, if that's what you were afraid of."

"I wouldn't care for that, Captain." Her own lips were twitching and it was written on the face of every silent, open-mouthed man in the room that they were wondering what the hell these two were talking about.

Adam Cooper continued to smile as he held out his hand to her, relieved beyond measure when she took it. He had the answer, of course. It had come to him weeks ago though he would not admit to it at the time, when she had confessed to having nightmares, when she fell asleep in his company, when he had watched her and known she was on the very edge of some abyss which, if no one dragged her back, she would fall into.

Sally Grimshaw was not quite the self-reliant creature she thought herself to be, though he would not have dared say so.

"No, I didn't think you would." He grinned. "But I thought you might care to take a job I have on offer. May I tell you about it?"

10

The servants were flabbergasted and they told one another so repeatedly, all eleven of them who worked in the house, as their master handed down the plainly dressed woman he had gone to fetch from an alehouse in Prescot.

Almost before the carriage had been ordered and Alec told to bring it round to the front of the house, they all knew about it, and her. Well, they could hardly miss the large, silent man, gaunt-faced, wild-eyed, from whom the women shrank back in alarm and the menservants gave a wide berth to. Mr Henton had been incensed and had, in fact, threatened to resign – only to them, of course, since he really had no intention of doing so – when Captain Cooper had instructed him to see that the man was fed *again*, bathed in whatever place the menservants bathed, allowed to shave and then be put into some decent clothing. That is if any could be found to fit him since he was well over six feet tall. Perhaps Henton might take a look in the captain's own wardrobe, he said, since he and Job – that apparently was the man's name – were of similar height, he added, as he shrugged into his good merino frock coat and adjusted his cravat. There must be a pair of breeches, a shirt or two, an old riding jacket that might be suitable. Would Henton ask Mrs Chidlow to see that the maids prepared a room . . . which one? . . . he didn't know, he'd leave it to

Mrs Chidlow, for he was expecting to bring a lady guest back with him.

A lady! A *lady*! It was no lady who stepped down lightly from the carriage, her back like a poker, her bonnet held high, her nose in the air. She was as regal as though she were a duchess who had come to take tea with the master as she moved into the wide, well-proportioned hallway of Coopers Edge, but she was recognised at once. It was Sally Grimshaw from the Grimshaw Arms and when they were told of it, those in the kitchen, by Tipper the footman, who drank there on his night off, they couldn't, wouldn't believe it. Not that the maids knew her, naturally, since they did not frequent beer-houses, or even inns, as the Grimshaw Arms was called. They had all heard, as who in the district had not, of her brother's profligacy at the gaming tables which had lost him the inn and of his marriage to the daughter of one of the local farmers. There was not much went on that they didn't hear of on the grapevine of servants who were employed in the big houses in the parish of West Derby.

So what was the man's sister who, when all was said and done, was no more than a barmaid, and were such creatures respectable? they asked one another, doing in the captain's carriage, in his hallway and even, so Mrs Chidlow told Cook, to be put in one of the guest bedrooms on the first floor? It was one Mrs Chidlow had thought fit for a single woman of her station. Not the best by any means and she'd not lit the fire, even though it was damp and cold outside and would not do so until ordered. This . . . this person was not a lady. In fact she and Cook wondered what the captain had in mind for her since she was exceedingly plain. Tidy, they'd give her that but not the kind of woman men seemed to require in their beds. Not that Mrs Chidlow nor Cook had ever been in any man's bed but they recognised the type of woman who had and this was not one of them.

"Is there a fire in the drawing-room, Henton?" was the first thing the master said as he helped the woman off with her coat, handing it to the butler, who took it between his thumb and forefinger as though it had just been dragged through a cowpat. Henton did not notice Sally Grimshaw's gimlet eyes on him and if he had he would not have understood what a sorry mistake he had just made.

"No, sir, I was not aware . . ."

"Where is there a fire, then?"

"Well, I believe Fletcher lit one in the small parlour, sir." The small parlour was where Mrs Chidlow and Henton were accustomed to drinking a pot of tea together now and then, since it was very comfortable and the master never went there. It was the room to where, had they had one, the mistress of the house would have summoned the housekeeper, asking her to fetch the books which would show the current expenses of the house and the tradesmen's bills. Where they would discuss the running of the house, the standards of the maids, the state of the household linen cupboard, the stillroom, the pantry and where Cook would go each morning to arrange the day's menus with her mistress. A lady's small and private sitting-room where visitors were never shown.

"That will have to do for the moment. Bring tea, will you?" He looked enquiringly at Sally. "Would tea be welcome, Miss Grimshaw?"

"Thank you, Captain." She nodded. "That would be nice. It is not . . . warm today, is it?" She shivered just a little as though she found the temperature of the hallway not to her liking though that was not the real cause. Adam Cooper was not to know, and neither was Henton, that Sally was doing her best to avoid standing in awestruck silence in front of the portrait of the most beautiful woman she had ever seen which hung over the empty fireplace.

"No, you're right, it's not." Adam Cooper looked about him. "Why hasn't the fire been lit here, Henton?" he asked the butler as though he had only just noticed the lack of one.

Henton shot a venomous look at Sally but she merely smiled. She would make short work of this one, her smile said, the smile her own staff had once known and dreaded, though Henton did not recognise it.

"Well, sir—" he began coolly.

"Never mind," his master interrupted him. "Have one lit now and in the drawing-room, too." He paused in the act of ushering his guest along the chilly hallway in the direction of the back parlour, looking for a moment over his shoulder.

"I take it there is a fire in Miss Grimshaw's room, Henton."

"I will make enquiries, sir. I'm sure—"

"See to it at once and send one of the maids with the tea immediately, if you please."

"Of course, sir."

The butler inclined his head a mere half-inch and began his ponderous march in the direction of the kitchen, his back indicating the degree of his offence.

Sally, who was to say later to Job that at that moment she didn't know whether she was on her head or her elbow, sat down where the captain indicated. It was a small but comfortable sofa which, with its partner opposite, stood out at right angles to the wall on either side of the good fire which crackled in the grate. They were both heaped with cushions, plump and, she supposed, restful to the back though hers did not touch them. There were a couple of footstools to match the sofas where Henshaw and Mrs Chidlow were wont to rest their cherished feet. Above the white marble fireplace, which was decorated in a relief of garlands and lover's knots, stood a clock of ormolu whose delicate carillon chimed as she sat down. There were attractive pottery oil lamps designed by Joshua Wedgwood in shades of blue and white on either side of the fireplace, standing on small, round tables. On the walls, which had been papered in a rich shade of raspberry, were framed pictures, watercolours mostly in subtle hues and misty images which were hard to define but pleasing, nevertheless, to the eye. Silk curtains hung at the three long, narrow windows in a pale dove grey with pelmets and tie-backs to match. The carpet was the same shade of grey but for a circle of raspberry pink roses in its centre. There were mirrors wherever there was a space on the wall and Sally wondered why the exquisite creature pictured in the hall had been so concerned with her own reflection that she must have it shining back at her wherever she sat.

She also noticed that the room had not been dusted that day!

They sipped their tea, she and Captain Cooper. Sally had to bury her nose in her cup a time or two to hide her smile, for he looked so out of place in this totally feminine room, and so ill at ease balancing the fragile porcelain cup and saucer on his knee. He was waiting for her to settle, to relax, to feel warm and comfortable before he took up again the astonishing offer he had made to her in the taproom of the Plough. She knew him well enough by now to be aware of that. He was a kind man and, despite his chosen career as a soldier and the tragedy of his private life which could have hardened him, or made him bitter, he was sweet-natured. That was not to say he was a man who suffered fools gladly, since he was neither soft-hearted nor lily-livered. Far from it, though she had to admit he certainly did not seem to care what his servants did in this house. Well, if he had meant what he had said in the carriage about needing someone to look after his home then she'd soon have that put right.

There were many matters to discuss first though, not the least being the fact that she was perfectly sure he already had a housekeeper though not a very efficient one by the look of things. Dust on the polished surfaces of the tables, in this room at least, and fires not lit where they should be, and this tea she was drinking was as weak as dishwater. Look after his home, he had said, which he knew she was well able to do since he had seen the order, the discipline of the Grimshaw Arms; the absolute perfection of the state of her floors, the shine on her brass, the sparkle of her windows. He had not tasted, sadly, her steak and kidney pies but then he did not require her to be his cook, or his housemaid. He wanted her to oversee it all, to run his household and all those who worked within its walls, as she had run the Grimshaw Arms. She was a decent, honest, hardworking woman and what other qualifications were required?

"Might I ask where Job is, Captain Cooper?" Her voice was crisp, giving the impression that she had to start somewhere, that is if she was to start at all, which had not yet been totally established.

"I'm not sure, Miss Grimshaw. Are you ready to come through to the kitchen and find out? Or would you prefer to go to your room first? Perhaps a rest before . . .?"

He lifted his dark eyebrows and smiled courteously and Sally realised that the informal and relaxed acquaintanceship they had shared on their meetings beyond Knotty Ash would soon be ended. He would always treat her civilly, but as a servant and not a friend. He would help her, support her in her new position, whatever that might be, should she need it, but their roles had altered, or would do the moment she took up employment at Coopers Edge. This would be the last time they would sit down together to drink tea, or indeed in any capacity since a gentleman did not socialise with his servant.

She was disturbed at the pang which struck her somewhere between her breasts. She had enjoyed their friendship, which had been easy and humorous. It had lightened many a bad hour over the last few months and she would be sorry to lose it, but she needed a job more than she needed a friend, she told herself sadly. Where else would she find a situation such as this one, for herself and for Job, who must be considered, particularly when she remembered what he had saved her from? She was afraid to close her eyes at night since it had happened lest she find Richard Keene waiting for her in her nightmares but surely here, in this lovely house, in the work she knew she was well qualified to do, she would find a decent life? A decent reward for a decent day's work. That was all she had ever wanted from life.

"Job first, I think, sir." She stood up. Her hands went automatically to her hair and she glanced in the mirror over the fireplace as she did so. He had risen to his feet when she did and she caught his eye as he watched her reflection. There was a strange expression on his face, sad, she thought, brooding, as though he were seeing another woman there whose going had left a hole in his life that had never been filled. But that was nothing to do with Sally Grimshaw, who had holes of her own to see to!

He led her along a passage beyond the door of the small sitting-room, turning left beneath the wide curving central staircase to where a green baize door stood. Leaning forward to open it for her, he indicated that she was to enter the kitchen, holding the door open as she passed through. As she moved into the enormous room she was aware that every movement within it ceased and so did every voice. There was total, thundering silence in which the ticking of the clock on the wall and the crackle of the flames in the blackleaded grate could distinctly be heard.

Knowing his master was "on the prowl" as Henton had muttered to Mrs Chidlow, though he had not expected him in the kitchen, they had between them made sure that every servant, from Clara the scullery maid, who was at the Brussels sprouts in readiness for dinner, right through the hierarchy up to himself at the top, was fully occupied. Tilly, who was kitchen maid and Cook's right hand, so to speak, was busy stirring something in a deep bowl at the kitchen table while Cissie and Maddy – Newton and Fletcher when they were in the "front" of the house – were buffing the silver which Tipper had cleaned an hour since. Tipper himself was behind a glass partition sharpening knives but even the grinding drone of the machine faltered to a halt as Sally Grimshaw and their master walked into the kitchen.

"Aah, Henton," their master said and at once all eyes turned away from the woman, going to him in deep anticipation of what he was to say. You could see it in their faces, that sly glint of excitement since not one of them could conceive that this woman, whatever she was to be to the captain, might in any way alter their lives.

"Yes, sir?" The butler, who was studying a bottle of wine, meant not for his master's consumption but his own, placed it carefully on the table, his narrow-eyed, tight-lipped face plainly telling Adam Cooper that he was not pleased. Master he might be but he knew as well as Henton that it was not done to stroll calmly into the kitchen, or the servants hall which was Henton's province, as though he had a perfect right to be there. It was the proper thing, if he wished to speak to any servant, to summon them to his study and say what he had to say there. This was the second time today Henton had been offended by Captain Cooper's behaviour. In a household such as this there was a strict code of conduct, which a mistress, a lady, that is, would have known, naturally, even between employer and employee and the master was abusing it. Henton did not like it. A butler of his calibre, who had once, when he was younger, worked in aristocratic circles, should be treated with the respect he deserved and he had not been so treated today.

"We were looking for Job, Henton," his master said, apparently unaware of the displeasure he had given to his butler.

"Job, sir?" Henton pretended ignorance though they all knew full well the name of the big chap who was at this moment straining Captain Cooper's corduroy jacket to bursting point across the shoulders as he chopped wood in the yard.

"Yes, Job. The man you showed into my study this morning."

"Aah, yes, sir. I believe he is . . . working."

"Working! Good God, man, he was done in when I went to fetch Miss Grimshaw. I left orders that he was to rest. There are empty rooms above the coach house, I believe, with beds in them. Could he not have been put in one of those?"

"Yes, sir." The butler's patience was icy. "But he refused to occupy one of them. He seemed to be . . . anxious about" – he let his high-nosed glance drift to Sally – "about the young lady, sir, and said he would chop wood until . . ."

Sally tutted and without so much as a glance at Cook, whose territory this was and whose permission should be sought, as a courtesy, to enter it, strode across the stone-flagged floor to the back door, forcing Cissie to jump smartly out of the way, startling her into a small curtsey.

"I might have known he'd do something like this, Captain Cooper. He's the very devil about independence and—"

"Like someone else I know," Adam Cooper said dryly.

"No, really, sir, he must be made to rest. He has barely slept these last ten days, watching over me while I did, refusing to do more than sit down beside me and as for eating, it was all I could do to get a bit of dry bread down him."

She flung open the door, looking out through the drizzle which drifted across the yard to where Job could be seen swinging an axe while every brain in the kitchen, except Adam Cooper's, grappled with the words the woman had spoken. *Watched over her while she slept*! Could she possibly mean what they thought she meant? That great ugly brute of a man with half of his ears missing and this woman, who was no beauty certainly, but surely . . . surely to God they were not . . . not what the words implied? Would their master allow in his house a ruffian with the smashed face of a prize fighter and a woman of low morals, a barmaid who only God knew what sort of men she consorted with. And him with two innocent daughters upstairs in the schoolroom!

They hardly dared look at one another, though Tilly managed to nudge Clara who dropped her paring knife with a squeak as the master followed the woman to the back kitchen door.

"Job," they heard her call, "will you come in out of the rain at once. Dear heavens, man, I can't leave you alone for an hour but you must do your best to kill yourself. You know you've been coughing these last few nights and this rain will do your chest no good at all."

She whirled about, turning her extraordinary eyes which were, Tilly thought, exactly like the golden ones in the face of the cat on the hearthrug, in the direction of Cook. She smiled but there was a look of resolution about her which seemed to say she would stand no nonsense, though of what sort they were not sure.

"You're the cook here?" she asked, politely enough.

Cook nodded, not at all sure she wanted to engage in conversation with a hussy.

"Then I'd be obliged if you could let me have a couple of lemons, a teaspoon or two of glycerine and a cup of honey. And some hot water in a mug, and perhaps a tot of whisky."

Adam cleared his throat warningly but Sally was too busy with her concern over Job to notice. She seemed to have no conception of what her treatment of Job Hawthorne was fermenting in the servants' minds. They were not to know of the loyalty and devotion which had grown between her and the ex-prize fighter in the turmoil which their lives had become over the past few months but it was too late now. Adam Cooper had made up his mind and he meant to stick to it.

Shaking himself like some grizzly bear which has just spent several hours lumbering about in a wet woodland, the man she had spoken to came slowly into the kitchen. He did not smile, nor even look particularly pleased to see her but there was something about him, a certain release of tension which told Adam a great weight had been lifted from his shoulders.

"Now I'm going to—" she began.

"Miss Grimshaw," Adam said gently, "let one of the maids see to that. I'm sure . . . er . . ." He looked about him until his eye fell on Tilly.

"Tilly, sir." Tilly sketched a curtsey and smiled shyly.

"I'm sure Tilly can be shown how to prepare . . . what was it?"

"I already know, sir. Me mam always give us honey, glycerine and lemon fer a cough. There were no whisky in it though," she added apologetically.

"Never mind, put some in anyway, and then Tipper can show Job where he is to sleep."

Sally glared at Tipper. "Plenty of blankets, mind, and is there a fireplace in—"

"I'm sure he will be well looked after, Miss Grimshaw."

"And that ear needs seeing to. Have you a disinfectant?"

"I'm sure we have. Cook?"

Cook nodded grudgingly.

"Excellent, now then, Miss Grimshaw . . ."

Sally looked with a worried frown at the enormous and patient man by the open door and Adam could have sworn she was about to put her hand to his forehead as one would to a child to check for a fever. He felt the irritation rise in him.

"Go on, Miss Sally," Job said gently, seeing it. "I'm right enough . . . now."

"You'll take the mixture?"

"Aye, I promise."

"And let . . . Tilly, is it . . . bathe your ear?"

"Yes, Miss Sally."

"Promise you'll go at once to your bed. You need a good night's sleep."

"Yes, Miss Sally."

"Well . . ." Sally allowed her gaze to travel round the kitchen, meeting one by one those of the servants and not one was other than cool, except perhaps for Tilly. She was a guest, an improbable one, true, in this house, and it seemed the big man was to work here but that did not mean they should show her anything other than the necessary politeness, their expressions told her.

"Then I'll go to my room now, sir, if you don't mind," they heard her say. "Perhaps . . . a bath . . . if it could be arranged?"

"Of course. Mrs Chidlow?" Adam turned back to the housekeeper who could hardly bring herself to nod.

"And a tray in your room?" he asked her courteously.

"That would be most kind . . . if one of the maids could show me where."

"Of course."

Maddy was thrust forward, her mouth still hanging open with the excitement of the scene that had taken place in the kitchen. She managed to pull herself together, exchanging a glance with Cissie, grimacing as she scuttled out into the hallway in front of the master and his guest.

"Then I'll bid you a goodnight, Miss Grimshaw," the captain said, even though it was no more than mid-afternoon.

"Yes, sir, thank you, sir. There is just one thing, sir."

Maddy waited at the bottom of the stairs as Miss Grimshaw turned to Captain Cooper who was making for his study.

"Yes, Miss Grimshaw?"

"I just wanted you to know that I'll be happy to help with the house."

The kitchen was in uproar when Maddy returned, having deposited "the woman", as they were all calling her, in the small back bedroom usually reserved in the past for young bachelor guests. She had begrudged every moment she was kept from running down the stairs to tell the others about the bewildering remark she had overheard the woman make to the master. And what would they make of Maddy's description of how the visitor had rudely run her finger along the mantelpiece and the dressing-table in the bedroom, given the curtains a twitch, then coughed dramatically as though they were full of dust, even turned down the bed to study the sheets and all without the slightest attempt to disguise her actions.

"Has this bed been aired?" she'd asked and when Maddy admitted she was not sure, since she had not aired it when she made it up earlier in the day, she'd only instructed her to bring up a hot-water bottle, if you please, two in fact, one for the bottom of the bed and one for the top. And some more coals and would Maddy make sure that the water for the bath was piping hot. She'd like to take it before her bedroom fire, when it had been made up, of course, looking contemptuously at the three or four tiny embers which burned in the fireplace. "I like a fire to *be* a fire, don't you?' she'd said to the flustered housemaid, who was furious with herself for being flustered!

Who in hell does she think she is? they asked one another as they sat down in the servants hall that evening to the indifferently cooked roast beef and Brussels sprouts put in front of them and to which, like their master, they had become accustomed. They quite enjoyed the meal for once since it had added to it the piquancy of the excited bustle the arrival of the big man and the small woman had whipped up in their drab lives and the speculation of what was to become of the pair of them. The man was easy enough since there was always work to be found outside, in the yard, the stables, the vast gardens, even beyond in the extensive parkland which surrounded it all.

But what of her? Where was she to fit in? As far as they knew there were no positions to be filled at Coopers Edge, not for a female, unless the captain had decided on an extra housemaid, but if that was the case she'd not be likely to be sleeping in a guest bedroom, would she, ordering up buckets of coal, hot water by the gallon and a meal of quite gargantuan proportions, of which she'd complained that the beef was overdone and would Maddy ask Cook what she put in the gravy in which it floated?

And that remark about "helping" with the captain's house was very perplexing. They went to their beds still ruminating on the future of "the woman" in their lives, that is if she was to have one.

In the room she had been allocated which, though warm and clean and infinitely less noisome than the one she had shared with Rosie at the Plough, and which she meant to move out of as soon as possible, the woman in question stared into the fire-flickered darkness.

The bed, despite the wool-wrapped stone hot-water bottles felt damp and the lumpy potatoes which had been served along with the watery Brussels sprouts sat uneasily on her stomach. She was at least clean, a state she had not been in for days, her hair washed and brushed until it snapped about her head and hung to her waist in a thick bush of gleaming curls. And beyond her window, somewhere above the stables she hoped – and if he wasn't she'd know the reason why – Job was resting in a bed for the first time since Richard Keene had turned them out, his cough soothed with the honey concoction, his ear bathed and beginning to heal, his exhausted body warm and lulled to sleep.

Wonderingly she let her mind drift back to the Grimshaw Arms. It seemed scarcely credible that what had been her home, her life, her very existence for the best part of twenty-odd years was now probably in some other woman's hand. Or perhaps a man had it in his charge, though it would need a woman's hand to provide the comfort, the good food, the welcoming word she herself had furnished for so long. There was one thing certain and that was that Keene himself would not be running it and did he realise, as he counted his profits, whatever they might be, what that little bit of nonsense between his legs had cost him? She had been leaving anyway, appalled at the thought of the illegal sporting activities which were to take place there, but even now she could scarcely credit that he had crept to her bedroom for the sole purpose of seducing Sally Grimshaw who, when they thought her to be out of earshot she had heard one farmhand describe to another as "old iron corsets"! No man had ever wanted her. No man had even attempted the saucy banter which they considered was due a barmaid. But Keene had seen something in her that no other man had fancied and, sighing, she wondered what it was.

She could hear small sounds in the night, unfamiliar sounds which, though she knew them to be harmless, impinged on her almost sleeping mind. An owl hooted, presumably from among the trees which lay like a battlement within the high stone wall that surrounded Coopers Edge. They had been so close together in their summer foliage she could barely get a glimpse of what lay beyond as she and the captain drove up the long, curving drive to the house.

She had never lived in a house. The inn had been on the main road out of Liverpool and though it was quieter at night there had sometimes been the sound of horses' hooves or the rumble of wheels beyond her bedroom window. Here there was absolute stillness, a silence so deep and heavy it seemed to press against her ears.

The silence was suddenly broken as a dog began to bark, close to the house, she thought, and then another took up the cry. Did they belong to one of the servants, her sleepy thoughts wondered, or was Adam Cooper their master as he was now hers?

Adam Cooper. Though her eyes were closed and her mind drifting, his face swam dreamily into her vision. His eyes were a warm, melting blue as he looked into hers and his wide, soft mouth moved and his lips parted across his teeth. His smile was engaging, merry as he put out a hand to her which she took in her dreaming sleep.

11

A small buzz of excitement tingled through her as she ran lightly down the wide, curving staircase. Her highly polished boots, which owed their gleam to her own spit and a certain amount of elbow grease since she had nothing else to hand in the bedroom where she had been put, barely touched the deep pile of the carpet. She felt as though she had wings on her heels. She was smiling absurdly, she knew she was, but there was no one to see her so it didn't matter.

It was seven o'clock and she could hardly wait to begin, to take up the challenge Captain Cooper had offered her, a new, exciting challenge but surely one she had been trained for all these years? Running a house could not be so different to running an inn since the concept of hospitality, the management of a kitchen, sound common sense, cleanliness and order were the same and she couldn't wait to get her teeth into it. To put her own unique stamp on this household which, it seemed to her, was surely in need of it.

But where were the servants? It was seven o'clock and as though to verify the fact the grandfather clock made a noise which might have been that of an old man clearing his throat, then, in a deep basso profundo, sounded the hour. Why was there no one about? A housemaid nimbly taking up hearthrugs in preparation for turning out the rooms she was to "do" before breakfast. There were carpets to be swept, ashes to remove from yesterday's fireplaces, fires to be laid and lit, grates to be cleaned, ornaments to be dusted, furniture to be polished and windows to be leathered. The list of duties was endless and yet where there should have been a bustle of activity and the sound of quiet voices, there was only stillness and silence.

Except for the clocks! She had never heard the sound of so many clocks and all at one and the same time. The grandfather at the foot of the stairs, which had given her quite a start, its booming notes going off in her ear as she passed it, seemed to bring to life a dozen others. As she peeped inside the small sitting-room, still expecting to find a housemaid busy at her duties, the delicate carillon of the timepiece on the mantelshelf tinkled prettily. As though at a signal sounds of pealing and tolling began, a positive explosion of clocks making their voices heard from the downstairs rooms of the house. From every room she peered into the noise came, clocks under domed glass, calendar clocks, bob clocks, pendulum clocks and a cuckoo clock which, for some reason, was hidden at the back of the staircase.

There was no one in the kitchen except for a thin, harassed young girl of no more than twelve or thirteen. She was on her knees before the kitchen range clearing out the remains of yesterday's ashes and as Sally entered briskly she turned, then fell back as though at the sight of an apparition. Her jaw dropped and her eyes were like saucers in her pale face. The ashes she had collected on the shovel slid off on to the hearthrug, and the cat, around which she was doing her best to work, squawked and leaped resentfully to its feet.

"Good morning," Sally said. "Put that cat outside, if you

please. It's no business being where food is cooked. And where is everyone? You and I seem to be the only ones up and about."

"Beg pardon, mum," the girl ventured, scrabbling frantically with the spilled ashes, at the same time doing her best to get a hold on the protesting cat. Her eyes went over Sally's shoulder for a sign of some sort of salvation in the form of another servant, one who was above her, which meant them all and who would surely know what to say to "the woman", as she had heard the rest of them describe her.

"Don't tell me they are all in their beds still?" Sally's voice was shocked as she looked round the room and the girl lowered her head in shame as though it were her fault. Sally noticed almost with one glance the signs which clearly showed the slackness of those who ran this kitchen, who ran this household, who had the ordering of the servants and this young girl who was looking at her as though she were a witch who was about to put a curse on her. There were cups and saucers unwashed from the night before, a half-eaten meat pie on a plate, a crumpled teacloth on the floor and a soiled apron flung on a bench. The place was clean enough, she supposed, at least for most folk, but there was a general air of slackness about it which told her, as it would tell any decent housekeeper, that there was no mistress in this house.

The girl continued to stare at her, leaning further back on her heels as Sally approached. She had given up on the cat which had flounced towards the back door, and her eyes were haunted in her sallow face, for if what they had been saying last night was true then this woman was no better than she should be and her mam would skin her alive if she associated with . . . with a harlot.

Sally's face softened imperceptibly. The girl was either paralysed with fear, probably to do with something the other servants had said about her and Job, or simple, and in either case was not to be blamed for what was going on here. Or rather what *should* be going on here! Gone seven o'clock and she and the skivvy the only ones up and she could only wonder what time the captain and his family got their breakfast. It really was disgraceful. There was much she could see needed to be done in this careless household and Sally Grimshaw was the right person to do it. She'd make it quite clear to the captain that she must have a free hand, no matter whose feelings were hurt, if she was to bring order, comfort, her own special brand of good management to his home, and what better time to begin than now?

Sally smiled and the girl was transfixed. Surely no one with a smile of such loveliness could be as bad and wicked as the others said she must be. The man, the big man, looked absolutely terrifying, but he too had smiled at her yesterday afternoon when she had given him some hot water to shave with, and there had been a twinkle in his green eyes. Ugly as the devil, he was, but being plain and put upon herself she had found she was shyly sympathetic with his awkward attempt to be friendly. She waited now, her heart in her mouth.

"What's your name?" Sally asked her.

"Clara, mum."

"Well, Clara, you finish cleaning out the range and those ashes on the mat. When you've lit the fire we'll have a cup of tea, shall we, while we wait for the others to come down. In the meanwhile, do you happen to know what the master has for breakfast?"

"Beg pardon, mum?"

"What does Cook make for the captain's breakfast?"

Anything that suits *her*, Clara would have liked to answer but she thought better of it.

"B . . . b . . . bacon, mum."

"Is that all, Clara?"

"Beg pardon, mum?"

"Does he have eggs or kidneys? Perhaps mushrooms?"

Clara was becoming bolder by the minute. "Well, aye . . . 'e does, mum."

"Does he like porridge, Clara? Or perhaps it's a favourite with the young ladies?"

Clara didn't know about that, she said.

"And where is it all kept, Clara?" Sally nodded encouragingly, waiting with a patience which was not usual to her, but Clara seemed to be struck dumb again.

"Well, never mind, we'll make some anyway, shall we?"

Clara felt the dread seep out of her completely and after she had shown "mum" where everything was and finished the fire they had a nice cup of tea together, though Clara could not be persuaded to sit down and drink it as "mum" begged her to.

Sally had to turn away and smile, she told Job afterwards, as, some time later, the maids began to drift into the kitchen, yawning and stretching, the early morning expressions on their faces turning to comical amazement as they caught sight of her. She had put on one of Cook's clean aprons by then, found in the drawer Clara had shyly pointed out to her, as she began to prepare one of her splendid Grimshaw Arms breakfasts for the captain who, Clara told her, breakfasted at eight thirty. She and Clara had rummaged about in a cupboard, discarding the enormous silver serving dishes normally used, scouring out several smaller ones and setting them to warm in the side oven.

"What about burners, Clara?"

"Burners, mum?"

"Mmm, to keep the food hot when it is taken to the breakfast-room."

"I seen summat like that in Mr Henton's pantry, mum, but 'e don't like no one messin' about in there."

"Show me, Clara, and we'll see what can be done with them."

It was clear that Clara's new-found confidence was appalled at the thought of entering the butler's private sanctum but somehow, trusting this woman who it seemed to her feared no one, the burners were found and by eight o'clock, when the servants began to dribble into the kitchen, were lit and in their rightful place on the serving-table in the breakfast-room.

It was Cook herself who totally annihilated Clara's slowly blossoming assurance and she shrank back into the safety of the scullery which was her private sanctum since no one else scoured pans and washed pots, nor scrubbed and peeled vegetables, which activities were performed there.

"May I ask, miss, what's going on in my kitchen?" Cook's voice was icy, flowing like a winterbound river from the kitchen doorway where she had come to an astounded halt. Her narrowed eyes surveyed the scene which was taking place in *her* territory and she was incensed, the maids could see that. They huddled together, for even though they were not at fault had they not in the past suffered at her hands and from her tongue? But this was more than just outrage, they could tell that, too, though what the other emotion they saw in her face could be was a mystery to them. You couldn't blame her though, could you? Here was the woman, whose exact position in this house was a riddle none of them could solve, dressed up as cocky as you please in Cook's own apron, wielding

Cook's own frying pan and Cook's own long-handled fork as she poked at something she was cooking on the range. And she wasn't dismayed at being caught, neither, that was obvious. She even turned to smile over her shoulder at the enraged, red-faced figure in the doorway. There was a lovely smell of bacon frying and the sizzle of it in the frying pan, along with what could only be the succulent aroma of fried kippers which the servants were well aware had been meant for Cook's, Mrs Chidlow's and Mr Henton's breakfast.

"Good morning, Cook," the cheeky madam said, just as though she had every right to be where she was. "Did your foot get caught in the sheets?"

The maids gasped. Cook's face turned an even deeper shade of brick red and her mouth snapped shut over her false teeth with a sound like a mousetrap being sprung. She banged the door violently behind her and in her cubby-hole Clara squeaked as though she were the mouse in the trap.

"What the devil d'you think you're up to?" Cook snarled, beyond caution or anything that might be called diplomacy. She took several menacing steps away from the kitchen door, moving towards the usurper at her range.

"Isn't that obvious, Cook?" the usurper responded calmly. "I've been told that the captain and his daughters take their breakfast at eight thirty." Sally glanced down at the watch which was pinned on her bodice beneath the bib of the apron. "And as it's now . . . ten past, I thought I had better make a start. Clara was kind enough to show me where everything is kept so . . ."

"I'll see to you later, you cheeky young devil," Cook hissed in Clara's general direction and Clara moaned. "And as for you" – glaring through slitted, puzzled eyes at Sally

– "I'd be obliged if you'd leave my kitchen at once. I'm the one who'll see to the captain's breakfast."

"In less than twenty minutes?"

"I could do it with one hand tied behind me back," Cook sneered through gritted teeth.

"Yes, I'm sure you could. As you no doubt cooked the meal I was forced to eat last night."

"No one forced you, miss, and if you don't like my cooking, there's the door. I don't know what you're doing here but let me say this. When the captain hears of your interference in what doesn't concern you . . ."

"Yes? You'll what?"

Sally was conscious of the breathless, slack-jawed, fascinated gaze of the three maids. There were all dressed alike in cotton uniforms of grey with white aprons and streamered caps. All clean, it appeared, but without that immaculacy Sally herself insisted upon. They stood in a mesmerised group, herded together just inside the door, Tilly and Cissie and Maddy, so that Cook had to push them aside to get by. Tilly was ready to dimple into a delighted smile, Sally could see it, as though it did her heart good to see someone get the better of Cook, but the other two were shocked and speechless at the sight of a fellow servant being put in such a dreadful position by this outsider who had imposed herself in their kitchen.

Sally found she didn't care, not one bit! Sally Grimshaw of the Grimshaw Arms was back. The quiet, sympathetic woman who had spoken patiently to the skivvy and even drunk a cup of tea with her had fled to be replaced by the confident, self-willed young woman who had reigned supreme in her own domain for so long. A clash of will meant nothing to her. Sally had known exactly what would happen even as she lifted down the heavy iron frying pan and tossed several rashers of bacon in it. No fat, of course. A cold pan, then on to the heat until the thin rashers curled at the edges. Six eggs poached, the yolks unbroken and, when cooked, all arranged attractively beneath the domed cover of the silver dishes with small squares of fried bread and expertly cooked tomatoes.

The servants could feel their mouths watering but not Cook. "The master'll hear of this," she hissed, taking another dangerous step towards Sally, "but I've things to do first." She elbowed Sally out of the way. She was a big woman who, even if no one else did, enjoyed her own cooking and it showed in her ample form. She was furious as she took her place at the range. Picking up the shining dish under the cover of which nestled her master's appetising breakfast, she passed it contemptuously to Cissie.

"Here, Cissie, get rid of this, will you, while I cook the master's breakfast. The scrap bucket's best place for it."

Cissie, in whose mind was the tantalising thought that she and Maddy would be glad to get their chops round what was in the dish, hesitated, glancing uncertainly from the woman who was removing her apron to Cook who was donning one.

"Go on, Cissie," Cook said warningly, reaching for the frying pan and dropping a great dollop of lard in it while Sally watched in horror.

"You're not frying good bacon in all that—"

"How I fry my bacon is nothing to do with you, miss. May I remind you that I am cook here and . . ."

Cook's words became indistinct, dying away to hum round in Sally's head like a swarm of angry wasps and Sally was aware as the servants stared at her, waiting to see what she would do next, that she had made a mistake. She had been so eager to start, to make a good impression, to give Captain Cooper the kind of breakfast he was entitled to expect, she had gone too far. There was no doubt in her mind that Cook would be got rid of since no one who worked with Sally Grimshaw would be allowed to turn out meals of a quality such as the one Sally had eaten the night before. And Mrs Chidlow, too, for there was no room for two housekeepers in a house this size but it was not up to her, Sally Grimshaw, to interfere in what was the captain's business. Time enough for that when she herself took up her duties. Then she would be entitled to rule the servants, at least the women, directing them in her ways as she had done at the inn. Mr Henton would be in charge of the indoor menservants but as that seemed to include only the footman and a young boy called Tom whose duties were vague, it appeared to follow that her powers would be the greater. And how would she and he manage together? she wondered. Their standards were obviously not of the same high level and it was pretty evident that the butler was of the opinion that he was taking a ride in a comfortable boat on smooth waters and he would not take kindly to having it rocked.

But rock it she must if she was to run this house in the only way her pride and her honesty let her. Carelessness had been allowed to gain a strong foothold and she had her own ideas of how to get rid of it. She was armed with the knowledge she had gained at the Grimshaw Arms and with her own passion for efficient housekeeping which she meant to put into practice as soon as she had discussed it with the captain. She had a strong will and it would take more than the high-nosed butler to crack it. Perhaps Henton, who must be in his mid-fifties and of an age where he would prefer an old situation rather than find a new, would be inclined to take the sensible view and work in harmony with her?

If not then he could go to the devil. Sally Grimshaw had been given this second chance to make a life for herself. A life that would be worth something and she meant to grasp it with both of her strong, capable hands.

Cook was smirking as Sally quietly left the kitchen. The old, enormous serving dishes – unheated – were being clattered on to the table. Into one of them she had carelessly tipped the dripping, soggy bacon and into another the overcooked eggs and the other items she had been serving in this house for the past eight or nine years. No one had complained and this . . . this hussy, whoever she was, would soon learn her place. The uneasy sensation that had attacked her in the pit of her stomach when she had entered her kitchen to find the woman at her range still trembled there, and she wondered why.

Sally gave Captain Cooper and his daughters time to eat their breakfast and the girls to return to the schoolroom before tapping on his study door. Two dogs rose to their feet as she entered the room, coming to sniff at the hem of her skirt before flopping down again on the rug before the fire in a joined tumble of legs and tails. They had reddish tan coats, harsh and dense and their eyes, which still studied her, were dark and keen.

"I think we had better discuss what I am to do in this house, Captain Cooper," she began, "that is if you meant what you said yesterday."

Sally's voice was brisk but she smiled politely as she stood before her employer's desk. She herself had eaten a good breakfast of fruit, and toast with creamy butter and strawberry jam and a pot of coffee. If Maddy Fletcher, who came to the small parlour when Sally rang the bell, was surprised to see her there, and she was, it seemed she could not quite bring herself to disobey a direct order.

Neither could Cook, though the coffee was barely warm and the toast slightly burned. Nevertheless Sally ate heartily in preparation for what lay ahead of her. She had slept well and though she had made a bad beginning in the kitchen, she was refreshed by her night's rest, and it showed.

Adam Cooper sat back in his chair and studied her. There was something about her that was different, he decided, knowing nothing of the contretemps in the kitchen which had put the zest back into Sally Grimshaw and brought colour to her cheeks, a sort of glow to her skin, he thought, and a certain air of determination which was vastly different to the calm, exhausted demeanour of the woman who had followed the housemaid up the stairs late yesterday afternoon.

"Of course I meant it, Miss Grimshaw, so won't you sit down?"

"Thank you, sir." She did so, smoothing the folds of her gown which was of a soft, cinnamon brown woollen material, well made and attractive, though the fit was not too good. It looked as though it had been fashioned for someone plumper than she was, hanging from her narrow shoulders, the bodice barely filled by the curve of her breast. Adam was not aware that it had been made for her last Christmas before she lost weight. A "best" dress she had never worn in the bar, simple but elegant with a deep band of brown satin about the plain neck, the wrists and hem of the full skirt. She had added a broad brown satin sash that was tied in a demure bow at the back. The colour suited her. Perhaps it was that which reflected in her smooth skin and put that deep amber in her long-lashed eyes. Had she long lashes? he asked himself curiously, quite surprised by the question and the answer was yes, long and brown but with a touch of gold at their roots. How extraordinary that he should suddenly notice it, he mused and into his head popped another thought and that was, what would she look like with her hair loose? He had never really seen her without that plain bonnet of hers until yesterday and then he had been too possessed with the need to get her away from that damned beer-house to notice her appearance, but now . . .

"You slept well, I hope?" he asked hurriedly, bewildered by the way his mind was wandering, needing to get back to the niceties a gentleman showed a lady.

"Oh, yes, indeed, thank you." She inclined her head, waiting.

"I'm glad."

"Thank you." She waited again.

"Your room was comfortable?"

"Yes, sir. It was . . . agreeable to sleep in a bed again. One does not realise what one has until it is no longer available." She smiled her lopsided smile, making light of an experience that must have been appalling to a woman of her upbringing.

"I'm sure it was, but of course the room you are in is only temporary, you realise that, don't you?"

He appeared to be flustered, inclined to fiddle with a letter-opener on his desk and she wondered why.

"Well, I did hope that . . . but whatever you say, Captain Cooper."

He fell silent then, his eyes still touching her though not in any way that could be called insulting.

"Captain?" she asked him questioningly, clearly bewildered by his scrutiny and at once he pulled himself together. For the past eight months he had considered her plain, shrewd, bright, with a stubborn jaw on her and a firm mouth. A woman not sexually attractive to a man but he had liked her. There was a strength of character in her he had admired, a steadiness, an alertness which he had never seen before in a female, at least of his class. Ladies of his own background were concerned with little more than fashion, marriage and how to get into that state, children, the running of their households and the submission they must show their husbands. They lived in a world where they must conform to the strict code of conduct laid down by their mamas who had been similarly taught by theirs. To deviate a fraction from this precept was to wander into a minefield of uncertainty and doubt and no lady of good breeding would consider it lest she be lost for ever. This woman with the thin, fascinating face and quite incredible eyes would never be lost, or uncertain, he hazarded. These last weeks had shown that. Sally Grimshaw was, by the standards of his social group, not a lady, but then did that matter? She was honest and loyal. You had only to see the devotion she showed to that big fellow who was probably about some gargantuan task in Adam's yard at this very moment. She was strong-willed and stubborn but she would need these characteristics if she was to take this house and shape it to suit her own standard of integrity. She had a humour that could be sharp and biting but at the same time she was inherently sweet-natured. There was a kindness in her he had sensed in many of the conversations they had shared, a generosity of spirit she kept well hidden and she would use that strength and generosity to transform this house of his into what he knew it had not been for a long, long time. A home!

Sally smiled at him expectantly, waiting for him to continue the interview. It was up to him, as her prospective employer, to start, surely? There were many things to be discussed, things that another woman, the mistress of the house, would have known instinctively. There were many things Sally must know if she was to take in hand the motley collection of men and women who were the servants in this household. One thing was certain and that was that she would get no help from the servants themselves. She was to start at a disadvantage since they had all been here before she came and would definitely not put themselves out for a woman they saw as an upstart, a usurper, for one of them would have to go if she was to be fitted in. It would be a daunting task but one she relished, for Sally Grimshaw had never in her life shrunk from a challenge.

It seemed Captain Cooper was at a loss where to begin, which was understandable. A gentleman knew nothing about the workings of his household. He left that to his wife, or if he had no wife, to his housekeeper. It was plain he was uncertain what questions to put to her so she supposed she'd best begin. Tell him what she intended doing, that's if he had meant what he had said yesterday about employing her, which it seemed he did. What other purpose could he have for rescuing her from the Plough and bringing her here?

The captain was still looking at her in that strange, distracted way as though he was not quite sure why she was sitting opposite him and Sally found it hard not to fidget beneath his steady gaze. She was not a fidgeting sort of woman, thank God, but it was difficult to keep her head high and her own eyes unclouded as he studied her.

She cleared her throat and she was startled when he jumped.

"Captain?" she asked questioningly.

"I'm sorry, Miss Grimshaw." He jerked himself from his reverie and leaned forward. Putting his elbow on the table he supported his chin on one fist. "You were saying?"

"I was saying nothing, Captain Cooper, but something should be said and though you may not care for it I feel bound to speak up."

He seemed to find this amusing but he said nothing so she continued.

"I'll be completely honest with you."

"You have never been anything else, Miss Grimshaw." His mouth twitched slightly.

"That is my way, Captain Cooper." She held her head a little more regally on her rigid neck and shoulders, wondering why she had the feeling he was finding this interview, and her, highly diverting.

"Please go on, Miss Grimshaw."

She looked down for a moment, her hands caressing the châtelaine which hung from her belt, then, as though she had made up her mind that she might as well be hung for a sheep as a lamb, she lifted her head and stared, or rather, glared, directly into his eyes.

"Your servants are a disgrace, Captain Cooper. Or should I say some of them are. Those in a position of authority, particularly. Though naturally I have not been made privy to the housekeeper's account book nor to Mr Henton's method of . . . of . . . well, shall we call it bookkeeping, I'm sure they will both be found to be . . . wanting, if you take my meaning."

"I do indeed, Miss Grimshaw." His mouth twitched again.

"And that meal we ate last night was . . . well, all I can say is Job could have made a better job of it and though I did not personally sample it, the breakfast that was served you I would not feed to the cat."

He looked surprised. "You have already been in the kitchen then?"

She ducked her head for a moment, two bright spots of colour on her cheeks, then raised flashing eyes to his.

"Yes, I have. I . . . I shouldn't have gone there without your permission, I know that, but . . . I wanted to show you . . . give you . . . serve you a decent breakfast. Well" – she smiled ruefully— "Cook was not pleased. In fact she put what I had cooked into the pig bucket."

"Did she indeed?"

"So what I'm saying is that the chances of Cook and I getting on are very slim."

"I can see that, Miss Grimshaw."

"So you agree that she must go?"

"It is entirely up to you, Miss Grimshaw."

Sally looked surprised. "Up to me? What about Mrs Chidlow?"

"What about Mrs Chidlow?"

"She has the hiring and firing of those in her charge, surely, Captain, but what I'm getting at is that a household cannot be ruled by two housekeepers. If, as you implied yesterday, I am to be yours then I'm afraid that, along with Cook, Mrs Chidlow must be dismissed."

"You mean . . .?"

"As your housekeeper, sir, I must . . ."

He began to laugh. A deep throaty chuckle that she had never heard before. He leaned back in his chair, placing both strong hands flat on the desk top.

She took offence. "Well, I can see nothing humorous in that, Captain Cooper," she said tartly, "but please, if you think there is I wish you would share it with me."

The laughter stopped as abruptly as it had begun but a

smile remained, a warm smile which curled Adam Cooper's well-shaped mouth at the corners.

"I'm sorry, Miss Grimshaw, I shouldn't have laughed but it seems you have misunderstood me. I am not in need of a housekeeper. I am in need of a wife."

12

For perhaps thirty seconds after Adam Cooper had stopped speaking Sally sat completely still in the chair opposite him, her mouth hanging foolishly open. She could feel the blood drain away from her head, from her heart, and she remembered wondering helplessly why he should play such a cruel and foolish jest on her, since surely he was jesting? But why? What did it mean? What was he to gain by making her look such a complete idiot? A few moments of laughter at her agonising embarrassment? The knowledge that Sally Grimshaw could be got the better of? That she could be struck dumb? Caught off guard? It was cruel and it was not like him since he was not a cruel man.

She could not speak. For perhaps the first time in her life she had nothing to say as she became agonisingly aware with what delight, had he meant what he said, his words would have been received. For months now he had been the best, the sweetest part of her life, keeping her steady, giving her a reason to go on, bringing lightness to her days which had been dark and filled with drudgery. She had not really been aware of his importance to her. What she had felt for him was a grateful friendship, a thankfulness that he seemed to find pleasure in her company, as she did in his. Now, with a few stupid, ill-thought-of words, he had taken it from her, made a fool of her.

He stood up slowly and in the depth of her own painful bewilderment she was suddenly aware that his face had become as awkward as her own must surely be. His eyes, blue and deep as a lake in which a summer sky is reflected, widened with an expression which appeared to be remorse. With a small sound in the back of his throat, which might have been a groan, he moved round his desk, then, to her astonishment, sank down on to his haunches at her feet. Her hands, which, though she was not consciously aware of it, were gripping one another in a turmoil of confusion, were taken fiercely between his own.

"Miss Grimshaw . . . Dear God . . . Sally, will you ever forgive me for being so insensitive?" he beseeched her. "To laugh at such a moment was unpardonable . . . to blurt it out like that . . . please . . ."

He was looking up into her face with such contrition, such penitence she was tempted to put her hands, which he still held, to his face. To cup his cheeks as though he were a child, to tell him it was all right, that he must not condemn himself; that it was her fault for misunderstanding whatever it was he was actually saying to her. That he was not to blame. In the chaos of her feelings she yearned for nothing but to take that mortified expression from his face, to comfort what seemed to be his distress, but stirring urgently beneath this new sensation of hers was another, one that was very familiar to her. One that had plagued her and, more to the point, the person at whom it was directed – mainly Freddy – ever since she was a child. To hell with him, it said. It was, as yet, only a whisper inside her, but it was growing, becoming more insistent, that wild rage which was threatening, as it had always threatened, to explode and injure all those about her. Only one man had had the power to restrain it and that man had been

Richard Keene, for if she had let it out to confront him, as she had longed to do, she knew she would have lost what, at the time, she had valued most. Her place at the Grimshaw Arms.

Perhaps it was this, this constantly tamped-down need to repress her anger over so many months which now built up and fuelled what was within her.

With a violent movement she snatched her hands away from Adam Cooper and stood up. Losing his hold on her, and his balance, he sprawled back heavily and his face darkened with his own anger, since no man relishes being made to look foolish and Adam Cooper was conscious of how foolish he must look.

Quickly he sprang to his feet, rearranging his coat, his cravat, smoothing a somewhat trembling hand through the thick silver swathe of his hair before turning to face Sally Grimshaw who was doing some trembling of her own.

"Well, it seems my offer does not meet with your approval, Miss Grimshaw," he said coldly.

"Your offer, Captain Cooper?" She raised an imperious head to stare at him in astonishment. She swung about and began to pace backwards and forwards, moving from the window to the door and back again, her face like a peony, her eyes like chips of iced amber, then she stopped. Placing her hands on her hips she glared at him. "And what might that offer be? Whatever it was it seems it caused you a great deal of amusement. I don't think I have ever felt so insulted."

Why was she saying this? some small, bewildered part of her was asking. Why was she so mad with him, for God's sake? But the voice which asked the question was drowned out by the anger within her. How dare he make fun of Sally Grimshaw? Who in hell did he think he was to play fast and loose with emotions which were sore and tender in any woman who knows full well when she is being made to look ridiculous? A wife, indeed! Dear God, as far as anyone knew, he already had a wife and yet he was pretending for reasons best known to himself that he wanted another. A housekeeper, he had said . . . hadn't he? So what was she to make of this new offer? Dear God in heaven, it could only mean he wanted her to . . . to perform . . . *other* duties!

She glared about her, then, shaking her head in outraged mystification, began her pacing again, kicking back the full hem of her skirt at every turn. One of the dogs raised her head and studied her with suspicious eyes as though undecided whether Sally's actions constituted a threat to her, her companion or her master. After a moment or two she lowered her muzzle to her paws though she continued to watch Sally.

Adam Cooper shrugged irritably, tapping his fingertips on the polished top of the desk.

"Miss Grimshaw, I really would be obliged if you would return to your seat and listen to what I have to say."

"As I think I have told you before, Captain," she answered crisply, "I am not one of your foot soldiers who must—"

"Goddammit to hell." He clapped the palm of his hand to his forehead, whirling away from the desk and stamping to the fireplace. He took a cigar from a silver box on the mantelshelf, lit it with a taper from the fire, then jerked back to her. "I have never known a woman to take offence so easily. I was under the impression that females were pleased, perhaps even honoured to be offered a decent proposal of marriage but not Sally Grimshaw! Oh, no! You act as though I had made some lewd suggestion."

"No, not lewd, Captain, but one I cannot understand.

No woman likes to be made to look a fool, to be tricked—"

"Tricked!"

"Then laughed at when she makes the mistake of believing that an offer of employment is genuine."

His mouth dropped open in amazement and for a moment he was preoccupied with what to do with his cigar which he had been about to place between his teeth.

"What the bloody hell are you talking about, woman?" he asked her dazedly.

"No, what are *you* talking about, Captain Cooper? Do you wish me to take up employment here as your housekeeper or not, or is that joke you cracked at my expense—"

"What joke?"

She stiffened and her eyes flashed dangerously and Adam Cooper knew again that sudden perplexity of feeling which came with the awareness of how . . . how attractive . . . glowing . . . shining she was when she was roused.

"You know perfectly well what joke I mean. You may need a wife, as you said with such obvious amusement and perhaps you do but that has nothing to do with me. At the same time you imply, in fact state quite plainly, that you are perfectly satisfied with Mrs Chidlow, so perhaps you could tell me what in hell I'm doing here if I'm not to take her place?"

She tossed her head in that diverting way she had and several strands of her gleaming, silken hair fell about her face. She blew them upwards with great vigour and it was then, try as he might not to, and really it was not the time to do so, he began to laugh again. He could not help himself. It was all so bloody ridiculous and so bloody typical of Sally Grimshaw, who firmly believed there was no one in Liverpool who had as practical a mind as hers. Perhaps that was true but when it came to matters which needed, not common sense, but emotions, she was sadly lacking. She had not understood. God knows why not, but for some reason she thought . . . well, who knew what daft thoughts were in that muddled mind of hers? God, she was an aggravation but had he ever met a woman who entertained him as this one did? He shook his head, still grinning.

She was incensed. "Whatever it is that makes you grin like a monkey it is clearly not to be shared," she began, but having had more than enough of her arguing, his patience coming to an end, with a swift stride he was across the room. Before she had time to protest he dragged her unceremoniously to the chair in which she had been sitting originally and with little care for her feelings pushed her down into it. At once she tried to rise but with his hands on her shoulders he held her until she ceased to struggle.

"Well," she said loftily, "at least we have proved one thing."

"What is that, Miss Grimshaw?"

"That you are physically stronger than I am. As for strength of mind, we shall see."

"That we will. Now then, before you fling yourself from that chair and then, presumably, from my house in high dudgeon, may I tell you that I meant exactly what I said just now."

"Which was?" Her tone was disdainful.

"That I want you to be my wife. Not my damned housekeeper but my wife. That I would be glad, honoured, if you would marry me. There, will that do you?"

He stood back from her, his mouth curving into a wide grin.

"There you go again, grinning like some . . . some . . ."

"Dear God, woman, don't try my patience too far."

"Why?"

"Because it is not as deep and endless as you seem to think."

"I meant, why do you . . . you want me for . . . your wife?"

"Well, thank God that you appear to understand what I'm saying at last, though why it should be so difficult . . ."

"Captain Cooper . . ."

"Can you not bring yourself to call me Adam? If we are to be married—"

"That remains to be seen," she interrupted primly.

"Surely it needs merely a 'yes' or a 'no'?"

"Oh, don't be so . . ." She hesitated.

"What, Sally? I may call you Sally, mayn't I?"

"Please . . . please . . . I can't bear . . ."

"Can't bear what, Sally?"

"I can't bear to be teased, you see."

There was a small fire burning in the grate, its flames flickering cheerfully, lighting the reddish brown coats of the two terriers to cinnamon and toffee. Though one still dozed peacefully, not at all perturbed by the raised voices, the second continued to watch the man and woman, particularly the woman, distrustfully. The gilded and engraved carriage clock on the mantelshelf struck the half-hour and Sally looked up at it as though surprised to find how time had flown. The light from the flames pricked in her eyes and Adam was surprised at what appeared to be a glint of tears in them. Sally Grimshaw crying? Never, and as if to confirm that thought she squared her shoulders and stuck out her chin.

"This is absolute nonsense, you know that," she declared firmly.

"Since when was it nonsense for a gentleman to ask the lady of his choice if she will be his wife, Sally?"

"Stuff and nonsense, Captain Cooper."

"Adam, please."

"I can't call you that."

"You'll have to force yourself when you are my wife," he observed, smiling that droll smile of his.

"This is ridiculous."

"Why?"

She was calmer now and he turned away from her, crossing slowly to the wide bay window which looked out over the side of the garden. The striped lawns, velvety green and recently mown, rolled away down a gentle slope to where the trees began. Trees that had been there since before the house was built. Trees beneath which, it was said, Prince Rupert, a relative of the doomed King Charles I, hunted wild boar during a lull in a battle fought two hundred years ago. He was attempting, and succeeded, to take Liverpool for his king during the Civil War, but even wars had their lighter moments and it was rumoured that on a particular June night the excited cries of the hunters could clearly be heard. There were hedges of sweet bay bordering the lawns. In the flowerbeds lying parallel to them was an eruption of showy peonies, a rich and brilliant splash against the broad, glossy leaves of the hedge. There were asters in clumps of white, and delicate mauve with yellow centres. Dahlias nodding their enormous heads of gold, of dazzling pink, of yellow and torch-like red. Like the rest of the gardens which spread in dozens of acres about the house, it was all in the increasingly gnarled but infinitely patient hands of "young" Reuben. Young Reuben and his father, "old" Reuben, who everyone agreed must be a hundred if he was a day, and still interfering in what he considered to be his domain, had shared the task of caring for the gardens of Coopers Edge for the amazing span of over a hundred years between them. There were others, of course. Noah and Henry and young Eppie, who really was young, being a lad of twelve or so. Between them they created and cared for the splendour which was a beauty to the heart as well as the eye.

Adam turned away from the windows, having seen nothing of what was beyond them. His eyes were deep and unfocused as though they were directed at something visible only to himself. One hand was thrust in his trouser pocket, the other holding the cigar which still smouldered between his fingers. Slowly he moved back to his desk. He sat down heavily in the chair behind it. The dogs, who had raised their heads to watch him protectively, dropped their black button noses again when he was safely seated.

"I think it's time I told you exactly what happened nine years ago," he said quietly to Sally. There was a tenseness in his voice which infiltrated the room with a vibrancy Sally felt at once and yet he appeared to be calm. Only his mouth was inclined to show his disquiet, biting off each word with a snap.

She had been holding a glass paperweight in which was captured a net of milky white threads surrounding a perfect pansy. It was a beautiful thing, an object of great delicacy, totally out of place in this completely masculine room of Adam Cooper's. A woman's thing and, as though the thought had brought her to mind, Sally could suddenly see the exquisitely lovely woman whose picture still hung in the hall.

Hastily, as though guilty of an act of some indelicacy, she put it back on the desk, wincing a little as it clicked against the wood.

"My wife gave me that when . . . well, a long time ago." He said it without emotion and when she dared a quick glance at his face it was totally without expression. Her heart thudded in her chest and she longed to tell him she didn't want to hear what he was about to tell her. She was not ready to hear of his past, which was nothing to do with her anyway, nor did she wish to hear of the future he proposed. All she required was a decent job of housekeeper which was within her capabilities and this talk of "wives" was not for her. She didn't want to be one. She didn't want to know about one, particularly his.

"Captain Cooper, if I may I'd like to . . ." She began to rise but he frowned and for some reason not even she recognised she sat down again.

"You will have heard the gossip, the rumours." It was not a question and she made no answer.

"There was a good deal of speculation about where . . . Oralie . . . was but I kept it to myself for as long as I could." He sighed and Sally felt her heart move mysteriously. "The Liverpool Regiment in which I served had in its ranks, and among its officers, men from Liverpool. As they returned home, the scandal returned with them so it became common knowledge that . . . my wife had . . . gone away . . . left with a man . . . a fellow officer."

He paused, his eyes unseeing. "They say the husband is the last to know, don't they?" In his voice was infinite sadness. "It had been . . . it was known they had been lovers . . ."

His voice died away and from him in great waves, which Sally was sure he was not aware of, came the pain and humiliation, the torment and grief he had suffered, and still suffered, it seemed to her.

"Captain, please . . . if this is too painful for you," she heard herself say in an amazingly gentle voice.

"No, it must be said, Sally. There must be truth . . . and trust between us if we are to succeed."

Succeed! What a strange word to use in the context of the relationship he appeared to be proposing between them. As though they were to become partners. Not husband and wife, as he was intimating, but business partners. It was marriage he was after, he had told her that, and marriage was a contract, a partnership and being a business woman herself she could understand that, so perhaps the word was not unwisely chosen.

She was so conscious of herself she could hear every sound around her in the room. The crackle of the coals in the grate, one of the dogs yipping in her sleep and from somewhere outside a man's deep voice raised enquiringly and that of a boy answering.

"May I go on, Sally?" he asked at last.

"Yes," and they both knew she had answered his question regarding a marriage.

"We were married young, Oralie and I" – even her name was beautiful, exotic, not of the ordinary, Sally remembered thinking – "twelve years ago now. I was twenty-three and Oralie was just twenty. She was very wealthy, an heiress to a great shipping fortune, an only child and I had nothing but this house and an income just big enough to pay my mess bills. People wanted to believe I married her for her money but how could they think that? They had only to look at her."

Yes, Sally had seen her and knew that this man had loved her. Perhaps he still did.

"We went to India soon after that. I was a soldier and though I was willing to resign my commission Oralie wouldn't hear of it. She loved the life. She loved India. She loved being the wife of an officer and all that meant. The parties and balls and . . .

The social life was glittering and, of course, she was at its centre. She was very gregarious and was popular with the other officers' wives . . . and the officers."

He paused, that faraway look in his eyes again. She wanted to tell him it didn't matter. He owed her no explanation, but of course, he did. If they were to make anything of . . . Dear Lord in heaven . . . of this . . . this marriage he was proposing, they must be totally honest with one another. Anything that had happened, to either of them, in the past, if it had a bearing on their relationship, must be examined, discussed, so that each of them would have knowledge of and understand the difficulties which were bound to arise. There was no love in this partnership but there must be honesty and respect. He needed her to look after him and his home, to help in the bringing up of his daughters, she understood that. She needed shelter, protection, stability, a worthwhile occupation and to be valued for the qualities she knew she possessed.

But there was more to be said about . . . about Oralie.

He said it. "They simply disappeared together. My regiment was involved at the time in the Battle of the Punjab. The first Sikh war. In February 1846 it ended and when I returned to Meerut they were gone. She left her daughters behind. Leila was two years old and Aisha just nine months. He – the man – was forced to resign his commission, naturally, and it was said – I don't know the details – that they had set up house together in Calcutta." A spasm rippled his face like a breeze on water. His eyes were hooded. "They had a child two months later. Both the child and Oralie died."

It was said in a calm, dispassionate voice. His face was set in an image of what seemed to be cold indifference but a pulse beat rapidly in his throat and his eyes had a strange blue sheen to them, not tears but a film of something that spoke of some deep, emotional distress.

"I couldn't leave the children to be brought up by ayahs, so I brought them home. Settled them here with a nanny and a governess then returned to my duties as a soldier. Oralie's money came to me when we married, of course, so . . ."

His voice faltered as though he had lost the thread of what he was saying and a long, painful silence followed. He appeared to have withdrawn himself to some place where Sally could not follow. Perhaps to a place he had made to hide in all those years ago when the pain he had known was too much to bear. He sat in his chair, his elbows on the arms, his slender brown hands hanging limply over the ends. He was relaxed, his face turned to the windows but the light from them revealed the paleness of his flesh.

Sally sat as she always sat, her back straight, her head set gracefully on her neck, her hands folded in her lap. She felt she should say something since he was evidently at the end of his disclosure but there seemed nothing to be said. It was out of the question to mouth platitudes about how sorry she was, even though she was sorry, grieved at the pain he had obviously known, so she waited quietly for him to return to her.

The breath suddenly left him on a long, shuddering sigh but he did not turn to her at once. He spoke though.

"I want no one's sympathy or pity, Sally." It seemed to be a warning.

"I know that, Adam."

He turned then and smiled and it was a smile with no ghosts in it, no memories, nothing of the past to haunt him. A smile of whimsical humour and pleasure that she had spoken his name. He lifted an eyebrow and his mouth curled.

"At last! My God, woman, you're a tough nut to crack."

"Not really. I just like to know exactly where I stand. Your past is not really my business, though of course it was right for you to tell me about it. But your future" – she bent her head in what looked like confusion – "your future . . . our future . . . is of vital concern to me. If we are to . . ."

"To be married?" He bent forward and peered up into her averted face.

"As you say . . ."

"Sally, Goddammit, will you stop prevaricating and give me a proper answer? Surely you can see how . . . how beneficial it would be for both of us. We have found one another's company most enjoyable in the past. Can you deny it?"

Without looking up she shook her head slightly.

"There you are then. I am badly in need of someone who will take me and my household in hand. I am guilty of neglecting my daughters but now, with your help, perhaps we can make a proper family for them. We need you, Sally, and I believe you need us." The last few words were spoken sincerely and with such gentleness she felt herself begin to tremble.

She stood up, her legs far from steady, her heart strained with an emotion only she, at last, recognised. An emotion she must at all cost keep to herself. She crossed to the window, watching as an old man, accompanied by a young boy who trundled a wheelbarrow, ambled along a path which cut across the lawn. It was beautiful. The peace of the gardens. The trees at the bottom of the slope. The sudden explosion of rooks which lifted across the blue of the cloudless sky like black confetti. The rain of the day before had left a freshness, a sweetness, a sparkle to the vista spread out before her and the essence of it settled in her heart, finding a place there which she knew it would never leave. She had been content in the home into which she had been born and in which she had lived for twenty-four years. She had taken great pride in it. It had been her warmth and protection, her comfort, her solace, but she had never once seen it as a place of visual appeal. It had not occurred to her. Truth to tell she had never had time to study it. She had not looked at it with a newcomer's eyes, as she was now looking at the surroundings which held the house, Coopers Edge, in its loving arms. This was beauty. This was perfection. And Adam Cooper was offering it to Sally Grimshaw.

"You will be mistress here, Sally," he said behind her. "This house will be yours to run as you think fit. And you can do it. Dammit, any woman who can rule the Grimshaw Arms and all beneath its roof, as you did, will have no difficulty knocking this lot into shape. Oh yes, I know I am badly served. I have eyes in my head and I have seen the disorder, the sloppiness, the lack of discipline among the servants, as servants will be with no mistress to answer to. They're perfectly polite, of course, knowing exactly where the line is between laxity and bloody-minded defiance. They want to keep their jobs. The three highest ranking servants, Cook, Henton and Mrs Chidlow have, for the past nine years, done exactly as they pleased. I have no female relatives to oversee them and my solicitor, whom I paid to visit once a month to check and report on, not only the state of the accounts but the welfare of the children, seemed to find no fault. But it is I who have been at fault. My daughters are strangers to me. Oh, we all three do our best but they find me quite alarming. My attempts at a joke are misunderstood and when I try to interest them in what interests me and what I think will interest them, they are bewildered. With what relief they scurry back to the nursery and Nanny when I release them. Their governess was highly recommended by the matron and head governess of the Girls High School in Mount Street."

"Miss Davies?"

He stopped, surprised.

"Yes, do you know her?"

She turned back to him, smiling at some memory. "Oh yes, I was educated there. My father, having not a great deal of learning himself, believed in giving Violet, Freddy and me a decent start in life. Not that it did Vi or Freddy much good," she added disparagingly. Her smile deepened. "Mind you, I was a rebellious pupil since I had been led to believe by my parents that I was never wrong. Miss Davies did not agree. But she and the others, Miss Jones, Mrs Pedder . . . oh, and Miss Gallagher, who taught me how to add up in my head which proved a boon, were splendid teachers."

He studied her for a long moment, tapping his clasped hands against his lips, his eyes narrowed in concentration.

"D'you know, Sally Grimshaw, you never fail to surprise me and you have given me an idea. My girls have never mixed with others but I'm certain it would do them the world of good to do so. What d'you think? Would they benefit from being educated at the High School?"

"They're not all daughters of gentlemen at the school, Captain . . . er, Adam." She grinned, her eyes sparkling with mischief. "Look at me."

He had been ready to smile with her, his own eyes crinkling into deep laughter lines, then he sobered.

"Miss Grimshaw . . . Sally, if they turn out as splendidly as you have done than I shall be more than satisfied. You see, I do need your help, your support, your advice. Already we are halfway to solving one of my problems."

He stood up and came round the desk, crossing the rather

strange-looking carpet which Sally thought might have come from India, to stand before her. Taking her hands in his he brought them, first one then the other, to his lips. His mouth was warm and soft and inside her something quivered and sang with the joy of it.

"My dear Miss Grimshaw, can you not see what a . . . a salvation we can be to one another? I realise that we barely know each other but it seems to me that we would make a good match. Don't you agree?" In his eyes was warmth and sincerity. It softened his mouth in a smile and Sally felt her insides melt and flow.

"So marry me, I beg you, Miss Grimshaw," he went on. "It really would be churlish to refuse. Say yes, please say yes."

Sally looked down at their clasped hands. As Mrs Adam Cooper she would be well provided for. There would be consternation among the society of which the captain was a part but he didn't seem to care about that, or if he thought about it at all it was not important to him. She would have a position in life. A worthwhile "job" to do, which was all she had ever asked. Looking up, her eyes smoky as quartz, she said, "Yes."

He sighed thankfully, turning his face up to the ceiling for a moment as though in relief, then he let go of her hands and she felt the loss of his touch replace the joy it had given her.

"Thank you, Sally. You won't regret it, I promise you. I'll do my best to be a good husband. You're a fine, strong woman and we'll do very well together. Now, I'll ring the bell for the girls to be brought down since they must be the first to know."

13

They were married three weeks later at the small parish church of St James in Old Swan. They were accompanied by Adam's two lovely, bewildered daughters who stood behind them in the role of bridesmaids clutching small posies of pale pink and white rosebuds. Freddy gave her away and some anonymous friend of Adam's acted as best man.

Freddy was cock-a-hoop at being made into the brother-in-law of a member of one of Liverpool's leading families. Though he himself had done well in marrying the daughter of a well-to-do yeoman farmer, strengthening his own position with her father by immediately putting her in the family way, Sally, the sly minx, had gone one better by snaring Captain Adam Cooper and how she'd managed it was a question he and all those in the congregation were asking. A bit of a strange situation to say the least and one which Sally herself refused to explain, telling him merely that she had not been satisfied with her position at the Grimshaw Arms with Richard Keene and when she had been offered a better one she had taken it. That was all. A better one, if you please! You would have thought by her manner that she was to be upper parlourmaid, or perhaps Cook, Freddy told his astonished wife later, but his sister had simply shrugged in a careless sort of way and what did Dorothy make of that? Dorothy could make nothing of it and didn't really care since the dazzle of being the sister-in-law of Mrs Adam Cooper was more than enough for her.

When, having gone over the water to tell Violet and to invite her and Arthur casually to the wedding, Sally was so cool about it she gave the impression she was to marry one of the grooms, or perhaps the coachman, her sister protested in amazement. She couldn't believe it, really she couldn't, she kept repeating and if Sally didn't tell her exactly how it all came about she'd give her a clip round't lug, which, bearing in mind Violet's pretensions towards gentility, highlighted her consternation.

There was an autumn-scented haze hanging in silken drifts beneath the trees which bordered the churchyard. The year was growing old but a mellow curtain of amber sunlight slanted through the broad, spread branches of the great oaks. It fell gently about the bride and groom as they stepped hesitantly from beneath the church porch, and those who watched – not many of them to be sure since it appeared Adam had no friends he cared to invite – wondered at it, for this was the second time around for him. He looked very distinguished in his mulberry-coloured frock coat with a velvet collar which fitted his tall, lean frame quite magnificently. His trousers were of pale grey doeskin and his waistcoat of white drill. His silk cravat was tied in a flat bow and he carried a black top hat. The sunlight touched his prematurely grey hair, turning it to polished silver and with the amber and bronze tint of his skin, the piercing blue of his eyes, he was undeniably attractive.

But could they say the same about his bride? the spectators asked one another, the bride about whom the whole of Lancashire society had been gossiping for the last three weeks. She was a plain little thing, coming barely to his shoulder and though it was evident that her gown was of the very best quality and cut and must have cost a pretty penny, it was of a neutral shade nobody could quite name. Was it a pearly grey, or perhaps the colour of sand, or a combination of the two? It had a modest touch of white at the neck and the same under the brim of her small bonnet, but no other decoration. Not a frill or a bow or a bit of ribbon. But for the small posy of white rosebuds she held you would have been hard pressed to realise that it was her wedding day, Cissie was overheard to say to Maddy. Talk about the peacock and the peahen, with the master looking so splendid and their new mistress traipsing along beside him, totally lacking claim to either beauty or style. The little girls looked quite lovely, though, in their white muslin ankle-length dresses with broad pink velvet sashes which their new mama, or so it was rumoured, had chosen for them. But then, put them in a length of sackcloth and they'd still be the prettiest creatures you ever did see. Apparently their mama, their *real* mama, had been just the same. What was the master thinking of? they asked one another, shaking their heads, and for the life of them they could find no answer.

What a three weeks it had been!

To say the servants were stunned was an understatement that fell far short of the truth, and after they had been told of it, Cook, Mrs Chidlow and Mr Henton were ready to hand in their notice. They'd not work for a woman who was no better than she should be, they said indignantly. A woman who had once been a barmaid and only God knows what else. Barmaids were notoriously free with their favours, or so they had heard, working in close quarters with men who had drink in them. It could only lead to immorality and degradation and how could they, who were respectable and virtuous, be expected to serve under her? It was not as though there weren't dozens of well-bred young ladies who would jump at the chance to be the wife of a handsome, well-set-up widower like the captain, the mistress of his magnificent home and a mother to his motherless children. So why did he have to choose this one?

Sally couldn't help but smile and she fancied Adam knew the reason why, every time she remembered that morning just after the girls had gone back to the nursery.

"Well," he had said, man-like, as the door closed on his daughters, "that wasn't too bad, was it?" and it had not been bad at all since Leila and Aisha had shown nothing but polite indifference when Sally was introduced to them as their new mama.

"Oh, hardly that, Captain . . . er . . . Adam," Sally had remonstrated with him mildly, for surely these two flawlessly dressed little dolls would not care to have her, a perfect stranger, taking not only the place but the name of their own dead mama. "Surely Stepmama . . . or better yet, Sally," she added wistfully.

'They can hardly call you Sally . . . er, Sally. It wouldn't be at all suitable." Adam had frowned. "I believe Nanny has taught them the correct way to address an adult and it is not by their Christian name only."

"Why? I'm not their mother and neither am I – or will not be – an acquaintance so it would hardly hurt to call me Sally."

The girls were beginning to look slightly alarmed, that blank-eyed expression of indifference with what these two strangers were proposing to do fading away. Their velvet grey eyes swivelled from their father to Sally and back again. They were doing their best to understand what was to happen, what their papa was explaining to them, but it was clear they were both totally confused.

Adam took pity on them. "Do you realise what I am saying, girls? Miss Grimshaw and I are to be married and so she will live with us here at Coopers Edge. Will you like that?"

"Yes, thank you, papa," they chorused, their eyes wide with apprehension, clearly longing to leave, for they could see no reason why this news should be of importance to them.

"Will you not congratulate us, then? Leila? Aisha?" He smiled at them kindly. "It is the custom."

"Yes, Papa, congratulations, Papa."

"And Miss Grimshaw."

"Congratulations, Miss Grimshaw." They chanced a swift peep at Miss Grimshaw.

"Thank you. We wanted you to be the first to know." Sally could see they were wondering why. "Well, we will decide what you are to call Miss Grimshaw at a later date so off you go back to Miss Digby."

"Thank you, Papa."

They bobbed a curtsey and left, timorous as mice, eyes cast down as Nanny had taught them and Sally wondered, as they quietly shut the door behind them, if it had ever entered what seemed to her to be their empty, innocent heads that she, Sally, could not only turn this household upside down but everyone in it, them included.

That was when Adam voiced his opinion that the interview had gone well and Sally decided it was too soon to disagree with him. After all, they had been affianced – was that the word, oh dear God? – to one another for no more than an hour!

She was not herself, she knew that. She had had what

she could only describe as the wind well and truly taken out of her sails by what had happened this morning and her normal fighting spirit and positive determination that she knew what was best for Sally Grimshaw was at a low ebb. Frankly she didn't know whether she was on her head or her elbow and could you blame her? Things were not right, not normal, with Adam's daughters and, in time, when she had been restored to the real Sally Grimshaw, she would make it her business to correct it. In the meanwhile best hold her tongue.

Adam rang the bell and when Maddy appeared, neat and tidy in her print morning dress, cap and apron, Sally noticed her apron had a stain on the bib. Something else to correct!

"We'll have coffee please, Fletcher."

"Yes, sir . . . for two?" Her eyes ran familiarly over Sally and Sally was aware of the gleam of excitement in them.

Adam looked surprised. "Of course for two."

"Yes, sir." Like the young ladies of the house she sketched a curtsey but it was perfunctory at best and Sally realised that Adam had for so long not complained, nor even noticed such small things, the servants could not be blamed for their own negligence.

They drank their coffee while Sally admired the room in which they sat. It was a big room with long windows to the floor and a bay to the side which allowed in shafts of bright sunshine. It was, though Sally was not aware of it, not just a study but a smoking-room and library combined. The walls were taken up with shelf upon shelf of books in which were set not only the windows but the fireplace and the door. Every scrap of available wall space had books displayed on it. It was to this room that the master of the house retired to smoke his pipe or cigar since no self-respecting mistress would tolerate carpets and curtains reeking of tobacco. It was a totally masculine preserve where a gentleman and his male guests might escape the polite conversation of the drawing-room. There were deep, comfortable chairs and a sofa of definitely eastern origin with fat, sausage-shaped tasselled cushions at each end and a great pile, square this time but of the same design, at its back. All in a shade of rich, coffee-coloured silk. In fact the whole room spoke of Adam's travels in India with intricately carved wooden tables and one which was eight-sided and made from a delicate tracery of beaten copper scrollwork. There were dozens of beautifully carved figurines in ivory and jade and other materials Sally could not identify. There was a large, elaborately carved, gilt-framed looking-glass over the fireplace, on either side of which was an exquisite watercolour, framed in silver, of birds in flight, no more really than a suggestion of wings, a bright eye, with barely any colour. They had obviously been done by the same artist as those in the small parlour.

On shelves which did not contain books were set out a collection of medals, several guns of some sort and the very sword which had clanked so horribly on Sally's stone-flagged floor on the day she and Adam met. There were cases in tooled leather and tortoiseshell, more figurines, this time of animals, a tiger snarling, an elephant with its trunk raised. Draped over the chair backs were richly coloured rugs, the designs bizarre and yet quite beautiful. Cane baskets held palm trees which almost reached the ceiling.

"You like my room, Sally?" Adam asked almost shyly. He was standing in front of the fireplace, one foot resting on the fender, his elbow on the mantelshelf as he sipped his coffee. In the brightness of the room his vivid eyes were the colour of the speedwell which grew in the wild wherever there was a damp spot in a ditch or cart rut. A blue so bright it seemed quite unreal and yet was devastatingly beautiful. His face was calm as though, having made some momentous decision, he was at last at peace with himself. It was a kind face and Sally felt a great longing inside her to have the power to change that kindness to something . . . what? . . . something stronger, warmer, something that declared that Sally Grimshaw meant more to him than a capable, resourceful woman who was to take over the running of his household. An hour ago she would have chided herself for being foolish, for that was exactly what she was. A capable, resourceful woman who was to take over the running of his household. But that was before she had been struck by the lightning, the thunder, the tempest of emotions which had led to the incredible realisation that she loved him and probably had done so since the day they met. She was ignorant, innocent, naive, she supposed, where human emotions were concerned and what had stirred inside her on several occasions had not been recognised. Those small and unfamiliar sensations which might have been delight had gone, not unnoticed, but unnamed since she had not known what they were.

Now she knew.

She kept her eyes from looking into his, turning her head to look about the room.

"It's very . . . unusual," she said hesitantly.

"But do you like it?" he persisted.

"I think I do. The furniture and rugs come from India, I suppose?"

"Yes, they do. There were many things about India which appealed to me. I brought a small part of what I liked back with me. Including a need for light."

"Light?"

"Yes, I don't care for the present fashion of heavy furnishings and dark rooms but, naturally, when we are married you may do as you please."

"In what way?" She turned then and gave him her full, bewildered attention, doing her best to disguise the fact that her heart was doing the most peculiar things in her breast, which seemed to be its predisposition every time marriage was mentioned.

"Sally, this will be your home and you may alter whatever you wish to alter. Except this room."

She was deeply shocked. "Captain Cooper, I would not dream . . ."

"My name is Adam and yours is Sally and if we are to be . . . friends then you'll oblige me by remembering it."

"Of course, but . . ."

"No buts, no maybes. We will be married within the month, I think and then . . ."

Her face paled and her eyes widened.

"As soon as that?"

"Oh, yes. You must realise that, as a single lady, your reputation will be seriously damaged if you spend a night under my roof without a proper chaperon. We must let it be known at once that we are to become man and wife. Your character will be in question already if the servants talk, especially if they mention the . . . period you and your servant spent alone together. I suggest you stay either with your brother, or your sister until . . ."

For several seconds Adam had become aware that Sally's face had begun to twitch, her mouth lifting into that lopsided smile with which he was becoming increasingly familiar. She put up a hand as though to hide it, bending her head a little, then, suddenly she began to shake. An explosion occurred somewhere beneath her hand and a great shout of laughter erupted, noisy and uncontrolled, startling the two dogs who lay in the bay in a square of sunlight. Sally's mouth opened wide and her even white teeth gleamed in her suddenly rosy face.

Adam watched her in amazement, his eyes narrowing suspiciously. His mouth clamped into a line of what might have been anger but her laughter was very infectious and, despite his annoyance at her levity on what was a very serious subject, he found himself unable to resist the sudden leap of gladness in his heart and the wry curl of his own lips.

"Dear God, Adam, if you could hear yourself prattling on about chaperons and reputations you would realise how foolish it all is. I am no young girl whose family has guarded and treasured her since birth. I come from what are known as the working classes. I am my own woman, a woman who has been among men all her life. I have nothing to hide and nothing of which I am ashamed." She was still laughing, great gasps of it coming from her, pure and uncomplicated, like that of a merry child.

"But . . ."

"Don't . . . don't, Adam. Can't you see how humorous it all is? How foolish the conventions of your society are? Don't you realise that already I am compromised merely by being who I am? The daughter of an innkeeper. Let's not do this as others dictate but as it suits us. Oh, Lord, I'm sorry, I can't stop laughing at the idea of . . ."

"Sally, it's not funny," but his face had crinkled into a laconic smile and he was beginning to chuckle.

"It is, Adam, it is. Can't you see it?"

For several seconds he continued to resist, then his own laughter broke free and harmonised with hers.

The two dogs stood up and yawned. They both stretched one back leg and then the other, strolling over to their master and treating his visitor to another tentative sniff.

Adam took Sally's hand and tucked it into the crook of his arm. She did her best not to quiver at his touch.

They were still inclined towards laughter, much to the amazement of the servants when they were all summoned to the servants hall a few minutes later.

Sally made up her mind to begin as she meant to go on. Just as Adam was about to speak she put a hand on his arm and when he looked down at her enquiringly her face was cool and her voice unhurried. The servants were tantalised by her action, all agog with fascinated curiosity, for what could that familiarity mean? They were inclined to think the worst.

"Is everyone here, Mr Henton?" she asked the butler, who looked as though he would like nothing better than to show her the door.

"They are," he answered in his impassive butler's voice. He had no idea how to address her since he had no idea what her position was to be in this house, but by God, whatever it was, he'd make her life a bloody misery.

"I cannot see Clara, or Tom. Were they not told to be here?"

"Clara? Tom?" Henton looked quite blank as though no one of those names had ever come to his attention.

"Yes, I believe she is the scullery maid and Tom the boot boy," Sally went on pleasantly enough. Adam waited patiently, his face quite expressionless, knowing that this was her first test, since Henton was no mean adversary.

"Aah, yes," Mrs Chidlow chipped in. "That is so but I hardly thought it necessary for them to be present." She smiled thinly, the emphasis on *them* showing her contempt for such lowly beings.

"That is for the master of the house to decide, Mrs Chidlow. He asked that all the indoor staff were to be summoned since he wished to speak with you."

"I can tell them whatever the master has to say."

"Fetch them, if you please, Mrs Chidlow," the master himself said quietly.

Clara and Tom looked like two convicted felons being led to the gallows, Mrs Chidlow's vicious hand at the scruff of each cringing neck, dragging their heels and shrinking into a corner at the sight of their master whom they scarcely knew except from a vast distance. But the lady smiled at them which helped a bit.

Sally was aware that there was still another servant whom the butler had contemptuously excluded and that was Job. Perhaps it was for the best since he was to be outdoor staff. And she would rather tell the man who had surely saved her life and led her to this haven when they were alone. She owed him that much. They were safe now, she and Job, and as soon as this was over she meant to seek him in the yard or wherever he was and tell him what was to happen. He would be pleased.

She turned to look up at Adam. "Captain?" she said in a low, strangely soft voice.

"Yes, thank you, Miss Grimshaw." He was perfectly composed, for after all it was nothing to do with his servants whom he chose to marry. He had been served by men and women such as these all his life. He was used to obedience and respect from those in a station of life below his own. He was not intimidated. They were servants.

He said, "I have gathered you together to inform you that in three or four weeks' time you are to have a new mistress. This house has been seriously . . . depleted for some time now but that is to be rectified."

Looking down at Sally, his normally humorous face stern and uncompromising, he took her hand and placed it in the crook of his left arm, holding it with his right. He was going to do this thing properly, he was telling her, despite her amusement of a few minutes ago. But a smile played about her mouth and again he felt the inclination to break into laughter, like a boy who knows no better, or some young man with his first sweetheart. What a strange effect this young woman had on him, he remembered thinking before he spoke.

"Miss Grimshaw has done me the honour of agreeing to become my wife," he said and because his eyes were on her and not on them, he missed the thunderstruck reaction which swept through the company like wind through a field of grass. It literally moved each one of them, making them sway in shock, only Clara and Tom, uncomprehending and still as mice in their corner, continuing unmoved.

Sally not only heard but felt the silence which followed. It was like a wall, solid and immovable, ready to hurt her should she fling herself at it which, several months ago, she might have done. The old Sally Grimshaw, the one who, temporarily, seemed to have been swept away on the wave of her new-found joy, would have snapped out something in the order of "Cat got your tongue, has it?" or "Well, has nobody got anything to say?" She would have straightened her spine, pulled back her shoulders and lifted her head, fixing them with a cold eye as if daring one of them to step out of line with a word or even an expression she did not care for.

She still stood arrow-straight but the hand Adam held was icy, ready to tremble, for these people were not like Bridie or Jane, Tim-Pat or Flo. These were men and women who had been employed by some other woman. They were not of Sally Grimshaw's choosing. They had, some of them, perhaps known the beautiful woman who had been Oralie, Mrs Adam Cooper, a real lady who would have soon made it clear to them that they were in this house for one reason only and that was to serve *her*. Unquestioningly. Respectfully. Unobtrusively. Efficiently. As Sally Grimshaw would have demanded had she been housekeeper!

But she was to be wife, mistress of the house, perhaps mother to the two unsuspecting little girls in the schoolroom and for the moment she could not quite get her bearings. She would, once she had a firm hold on it all. She had made her position felt when she had demanded the scullery maid and the boot boy be brought to hear Adam's announcement, a token gesture but they would have known what she was about. Naturally, with Adam beside her they could be no other than deferential. Deferential and silent until Henton spoke.

"May I and the servants offer you our congratulations, sir," he proffered, his mouth set as though he had a slice of lemon on his tongue. "We hope you will be very happy," though I very much doubt it, his expression said. Not once did he look at Sally.

"Thank you, Henton."

"Thank *you*, sir. Will that be all, sir?" His tone was fulsome, his face bland.

"Yes, thank you, Henton."

The butler ushered out the stunned servants.

For the next three weeks, while she prepared for her wedding day and consulted with Miss Riley, the seamstress who had always made her gowns, on the colour and style of the one she was to wear as a bride, the servants acted as though she simply didn't exist. Oh, they brought her hot water to the small room in which she still slept, kept the fire in, laundered her undergarments and nightgowns, served her with whatever food Cook thought fit to offer and were polite when the captain was present. They silently obeyed her orders as she supervised them in the "bottoming" of the room she and Adam were to share, cleaning curtains and carpets, windows and mirrors, shifting this and that from here to there. But if they passed her on the stairs or in the hallway they went by as though she were invisible, only speaking if she spoke to them.

Sally, floating in the enchantment created by Adam's pleasant company, in the meals they ate together with the silent children at the unpolished dining-table, in the walks they shared, the plans he told her of for their future, scarcely noticed. She knew she was bemused, in thrall to Adam Cooper and so she was not, at the moment, the true Sally Grimshaw. She knew he did not love her. How could he after being married to that exquisite creature who still smiled down at her from the wall in the hallway, but he seemed to like her and that was enough. Let her drift in it for a while and later, when they were man and wife, when she was truly mistress of Coopers Edge, she would face the antipathy of the servants as she had faced every obstacle in her life.

Though she could feel their antagonism at her back during the wedding ceremony and see the contemptuous lift to their lips as she moved down the aisle on her husband's arm, she was not at all disconcerted, for that was where she was. On her husband's arm. The husband, the man she loved with all her heart. The man to whom she meant to devote her life and her considerable talent as a home-maker. His daughters whom she would get to know and make friends of, were at her back and before her stretched her wondrous future as Mrs Adam Cooper.

She allowed the wondering happiness to thrill along her veins and pulse in her wrists and when she saw Violet's envious face among those who stared at her, she smiled with such radiance they were forced to agree, those who saw it, that the innkeeper's daughter might have some claim to looks after all.

Job stood at the back of the church. He wore a discarded frock coat and trousers of Adam's. His hair was neatly brushed, his chin smoothly shaved and his eyes were a pale green smile in the returning bronzed health of his face. He nodded his head slightly, telling her he was well satisfied. She was protected from now on from Richard Keene and men like him and as long as he could work for her, serve her, see her now and again in her capacity of lady of the manor, then he was content. They had both come home to rest.

Neither he nor Sally noticed the tall, thin but extremely well-dressed gentleman by the church gate who climbed on to the back of a fine mare and, kicking the animal viciously in its side, galloped off in the direction of Liverpool.

Sally scarcely remembered the rest of the day. She was kissed on the cheek by Violet and Arthur – who could not wait to take Captain Cooper's hand – by Freddy and Dorothy and even by Jacky Norton and his father and mother whom, with his casual attitude to protocol, Freddy had invited.

Tomorrow morning she meant to demand the household keys, the accounts, the menu book and even Oralie's guest list though she didn't for a minute expect to use it.

But she had tonight to get through first. Her mind and body, she admitted it, were excited at the thought but she shied away from it, not because she dreaded it but because she longed for it with every beat of her loving, passionate heart.

14

Though she had known it would happen, naturally, for had not her things been moved by the slyly smiling housemaids into the bedroom she and Adam were to share, she was considerably startled when he walked in on her.

They had not even kissed. For three weeks he had been the most attentive companion, taking her round the estate, introducing her to his tenants, her arm through his, his head bent to hers as he explained to her the duties and often the family background of all the outside workers. There were ten men in the stables and gardens, that's if you counted Eppie he told her, who was only twelve, young Reuben's grandson and probable successor to the Reubens' kingdom.

The stable block which Sally thought was almost as grand as the house, the entrance being crowned by an enormous clock turret, was run by the coachman, Alec. It was his job to maintain the five horses and carriage in the coach house and beneath him were the grooms, John and Jimmy. Alec wore special livery when he drove the splendid maroon-painted carriage which was pulled by two coal black carriage horses. Sally knew this, for hadn't she ridden in the grand equipage with the coachman up on his box in all his glory, not just on that first day when Adam had come to fetch her from the Plough but since on numerous journeys into Liverpool to visit the dressmaker.

"We must look out a mount for you," Adam told her, laughing away her protests, ignoring her protestations that she had never been on a horse's back in her life.

"Jimmy'll teach you to ride, won't you, Jimmy? He taught me when I was barely able to walk."

"Aye, sir, an' if miss turns out as well as you she'll do." The elderly groom grinned, touching a respectful finger to his steel grey curly hair and nodding in Sally's direction.

Sally noted that none of these men seemed tainted with the same sly contempt the indoor servants treated her with.

She had been shown the tack room where the riding equipment was kept clean and stored and which was as spick and span as Sally's kitchen at the Grimshaw Arms. She nodded back approvingly.

There was a walled garden with a small dovecote in the middle, reached by a smoothly raked path bordered by a low box hedge which looked as though it had been shaved by a cut-throat razor. Glasshouses, vast vegetable gardens, lawns as smooth and green as the billiard table in the house and which no one seemed to use. There were terraces with steps leading down to more lawns and flowerbeds crammed with wallflowers and Canterbury bells. There was a small pond on which ducks floated serenely, oblivious to the excited scurries of the terriers round its edge. There was woodland and pasture where in the distance Sally could see Job scything the grass. He lifted his hand in greeting but though she had returned it something in Adam's manner had prevented her from going over to him. She and Job did their talking in private.

The bedroom which, she had been told considerately and diplomatically by Adam, had never been slept in since his mother died and therefore had not been shared by himself and Oralie, though he had no need to say this last, had been turned out and refurbished to Sally's own taste though she was not awfully sure what that was at the moment. Remembering Adam's declaration that he liked light, she had done her best to make it bright and airy.

She had not changed any of the furniture since she found the deeply glowing satinwood of the tallboy and the dressing-table pleased her. There were pretty little chairs of the same wood which she had had reupholstered in apricot velvet, amazed by the speed with which such things could be accomplished when one's name was Cooper and money was of no consequence. There was a sofa to match which she drew up to the fireplace. Cut flowers from the gardens and glasshouses were arranged, somewhat haphazardly to be sure, in crystal vases, ordered by Adam, she knew and on every surface were dozens of delicate ornaments collected and treasured by Adam's mother. There was nothing of Oralie Cooper in the room.

The bed was enormous, a half tester which Sally had experimentally draped in cream-coloured muslin. The carpet, in a muted shade of apricot and sand and unusually plain, matched the new ties on the bed curtains and those at the windows which were of cream silk. Sally was inordinately pleased with her handiwork, feeling that a small step towards putting her own identity on this new home of hers had been taken. The windows themselves, three of them, looked out to the front of the house where the rolling lawns were dissected by a complex ornamental garden of exquisite design. There were four squares inside each of which was a shamrock-shaped pattern of box which contained, at the right season, young Reuben patiently told her since it was obvious the new young missis knew nothing of gardening, flowers of a dozen different colours. The deep pink of asters, the scarlet of zinnia, purple blue of viola, orange of tagetes, the delicate mauve of lavender and the vivid yellow of iberis.

But it was not these, nor the fire-glowed elegance of the bedroom that Sally Grimshaw, Sally Cooper now, was concerned with as her new husband crossed the room to stand beside the bed they were to share. He wore a rich, brocade robe which almost touched the carpet, tied about his lean hips with a loosely knotted sash. His feet were bare and even in the midst of so much heart-thudding tension Sally noticed how fine and slender they were. His hair was neatly brushed, a soft, silvery grey in the light from the lamp which stood beside the bed and his eyes were as dark a blue as the evening sky just before total night falls.

She was sitting up in the kind of modest cotton nightgown she had worn all her life and had seen no reason to change now. It was plain and sensible and covered her beneath the bedclothes from her chin to her toes but there the severity ended, for Sally had let down her hair. She had brushed it and brushed it, snapping the brush through the long mass of tawny gold and silver until it had curled about the bristles. Now it lay in a glorious cape of living brilliance across her shoulders and breast, and down her back to the pillow, transforming her, and her nightgown, into a breathtaking picture Adam could not quite believe. She was pale, her hands folded tightly on the top of the sheet, her mouth folded primly to stop it trembling, her eyes deep, apprehensive pools of smoky amber and around her flowed her hair, that which had set Richard Keene on fire for her.

"You look about twelve years old in that nightgown." Adam smiled. His eyes were shadowed with some emotion, "And I don't think I have ever seen anything more beautiful than your hair."

She swallowed. He saw her throat work but he could tell he had pleased her. He sat down on the edge of the bed. Leaning forward he took a strand of her hair and wound it round his finger, watching it as it sprang into a curl when he released it. She kept very still, her breathing light and rapid.

"As we're man and wife now, Sally, would you object if I kissed you?" he ventured smilingly.

"No," she said through clenched teeth as though, come what may, she meant to grin and bear it.

"I promise it won't hurt," attempting a lightness he did not feel. His own hands had begun to tremble slightly and his breathing quickened. Though she looked far from the image most men dream of in her nun-like nightgown, the sight of all that glorious hair covering her almost like a veil was quite devastating. He brushed it back lingeringly and placed his hands on her shoulders. He laid his lips on the pulse which beat frantically beneath the curve of her jawline then let his mouth drift to her cheek. He could feel the tension in her but something told him it was not the strain of rejection but a wondering, a curiosity, a wanting to move on and make some sense of what she was feeling.

He kissed her neck and throat, then with quiet, unhurried fingers undid the top buttons of her nightgown and, pushing it to one side, kissed her shoulder. She was trembling violently now, so with a gentle but steady pressure he made her lie back on the pillow. She looked up at him, her eyes enormous and unblinking in her small white face and, bending his head, he laid his lips for the first time on hers. They parted as though in surprise so he continued, touching them caressingly with his tongue. She was still looking up at him as though waiting for further instructions on how to proceed but her face had become flushed and her mouth was rosy.

"Sally?" he said.

"Yes?" she answered, obedient as a child.

"Sally, was that the first time you have been kissed by a man?"

"Yes," she whispered.

"Did you like it?"

"Yes."

"So did I. Shall we try it again?"

"Yes, please."

He felt her begin to relax, to make small movements as though she wanted to take a more active part in this pleasant pastime but was not sure how to go about it.

As though by accident he let his hand brush against her breast, then very gently and very carefully he cupped it. She gasped and her nipple hardened against his palm. He lifted his head and she looked up at him with drowning, feverishly bright eyes.

"Sally, what is it?"

"I don't know."

"Do you want me to stop?"

"Oh, no . . ."

"Very well then." He pushed the neck of her nightgown lower, slipping his hand inside to hold her naked breast, finding the nipple as hard and smooth as a pearl. Her breathing was becoming erratic and he thanked God that she appeared not to object. Just the opposite, in fact, for her arms had crept about his neck.

"May I get in with you?" he whispered into the satin flesh of her throat.

"Oh, please . . . please . . ."

Quickly, lest he lose this willingness she was revealing, he threw off his robe. He was naked beneath it and as her startled gaze took in the jaunty size of his erection, which cared not a jot for Sally Cooper's innocent sensibilities, he slid into the bed beside her. She had become rigid again under the sheets.

Adam forced himself to hold her quietly, knowing that if he charged ahead and tore into her he would never have her confidence and trust again. He had the curious feeling that beneath her virginal nightgown, her prim exterior, the impregnable prudery she showed to the world, was a woman of excitement, of sensuality, a partner for his lonely bed who would prove worthwhile. He already knew she would transform his home into the peace and order and tranquillity which, recently, he had begun to crave. Perhaps in this, their private world, she would do the same. Well, not order and peace, but a pleasant place to be.

Putting his lips to her cheek, he turned her face towards him, taking her lips again, this time with more force.

"Tell me what you feel, Sally," he murmured against her sweet flesh, since he believed that as human creatures they should give and take love with words as well as actions. "Does it feel good to you? Do you like my hands on your breasts?"

"Yes . . . yes, I do, Adam." Her voice was shy. "I had no idea."

"I'm glad I please you but there is more, my lovely girl."

It was though with these last three words Adam Cooper had turned the key in the locked-up heart of Sally Grimshaw, letting out all the stored-up love she had kept there since she was a young girl. Lovely girl . . . *his* lovely girl, he had called her and she wanted to be nothing else. She could sense the need in him, the need he had of her, and her body, and she gloried in it. She could give him everything a man wanted from a woman, in and out of their bed and, by God, she would. Just as she had set about making the Grimshaw Arms the best in Lancashire so would Sally Grimshaw's marriage to Adam Cooper be the most successful in the kingdom.

Gently he removed her nightgown. His hands were at her waist and belly, caressing her slowly and she could feel her skin ripple in the aftermath of his warm, strong hand. Her back wanted to arch like that of a cat in a shaft of bright sunshine, to lift itself to meet his touch and when his fingers reached that part of her which was totally private she could hear herself begin to moan in the back of her throat.

"Is that pleasing, lovely girl?" he asked her, his own voice hoarse, as he buried himself in the web of her silken hair, wrapping it about him like a drifting cloak.

She could not speak. Pleasing? Was that how she would describe the utterly exquisite sensations which had begun to throb where his hand was, the sensations that burned her flesh and compelled her to a melting, quivering, clamouring need to go on, to go on and on until the core of her erupted and separated and sped away to every part of her body?

For a moment only she held back. She turned her head and looked into his dear, familiar face. She longed, hungered to tell him how much she loved him but she knew it was not possible. He would be kind but horribly embarrassed since his own heart was surely buried in a grave in some Godforsaken spot on the map of India.

He smiled warmly into her face, putting a hand to her cheek as though he sensed something strange in her.

"What is it?" he asked her, tenderness in his voice. "Are you ready for more?"

"Yes."

"Tell me then."

"I want more, Adam. I want you."

"Then you shall have me, lovely girl."

Lifting himself from her side he stretched his body over hers and the strange, hard shaft which stood out from his loins touched her between her legs which he had spread. He propped himself up so that they could look into one another's eyes, then pushed himself quickly into her. There was a pain, burning and she gasped and bit her lip, then he bent his head and took her nipple between his teeth and the pain was gone, leaving only pleasure. He moved inside her and some essential part of her which slept, awoke and clenched and held him, and in a moment so glorious she felt the tears come to her eyes as her world simply exploded within her, was filled with colour and yet was so dark and lovely every nerve in her body felt it too.

When she regained her senses – she could not describe it in any other way – Adam was striving with something she could not understand. His head was thrown back and his body reared, fixed only to hers at that mysterious junction which was the source of their pleasure, then with a shout which surely must have been heard in the kitchen, what had happened to her, happened to him. His face contorted and she thought he must be in pain, then he shuddered, relaxed slowly and his limp body fell across hers. His face seemed naturally somehow to come to rest in the curve beneath her jaw where his parted lips sighed against her flesh.

"Dear God," he breathed. "Dear God . . ."

"Was it . . . that bad?" she asked him, her arms going round him, smiling in her new-found knowledge.

"Dear God," he said again, sighing now as he settled against her, their naked bodies, despite the difference in their height, fitting together in sweet perfection. She could smell him now she had her senses back, smell his skin and some musky odour she could not identify, not an unpleasant odour but one which she knew she would always associate with this moment, this first time they had made love. She supposed it was on her too and as though he had read her thoughts he said against her throat, "You have the scent of sensuality on you, lovely girl."

"What does that mean?" she asked cautiously.

"It means you are a woman made for loving."

She felt absurdly pleased. "How do you know?"

He raised his head and grinned down at her, his teeth very white in his sun-bronzed face. "Sally, I have known . . . well, there have been others before you."

"I don't want to know about that," she said, prim as a parson's wife, and again he shouted out loud in laughter.

"My sweet girl, after what you have been a party to in the last hour how can you still manage to act as though you had never known a . . . a lusty moment in your life?"

"Well, it's different now. I'm a married woman. I can be as lusty as I like." She grinned back impishly.

"And so you have been, lovely girl. As lusty as any man could wish for. You were a delight."

"Was I really, Adam?" She wriggled and blushed, pulling up the sheet to her chin but he tossed it aside, knowing her now, knowing her true nature. He took her hands and held them above her head while he carefully inspected her breasts, which were small but rounded, her waist, the curve of her hips and the deep, golden-haired cleft between her legs. He kissed and nuzzled and caressed her until she felt the heat come back to the pit of her belly. She began to sigh and stretch and with great delight he took her again, pulling her astride him as he plunged deep inside her. It was she who shouted this time.

"You've taken to this like a bird to flight, my lovely girl," he murmured into her hair after he had adjusted their bodies to his own satisfaction before they slept. "Like a bloody bird to flight."

They slept then, blending together as though their bodies had been fashioned especially for one another, limbs entwined and Sally's last drowsing thought was that this must be the happiest moment of her life.

When she awoke the next morning he was gone.

She breakfasted alone for the first time in three weeks. She had no idea where Adam was and was too proud to ask the sly-eyed Maddy who slapped the plate of indifferently cooked bacon and eggs in front of her. She could tell by the maid's manner that she was intrigued and not displeased by her master's absence on what should have been the first day of the newly married couple's new life together. Even her stepdaughters were missing as though without their father's presence they had no need to be polite to her, or even bother to appear.

She took her time, eating slowly, hoping he would come in, flushed and vital perhaps from a gallop on his bay, Harry, apologetic, ready to kiss her when the housemaid had gone, but he did not come and Sally felt the pain of it enter her heart. After the wonder and magic of last night when he had been, she was well aware of it, a considerate and tender lover; when he had called her his lovely girl and praised her looks and her ability to please him she had expected . . . what? What had she expected? Not protestations of love, naturally, since he did not love her and was honest enough not to lie about it. Not his constant presence nor attention even, which he had given her for the past three weeks, but a shared companionship at mealtimes, a continuation of the discussions, the arguments, the laughter, the interest they seemed to find agreeable to both, all leading at the end of the day to that joy they had shared last night.

Suddenly she shook herself irritably. Dear God, what was wrong with her? Just because Adam had been warm and eager when he made love to her last night did not mean that he meant to be a husband to her, as newly married husbands should be. She had no illusions as to why he had married her, so why was she moping about at the breakfast-table like some love-lorn young maiden? She had a job to do. A job Adam had given her and she meant to do it. Properly. Starting right now. If Adam had some task to perform this morning then it was nothing to do with her. This house was to do with her. Those unnatural children upstairs were to do with her. That was her domain, the household and all in it and by all that was sensible she meant to set it all to rights if she had to sack every servant in the house to do it. Adam had said she was to do as she liked, whatever she thought needed doing and she might as well get started right this minute. It was not as if she had anything else to do, was it? Determinedly she ignored the solid wave of despondency which washed over her as she turned her mind to what were, after all, her duties.

The first thing she must tackle was the marshalling of Cook, Mrs Chidlow and Mr Henton into some sort of disciplined routine which suited *her*, not them. Get them set to rights and knowing what was expected of them, no, demanded of them, the rest would follow.

But she did wish she knew where Adam was. Maddy had gone, clattering noisily as she cleared the table and Sally put her chin in her hands, staring with unseeing eyes at the disorder that had been left on the serving-table. Tablecloths askew and crumpled. A spoon fallen to the floor and left unnoticed. The silver condiment set which was slightly tarnished. She saw them and her tidy mind tucked them away to be dealt with later, but they made no concrete impression on her since Sally Cooper's thoughts had gone off with Adam wherever he was.

She straightened up and shook herself, then, pushing back her chair, rose to her feet and wandered to the window. It was a brisk October day, bright and cold. A robin was singing as it pecked diligently for tit-bits beneath a wooden bench at the side of the lawn. Sparrows were fluttering and hopping and hanging for dear life on to the heads of the sunflowers which had gone to seed. Moving to the side window she looked out on a flaunting bed of chrysanthemums, gold and tawny. It filled her heart with delight but still she sighed.

Dammit . . . dammit . . . dammit . . . what was the matter with her? Why couldn't she just walk briskly to the stable block and find out if Adam's horse was there? If it was not, then at least she'd know if he'd gone riding, or whatever it was gentlemen of his class got up to at this time of day. Hadn't she heard somewhere that October to Christmas was the season when pheasants were shot, but if that was where he had gone surely he could have told her? Perhaps he had tramped off into the woods which stretched across his land, his gun under his arm, those two dogs of his – whose names she had learned were Trixie and Bess – at his heels.

She was just about to turn briskly away, chiding herself for her foolishness, since Adam had married her to take care of his household, not sigh over where he might be, when he appeared at the bottom of the slope of lawn where it met the trees. The dogs appeared first, busy in that brisk way terriers have, scuttling from one spot to another, sniffing and snuffling over the ground as a scent caught their interest.

Adam came slowly behind them from beneath the trees which were beginning to turn to the bright-hued glory of autumn, a canopy over his head of bronze and copper and amber, rose and burgundy, yellow and gold and tangerine. As he walked his booted feet kicked up a small drift of leaves which had already fallen. His head was bent, his tread slow.

As though his thoughts were a thousand miles from where his body was, he appeared to idle along, not aware of his surroundings and when he reached the bench beneath which the robin had been foraging he sat down heavily. He leaned forward, his elbows on his parted knees, his hands dangling between them, his head down.

For two or three minutes he remained in this position while Sally's heart twisted painfully in her breast then he lifted his head to stare across the garden. On his face was an expression of such unutterable sadness she almost cried out.

Fumbling blindly with the curtains as though for support she turned away, unwilling to be a spectator to her husband's obvious wretchedness.

15

The servants were surprised when the bell rang summoning one of them to the small sitting-room. It was not that the summons was totally unexpected since the woman was the mistress of the house now and could do as she pleased but they had been of the opinion that, being who she was, who she *really* was, she would be out of her depth to start with and would leave them alone.

When Maddy knocked on the door and entered, Sally was sitting on one of the two sofas beside a fire which was struggling for life. She turned and smiled coolly at the housemaid. She had been studying the framed watercolours on the walls, the paint so delicately applied to the canvas the subject was hard to define and yet so pleasing to the eye she found she wanted to stand and look at them indefinitely. They had been done by Oralie, Adam had told her awkwardly when she asked and she remembered how her thoughts had turned to sheer misery. Was there no end to the talents of this woman who had been his wife?

"Yes . . . mum?" Maddy felt compelled to add the "mum" since there was no way she was going to address this upstart by the correct title of "madam".

"I believe your name is Maddy Fletcher?" Sally began crisply.

"Yes, mum."

"Well, Maddy, perhaps you could tell me whose duty it is to replenish the coal scuttle?"

"Pardon?"

"I think you heard me. The fire is almost out and the coal scuttle is empty. See that it is filled and make up the fire, please. Then ask Mr Henton to come and see me."

Maddy's face turned sullen. "I think he's busy, mum. Last time I saw him he was off down the wine cellar and—"

"Well, fetch him up from the wine cellar and send him to me. Tell him the mistress wants to see him in her sitting-room at once."

Maddy's mouth fell open. Sally could see the expressions flitting across her face – disbelief, indignation, scorn – and she knew the maid would have given a year's wages to ask "the mistress" who the hell she thought she was but discretion took the upper hand. Besides, the idea of "sending" Mr Henton anywhere, and "at once" was evidently a novel one to her and she actually began to smile.

"Well, I don't know as . . ."

Sally took a deep breath. She kept her voice impersonal and her face expressionless. "How long have you been here, Maddy?" she asked.

Maddy looked startled. "Three years, mum."

"And you are happy working for Captain Cooper?"

"Oh, yes." Who wouldn't be? It was the most undemanding job Maddy had ever had in the eight years since she had taken up domestic service. There was a certain amount of work to be shared out among her and the other maids but with Mrs Chidlow and Mr Henton, who were both getting on a bit, inclined to take it easy in the declining years of their working lives, they all drifted most pleasantly through their working day.

"And do you wish to keep this job with which you say you are so content?"

"Well . . ."

"Yes or no, Maddy, bearing in mind that maidservants are ten a penny in Liverpool. I could lay my hands on half a dozen good ones by the end of the day. And I know a good one when I see her. So, what is it to be?"

"Yes . . . madam."

"Then the first lesson you will learn is that I am mistress of this house. That fact is unchangeable. I am here to stay, unlike the rest of you, so you will accept that it is *my* orders which will be obeyed. When I ask you, or any of the servants, to do something, I want you to do whatever it is at once, without question. Is that understood?"

"Yes, madam, but I can—"

"Maddy, you are trying my patience of which, when you know me better, you will learn I have very little. Now then, the coal, the fire and Mr Henton, in that order."

Maddy almost ran back to the kitchen in her eagerness to tell the rest of them about the "sauce" of that woman, and for several minutes there was pandemonium as they all gave their opinion at once, only Clara, who was not sure what all the fuss was about anyway, keeping out of it. Words like "hussy", "impertinence", "cheek" and "shameless" were bandied about but had they any option but to do as their mistress – Ha! – ordered them?

The coal scuttle was filled, the fire fed until it burned cheerfully, the grate itself brushed until it was as neat as a pin. Maddy, whose job it appeared it was, being under-parlourmaid, attended to it deftly and quietly and, having let off all the steam she was allowed to the others and being a sensible girl who valued her job, bobbed a respectable curtsey as she left the room. Her face said she didn't like it but she was prepared to lump it for now.

Sally was only too well aware that because of who she was and where she had come from, no matter what her position now, the servants had been of the opinion that she could easily be disregarded and she must make it clear right from the start that they were mistaken. This mission of marriage she had embarked on was of vital importance to her and with the full force of her nature which had come from Grandpa Grimshaw, she meant to make a success of it. She had made a start with Maddy.

Henton who, she was well aware, had found life very easy in this household of which, for the past eight or nine years, he had been the virtual head, would not be so easily persuaded to compromise that position. His views were very clear as he made an ill-advised attempt to treat her like the ignorant vulgarian he undoubtedly thought her to be, doing his best to intimidate her with his overbearing butler's manner which he had learned over the years.

Sally was about to be made aware of the fact.

"You wished to see me, madam?" he began loftily, his manner showing clearly his wonderment at her nerve in even summoning him here.

"Yes, I did. I think it best to let you know right from the start what I expect of you, and the rest of the staff whom I shall interview separately later."

"Very well, madam," he murmured icily, his eyes fixed on some point above her head, "but might I say that this house has always been run to the satisfaction of the master, *and* the mistress before her sad demise."

"You may think so, Henton, and perhaps it was but I imagine my standards are considerably more demanding than . . . the first Mrs Cooper."

"Indeed, madam." It was obvious from the sneer about his mouth that he found this difficult to believe since Mrs Cooper, *all* the Mrs Coopers who had gone before this one, were ladies.

"Indeed, Henton. Now you may fall in with my ways, serve this house to the standards I set, obeying my orders to the letter, or you may decide that, at your age, you are not equal to a new régime which, believe me, will be stringent, and which I intend to begin this very day. If that is the case then I think we'd best part company at once. I require, my husband requires" – it nearly stuck in her dry throat and she fought her need to swallow forcibly as she said this last – "a man who can be trusted to—"

"Really, madam, you are most insulting." Henton's face was blood red with rage and his eyes narrowed to slits. "I would like to speak to the master at once. I have given service to this house honestly and efficiently—"

"No, you have not, Henton. You are the butler and under you, and Mrs Chidlow, who shares your responsibilities, the staff have become lax and inefficient, the house kept barely clean and the food appalling. That, in my opinion, is dishonest. You have not earned the wages you have been paid. I have not yet had access to the accounts but I intend to do so at the first opportunity. I have, during the last three weeks, inspected many of the rooms and what I found there is not at all what I am used to."

"No, I'm sure it's not."

"Be careful what you say, Henton, in case you should decide to remain with me. Now, I mean to examine every room, every cupboard in every room, the servants' quarters, the dairy, the laundry, the stillroom and the wine cellars. You see I know something about wine, Henton, its quality and its cost. Your pantry and the servants hall will suffer close scrutiny, as will the kitchens and sculleries. I need absolute cleanliness, decency and hygiene. I loathe dirt, Henton, as much as I loathe laziness, and I must have those who feel the same working under me. I am very pleasant to those I consider hardworking, loyal and honest and have been known to reward them for it. Am I making myself understood, Henton?"

"You are, madam, and I find it hard to believe the master is in agreement with you over this. I have served—"

"You have already said that, Henton, and before you say more I think it would be wise if you were to go away and consider what I have said, and your position here."

"I demand to see the master." He was ready to smack her about her insolent face, just as he might a scullery maid who had displeased him, since she was no better in his opinion. He couldn't believe it, his thunderstruck expression said, to be spoken to in such an offensive tone and by a woman whose background and upbringing were no better than his own. She would pay dearly for this, his manner said, but then he could not be blamed for it since he barely knew the Sally Grimshaw who had ruled with a rod of iron at the Grimshaw Arms.

"I believe he is in the garden," she told him, her eyes a steady gleam of golden amber as they stared unwaveringly into his.

"Thank you, madam." He turned ponderously and began a slow tread towards the door.

"Oh, Henton, send in Mrs Chidlow, will you?"

Mrs Chidlow proved to be as entrenched as Henton in her belief that Coopers Edge was a model of a well-run household, claiming to be amazed that any fault should be found with her. She had been in charge of the captain's home ever since the little girls, babies then, of course, had been brought back here after their mama . . . well, that was nine years ago and not once had a complaint been made against her.

"Perhaps that was because there was no one to make a complaint, Mrs Chidlow. The lawyer my husband" – she felt herself tremble again as she said the last words, hoping the housekeeper wouldn't see it – "the lawyer my husband employed to oversee this house was not qualified to judge the standard of service those two little girls were getting, though I must admit they appear not to have suffered from it."

At least physically, she thought, though their spirit seemed to her to be appallingly lacking when compared with the din made by her own nephews and nieces. God forbid that Leila and Aisha should be as rowdy and out of hand as Vi's lot but in the three weeks she had been at Coopers Edge she could honestly say she had never heard a peep out of them, nor seen them break into anything that might be described as a run. Round and round the garden they were led by Miss Digby, their booted feet gliding along the gravel path, their curls, dark wine red and gleaming, closely bonneted. They even wore gloves, for heaven's sake, no matter what the temperature and when old Reuben, or young Eppie, at their approach, stood respectfully to one side they did not smile, merely dipping their heads like two dowagers. They sat decorously at the table, barely raising their eyes from their plates, speaking only when spoken to and even then appearing to find her questions quite incomprehensible.

"Do you like croquet?" she had asked, having seen the hoops and mallets in the cupboard under the stairs on one of her forays.

Exchanging glances, they said together, "Croquet?"

"Yes, you know, on the lawn." She had smiled encouragingly, aware that Adam was watching approvingly.

"I don't think we have ever played it, ma'am," Leila, who was the elder, piped.

"Perhaps we can have a game one day."

"That would be lovely," she answered politely.

And on another occasion, "What kind of books do you like to read? Have you tried Mr Dickens's *David Copperfield*? It's a great favourite of mine. And what about *The Children of the New Forest* and *The Last of the Mohicans*? I used to read that to my brother Freddy." Freddy had always been a lazy scholar.

"I don't think . . . Nanny says . . ."

"What? What does Nanny say?" Sally leaned forward, turning to Adam for some support with these two beautiful but totally repressed little daughters of his but, coming from the class where, for the first ten or twelve years a child's life belonged to Nanny and where her word was law, he seemed out of his depth.

"Doesn't Miss . . . Miss What's-her-name . . . your governess allow you to read?" She shrugged and raised her eyebrows, hoping for some response from one of them.

"We have Hans Christian Andersen and . . . and . . ." They looked at one another helplessly. "And *The Fairchild Family* and . . . and *The Swiss Family Robinson*."

"So did Freddy and Violet and I. We used to play Swiss Family Robinson in the tree at the back of . . . of my home."

They seemed to be so thunderstruck at the idea of anyone "playing" what they only read about they could say no more and Sally gave up, vowing that when she and Adam were married she'd stir up that nursery floor like a hornets' nest. She wasn't even sure why she should do so really, since she had never particularly cared for nor had any interest in children. She had had no real childhood herself, working as she had with her mother about the inn, so perhaps that was it. Perhaps it would be pleasant to have one now with these two who surely needed it.

But first she must see to the house and the servants, speak to them, and the third to march steadfastly into the sitting-room was Cook. She looked so formidable and so totally prepared to stand no nonsense Sally wouldn't have been surprised to see her armed with her large wooden baking spoon. She was an ample-bosomed woman with a peevish face and it was made clear from the start that any criticism of her work would be met with fierce disapproval. Her cap hung untidily to one side of her bird's-nest hair and there was egg yolk on the bib of her apron. She carried the war immediately into the enemy's camp.

"I've been told by Mr Henton you don't think much of my cooking, madam," she said accusingly and Sally was made fully aware that the title "madam" was not used in the sense a servant addresses a mistress.

"That's true, Cook, and it seems to me that—"

"I don't care what it seems to you. I'm not standing here being insulted by someone who's no idea how to boil an egg, like as not."

Cook folded her arms beneath her bosom and hefted it several inches higher. Cook was sixty-five and had been vaguely considering retirement for some while now and had it not been for the easy and comfortable job she had been lucky enough to idle through for the past eight years, would have done so. Now seemed as good a time as any, especially after what Mr Henton and Mrs Chidlow had muttered to her about "new brooms" as they returned to the kitchen. She said so now.

"New brooms sweep clean, so I'm told, *madam*, but I

reckon I'm too old to bother with such things so I'll hand me notice in right now."

She was triumphant in her belief that the household would go hungry without her as she tossed her head, her cap becoming even more dangerously tilted, and heaved her bosom an inch or two higher.

"A week's notice I'll give you," she went on, with an air of someone making a great concession. "You should be able to find someone by then." And if you don't what do I care! It was not as if she needed a character reference from this jumped-up little tart. She and her friend, Emmy Agnew, who was a lady's maid with a respectable Liverpool family, had their eye on a nice little terraced villa in Everton and, with their combined savings and perhaps a quiet gentleman lodger or two, would manage very nicely.

"There's no need for that, Cook. You may go now. I want no one working for me who does so reluctantly."

Cook's jaw dropped. "Well I never. Here am I prepared to help you out for a week and what do I get?"

"Thank you, Cook, that will be all. Henton will have your wages for you when you're ready."

"But who's going to see to the . . .?"

"That is no longer your concern, Cook. Contrary to your belief that I can't boil an egg perhaps you may have heard of the . . . the hospitality for which the Grimshaw Arms was famous."

"Oh, that," Cook sneered. "Inn food."

"The best in Lancashire and until I find someone who meets my requirements I shall supervise the cooking myself. There are three maids in the kitchen, plus three housemaids."

"What! Them cack-handed half-wits."

"That's enough, Cook. Now, I'll have the menu books, if

you please, and I would like all the indoor servants assembled in the servants hall where I will speak to them."

The maidservants, accompanied by Tipper, the footman, Tom the boot boy and Clara from the scullery, stood in a silent line along the length of the big table where they ate their meals. They had been warned, not only by Maddy who was almost in tears over what she saw as "brass neck" provocation, coming from someone who was no better than she was in the social way of things, but by the three head servants. Cook was off to pack her bags, she'd told them in high dudgeon. Henton was with the master and what would come of that remained to be seen and Mrs Chidlow was drinking tea by the gallon, laced with the drop of gin she was fond of and what she intended to do was anyone's guess. They'd heard her say to Cook that *madam* was prepared to keep her on if . . . What that *if* was, was lost in Mrs Chidlow's fourth cup of tea.

Sally, believing that what had been said to Henton, Mrs Chidlow, Cook and Maddy would be sufficient to let the others know exactly what was expected of them, merely spoke briefly to each servant in turn along the line, confirming their names and their duties as though the past three weeks when they had assiduously acted as though she were invisible had not existed. She was their new mistress, her manner said, like it or not and, having done that, convinced that she had made a good start, she ordered coffee and returned to the sitting-room to study the menu books and the guest books, going back into the days when Adam's mother had been alive, which had been unearthed for her.

Adam stood up politely as she entered the room and at once her heart moved in a helpless, melting sort of way. She could feel the flush begin somewhere under her clothes, she couldn't say exactly where and her heart lurched uncomfortably against the bodice of her plain, high-necked white blouse.

"Oh . . . I thought you were . . . let me order you some coffee," she stammered, reaching for the bell in some confusion, wondering why, suddenly, this man had the power to reduce the redoubtable Sally Grimshaw who had just routed a houseful of surly servants to the nervousness of a new scullery maid. She was unable to meet his eyes as the memory of what they had done last night came flooding back. The last time she had seen him they had both been totally naked, a glorious nakedness which had, unexpectedly, delighted her. She had gloried in it, and in him, since he seemed to enjoy it as much as she did. She had known nothing like it, had not even guessed that two human beings could share such pleasure and had fallen asleep in his arms in the absolute conviction that something so lovely would, having been found, never be lost.

She had been mistaken. Some time in the night he had left her, slipped away to commune with his own private thoughts, no doubt about the unsuitability of this marriage he had foolishly undertaken. Probably standing beneath the portrait of the lovely, laughing woman who had been his first wife with regret in his heart and the inexpressible sadness she herself had witnessed this morning.

His first words confirmed it. "What on earth have you been saying to Henton? The poor old beggar's devastated. Accused of dishonest practice, of inefficiency and laxity with the housemaids. Dear God, he was almost in tears."

Without a pang of remorse her anger sprang, fully roused, to the surface and she was glad of it, since it swept away the memories of last night which would get in her way. It swamped the hurtful love which seemed to multiply with every heartbeat, gripping her in its painful, unwanted embrace. There is nothing more agonising than a love unreturned but Adam's words sent that agony and love hurtling away on a hazardous torrent as rage corroded its beginnings.

"I beg your pardon," she hissed. Her back stiffened as though her spine had been touched to steel and her eyes, which had been a soft, smoky quartz at the sight of him, flashed to a glittering, burning amber, like the eyes of a leopard Adam had once had in his gun sights in India. But he had no time to consider this phenomenon as she went on the attack.

"Do my ears deceive me? Am I to believe that after all your protestations about turning this ill-served, undisciplined, neglected and downright filthy house—"

"Oh, come now . . ." Adam's own face had darkened with anger but he might not have spoken for all the good it did.

"—into a home fit for a decent family to live in, you are taking the part of that disagreeable old man? I can't believe it. You yourself said the servants were disorderly and sloppy . . . oh, yes, your very words and surely the person to blame for this can only be Henton and probably Mrs Chidlow. Knock them into shape, you said."

"I know I did but that doesn't mean you may—"

"And return this house to the order it should have."

"I know and if you—"

"And I cannot do it unless I have the respect and obedience of those who serve you. That old fool . . . no, not fool since he has been lining his pockets."

"You don't know that."

"You don't know that he wasn't since you were not here."

"That is no excuse to accuse him without proof."

"Just let me get my hands on the accounts if you want proof. I ran an inn for nearly sixteen years, if you remember, and there is nothing I don't know about provisions, the cost of them, their usage."

He thought she might be ready to strike him and, as he had done in the past, he was riveted by the quite miraculous change in her appearance. When her passions were roused, whether in a drama such as this, or in the passion of their bed last night, she took on a lustrous gloss, a fiery ardour that whipped her into the kind of woman men could not resist. Dammit, he could feel himself becoming aroused as her rounded breasts heaved and that glorious, ridiculous hair of hers began its usual slipping glide into disarray. But this was no time for such things, even if the fury she was in would allow it.

He deliberately made his expression hard. "Will you listen to me," he snapped. "Sit down and pull yourself together, woman. The servants can hear you and—"

"Damn the servants and damn you. I'm off. When I took on this job it was with the clear understanding that I was to have a free hand in its performance. If I'm not allowed a free hand then be damned to you. Dear God, not a day gone by and you're already interfering and—"

"Is that all this is to you, Sally, a job?"

"It's all it is to *you*, Captain Cooper."

The change in Adam was dramatic. He had been as flushed and angry as she was with an underlying sense of peril which boded ill for her if she continued with this, but suddenly, as though in the realisation of who he was and, more to the point, who she was, his face and bearing took on an air which was remote and forbidding. Cold, he was, and ready to be cutting and Sally felt that cold chill her bones and enter her despairing heart.

"May I remind you that you are now my wife." His voice had ice chippings which froze her soul. "As my wife you will act as becomes—"

"Fiddlesticks!" she exploded. "Have you any idea what a pompous ass you sound? Have you? And yes, I had forgotten I was your wife, I must admit. You see I was embarking on the job you had engaged me for but I see it is to be useless."

"Will you lower your voice and sit down."

"What for?"

"For the sake of . . . Goddammit, I don't know." He ran his hands through his hair and turned away, moving across the room to stare at one of the lovely, soft-hued paintings on the wall and again Sally's heart felt as though a knife were being turned in it. It was as though he was linking himself, through her painting, with the woman who, it seemed to Sally, was never far from his thoughts. Surely this morning confirmed that.

When at last he turned back to her his air of cool detachment was complete. On the other hand Sally Grimshaw felt as though she had been dragged through a hedge backwards, hauled up the drive and across the threshold of the house, then tossed carelessly in a dishevelled heap on Oralie Cooper's beautiful carpet. She knew her damned hair was drifting about her head in a demented storm and in the midst of all the chaos her cool mind was beleaguered with the thought that perhaps, now that she was a married woman, she should start to wear one of those indoor caps with floating ribbons dangling down her back. It might at least keep her hair in place!

"Well," she said witheringly. "Am I to do this thing or not?

I am quite well able to sit back with my embroidery for the rest of my days if you prefer. Let Henton and Mrs Chidlow continue as they are, though I'd best warn you that Cook is at this moment packing her bags. Of course, one of the kitchen maids can prepare your meals until Mrs Chidlow finds another cook who I'm sure can be no worse than the one you have now."

He whirled away from her again, this time striding to the window, the set of his shoulders fierce, his hair sticking up about his head where his hand had disturbed it. She watched him, her own shoulders doing their best not to slump. She wanted to sigh, loudly and long, as near to tears as she had ever been, for her lovely, bright bubble of joy had lasted such a short time, but her passionate spirit drove her to stand upright, her head high, her hands clasped tightly in front of her.

"My mind is doing its best to picture you at your embroidery until the end of your days." His voice was low and there was a quiver in it.

Sally frowned, staring at his back, waiting for him to go on but he continued to stand at the window. He seemed to be trembling slightly.

"Well," she said at last, "is that what you want?"

"Is that what you want, Sally?"

"You know it's not." Her tone was challenging and she moved impatiently. Was he to stand there transfixed for all eternity or was he to turn and order her to run upstairs for her sewing since that was to be her sole occupation from now on? Despite what she'd said about embroidery surely he knew she didn't mean it? She'd not back down. She'd not let that puffed-up old man rule this household for another minute, not if she'd to fight him, and Adam, every step of the way. Could you imagine what her position would be at

Coopers Edge when the servants heard that the master had taken Henton's side? Sly, sneering glances, orders sullenly obeyed, a running to their master at every imagined slight. It would be insufferable, but if she had to do it, she damn well would, and with style. After all she was Sally Grimshaw of the Grimshaw Arms!

When he turned he was still cool, unapproachable, no expression on his face she could indentify. His eyes seemed to have a light behind them though, a clear gleaming blue light, the blue surrounded by a thin black line, so beautiful and yet declaring quite vehemently his unapproachability.

"Sally, you're my wife now, in every way. You understand what I'm saying?" His voice was grave and she nodded, ducking her head a little in shyness before bringing it up proudly again. "You are a Cooper and do you honestly believe I would allow anyone, servant or otherwise, to come to me with tales of grievances against anyone of my name, whether they be true or untrue? As my wife you're entitled to my support, my protection, my loyalty and for the remainder of our lives together you shall have it."

Whether there is love between us or not! He didn't have to say it.

"I know Henton is a rogue and though I believe . . . well, you are very forthright, Sally, so I imagine you will have no further trouble with him. He knows which side his bread is buttered, does Henton, and after he and I had a little talk he was convinced that you hold the household reins with my absolute backing. If I seemed to be initially disapproving, then I'm sorry but, in his way, he has been loyal to me and has protected my daughters."

"And that's another thing, Adam," she began, emboldened by his words but he held up his hands, stepping back a little as though her zeal was too much for him

"Not now, Sally, there's a good girl. We will attend to them shortly. The servants are in a turmoil but I'm certain, in your own particular way, you'll soon have them working to your high standards. Now . . ."

"Adam, if I may . . ."

"No, Sally, I . . . I have things to do so if you'll excuse me I'll . . ."

It was not vouchsafed to her what it was he was about to do. There was a tap at the door and Henton entered, not by the flicker of an eyelash revealing his thoughts about the last hour. It might never have happened, so deferential was his manner, and Sally knew she had won.

"There are two gentlemen to see you, sir," he intoned, his eyebrows climbing in sharp surprise as though the identity of the gentlemen would come as a shock.

"Who are they, Henton?" his master asked, frowning.

"A police inspector and a constable, sir. They did not give me a card."

"Did they say what it was about?"

"It's about Job Hawthorne, sir," and this time Henton could not resist shooting the new Mrs Cooper a triumphant glance.

16

"I have never heard anything so ridiculous in my life and I refuse absolutely to let him be brought here. This is just a trick of Keene's to try and get his own back on me because . . . because of certain things that happened. No, Adam, you must send these men away at once."

Sally was backed up against the glass-fronted rosewood secretaire cabinet in which were displayed many of the ornaments gathered by the Cooper women for the past one hundred and fifty years. It was as though she were defending it, her arms outstretched just as if Job himself was hidden in one of the drawers which divided it.

"Sally, please, this is not something that can be ignored. I have no power to send them away. They are officers of the law and have a right to speak to any man who has been accused of a crime. A serious charge has been laid against Job and it is the inspector's job to investigate it. Job must go with them to the police station where he will be questioned."

"I will go with him."

"No, you will not. I will send for my lawyer to speak for him."

"I am the only one who can speak for him, Adam. I was there. I know what happened, your lawyer doesn't. They will try to make Job say things which will go against him and I must be there."

"They will not. My lawyer . . ."

"Oh, please . . . please, Adam."

"Sally, you will not go and that is an end to it. As my wife . . ."

"Rubbish, rubbish and you know it and I care nothing for being your wife if it means discarding a man who is a . . . friend to me."

The inspector and his constable exchanged a furtive glance but Adam intercepted it and his irritation with Sally mounted. Hell's teeth, he had known her to be a spirited, determined woman when he had proposed marriage to her. It was one of the reasons he had done so. It was what was needed to pull him, his daughters and this house out of the trough of lethargy they had fallen into over the years. Oralie's desertion and death had swamped him with despondency and hopelessness for a long, long time and for years he had been unable to face returning to Coopers Edge where, briefly, he had known an exaltation, an enchantment that could not be described, nor repeated. Oralie had bewitched him, held him in thrall, blinded and deafened him to everything but her beauty and it was not until Sally Grimshaw, plain Sally Grimshaw with her pugnacious jaw, with her guts and her backbone, her doughty sense of humour and her curious lopsided grin, had come into his life, that he had known the renewal of hope.

But she was so bloody-minded, so independent, so positive that only what she thought was right, that only she could bring order where none had been, dispose of trouble, tidy up any knotty problems which might befall those she considered to be her responsibility. You had only to look at the squall which she had already blown up this morning with Henton and the rest of his servants. He had told her, true, that she had a free hand, but, God almighty, it was not even lunchtime and he felt as though he had been put through one of the mangles in the laundry.

Yet her loyalty was manifold, ready to be dispensed hugely to those she considered worthy of it. Just look at her over this man, this ex-prize fighter, this battered piece of human flotsam she had taken under her wing and who, because he had supported her, defended her, been a friend to her when she needed one, she would defend in her turn, and to the death.

"Inspector, would you mind waiting in the hall," he asked apologetically. "I will send for Hawthorne but in the meanwhile I must speak to my wife."

"No, you will not, Adam. You will not send for him. I will not allow these men to cart him off to gaol like a common criminal. He has done no wrong. He was defending me against a man who had . . . had designs upon me."

"Which you will speak of in court, Sally. Please, Inspector . . ." and when the policeman had sidled unobtrusively into the hall, taking his pop-eyed, red-faced constable with him, Adam put his arms about her and drew her to his chest. In normal circumstances she would have been filled with joy to be in his arms but her fears for Job were so strong his embrace meant nothing to her. She struggled to free herself but Adam held her firmly, smoothing her hair, her face against his chest.

"Don't, Sally, let him go. Trust me. I have some influence in this city and nothing will happen to Job. If you have to go to court to tell the judge what happened then you shall do so." He smiled a little into the curly tumble of her hair, then, cupping her face with his hands, he looked down into her anguished eyes. "You're the wife of an important man now, Sally, though I hate to sound so . . . pompous. Is that what you called me? Yes, let me see you smile, there . . ." and he kissed her gently, a mere brushing of his warm lips on hers, but calming. She was calmed.

She watched, her hand to her mouth, as Job was put in a hansom cab between the inspector and the police constable. In deference to the man whose servant he was, they had not manacled him, despite the serious allegation of violence that had been brought against him. They had allowed him to change into his decent Sunday clothes, at Adam's insistence, since he knew Job would make a better impression at the assizes dressed as a respectable artisan and as Job lifted his hand in a small salute to Sally his eyes had looked into hers, allowing her at last to see the depth of his feelings for her.

He did not come back that day and Sally was glad of the activity in the kitchen where, in the businesslike way she had acquired at the Grimshaw Arms, she supervised the preparation and cooking of a meal for approximately two dozen people, the first decent meal the household had eaten for years. Adam let her do it, though by the precepts of the society in which he had been raised, no lady would be so ill-bred as to take over her own kitchen. No lady would know *how* to take over her own kitchen. The sight of his wife, small and vulnerable, but resolute, in Cook's vast apron did not please him but he put aside his own misgivings and left her, deep in a bowl of stale bread which she assured him was to be a summer pudding. He was aware of her deep worry, her distress, the apprehension in her that in some way Richard Keene would hoodwink not only the police but the judge and jury into believing that Job's attack on him had been vicious and unprovoked. That he had been seriously injured by it and that Job Hawthorne should receive a long prison sentence.

Thank the Lord that the transporting of convicted felons to Australia had ended some years ago but it wouldn't come to that, Adam told her sternly, as he watched her toy with the delicious meal she had prepared.

They were eating a piece of roast pork, a loin which Cook had been saving for the upper servants' Sunday dinner. Pork was not considered to be the fare of a wealthy household since it was associated with the working man who kept a pig in his yard and fed it on household scraps. Sucking pig, on the other hand, had become increasingly popular, making for variety at dinner parties, but this was a plain loin, plain at least until Sally set about it. She had scored it and rubbed it over with a little salad oil and, admonishing Tilly to keep it well basted, put it to roast at the correct distance from the fire. It must be thoroughly cooked but not dry, she had told the kitchen maid. They were all given a job to do. Clara was at the scullery sink with the vegetables. Gracie, the second kitchen maid, was making apple sauce and Maddy, who was surprised to find she was beginning to enjoy herself under this calm, efficient woman who obviously knew a basting spoon from a roasting fork, was sent to the herb garden to gather the sage for the sage and onion stuffing. The potatoes, both roasted and boiled, were Cissie's task, though it was clear the head parlourmaid was vastly offended by the menial task her mistress put in her hands. Sally made a mental note that Newton, as it seemed Cissie liked to be called, would have to be carefully watched lest she undermine the delicate structure Sally was beginning to build.

Fresh asparagus was brought to the kitchen door by the boy, Eppie, just cut in the heated greenhouse, he explained, and could the "missis" make use of these fruits, damson and plum, raspberries – double-bearing which crop in the autumn – and blackberries – hence the summer pudding. Did she fancy some nice caulis, Mr Reuben wanted to know or a few peas and the salad stuff was still at its best if she needed it. Sally wondered, as the abundance of fresh fruit and vegetables continued to flow across the back kitchen doorstep, how Cook had managed to turn out, day after day, the badly prepared and poorly cooked meals which had been her habit with such quality and quantity always at hand.

The servants, indoor and out, after the master and mistress had eaten, had the same thoughts, some of them spoken out loud, as they sat down in the servants hall to the same meal which had been put in front of Captain and Mrs Cooper. Mrs Chidlow and Mr Henton had little to say, true, but it did not go unnoticed that they tucked into their food with every sign of enjoyment. It was also noticed that for the first time since any of them could remember, the butler had not helped himself to a bottle of the master's fine white wine. Perhaps it was due to the fact that the mistress had been down in the cellar with him.

Sally felt a pang of guilty shame strike her several hours later as she realised that not once since she and Adam had entered their sweet-smelling, fire-glowed bedroom had she given a thought to Job. All through dinner, which Adam ate like a man who has been seated with the gods and is partaking of their ambrosia and nectar, eagerly holding out his plate to Henton for a second helping, she had pictured Job in a tiny cell, cold and damp and eating slops, no doubt. She had been unable to manage more than a morsel or two, though she had to admit it gave her a great deal of pleasure to see Adam eat with such evident enjoyment.

"No wonder your establishment had such a good name, Sally," he said round a succulent mouthful of pork crackling.

"I've never eaten better than this. I've a good mind to employ you as my full-time cook."

Henton and Cissie exchanged glances. It was not Henton's practice to communicate with the underservants, unless it was to issue an order, but this last remark startled him into an expressively horrified look. Dear God, it said, what next? Surely they were not to be submitted to this woman's presence in their domain on a permanent basis?

"I wouldn't mind, Adam," Sally answered absently.

"I'm joking, Sally," and from the sideboard came an almost audible sigh of relief. Adam smiled at her and reached for her hand. She had refused absolutely to sit at the other end of the big table which seated a score of people, preferring to be on his left side, where they could hold a proper conversation, she had told him, without the servants cocking their ears. This practice the gentry had of shouting to one another down the length of a twenty- to thirty-foot table, treating those who served them as though they were not there, allowing all kinds of private family matters to be overheard, was one she could not understand. Henton had made it clear he did not care for the change, creating a drama out of moving the mat and napkin, the cutlery and glassware, but Adam ignored him. Sally had a way of doing as she wished, unconcerned with the servants' approval and he did admit it was more intimate, or should he say companionable, to have her beside him. Tonight especially since he could see she was on edge, her mind far away from the wonderful meal she had prepared from what was handy in the pantry.

"You know you must employ another cook, don't you, Sally?" he said gently, his blue eyes soft in the lamplight. "There will be other things to occupy you which will leave you little time for the kitchen."

"I suppose so," she said listlessly. She had changed into the apple green silk dress made for Violet and Arthur's wedding and worn earlier this year when Freddy married his Dorothy and, though her face was pale and strained and her eyes woeful, Adam thought she looked . . . well . . . attractive. She had done something with her hair so that it was soft about her face, gleaming silky tendrils drifting in loose curls to her shoulders. He was not to know that she had done precisely nothing to her hair, which was why it looked as it did. She had brushed it and bundled it up casually, holding it all together with an apple green ribbon snipped from her gown.

"I wish I knew what they were, these things which are to occupy me," she went on, sorry when he took his hand away after giving hers a little squeeze. "You know I don't care for . . . for sitting about."

He grinned and she thought how lovely he was, yes, lovely with his gleaming silvery hair, his long-lashed blue eyes which looked almost the colour of hyacinths in this light, the flash of his white teeth in his brown face.

"I know that, Sally, and the image of Sally Grimshaw . . . I beg your pardon, Sally Cooper, sitting about doing nothing is one I just can't bring to mind, but there are . . ."

He was suddenly aware of the two servants who, in their eagerness to hear what was being said, were almost leaning out from the sideboard. They were about to serve the summer pudding with thick, whipped cream but he waved them from the room.

"Put the dishes on the table, Henton. My wife will serve us," he said, reaching for his wife's hand again.

Sally felt the delight wash over her and she longed to lean into the lamplight and smile adoringly into his eyes. My wife! For twenty-four hours she had been just that. Adam Cooper's wife and now, at this precise moment, she had the feeling that he was glad about it. That remote, forbidding man she had quarrelled with this morning had disappeared, leaving behind one with warmth and humour and – dare she say it? – admiration for Sally Grimshaw.

Reluctantly she let go of his hand. She took up the serving spoon which Henton had laid ceremoniously beside the dish, the rich smell of damson and plum, raspberries and blackberries drifting from the pudding with its steam as she cut into it. Spooning the juices and a vast amount of cream on to his plate, since she was still of the opinion that her husband was far too thin, she passed it to him, feeling, with this small domestic task, for the first time as though she were serving him as a wife should serve her husband.

When he was eating with evident relish she cupped her face in her hands and watched him.

"What about you?" he said, looking up at her, "aren't you having any?"

"I'm not hungry. Tell me about my duties as your wife."

"Well," he said, licking cream from his spoon with great care, "there's me."

"You?" Her heart began to warm deliciously.

He grinned. "I shall need food like this at every meal from now on and you must see that our new cook, when you find her, can make summer pudding as well as you."

"No one can do that," she said, meaning it.

"I'm sure of that, but you will do your best with her, won't you?"

"Yes, what else?"

"There are the girls."

"Of course."

"I want you to help me to turn them into . . . hoydens."

"Hoydens?" She leaned back and clasped her hands together at her lips.

"Yes, tomboys who will race round the garden and play games like tig and leapfrog and the Chimes. They will go to school and learn something other than sewing and singing. In fact they will become little Sally Grimshaws."

"Oh, Adam."

"And then there is . . ."

"Yes?"

"Do you particularly want coffee?"

"Pardon?"

"If not, come upstairs and I'll show you what else there is. My needs are many and varied, lovely girl, and your job is to find out what they are and satisfy them."

"Naturally," she said breathlessly, "it's a wife's duty."

"Indeed."

At the back of her bemused mind she was well aware that Adam was doing his best to divert her thoughts away from Job who was at this moment incarcerated in Kirkdale gaol. He was teasing her, making her smile, making her dizzy with his nearness, making her flustered and flushed as the meaning of his words became clear. And yet it was in his narrowed eyes too. What she thought might be desire perhaps, an anticipation, an excitement which matched her own. It told her that her husband was not totally oblivious to her charms. She leaned into the lamplight and the front of her bodice dipped slightly, revealing the tops of her breasts. She was amazed at herself, for she knew she had done so deliberately. She, Sally Grimshaw, who had never tantalised any man by showing an inch of her flesh, and what's more despised women who did.

He leaned forward, bending his head and placed his

warm lips on her breast. Taking her hand in his he drew her from her chair, across the room, up the stairs and into their bedroom, closing the door firmly behind them.

The servants were dumbfounded. After all it was only eight thirty!

The next morning they drove together down to the crown court in Chapel Street where Job had apparently been transferred. The splendid maroon-coloured carriage was pulled by the two glossy black horses whose coats were polished to the sheen of wet coal. On the box Alec was just as magnificent in his navy blue velvet livery and cockaded top hat. The coat he wore was braided in gold at its edges, as was his waistcoat and knee-length trousers. Gold buttons bristled down the front of the coat and his epaulettes were as fine as any general's. His black boots had been polished by young Tom who had been told by Alec he wanted to be able to see his face in them.

All this splendour, all this finery, all the magnificence of Coopers Edge had been purchased with Oralie Cooper's money by Oralie herself when she came to the house as a young bride, and before she and her husband had set sail for India. Some of the servants, including Alec, had been newly employed by her and in the twelve years since nothing had been changed. Everything she had put in place still continued and if Adam had considered it at all, it seemed it had not occurred to him to alter anything.

Adam's lawyer, a competent and expensive gentleman by the name of Ernest Saunders, had, when Sally and Adam arrived, already arranged for the charged man, Job Hawthorne, to be released into the custody of Captain Adam Cooper who was to guarantee his presence at his trial which would take place next month.

Job stood impassively by Mr Saunders's side, crumpled

and unshaven since he had spent the night in a cell with several other prisoners. They had not interfered with him, despite his good clothes. It would take a brave or foolish man to tackle Job Hawthorne, despite his age. He smiled gently at Sally and nodded respectfully at Adam.

The crown court was used as a police court when it was not occupied at sessions or the assizes. It was here that the magistrate, presiding for the daily hearing of disorderly cases and the preliminary examination of persons in custody for graver offences, such as Job, had made his decision. There were barristers in wigs, clerks of the court and sundry persons jostling one another on the steps and further up Chapel Street, at another entrance, a gaol waggon was debouching more prisoners from Kirkdale prison to be tried.

Oh yes, Mr Saunders said, unfortunately there would have to be a trial since the accuser, one Mr Richard Keene, had produced evidence. What? A doctor's note and the presence of a witness at the time of the attack. Who? One Mary Clarke, barmaid, who said she saw Mr Hawthorne go for Mr Keene in August of this year.

"But Job was only defending me, Mr Saunders," Sally protested hotly. "And besides which, why has it taken him so long to bring this charge? It happened two months ago."

Mr Saunders turned with exquisite politeness to Mrs Cooper, for after all Captain Cooper was a very wealthy and therefore influential man in Liverpool which was probably why this chap of his had been released on bail. Most men of Hawthorne's class, charged with assault, particularly against a gentleman, could fester for months in an overcrowded gaol until his trial came up for all anyone cared. Job Hawthorne was lucky to have such a sponsor.

"Mr Keene states that initially he was so cruelly beaten he had not the strength to start proceedings against

Mr Hawthorne. Then, when he had recovered enough to go to the police, Mr Hawthorne could not be found. It was not until you, Mrs Cooper, married the captain a few days ago that Mr Hawthorne was located."

"What utter rubbish." Mr Saunders blinked as Sally drew herself up and gave him the the full benefit of her Grimshaw Arms glare. Mr Saunders was not intimidated though he did admit to himself that the plain, plainly dressed young woman the captain had married certainly improved with a bit of vitality in her. Mind you, there was a certain . . . rosy look about her. A look, being a sensualist himself, he recognised. Her lips were pink and swollen, bee-stung, he believed the expression was, and was that what was known as a "love-bite" just inside the high standing collar of her blouse? Still waters can run very deep, it seemed.

"What makes you say that, Mrs Cooper?" he asked mildly, moving to one side of the wide, shallow steps which led down into Chapel Street, drawing her with him out of the path of the multitude who poured in and out of the building. It seemed crime was very brisk that morning.

"Because I was there, Mr Saunders. Mr Hawthorne did . . . restrain Mr Keene, probably quite forcibly" – remembering Job's ear in her mouth and the taste of his blood – "but he certainly did not beat him. I would be glad of a look at this document which his doctor has provided, and a word with Mary Clarke who has the brain of a pea-hen attached to the body of a bull. She saw nothing."

"Mrs Cooper, do forgive me, but it is the judge you need to convince, not me. I am here to defend Mr Hawthorne."

"Yes, Sally. Mr Saunders has done all he can for the moment so let's get Job home. You will have your say next month." Adam took her arm but it seemed she was of the opinion that if she could just convince Mr Saunders of

Job's innocence, they could all go home, with this nonsense cleared up right here and now. She twitched her arm from Adam's grasp and he sighed wearily. None of them noticed Richard Keene lurking in the shadows of one of the many pillars which decorated the front of the building. It was evident from the expression on his foxy face that something had badly upset him. His mouth was drawn into a thin line of venom and in his eyes lurked a menace which might have alarmed Sally Cooper and even Job Hawthorne, who was afraid of no one, on his own behalf, that is.

He watched them move slowly down the steps, catching a word here and there above the racket which echoed about the court house. He could barely contain his loathing as he saw the lawyer, after shaking hands with the lunatic who had married Sally Grimshaw, hail a hansom cab and drive off in it. He watched with ill-concealed antipathy as the captain, God rot his soul, handed his wife into his own magnificent equipage, climbed in himself and then did his best to persuade that oaf, whom Richard Keene had expected to see behind bars again before the end of the day, to climb in with them. There seemed to be some argument then he distinctly heard the clear voice of the woman he hated above all others over the commotion of the street.

"Oh, get in, Job, for God's sake. You cannot go home alone."

The oaf murmured something and again Sally Grimshaw's voice rose.

"Don't you realise that you have been placed in Captain Cooper's custody. You are not allowed to wander about Liverpool by yourself until the trial is over. The captain has guaranteed to the court that . . ."

An enormous beer waggon lumbered past, the hooves

of the shire horses which pulled it making an ear-splitting clatter on the cobblestones, drowning out the bitch's words. The oaf climbed in, the door of the carriage banged to and it drove off.

Slowly he moved down the steps, the acrimony in him so great, his eyes so dangerous with it, several men moved hastily out of his path. He did not see them. All he could see was that bitch's face, across which passed the many expressions he had seen there in the six months she had worked for him. She had the sort of face that revealed exactly what was in her thoughts. Sally Grimshaw had had no need in the years she had been the virtual master of the Grimshaw Arms to hide what she thought of any man. She was always polite, of course, providing she received politeness, but if she thought you were a fool, a half-wit, a numbskull, a barbarian, vulgar and mannerless, it was there on her face to see. Her manner towards him had been derisive though she was careful not to speak out of turn. Nevertheless he had known she had considered him not worth a moment of her time.

But she had made him a lot of money and he had had to put up with it and, given an hour to pull himself together after the incident, as the police called it, would have called her back, perhaps even apologised, tongue in cheek, of course, waiting for an opportunity to catch her again when the oaf was out of the way, permanently. Keep her on as manager of the inn which had proved to be a little gold mine for him.

It was not that now. In the two months since Sally Grimshaw had left, Mary Clarke, plus the barmaid and cellarman Richard Keene had been forced to employ to run the place, had let it all slip away to nothing. Customers, used to good, simple meals, a decent glass of ale, value for their money, cleanliness and comfort, which had gone with Sally Grimshaw, had drifted away to the Bull in Knotty Ash, the Masons Arms in Old Swan or even as far as the Plough which was a good walk after a day's work.

And the strange thing was, he really didn't know why he had been so eager to get into Sally Grimshaw's prim drawers. She wasn't a looker, that was for sure, but there was something about her . . . a sort of . . . heat. Was that it, or was it simply that she was a challenge to him? That hair of hers, for a start, was something he would like to sink his hands into and those ripe breasts – smaller now, he had noticed – above the tiny handspan of her waist had driven him wild.

But, dear God, he hated her. May she rot in hell and that hulk of a man with her. He had known he could do nothing to get at her, not now she was the wife of a prominent citizen like Cooper but he could hurt her through Job Hawthorne. There had been something between those two . . . oh, not physical, he would swear to that, but a bond which had baffled and nauseated him. If he could vent his hatred on the big man then he would avenge himself on Sally Grimshaw. Now he would have to wait until next month to see if his plan came to fruition. He had been jubilant at the thought of Hawthorne rotting in Kirkdale gaol this very night and perhaps for several years to come, but now it seemed the whole thing might come a cropper. That bloody, silver-tongued lawyer of Cooper's had won the judge round. The old sod had probably been a friend of Cooper's, for weren't the gentry hand in glove with one another, returning favour for favour!

A month later, as he gave his own evidence, as the barrister he had hired questioned first the doctor who had been persuaded that a bruise or two on his client's throat constituted grounds for a conviction, as the barrister did his best to elicit from a terrified Mary Clarke what exactly she had seen on the night in question, which seemed to be nothing, Richard Keene knew he was beaten.

Mrs Adam Cooper stood up calmly in court, dressed very elegantly in what was evidently a new outfit and in a clear voice told the hushed and titillated jury of men exactly what Richard Keene had tried to do to her, a defenceless woman who had at the time been forced to earn her own living. The accused, Job Hawthorne, had done nothing that any decent man would not do, she told them, her lovely eyes letting them know that she believed they would have done the same. Most nodded their heads and again Richard Keene knew he was defeated.

His barrister was quite specific in his belief that Keene was lucky not to have a charge made against *him* by Mrs Adam Cooper and his advice was to get out of town as soon as possible.

He did, leaving on a train for London where a man might hide for years but not until he had knelt silently at the gates of Coopers Edge and vowed, like a man before an altar, that one day he would come back and no matter how long it took he would drag Sally Grimshaw into the foulness of his revenge.

17

It was in December that Sally knew she was pregnant and it was in December when she heard the child crying.

They had been satisfying weeks, those that followed the trial, and Sally had taken up the challenge of her new life with the vigorous determination she had shown since she was a small girl at her mother's side. She had advertised for, and found a cook who, she believed, would meet her own high standards. Mrs Trimble, a plain-spoken woman in her early forties, had worked for the last ten years in the household of a landed gentleman in Warwickshire, she told Sally. But she was a North Country woman, born in the village of Skelmersdale where she had gone into service at the age of thirteen, and she'd a hankering to come back to her roots.

She had been lucky, she told Mrs Cooper, for the cook where she'd first worked as a scullery maid had taken a shine to her.

"Well, I were always a beggar for work, madam, right from being a nipper, and she liked that."

Sally liked it too! "I worked me way up to kitchen maid. She taught me everything she knew and when she retired I were offered her job. But I'd itchy feet. I'd never known anywhere but Skem – that's what we call Skelmersdale – and I wanted to see a bit of the world. I were only a young lass, you see, so when I were offered a post down south I took it. I've had three jobs, counting the first and at each one I spent nearly ten years, leaving of me own accord. I were married once, to the gamekeeper on the estate but when he died in an accident I moved on. I'm a good cook, madam," she said simply, with no intent to boast.

"I am a demanding mistress, Mrs Trimble, with high standards," Sally told her. "I'm a good cook myself."

If Mrs Trimble was surprised by this admission from the lady of the house she did not show it. She sat on the sofa opposite Sally, just as straight-backed, not imperious by any means but with a quiet dignity which said she knew her own worth.

"Really, madam?" was all she said.

"Yes, I ran an inn for many years before I married." Sally saw no reason to hide her humble beginnings from this woman who, the moment she set foot in the kitchen, would be told of them anyway.

Mrs Trimble took up her duties the next week, she and her mistress making a most satisfactory pact that it was to be on a month's trial. The month came and went without being mentioned, as both of them, recognising what was in the other, had known from the first that it would. Mrs Trimble, Sally had to admit, if only to Job, was a better cook than she was.

Adam was very keen to initiate Sally into the joys of horse riding and had bought her a dainty sorrel mare whom Sally had called Flame. Sally was to have made for her a proper riding habit, her husband told her, and as soon as it was ready Jimmy would begin her lessons. In the meanwhile she was to go with him to the stables and make friends with the mare. It wouldn't hurt to walk with her into Near Paddock, under Jimmy's supervision, naturally. Adam rode every day, going off with enormous dash and vigour from the stable yard, across the paddock and into the great stretches of parkland which surrounded Coopers Edge. He would ride for an hour or two, inspecting his land, discussing crops and the weather with Albert Lord who ran the Home Farm on the far side of the estate. He would inspect the cottages in which the farm workers and other labourers on his land lived and talk to the man whose job it was to look after his game and keep down the vermin which threatened it. He had pheasants in what was known as Pheasant Clump, woodcock, grey partridge and wood pigeon in a covert which ran round the inside of the high walls surrounding the perimeter of his estate and with an old army friend or two, he told Sally, liked to shoot in season.

He took very seriously his responsibility to his land and those who worked it for him, spending time in what he called his estate office where he was available to any man who wished to discuss something with him, to receive reports, attend to the accounts and to pay their wages.

His job, apart from being outside instead of inside, was exactly like hers, she said, and he agreed with her.

Sally often talked to Job for ten minutes or so if he was about on one of her walks. Not with Flame but on her own, taking the path through the thinning, shadowy woodland, or across the vastness of the rolling parkland where shy deer grazed. Job was taciturn, barely stopping whatever task he was at but she, who knew him well, was aware that he was glad to see her.

On one occasion she had spied him talking to Tilly by the corner of the laundry building which was situated near the stables. An enormous line of laundered sheets had just been hung out in the special walled garden which was planted with lavender and rosemary to scent the linen and garments which were put out on a fine day by Mary, one of the laundry maids. Tilly had no business being there since she was not a laundry maid but Sally had turned away, glad that someone in this great house of servants appeared to like Job Hawthorne. He was smiling as he bent his head to listen to Tilly who, Sally was aware, could talk the hind leg off a donkey which was just as well since Job had nothing much to say for himself.

He was often to be found alongside Dicky, the carpenter, repairing walls and footpaths, making fences and gates, reroofing cottages or fashioning some article of furniture, a chair or a plain deal table, for one of the cottagers. He was a man of many trades, turning his hand to most things he was asked for and Sally knew he was content.

Later that day, when she came across him clipping the hedge which surrounded the ice-house, she was careful not to embarrass him as she brought up the subject of Tilly.

"You're settled now, Job?" she asked him, idling along behind him as his shears continued to click. "Comfortable in that room of yours above the coach house?"

"Aye, Miss Sally, I'm well settled."

"So am I, Job." He stopped and gave her one of his rare and attractive smiles.

"I can see that, Miss Sally." You look a picture, he wanted to say, in your love for the man who is your husband. He had recognised it in her, for was he not himself a man who loved. He had been glad for her, glad she was safe at last from that bastard who had tried to get Job into trouble with the law. If it hadn't been for Captain Cooper Job was sure he himself would be mouldering in Kirkdale prison right now, with a sentence of at least two years' hard labour. He would never be able to thank him for what he had done, for both of them, though he had been dumbfounded when the captain had married Miss Sally. Not that Miss Sally was not worth marrying, but housekeeper was what Job had hoped for. Wife was better though, even if it did break Job's heart in two.

"Don't you ever get lonely, Job?" she asked him artlessly and he bent his head to hide his smile since he knew where this was leading. She'd seen him with Tilly from the kitchen who, though he couldn't think why for she was a comely young lass, seemed to single him out despite his years and battered face.

"Not really, Miss Sally. I'm too busy to be lonely an' glad of it an' all."

"But what about the evening?" picturing him alone in his lonely room above the coach house.

"Oh, I have a game of dominoes with Dicky, or cards with the stable lads."

She was surprised. "Do you really? I didn't know."

"Well, you wouldn't, Miss Sally. You're the master's wife and have nowt to do with the outdoor staff."

"You're not just outdoor staff, Job. You're my friend and I don't know what I would have done without you."

"Nay, Miss Sally, give over, do. An' you're not to bother about me. I'm as happy as a pig in muck." He turned then and winked, startling her. "An' that Tilly's a right bonny lass even if she's a gob on her like the Woodhead tunnel."

Sally smiled. "I'm glad for you, Job," she said softly, putting a hand on his arm but he turned away abruptly. Miss Sally talking to him was one thing. Miss Sally touching him was another.

By now the house was immaculately polished, deep-scoured and scrubbed as once the Grimshaw Arms had been. Along with Mrs Trimble, Sally had taken on another housemaid to help with the extra cleaning she considered necessary. She was called Hilda and she brought the number of maids, counting Mary and Doris in the laundry and Annie and Jane in the dairy, up to eleven. There was a nurserymaid upstairs, and had been for six years, Mrs Chidlow had told Sally, whose name was Lucy. She helped Nanny in the nursery, though Sally often wondered what the dickens they did up there all day long, for Leila and Aisha were for the most part in the schoolroom with Miss Digby. When Sally had brought back order and efficiency to the housemaids, the dairy maids, the laundry maids and specified what their exact duties were to be and they were doing it to her satisfaction, she meant to make it her business, with her usual vigour and hatred of slackers, to find out exactly what Lucy did. Nanny was an old crone who was entitled to be left to finish out her days in peace but Lucy was no more than twenty or so and could be found other work to justify her wages.

After Christmas Leila and Aisha were to attend daily the High School in Mount Street, much to their own apprehension and Nanny Mottram's absolute horror, for who knew what kind of girl they might meet there and what kind of diseases those girls, who she was convinced would be of the lower orders, might pass on to her charges. She had wielded great influence over them for nine years now and before that, Miss Oralie, their mama, and she could see it becoming eroded by this new situation which she was sure was down to Captain Cooper's second wife.

In the weeks following their wedding Sally and Adam had enjoyed a great deal of mutual well-being in what she knew was a marriage of convenience, at least to Adam. His home ran smoothly. Every room was warm and comfortable. Fires were laid and lit every morning where fires should be, even if no one sat by them. Hot water and warm towels were in constant supply. The housemaids, even Cissie, who had all been told in no uncertain manner what was expected of them, did it efficiently and on time. Henton received callers, the few who came, so far only Violet and Arthur and Freddy with his pregnant wife. Meals were splendidly cooked and served punctually. Beds were aired, linen immaculately laundered and pressed. Sally had set the wheels in motion as she had been trained to do and they ran with silently efficient and well-oiled professionalism. The accounts were in her hands, the menus and guest lists – which had not yet been used – studied and discussed each day with Mrs Trimble, and though it was Henton's job to see to the wines and spirits, Sally made it her business to check the wine cellar when he least expected it. From his pantry he would oversee the cleaning of the silverware, including the cutlery. Tipper, the footman, helped to wait at table and looked after the fires and lamps which had to be filled and lit every day.

Mrs Chidlow was Sally's only failure and she supposed that was *her* fault. After all she was doing Mrs Chidlow's job as she ordered provisions, kept the accounts, checked on the women servants, overlooked the linen cupboards, the stillroom where preserves and cordial from the garden produce were made and generally made Mrs Chidlow redundant.

She had even, to her own surprise, become quite fond of Trixie and Bess since it had always been her opinion that dogs were messy creatures who brought in God alone knew what on their paws. They trailed everywhere at Adam's heels, everywhere except the bedroom and even then they curled up at the bottom of the stairs until he brought them to life by coming down them again. When he was riding they raced behind Harry, in danger of being clipped by the bay's hooves, their ears back, their rough coats whipped by the movement of this passage into a ripple of reddish brown. They treated her in a friendly if slightly offhand manner, their total devotion given to the man who was their master. Though they were only nine months old they made it plain he was the only thing that mattered in their lives.

Sally knew how they felt!

But it was in their bedroom where, each night, they made love with increasing ardour and satisfaction, that Sally was most truly happy. He was hers there, hers alone, his body rousing to hers with a male rapture and delight she found utterly satisfying, then, afterwards, falling asleep together with their boneless bodies wrapped in bonds of endless, depthless peace.

It would begin in the lamplight and fireglow, an incandescence which turned their naked bodies to honeyed gold as they explored one another with minute attention as though not a square inch of flesh must be overlooked. Adam's body was to Sally a miracle of male beauty lovingly put together with long graceful bones and flat muscles which flowed smoothly from the curve of his chest and shoulders to the slight concavity of his belly and thighs. His penis flaunted from a thicket of dark hair at his loins and from there the smooth line of muscle from his hip to his knee rippled. He had long, slender feet with high arches and when she kissed their soles he jerked and groaned in delight.

He bore the livid scar down from the back of his neck to his elbow given him by the Russian sabre on the Crimean Peninsula and she kissed that too, smiling with him at the play of "making it better". He was no longer the emaciated survivor she had first seen almost a year ago and her love for him grew inside her like the child she knew she was carrying. She had not told him yet, for it was in her mind that he might put a stop to this magic they wove together each night. She didn't know. She didn't know anything about childbearing or if, being pregnant, this . . . this diversion they undertook so joyfully at least once a day might be harmful. Perhaps it was but she couldn't bear to give it up. She knew, as she sat astride him, her hair about them both in a cloud, with him deep inside her, his hands at her breasts, that she must have this and this and this for just a little while longer since they had been married such a short time.

But dare she chance harming the child they had made? *His* child. *Their* child who would surely be dear to Adam if not to her. She had no conception of how she would feel about it but she hadn't the right to harm it, had she, for the sake of her own pleasure?

"I have a Christmas present for you, Adam," she told him gravely on Christmas morning, sitting up in bed with her naked breasts, rich as cream tipped in rose, already fuller, peeping through the fall of her hair. They had made love and it tumbled in a silken confusion of curls about her.

He lay beside her on his back. He groaned, his arm across his eyes.

"You have just given me one, lovely girl. I don't think I'm up to another. Give me five minutes though." She watched as his mouth twitched into a grin.

"No, this . . . this, I hope, is special."

"What we have just done was special, lovely girl," but something in the tone of her voice caught his attention and he lowered his arm, looking up at her. He sat up and the sheet fell away from them both but this time he made no move to touch her.

"What is it, Sally?" He put a finger to her chin and turned her face to look at him.

She sighed deeply as though in desolate sadness and his

heart twisted painfully, frighteningly. This woman had, in a few short weeks, brought him peace, and peace of mind. Comfort he had not dreamed of and a delight in their bed which he had never . . . *never* before experienced. Not even with Oralie in the first passionate weeks of their marriage. And she asked nothing of him. She gave and gave, which was her nature, he knew that now, the nature of a home-maker, which, despite being called an inn, she had made of the Grimshaw Arms. Now she was troubled and he found he had an urgent desire to take her troubles from her. Pile them on his own shoulders since hers were so fragile, or so it seemed in the pale light of the winter morning. Little bit of a thing she was and yet she tackled jobs, and people who might intimidate another. Brave as a lion with a courage and will that never failed to amaze him. His regard for his new wife knew no bounds and he meant to tell her so with the magnificent gift he had bought her for Christmas.

"Well, it seems . . ."

"What, for God's sake? What is it?"

"I'm . . . to have a child," she mumbled, dipping her head in what appeared to be embarrassment.

"What!"

"I'm . . ." but she had no need to go on as he gathered her up in his eager, enchanted arms and began to kiss her, scattering them from her hairline in tiny butterflies right down to her knees and back again.

"Oh, Adam . . ." She began to laugh, clutching at his head in an effort to bring it up to where she could see his face.

"Oh, Sally . . . my lovely girl . . . my lovely, lovely girl," was all he could gasp and she swore there were tears in his eyes.

"You're . . . you're pleased then?"

"Jesus Christ . . . *pleased*!"

"Don't blaspheme, Adam," she told him primly, in the manner of the old Sally Grimshaw, but he held her and rocked her and beamed at her and she knew it was all right.

"There's just one thing," she said breathlessly when she could free her mouth from his kisses.

"What?" He raised his head and gazed at her warily.

"Should we be . . . well . . ." She blinked and blushed a little.

"What, for Christ's sake?"

"There you go again, Adam Cooper, you know I can't abide . . ."

"If you don't tell me what it is I'll throttle you, Sally Cooper."

"Well, should we be making love with one another?"

He became still then, his expression hard to read but in his eyes was a blue warmth which, had she recognised it, would have filled her with joy.

"Is that how you see it, Sally?" he said at last.

"Well . . . isn't that right?"

"It's exactly right. Most men believe that they make love *to* a woman, and most women would say the same, as though they were not equals but you, my lovely girl, know exactly how it is. We make love with one another and we shall continue to do so for as long as it is physically possible, bearing in mind how enormous that belly of yours will become. Bugger the infant. He or she will have to put up with it."

It was a day of utmost perfection. Wherever she was and whatever she was doing she was conscious of Adam's eyes on her, warm with approval and something else which she liked but was not sure of.

She had insisted that Leila and Aisha should spend the whole day with them. Just as she had insisted a week ago that they should help her to decorate the Christmas tree, the tree of love the husband of their dear queen had introduced.

The first step had been to wrest them from Miss Digby's stiff-faced grasp, bundle them up in warm coats and take them, startled as young fawns, into the wood known as the Old Wood. Job had been roped in to go with them and bring the small dog cart pulled by the mowing pony.

"We want lots of evergreen, girls," she had called out as they trailed hesitantly behind her. "And mistletoe. Do you know what mistletoe is?"

"No, miss . . ."

"My name is Sally. I have told you and told you so. Repeat it if you please."

"S . . . Sally," they quavered and Sally could feel Job's smile at her back. Well, she had to get them out of this carapace of lady-like behaviour somehow, hadn't she?

"Now, that's holly which I'm sure you've heard of but we want some with lots of red berries. A big bunch, please, Job. No, more than that. Good, you help him, Aisha, and some ivy. Oh, and laurel as well. Mr Reuben has done us several pots of Christmas roses which will look grand on the table in the dining-room but first we must find exactly the right fir tree for Job to cut down. What d'you think?" indicating with a dramatic sweep of her hand the trees that were available to them. "Job will put it up in the hall and then the three of us will decorate it. I've found some lovely stuff in the attic, things to hang on the tree but I shall need your help. They were a bit dusty."

Things! Attic! Dusty! It was as though they were two little creatures from an alien planet who for the life of them could make neither head nor tail of this new and forceful stepmama of theirs.

They had been awkward then and they were awkward now, glancing continuously at their father, who apparently alarmed them enormously. But somehow, probably because of her own great happiness and the feeling that she was a cat basking in a shaft of unexpected and sublime sunshine, she began to draw them ever so slightly from their well-mannered shell of reserve. She had gone to great trouble to buy them something completely frivolous for their Christmas gifts, something to make them laugh, if such a thing was possible. She had seen their samplers, exquisite things, framed and set on the nursery wall. GLORY BE TO GOD with the message AISHA COOPER IS MY NAME after it and the date MAY 1852. Leila's had been even more intricate with every letter of the alphabet in tiny cross-stitch upon it, with birds and flowers and her name and the date. Had these children ever been children? she wondered, remembering another little girl whose delight it had been to make a batch of bread, knock up a few scones then scrub the kitchen floor because flour had been spilled on it.

Sally, to please her husband, had commissioned the Misses Yeoland in Bold Street, who were known to be very clever, very fashionable and very expensive, to make her a gown for Christmas Day. It, and the one she had worn to the assizes, were the first gowns she had ordered since she had become Mrs Adam Cooper and she was startled by the fuss that was made of her in the salon. Her Christmas gown was of rich satin, corn-coloured, with a sheen to it that turned it to gold. The neck was cut low and square revealing the upper curve of her breasts. It was perfectly plain with huge, puffed, elbow-length sleeves and a full skirt, and suited her figure and colouring to perfection as

Miss Gladys Yeoland had said it would. Adam's eyes told her he agreed. She had allowed Tilly, who had ambitions to be a lady's maid and was clever at such things, Mrs Trimble had privately told Sally, to dress her hair. It was piled high on top of her head in a loose tumble of curls threaded with gold satin ribbon. She looked taller, younger, quite . . . frivolous, in fact, she thought, and Tilly was entranced.

"Oh, madam, you look grand. You've such lovely hair and so much of it, an' all, with no need of tongs or curling papers. See, with them curls hanging here an' here, well, you look a proper picture."

"Oh, get away with you, Tilly." Sally tutted as though with impatience but secretly she was pleased and even sneaked another look at her new self in the mirror before she went down to join Adam. She was discovering that there was nothing she wouldn't do to keep her husband looking at her as he had begun to do quite recently.

The presents were opened after – in Adam's words – the best Christmas dinner he had ever eaten and if he wasn't already taken he'd marry Mrs Trimble tomorrow. Even the girls had smiled shyly, relishing not only the good food but recognising the joke.

The gaily wrapped gifts were heaped beneath the Christmas tree at the foot of the stairs. Dozens of them, for Sally meant this to be a beginning, a day Leila and Aisha would always look back on and remember as the start of their life as a family, a family which was already starting to grow, her hand to her belly.

"Now then, this is for you, Leila, and this one's for Aisha. Oh, and another, and another . . . and this is for your papa. Will you take it to him, Aisha . . . and this one seems to be for me."

Adam stood, one elbow on the mantelpiece, a cigar

between his teeth, a glass of brandy in his hand. He was smiling, relaxed, the personification of a man replete and satisfied with his lot.

"You may open your presents, girls," Sally told them encouragingly, since they seemed inclined to stand about, arms full and overflowing as though they were not at all sure what was expected of them. They had already exchanged the usual Christmas gifts in the nursery with Nanny and Miss Digby and Lucy. Handkerchiefs, a handknitted scarf apiece, new stockings and several books of an edifying nature.

But these were not of that sort at all. There were spinning tops and skipping ropes, a "diablo" apiece, a ball and stick, the ball with a small hole in it which, when thrown, should be caught on the pointed stick. There were paints and colouring books, "Knucklebones" which were to be thrown in the air and then caught, as many as possible, on the back of the hand. There were hoops and beautiful sets of marbles made of glass with swirls of colour inside and two exquisite and exquisitely dressed dolls. There was for each of them the prettiest necklace, bracelet, brooch and earrings to match, made from pale flushed coral, suitable for young girls, and tiny but elegantly filigreed scent bottles filled with lavender water. Enough to delight the most exacting child. Enough to delight the heart of a young girl growing up.

For an hour Sally and Adam watched them as, tentatively at first, the two little girls opened and displayed the treasures within each glitteringly wrapped parcel. They were overwhelmed at first, ready to gaze in awe, to touch reverently, speechless with wonder, turning again and again to Sally and their papa as though they could not believe that all this was from them, as though they did not know what all this was! They were both beautifully dressed. They had never gone hungry. They had lacked for nothing in their lives, cosseted and protected from anything that might offend or alarm them and yet they were, in a sense, as deprived as many a child from the gutters of the slums. They did not know they were deprived, for their lives were safe, bland and uneventful as one of their daily walks with Miss Digby, with nothing of frivolity, light-heartedness, silliness, child-like naughtiness in it.

For a while it looked as though it would be too much for them, then, suddenly, the first excitement they had ever known, or at least remembered, struck them a happy blow. They became flushed and rosy, laughing as children should when Sally tried to show them how the spinning top worked and to explain what to do with marbles, doing her best to remember, since Freddy had once owned some.

The two terriers, clearly amazed since they had never seen anything like it in their short lives and, being young dogs, still puppies really, became as over-excited as the children, nosing and chewing the torn wrapping paper with great enjoyment. They ran after the marbles which whizzed across the carpet, making everyone laugh, their own faces comical as though they could not understand this new phenomenon which had come into their lives. They did not know it was called "fun".

And neither did the girls. They exclaimed over the dolls, peeping under the silk ruffles of their skirts at their lace-trimmed drawers and giggling at their own daring. They helped one another to put on their necklaces and bracelets and were filled with excited alarm when their stepmama explained they would have to have their ears pierced to wear the earrings.

"Will it hurt, Sally?" Aisha whispered, leaning trustingly at Sally's knee, looking with wondering eyes at Sally's own simple gold ear-bobs which hung from her lobes and the tiny holes which pierced them.

"Only for the tiniest bit of a second, sweetheart.'

Aisha cradled her doll to her, her eyes filled with this wonderful person who had called her "sweetheart', then, with a verve which Henton was to describe as "quite disorderly" to the rest of the amazed staff who were eating their own Christmas dinner in the servants hall, rushed with her sister to the conservatory where they engaged in a mad game of "whip and top" on the polished tiled floor.

"Never!" Cissie gasped. "And didn't the mistress have anything to say about it? What if them tops had scuffed the tiles." Cissie still harboured a small pocket of resentment towards her new mistress who seemed not to care about Cissie's own standing in the hierarchy of the servants and saw no reason why the head parlourmaid should not turn her hand to anything the mistress thought fit, including polishing the windows or cleaning out a grate.

Sally would not have minded in the least had she seen the little girls playing hopscotch, or even a hectic game of rubgy football across the glossy tiles of the "winter garden", as Adam still called it. Her attention was fixed with an icy breathlessness on her husband and she had no interest in his children. He had turned away from the excited chatter of his daughters and the rich happiness of his wife and, believing himself to be alone, was looking up at the portrait of Oralie Cooper which still hung on the wall above the mantelshelf. Though Sally saw it, *really* saw it every day, she was still mesmerised by the slumbrous and exotic beauty of Adam's first wife. The grey velvet of her eyes which seemed to promise a sharing in something only she possessed. The white skin, almost transparent without a hint of colour in it and as smooth as a pearl. The hair, glossy and tumbled carelessly about her shoulders, the exact shade of dark red wine and the full, rosy mouth, slightly parted in what seemed to be a mocking smile to reveal perfect white teeth. In the conservatory Oralie's two daughters, such exact replicas of her it was uncanny, shrieked in a most unladylike way as they whipped their new tops into a frenzy of noise and colour.

Sally didn't hear them and if she had would not have cared. It was their father who was hammering spikes into her heart. He was standing, hands thrust deep in his trouser pockets, his brandy glass and half-smoked cigar neglected on the mantelshelf. His head was tilted back as he stared at the portrait of Oralie Cooper and on his face was a look of such haunting sadness Sally felt the light go from her day. He had not seen her come back from the conservatory where she had gone for a moment to check, at Aisha's insistence, on the smooth running of the spinning tops and she stood, transfixed and devastated at the image of the husband she loved above all else in her life, locked in the misery of his loss. The loss of the woman who had been Sally's predecessor. A woman long dead but still alive to the man who, it seemed, would continue to love her for ever.

She must have made some small sound, for he turned and his face became alive again with warmth. He held out his hand and she moved slowly towards him and took it.

He sensed the change in her and at once he was overcome with concern and the thought was in her head before she could stop it. It would not do for the woman who was to bear his child, perhaps his son, to be upset in any way on Christmas Day.

The coldness settled about her heart.

"What is it?" he asked her, his tenderness genuine.

"Nothing, a ghost walked over my grave."

"Never mind ghosts. Aren't you going to open my gift? You can give me yours later, much later," and he gave her a wicked wink.

It was the most beautiful thing she had ever seen. A long, delicate link of intricate gold chain in which was set at one-inch intervals, a perfect golden topaz. The dozens of links of the chain were decorated with small diamonds, each one perfectly matched. It meant nothing to Sally now.

"I cheated," he said as he watched her lift the necklace out of the velvet-lined box. "I begged Miss Yeoland for a snippet of fabric from your gown and then had the jeweller match it. And of course, the gems are the same shade as your eyes. Don't you think you have a clever husband?"

"Indeed I do, and it's beautiful. Thank you, Adam."

The children had gone to bed and, pleading tiredness which she was aware surprised her husband as much as her impassive acceptance of his gift, she made her way slowly up the wide staircase to the first floor. She had no idea why she should feel as she did. She had known that Adam loved and would always love Oralie. She had accepted it from the first. She, Sally Grimshaw, was his housekeeper and the fact that she shared his bed and was to bear his child changed nothing. She must not become entrenched in this . . . this feeling she sometimes sensed in him that seemed to speak of something stronger than friendship. He was a kind man who was doing his best to help her to settle into her new surroundings, her new *job*, her new life, and that was all. But it was hard, especially after . . .

Just beyond her bedroom door lay the stairs to the nursery floor and the schoolroom. They were dark stairs and narrow, carpeted in a plain drugget and she remembered wondering why. Out of the darkness came a sound, a sound which, though it was stifled, was distinctly recognisable as that of a child crying.

Lifting the hem of her beautiful new dress, Sally began to climb the stairs.

18

"I will have those women out of this house first thing tomorrow morning. The old one can be found a . . . a cottage or something on the estate but if that governess imagines she will get a character reference from me after this, then she is sadly mistaken. How could anyone be so cruel, so thoughtless and on a day when love in the shape of gifts is supposed to be exchanged? Dear God, you'd think the child had committed some dreadful crime and it wasn't even her doing. I'm to blame, me . . . I'm the one who excited her with all those presents and encouraged her to drink gallons of Mrs Trimble's lemonade."

"Sally . . . Sally, will you calm down and tell me what all this is about?"

"How could we have let this happen to them? I'm not . . . not overfond of children, Adam, but I would not allow those two dogs of yours to be treated as . . ." Her voice stuttered as Sally flung herself from one end of the drawing-room to the other, the skirt of her lovely gown swinging like a bell. Adam had noticed this about her before; when she was incensed about something as she was now she could not contain it and must swirl about the room like a tornado. The dogs eyed her apprehensively then retired behind the sofa to avoid the danger.

His voice was patient though he did not feel it. "I'm trying to determine exactly what has been done to . . ." It was clear he was becoming irritated. He had stood up as Sally burst into the room, spilling the brandy he had poured himself down the front of his shirt. Now he tried to intercept her in her mad pacing, but she shrugged him off violently.

"And how long has it been going on, that's what I would like to know?" she went on furiously. "She was rigid with terror and Leila was not much better. Demons and horned devils she was babbling about, and in total darkness. Well, I had that old woman out of her cosy sitting-room so fast she almost tripped over her witch's skirt and hot on her heels was Miss What's-Her-Name whom I've never liked from the first time I saw her. Something about her eyes, have you noticed? Set too close together so that her nose gets in the way. 'What's to do?' the old crone was saying and when I pointed out that one of her charges was lying in a wet bed in total darkness, terrified out of her mind, she had the effrontery to tell me that children need to be disciplined."

"Dear God." Adam put his hand wearily to his head, giving up trying to confront the virago who raged about him. The virago who had, half an hour ago, crept up the stairs like a mouse complaining she was tired.

"So," she continued, stopping her mad stampede at last, her hands on her hips, an expression on her face he knew so well. "What are you to do?"

"It seems as if it's already done. If you have given the entire nursery staff the sack then they must go."

"Is that all you have to say? Your daughters have been repressed for years . . . no, I know you weren't here but, by God, Adam, you should have been. To leave two small children in the hands of those . . . wardresses is . . . is . . . I'm sorry, I'm upset and I know I should not have said that but . . ."

"No, you should not, Sally. You know nothing about me nor my circumstances before we met except what I've told you. There are things . . . well . . ." He pushed his hand through his hair. "Perhaps you should not judge."

"I know, and I'm sorry but that is not the issue at the moment. That woman . . . that old woman, who has ruled their lives for so long, for reasons of her own which I can only put down to jealousy and having her position usurped, has taken all their Christmas presents and locked them up in a cupboard saying – listen to this – that they were to stay there until they learned to behave like ladies and not ragamuffins. I think that was what Leila said. She has punished them simply because they have, for the first time since they came back from India – I can't speak for what their lives were there – they have had some fun."

She whirled about again, throwing up her hands in disgust, her lovely golden dress shimmering as she moved, the exquisite necklace at her throat catching the light and Adam thought how beautiful she really was. He hadn't noticed it when they first met, in fact he had thought her plain, but she had just sort of grown on him and he was stunned by it. It was not just beauty of face and figure, though that was there now in her temper, but an inner beauty which, even now, was driving her to take up arms in defence of these two children she barely knew. She could be hard, even abrasive with those who displeased her, letting them know in no uncertain terms that they had better "shape" or they'd feel the length of her tongue, but now her protective instinct had risen up and swamped her and without a thought for the consequences she had peremptorily given notice to the three servants who she believed were to blame for it. Of course, in a week or so, those three servants would be redundant in any case when the girls went to school but in the meantime what was to be done?

"Sit down, Sally, please."

"I can't, I'm too damned mad."

"I know, I can see that, but try. Sit down and tell me exactly what's happened."

"I don't know what to say."

"I find that hard to believe." He smiled a little.

"If you're going to treat this as a joke then there's not another word to be said. It's not funny, Adam. Those two . . ."

"I know and I'm smiling at you, not the situation. Sit down, lovely girl, and tell me from beginning to end."

She did, omitting nothing. Aisha's soft cries of terror, soft because she knew Nanny would be cross if she made a "fuss". The bedroom without a wink of light anywhere in which the girls slept in two little beds, the absence of even the smallest fire. They were not allowed to get out of bed, Leila had explained in a trembling voice, not even to comfort one another in their distress. So great was their fear of Nanny's disapproval, even when she was absent, they would not dream of disobeying her because if they did the demons and devils who punished naughty little girls would come and get them. The final horror of Aisha's wet bed had so demoralised her she had begun to cry though she knew she shouldn't, and in the day nursery the three women who had her in their charge toasted their feet and a huge pile of muffins at the leaping fire and ignored her piteous cries since children must be disciplined. Leila begged Sally not to tell Nanny about Aisha for she would be so cross with her and Aisha was so sorry, really she was and wouldn't do it again, she was sure and all this in a high, unnatural voice. Aisha was beyond uttering a word in her own defence.

"Where are they now?" Adam asked when she had finished speaking.

"The old witch and her cronies are sitting outside in the hall where I put them, waiting to speak to you, I believe, since Nanny seems to think she has a case to plead. I changed Aisha, much against Nanny's wishes, I can tell you, since it is her opinion that naughty girls who wet their bed should be left to lie in it."

"Jesus Christ!" This time Sally did not admonish him.

"Exactly, then I put them both in our bed."

His head shot up and his mouth fell open.

"You did what?"

"I couldn't leave them up there on their own, could I? Besides being out of their minds with fear and with no fire . . . no fire, I ask you at this time of the year, they were cold and frightened. They seemed quite happy to snuggle down in our bed with their dolls. I built up the fire, lit all the lamps and sent for Tilly to sit with them. She's a good heart, that girl."

For a moment she seemed distracted by some thought that had occurred to her and Adam was not to know that it concerned Job Hawthorne, then she continued.

"They were falling asleep when I left them, cuddling their dolls and each other, surrounded by whips and tops and skipping ropes as though they couldn't bear them out of their sight. I was ready to cry, really I was," and without further ado, for some reason she couldn't explain since she was not aware that pregnancy often caused this reaction, she burst into tears.

At once Adam was by her side, drawing her into his arms, kissing her wet face, smoothing back the wild tangle of her hair, then, sitting down again, pulling her on to his lap. His arms held her tight and Sally marvelled at this man who, though he loved his dead wife with unswerving devotion, could be such a comfort to the one who was alive.

The servants were thrown into a great hullabaloo with Mrs Cooper's crisp instructions, the captain's cursing which was quite uncalled for, Mrs Chidlow said disapprovingly to Mr Henton, with Nanny Mottram's wailing, well, screeching really, like the witch Mrs Cooper accused her of being. Miss Digby was loud in her own defence, saying that her responsibility to Captain Cooper's daughters ended in the schoolroom and it was not her place to interfere with Nanny's domain in the nursery. Lucy wept and begged for a second chance since she herself had been totally under Nanny's domination, while the master tore his hair and the mistress calmly went about the reshaping of her stepdaughters' lives.

The nursery beds were to be changed and aired, the fire lit and never, never allowed to go out. Lamps were to be placed on every flat surface in the room and tomorrow first thing she would personally see to planning the complete refurnishing of the nursery floor and schoolroom since it would be needed soon anyway. What were they to make of that remark? they asked one another, slack-jawed, somewhat disinclined to believe what they thought she meant. Not already, surely? She and the captain had only been married a matter of weeks, Cissie remarked somewhat stringently and was amazed when Tilly rounded on her.

"You're a spiteful cow, Cissie Newton. You've had it in for madam ever since she let it be known she expects you to pull your weight like the rest of us instead of prancing about all day long with a feather duster. She's a good mistress. Oh, I know she's a beggar for work and expects us to be the same but she's fair. And she's taken up them girls like they was her own an' I for one won't have you calling her."

"I never called her and I'll thank you to keep a civil tongue in your head, Tilly Jones and remember I'm head parlourmaid here and won't be spoken to by—"

"That will do, both of you." The quiet, but determined-to-be-heard voice of Mrs Trimble brought them both to silence. It was Mrs Chidlow's job to keep the women servants in order but Mrs Chidlow seemed totally uninterested these days in what went on in the kitchen, spending most of her time in her own room, pretending to be busy and, so the rumour went, taking frequent nips from the gin bottle she smuggled in under her cloak. Wait until the mistress caught her, there'd be skin and hair flying then. In the meanwhile, scarcely without any of them really noticing it, Mrs Trimble's voice had become the one they all listened to.

That night they were all aware that their master and mistress slept together in the narrow bed which was in the master's dressing-room and which, to their knowledge, had never been used since they married. It seemed they couldn't bear to be apart even for one night though there were plenty of empty beds in the house. There was barely enough room for one, never mind two, so was it any wonder, if it was true, that she was already in the family way. The door between it and their own bedroom was left open, Tilly told Mrs Trimble, almost as tearful as her mistress, lest the young ladies were fretful in the night. They would need to be watched over for a while, they privately agreed, finding they were in complete accord in their opinion of their mistress. There would be new staff on the nursery floor eventually and in the meantime cheerful, good-natured Tilly Jones was to look after the master's daughters, she was told.

In the weeks that followed it became a constant source of open-mouthed amazement among the servants, indoor and out, to see the emergence, like butterflies from a chrysalis, of Leila and Aisha Cooper. Not all at once, of course, since they had been subdued for so long, but gradually, under the sensible influence of their stepmother and the blithe influence of their stepmother's kitchen maid, they began to be children.

They must not get mud on their boots they had at first told Tilly, looking fearfully over their shoulders as though Nanny might be watching. It had been raining and the path through the wood had small pools of water along it but when Tilly informed them that it was quite in order to pick up their skirts and jump the puddles they thought it was the most marvellous game, leaping as far and as high as they could and if their boots got muddy Tilly didn't seem to mind at all. Their laughter echoed where none had been before and the gardeners were inclined to look at one another in wonderment, shaking their heads at the strangeness of it.

They must not go near the stables or speak to the grooms, they confided nervously as Tilly led them one day across the frozen white expanse of the park at the back of the house. It was January and the hazed circle of the orange sun floated in a winter pink sky that day, capturing the stark beauty of black, leafless trees and bringing poppy flags to the cheeks of Oralie Cooper's daughters. Deer raised their heads to stare at them from beneath a small stand of trees which seemed to float in the misted distance, the mist hanging in still veils, not moving in the windless air.

"Give over," Tilly told them, herself bright-eyed and pink-cheeked with the cold. "There's nothing wrong with having a chinwag with Jimmy or Alec or any of the grooms. They're the nicest chaps you'd ever wish to meet."

"Really?" Leila answered politely.

"Really. John's a right card. Put him an' Dicky together

and the pair of them are as good as a music-hall turn any day of the week."

"What's a music-hall turn, Tilly?" Leila ventured to ask, recovering more quickly than her younger sister from Nanny's harsh régime.

"Nay, you'll find out one day, my lass. It's a kind of . . . theatre."

"Like a Shakespeare play?"

"Well, I don't know about that, chuck." Tilly had never heard of Shakespeare, whoever he was, just as Leila could not get over the wonder of being called "chuck", "my lass" and "lamb" which was another favourite of Tilly's. Tilly, unlike many of the servants, could both read and write. She was shrewd and bright and kind and the girls began to unfurl like newly budding leaves under her cheerful warm-heartedness.

Though they did not know it and would not have understood the implications of it if they had, Tilly was more than a little taken with the "big feller", as Job was called in the kitchen. She had just seen him crossing the stable yard and surely now was as good a time as any to take the girls to see the horses in the stables. There was talk that the master was to get them a pony each, though Tilly was of the opinion that it was a bit soon for that yet. Their schooling had been put off until Easter for, as madam put it, these two were like chicks just come from the egg and must be given time to get used to this new world of theirs before entering another.

Job was quiet and patient with the little girls, hunkering down to their level as their big, velvet grey eyes studied him gravely. Nanny hadn't liked "men", the word uttered in a voice which seemed to convey they were the lowest form of human life, but they knew this one. He had come to pick evergreen branches and holly with them before Christmas when Sally had taken them into the woods and if Sally trusted him, so did they. They were beginning to believe there was no more comforting person in the world than Sally who called them "sweetheart" and, when they were alone, "darling". They liked Tilly, of course, who, almost against their will, made them laugh shyly, as though they weren't quite used to it, making every walk about the estate a big adventure. Tilly was a country girl, born in a farm labourer's cottage out Prescot way and knew every bird in the sky and every flower and tree that grew and every animal that crept about beneath it all. She even showed them where to get the best frogspawn though they were sure, when the time came, they would not care for the task of collecting it in jars as she suggested. They didn't like frogs, they told her politely, their faces apologetic since they wouldn't for the world upset this new friend of theirs who smiled at the big man with such a lovely look in her eyes.

"My name's Job, my lasses," he told them, watching as they clutched their dolls protectively against them. "Has Tilly fetched you to see't horses?" His heart-stopping smile transformed his battered, ugly face to a strange beauty. When they nodded warily he stood up and offered a hand to each of them, which they took. Though Nanny's words about the peculiarities of men still hissed in their ears it seemed they trusted him. His hands were warm and gentle as he led them along the stalls to meet Harry, their papa's bay and Flame, who was so pretty but would not be ridden for a while yet, at least not by their mistress whose mare she was. There were Jupiter and Mars who were the carriage horses, he explained, and Bunty the pony who pulled the lawnmower in the summer, and Piper and Wally who were hunters. These girls' mama had been a good horsewoman who had ridden to hounds since she was younger than they and Piper had been hers but neither they nor Job knew this.

A gleam of winter sun shone on the animals' glossy coats and striped the pale hay which Jimmy was forking into neat piles with yellow bars, lighting the drifting dust motes to showers of golden dust. There was the rich smell of horse manure, though the floor was swept clean, mixed with leather and polish and the honest reek of working men's sweat.

"'Appen you'd care to sit on Bunty's back for a minute?" Job asked Leila gravely, who he could see was not as nervous as Aisha.

"Well . . ." She hung back a little, for though the placid pony was no taller than she was she had never in her life been close to an animal of any sort. Even her papa's terriers who had been trained to be quiet in the house had been given a wide berth at breakfast time and when they visited his study.

"I'll hold you on," Job said encouragingly.

Aisha watched in speechless admiration as her sister, her skirts pushed up her legs to reveal her lace-trimmed drawers, which Nanny would have *fainted* over, sat astride the unconcerned pony.

Job was not surprised, since it seemed once Leila had braved something Aisha could be persuaded to follow, when the little girl said breathlessly, "I'd like to do that, Mr Job, if I may." She was exquisitely polite as she had been taught to be but there was a glint of silver excitement in her eyes and it was plain that another step had been taken into normality by the two little girls.

Sally took them to town with her the following day, accompanied by the new nursery maid who had arrived the day before. Lucy had gone, bewailing her misfortune and promising to do exactly as Mrs Cooper instructed her in future if she would only let her stay, but Sally told Adam she couldn't possibly be trusted again, particularly with the new baby to come in July.

"I should think not," Adam agreed, probably thinking of what he hoped would be a son, Sally imagined. They had been just as close as ever in their bed once the girls had been relocated in their warm, newly decorated and refurbished nursery quarters. Their lives continued in the pleasant even tempo which Sally set. She allowed no thought to whisper to her of the hope that Adam Cooper might one day feel for his living wife what he still felt for his dead one. If there should be a warmth in his eyes or a tenderness in his voice then it was for the mother of his expected and hoped-for son; for the woman who had turned his house into a home and who was becoming increasingly fond of his daughters. They got along well, Adam and his housekeeper-cum-mistress-cum-mother-to-be and if beneath it all Sally Grimshaw yearned to be free and given the chance to allow her love to flower and capture him with its passion and sweetness, Sally Cooper beat her down, battened her down and piled the cargo of her journey through life on top of her.

The new nurserymaid was called Alice Cartwright and from the first Sally let it be known to Leila and Aisha that she was to be called Alice. There were to be no "Nannies" or "Miss Cartwrights" in their life. Simply Alice. She was to be their friend and companion for now and soon . . . well, she would explain what was to happen soon later, and like the biddable and polite young ladies Nanny Mottram had made of them they did not think to question her.

Alice was tall, deep-bosomed and plain but with the kind of

smiling eyes and face that denote good humour and strength which Sally admired. She'd stand no nonsense, as if these two badly repressed little girls would have given her that, but she would be kind, fair, merry even in the games she and the girls would play, she told them. Did they like "snakes and ladders", "spillikins" and "Happy Families"? she asked them, since, to the continued astonishment of the servants, Mrs Cooper insisted upon the girls being present when she interviewed the long succession of hopeful nursery nurses. If the girls didn't care for Miss Benson or Miss Taylor or Miss Burton then there was no use in hiring them, was there? she asked reasonably enough and it seemed her husband agreed with her.

They all agreed they liked Alice, even Captain Cooper who was called in to look her up and down, and Leila and Aisha pronounced themselves eager to play "snakes and ladders", "spillikins" and "Happy Families" whatever they might turn out to be.

Tilly was quite sorry to lose her job as the girls' companion, she told Mrs Trimble, but she had reason to be hopeful that madam was considering her for her own personal maid which was what she was really after. Madam would need one when the baby came, which by now they had all guessed at, for surely she and the captain would begin to entertain and be entertained by the local gentry. She would need someone to look after the lovely gowns Tilly was convinced she would have made for her one day. Someone to dress her hair in some other way than that everlasting coil at the back of her head, said Tilly, who read all the latest ladies' fashion magazines such as *Ask Mamma*, *The English Gentlewoman* and *The Handbook of the Toilet* which were passed on to her by her friend Agnes Jackson who was already a lady's maid and whose mistress took all three publications. Tilly meant to be that someone though she told no one about it, not even Mrs Trimble.

And she would still see the little girls of whom she had grown fond since they were encouraged to come and go as they pleased in their stepmama's upstairs boudoir. When she had been in charge of them she had often taken them down to the kitchen where a great fuss was made of them; where they were beseeched to try Cook's gingerbread biscuits or coconut macaroons and she had implored them to continue to come and visit her there, and the rest of the staff, when Alice took over.

It was perhaps these children and their introduction to the men and women of the household who were the beginning of Sally Grimshaw's total acceptance as mistress of Coopers Edge. They had knuckled down to her authority since they had no other option, but as though they admired her stout defence and championship of the two "lambs", ones they had scarcely ever seen, they began to think kindly of her, even Mr Henton remarking on her good sense.

The little girls, bemused by so much attention, by the obvious warmth and interest they met in all the places, in and out of their home where they had never been before, promised Tilly that they would visit her and the kitchen every day, that is if Alice would let them, still not entirely believing in this magical world they found themselves in.

Today they were to go to Sally's dressmaker, Sally told them, since it was high time they all had new outfits for the spring, not mentioning to them that she could scarce get into anything she already owned. It would be April soon and what with the girls growing so quickly, as well as herself, it was high time they consulted with the Misses Yeoland.

She watched with pleasure their obvious and newly

awakened interest in everything that went on about them as they drove along Prescot Lane towards Liverpool. It seemed, until their papa came home, they had never been beyond the walls of Coopers Edge and then they had been so alarmed by the sheer enormity of venturing out with a stranger, they had hardly dared lift their eyes from their folded hands. Now their glance was almost bold and they asked a continual stream of questions Sally did her best to answer.

"What is that man doing, Sally?"

"Ploughing ready for the sowing of seeds."

"Like Mr Reuben plants seeds?"

"Yes, that's it, sweetheart."

"What is on that cart, Sally?"

"Milk churns, darling. The milkman delivers milk to the houses that don't have their own cows like us."

"Goodness!"

"What's that woman doing in her garden and what are those funny things?"

"Those are beehives and I suspect she's getting them ready for . . . well, when the bees make the honey."

"How do you know that?" And on and on until, as they drove at a spanking pace in the direction of Old Swan through which they must pass to get to Liverpool, they, Alice and Alec were considerably startled when Sally's voice rose in what was almost a shriek, calling on Alec to stop at once.

With a great deal of "whoa-ing" and "shushing" of his precious horses, which were not used to such sudden movements and were seriously alarmed, Alec brought the carriage to a halt. He took a moment to make sure all was well with Jupiter and Mars, then turned enquiringly to his mistress.

She was staring across the road at a building, a jumble of buildings really, with a cobbled strip to the front of it and a cobbled yard at the side which evidently led round to the back. It had an air of neglect, not in bad repair or anything like that, but as though no one gave a damn about it, and the place knew it.

Alec stared, first at it, then back at Mrs Cooper and it was then, as he told Jimmy and John later, when it all came out, that he knew why she sat there, on her face the saddest expression he had ever seen.

It was the Grimshaw Arms. It was empty, deserted and swinging from the sign was tacked a forlorn notice which said "FOR SALE".

They were in their bed, drowsing after the rather careful love-making they were both coming to realise was all they could manage for the time being, when she spoke.

"Do I please you, Adam?" she said in a husky voice, her hand at her belly where their child, as though disturbed by their endeavours, was making tiny, fluttery movements of annoyance.

"You know you do, Sally. Dear God, woman, can't you see that you do?" His voice was slightly irritated, for he had been almost asleep. His cheek rested comfortably on the lovely full curve of her bare breast and his legs were entwined with hers.

"I'm serious, Adam. This is not just a casual question."

There was silence for a moment then he lifted his head, leaning on one elbow, studying her face on the pillow. She looked quite lovely, he thought, her eyes deep, dark and dreaming, perhaps of the child to come, or was she still in that rapturous place they journeyed to together? Her hair was spread on the pillow in a magically patterned fan of silver and gold where it had pleased him to arrange it and he felt the warmth of needing her, not as a man needs a woman, but just needing her in his life. It entered sweetly into his heart and soul and he knew he could not manage life without her now. He didn't know when it had come. It had crept up on him, this feeling, catching him unawares and he could feel the smile begin somewhere round his heart, bursting to get out and be presented to her.

"Sally, lovely girl . . ." He was ready to tell her so, to kiss her and hold her to him, to tell her exactly how she pleased him but she put her hand up to his mouth to stop him.

"Can I say something before you answer?"

"Sally, you know . . ."

"No, I don't, not really. I know you . . . seem to be content."

"You know I am. It was the best day's work I ever did when I dragged you out of that bloody public house in Knotty Ash."

He gave a short laugh, then became serious again.

"So, you were saying?" she asked him patiently.

"I'm saying will you get on with it, woman, and then we can both get some sleep. I've arranged to be at the Home Farm at eight to help Albert with the new bull. Damned thing penned Fred Lockshaw in."

"I want something from you, Adam."

"Lovely girl, I am totally yours, you know that, but give me half an hour to recover from—"

"Adam, will you listen to me?"

He flung himself on to his back, his arms out in a pretence of total surrender.

"I'm listening, I'm listening."

Now she had his full attention she began to fumble with the words, a sure sign she was nervous.

"Well, this morning, Alice and the girls and I – well, me really – decided it was high time we had some new outfits. I'm getting so fat and they're growing so tall. I suppose it's because they spend a lot of time outdoors now . . . running and . . . well . . . things they never did before and they need things . . . clothes besides the frilly nonsense Nanny thought fitting and . . ."

"Is there an end to this epistle, Sally Cooper? If so, get to it before I fall asleep."

"Yes, there is. The Grimshaw Arms is for sale and I want it."

Very slowly he sat up. The lamps had been turned down to a glimmer but the fire in the tiled grate was alive with flames and crackling coals. Sally could see it reflected in his dark blue eyes, two tiny fires, leaping and merry. His face was amber shaded, as was his upper body and his expression was unreadable as he spoke.

"My wife has no need of an inn, Sally."

"No, but Sally Grimshaw has."

"What the hell does that mean?"

He was holding himself very still, very controlled, hiding what was in him, whatever it might be. The humour had gone, everything had gone, leaving only that arrogant officer she had first seen in the bar parlour of the very inn they were discussing. He had been deeply offended when she had spoken of his family, thinking her to be insulting him, and it seemed he was the same now.

With a small sound she could not identify he turned away from her, getting out of bed and padding to the mantelpiece where he kept a box of cigars. He took one, lit it with a taper from the fire, inhaled deeply then blew the smoke straight up to the ceiling. He leaned on both hands, staring into the fire, the cigar in his mouth, his back to her, long and lean and graceful, his buttocks taut, his legs in perfect proportion to the rest of his body. She loved him with everything that was in her, deeply, enduringly, as she had never before loved another human being and she knew she always would. So why was she gambling that love, this life, her home she had made, on an old inn which nobody wanted, particularly her husband, it seemed?

"Explain it," he said briefly, not looking at her.

"I have no real explanation except . . . it's part of me. It's part of the Grimshaw family as Coopers Edge is a part of your family. We, the Grimshaws, have owned it since . . . oh, not as long as you have been here, certainly, but long enough to . . . to make me value it. Three generations of us and into it went my mother's heart and soul . . . and mine. Between us, my mother and I, we made it what it is – was – and I want it back. I want to bring it back to life. Freddy wounded it but it was that bastard Keene who delivered the mortal blow and, if you agree, I would like to . . ."

"What?" He did not turn to her and she had no idea what he felt.

"Put it together again. Make it live again."

"You have a family now, Sally. Your duty is with them."

"I know, and . . . I want nothing else but to . . . serve it." His shoulders sagged a little as though he had relaxed. "But I feel I have a duty to the inn. I loved it, Adam. It was all I had and to see it today, dying before my eyes, was a . . . was a cruel blow. I . . ."

"Yes?"

"If you would buy it for me, in your name if you wish, when I am able to supervise it I would see it working again. Put people in it I can trust. I have asked you for nothing for myself."

"I know, and given me so much."

"Then?"

"I will see Saunders tomorrow."

Still he continued to look into the fire and some instinct, some sense which came alive just for him, warned her that he was afraid, perhaps that he would lose the serenity, the calm, the content she knew was in him and which she had brought him. Perhaps he was afraid he would see a return of the high-handed, ruthlessly determined woman who had once run the inn. Afraid that Coopers Edge, which was her home now, and all those in it who depended on her, would suffer.

"Adam, come back to bed," she said softly. "Come and hold me and our child in your arms. The inn will not really be mine. It will have tenants whom I will choose carefully. My place is here with you and our children. But it will be safe as I am safe with you."

He came then, shivering, though he was not cold and she was surprised by the rough strength of his possession of her far into the night.

19

Mrs Trimble said in a self-satisfied way which was not at all like her that she'd known for weeks that it would be twins. That there doctor hadn't known but she had! She'd never had a child herself but her lady down in Warwickshire had, twins, and twice, so Mrs Trimble knew what she was talking about. And you'd only to look at the size of Mrs Cooper, a belly jutting out on her you could cut bread on, her ankles the thickness of tree trunks, unable to walk more than a few steps and the captain almost out of his mind with worry, poor man.

What an anxious time it had been with those two little girls who went to school each day in the carriage now, tumbling out of it at the end of the afternoon, shrieking for Sally as they ran up the stairs. Hardly able to wait to get into the mistress's bedroom to make sure she was all right. They had been told that a baby was to be added to the family and though they had no idea where it was to come from since they were too young and innocent for such a revelation, they were as eager as the rest of them to get their hands on it. They hung about whenever they were let, begging to be allowed to read to their stepmama, brush her hair, stroke her back which ached all the time and generally fighting with their papa over who should do what, and next, for her.

Mind, they were all the same now, even Henton inclined to eavesdrop as the doctor and the master conferred on the front doorstep before the doctor drove away in his carriage.

"What did he say, Mr Henton?" the servants would beg to know, clustering round the butler when he returned to the kitchen.

"Just rest and more rest, Mrs Trimble," Henton would reply sorrowfully, addressing his answer to the person who was his equal, and no one seemed to find it ironic that this man who, almost a year ago, hadn't a good word for Mrs Cooper, saying she was a little upstart and no better than she should be, should now be as concerned as the rest of them over the condition of their breathlessly rotund little mistress. They made excuses, even Cissie, to run up to her room, bringing her hothouse peaches, the first strawberries from the garden, a posy of freesias from the gardener's boy, a little knitted jacket from Albert Lord's missis on the Home Farm.

Clara begged Mrs Trimble to be allowed to take her mistress the first egg that she, in her new role as kitchen maid, had boiled successfully. Maddy, who was clever with her needle, embroidered her an exquisite handkerchief and the outside staff sent her daily good wishes with the little girls, who were coming on a treat, Jimmy said, with their riding lessons. They'd to tell Mrs Cooper that, and soon, when she was able, he and Flame would be waiting for the mistress herself. Job was never off the back doorstep with something or other and had even been allowed up to see her a time or two since the captain knew of his devotion to the mistress.

Yes, she'd brought peace and order to this household, had the captain's new wife, laughter and love to its children, harmony between its servants and they wouldn't swop her for a gold clock for all her finicky ways. Of course the prospect of a baby had helped to lay the remainder of any resentment which might have been harboured in a breast or two, for a house with a baby in it was a grand thing indeed.

Tilly was her constant companion, when the captain wasn't there, naturally, helping her to get out of bed, to bathe and dress in the morning, though it seemed her services were not required in the evening, she said, her face aflame, the implication not missed by the rest of the servants who scattered at once, their own faces flushed, to their own suddenly urgent tasks.

Her pains began at just gone nine in the evening, two weeks earlier than expected. The girls were asleep, thank God, Mrs Trimble was heard to say, with Alice watching over them, or they'd have been getting under everybody's feet in their bewilderment and concern for their stepmama. The captain wasn't much better, galloping round like a horse that's taken fright, shouting for Tilly, for Mrs Trimble, for Tipper to run for the doctor, for hot water and hot tea and in the middle of it all, Tilly reported, the mistress calmly got on with the business of giving birth, orderly and efficient as she was in everything.

"Adam," Tilly heard her say, repeating it in private to Mrs Trimble with whom she got on well, the feeling returned despite the difference in their ages. "Adam, will you calm down. Come and sit beside me and hold my hand," which he did, wincing palely when she arched her back and gripped him like a vice. She did not cry out once.

"It's twins, a boy and a girl," Tilly yelled exultantly six hours later, bursting into the kitchen, not at all surprised to see every last one of them, even Henton and Tipper, lolling about the kitchen table at three o'clock in the morning. "Small but healthy, the doctor says, an' there's to be a bottle of champagne opened, Mr Henton, the master said, and he'll be down directly to wet the babies' head . . . *heads*!"

Dominic and Naomi Cooper, and if they weren't careful the pair of them would be totally ruined, their mother said firmly to their father – who was as bad as the rest – in the weeks that followed their birth. There was always someone hanging about waiting for them to wake up wherever they happened to be. In the garden where Alice took them for their daily walk; in the nursery when Alice's back was turned for a second, even in the small sitting-room where they often slept as their mother discussed the day's menus with Mrs Trimble. From Henton down to Flora, who was the new scullery maid, the gardeners who pushed gentle grubby fingers into the baby carriage and the stable lads who came charging out of the yard and across to the path where Alice strolled. The perambulator itself was quite charming though only suitable for summer walks. It was made of basketwork and looked like a bassinet on wheels. Over it hung a large parasol-type hood to keep the sun off its occupants, in this case two occupants, one at each end of the contraption. By the time winter came they would be sitting up, Sally told Adam confidently, since they were exceedingly clever babies and would be able to sit side by side in the sturdy, hooded, double perambulator, exhibited at the Great Exhibition in 1851 and which Sally had already ordered from the London shop which sold them.

There hadn't been a child born in this house since the captain himself some thirty-odd years ago and naturally, none of the present staff had been here then. As Mrs Trimble said, there was nothing like a baby, let alone two babies, for bringing joy to a place and with the two little girls ready to be quite . . . well, boisterous now, the old house had come alive again. Mrs Trimble liked to bestow her thoughts on those she considered to be in her dependency which the kitchen was now since the resignation of Mrs Chidlow the week before the twins were born. And good riddance too, in Mrs Trimble's opinion, for the woman had done nothing to earn her wage ever since Mrs Trimble had come to replace the old cook at Coopers Edge. Even when Mrs Cooper had been so incapacitated towards the end of her pregnancy, the housekeeper had not felt the need to take over what were really her own duties and it had been left to Mrs Trimble to be both cook and housekeeper, which she was perfectly capable of, naturally. With them babies to see to, her stepdaughters to whom she gave a lot of her time, and her husband who, it seemed, could hardly bear her out of his sight, the mistress no longer had the time, nor the inclination, Mrs Trimble privately thought, to bother with housekeeping duties. Mrs Trimble knew she was trusted and, being a sensible woman who could see no reason to complain of the extra work, got on efficiently with her job. Henton had mellowed beyond recognition under the firm but fair command of his new mistress and Mrs Trimble's tendency to stand no nonsense from him, being well used to butlers of his sort.

The maidservants, of whom there were now seven – not counting the laundry and the dairy – since Clara had been promoted to kitchen maid and Tilly to Mrs Cooper's personal maid, worked in harmony for the most part and it was woe betide those who didn't.

Tilly was made up with her new position, inclined to swank a bit, but settling finally to the task of looking after Mrs Cooper's new wardrobe which, when she had regained her figure, her husband insisted she had made for her.

"You've never looked better, lovely girl," Tilly heard him say to her. "Motherhood suits you and you've taken to it like a duck to water. But besides being a mother, you're my wife and I refuse any longer to have you going about in those prim, neutral garments, whatever they are, for a moment longer. You look as if you're off to a funeral."

Sally had discarded the full, pyramid-shaped skirts and mantles which the Misses Yeoland had made for her and which she had worn for the last three or four months of her pregnancy, reverting to the businesslike skirts and blouses she had always worn. Adam looked her up and down and pulled a face with the air of a man who is not pleased with what he sees.

Sally bristled at once as he knew she would. "What's wrong with what I wear? My clothes are well made and of good material and have years of wear in them."

"That's what I'm afraid of." He grinned amiably.

"What are you grinning at? I can see nothing amusing . . ."

"You look superb in that golden thing you wear to dinner, Sally," he wheedled, "but it's time you had another. Several others, in fact. Light colours – well, I don't know – summery things. Old Miss Yeoland will know what you need." He was suddenly serious. "Please, Sally, you're no longer a businesswoman and I don't want you to look like one. You're the mistress of Coopers Edge and should dress accordingly. Let me come with you and we'll choose together."

"The twins . . ."

". . . can manage without you."

"I'm quite happy with what I wear now."

"But I'm not," and how could she resist the slow curl of his impish grin, the twinkle in his blue eyes, his hands at her waist as he began to waltz her round the bedroom. She had become aware, an awareness which grew secretly, stealthily, one she was afraid to study too closely, that her husband's feelings towards her were changing. Warming. Strengthening in some way and she did not believe it was to do with the handsome son and daughter she had borne him. The atmosphere in the house was warm, pleasant, amicable, everything running on oiled wheels, but again she suspected that this growing approval of her was not concerned with that. She caught him watching her, his eyes deep and filled with warm regard and something else she could only guess at, shiver with delight at, and which it seemed he made no attempt to hide from her. He wanted her to look smart and pretty, he was telling her, as fashionable as many of the ladies she had seen in the Misses Yeolands' salon and now, now that her position in his house, not only as Mrs Adam Cooper, but the mother of his children was assured, could she refuse? She had always, as Sally Grimshaw of the Grimshaw Arms, despised fripperies and flounces, gee-gaws and baubles, indeed all the things women use to attract a man. Then, as Sally Grimshaw, she had not the faintest interest in attracting a man. Now, as Mrs Adam Cooper, she had, and that man was her husband.

They couldn't believe their eyes, the servants told one another, and they were becoming accustomed to madam's tendency to surprise and amaze them, when their mistress appeared in the first of the dozen new evening gowns the Misses Yeoland had designed and made for her. They'd seen her in the corn-coloured satin many times before the twins were born but now she drifted downstairs on her husband's arm in ivory silk, a rich ivory shot through with gold, a sheath which clung to what they had never realised was a perfectly proportioned and delicately rounded figure. The gown had no decoration but for an enormous golden rose of silk, just at the waist, simple but very chic, a word

Tilly used a lot, having seen it and liked it in *Ask Mama*. It seemed she had a hitherto undiscovered knack with clothes, Mrs Cooper, clever, as she was about most things, realising, when she had conferred with Miss Gladys and Miss Emily Yeoland, exactly what suited her. She had light summer dresses with sleeves of puffed tulle, pastel-tinted afternoon gowns of delicate creams and near whites, exotic, richly patterned shawls of silk, a coffee-coloured walking dress trimmed with black velvet, wrist bands and sashes of pearl and coral for the evening. And the evening gowns! A deep-cut black velvet which clung tightly to her figure as far as her knees where it exploded in a cloud of black gauze. Against the creamy white of her flawless skin, the smooth, well-brushed glory of her tawny hair and the golden amber of her eyes it looked quite magnificent. There were velvets, silks, satins, lutestring, which was a very fine, corded glossy silk, poult de soie in poppy red, rose pink, apple blossom, burned almond, honey and primrose. With the help of the Misses Yeoland, who knew about such things since they had been in business for many, many years, she learned and showed Tilly how to capture her abundant hair in a net of gold chains, another of pearls and with her beautifully cut riding habit she wore tight trousers and a pair of high, military boots.

"She's beautiful," breathed Tilly, who put her in her new gowns and dressed her hair on that first night. "Wait till you see her," and they had to agree, and would you look at the captain whose eyes said it all.

Mind you, she wasn't always tricked up like a dog's dinner, as she put it to her husband, since she was still Sally Grimshaw beneath the slow blooming of Sally Cooper. She was measured for some simple gowns which was only sensible, for after all she was the mother of four growing children and couldn't always be dressed up to the eyeballs, could she? she implored him.

"That's true, lovely girl," Adam agreed gravely, that soft, what she would almost call melting look in his eyes. "My mother used to look like a farm girl when she was out working in the garden."

"Your mother did!" the picture of Adam's ladylike mother digging in the flowerbeds refusing absolutely to come to her mind.

"Oh, yes. Though she was of good family, taught to sew and sing, to be a wife and mother and nothing else, like girls of good family were, and still are, she could not abide the dullness of it and when she married and came here she set to and made the gardens you see about you. She had the conservatory designed and built to her specifications so that she could carry on her planting and growing things even in the winter. She always had a trowel in her hand and her callers were often astonished to find it there when they visited her."

"Well, I never."

"A down-to-earth woman was Naomi Cooper. You remind me of her."

"Really?" Sally smiled, pleased beyond measure.

"Oh, yes, and then, though I wasn't here, of course, there was my great-great-great-grandmother – I'm not sure how many greats there should be – who helped my great-great-great-grandfather to build the business which made the family fortune. You can guess what that was, of course."

"Casks . . . barrels?"

"Clever girl."

"Well, I was in the business of selling beer."

"They called my great-great-great-grandfather a cooper,

and so he was by trade and by name and it's said my great-great-great-grandmother was not afraid to put on a leather apron and give a hand in the yard when they were busy. It was then that my venerable ancestor built Coopers Edge, so you see we were not all ladies and gentlemen. I come from working stock, as you do. This house has stood for over a hundred and fifty years, solid as the Rock Lighthouse in the mouth of the river, but gradually, over the years, the sons of the family became . . . well, I suppose you'd call them gentlemen and the wealth my ancestors accumulated by hard work and shrewdness melted away until there was nothing. There was a small income from some shipping shares my father managed to hold on to which bought me a commission in the army and paid my mess bills but until—"

He stopped speaking abruptly. They were in the hall, just about to stroll out on to the lawn in the sunwashed garden where Leila and Aisha were attempting a colourful game of croquet. Nobody seemed to know the rules since no one could remember ever playing it, even Adam, so between the four of them they had made up their own game which seemed to create no order, only slightly hysterical laughter. Alice was sitting on a chair beside the basketwork baby carriage in which Dominic and Naomi, now eight weeks old, were sleeping. They would not fit in it for much longer, Alice said, for they were growing fast and already were beginning to fight for room in it. It was September and warm with the somnolent drone of bees among the flowers, the busy twitter of swallows in the eaves of the house and a heavenly burst of song from the throat of a blackbird swinging on a high branch of an oak tree. It was all so lovely, so right, so perfect and Sally felt her heart tear as Adam walked slowly back up the hall and stood beneath the portrait of his first wife. For a long time he stared up at it, that sad, haunted look on his face she had come to dread. She felt the ice of it freeze her veins.

"She saved it," he said in a flat voice. "If it had not been for her I would have had to let it go. It was falling down, the roof going, a virtual ruin when my father died and I had no money to put it right."

Sally watched him, dying a thousand times, and in mortal agony as he looked up at Oralie Cooper.

"God, she was the loveliest thing . . ."

"Don't, oh, please don't . . ." It was more of a moan than words spoken and the unusualness of it turned Adam away from the portrait to look at her in surprise.

"Sally?" He began to walk towards her.

"Can't you see what it does to me when . . ."

"What, what is it, lovely girl?"

"Why do you call me that when . . . when you love her so much?"

It was as though she had thrown up some invisible wall into which he walked, so abruptly did he stop. His face lost all the lovely, sunwarmed colour he had acquired over the summer and in his eyes were astonishment and a pain she had never seen before. In it was a light of such sublime brilliance it blinded her.

"Love her," he said harshly. "Love her. Jesus God, I've never hated anyone in my life as much as I hated her and I've felt the shame of it and the guilt of it ever since she died. I wished it on her a thousand times and when I heard that she was dead I tried . . . tried to be sorry for her but I couldn't. I was glad . . . glad she'd gone . . . released me."

Sally stood completely still, like a frozen figure of marble. She had on a simple white dress, her hair carelessly tied back with a bit of blue ribbon. She looked about twelve years old, small and defenceless. During the summer her pale skin had been transformed to the lovely golden hue the sun had given it, rose amber glowing at each cheekbone. Now, like Adam's, it drained away to a greyness which resembled putty. She was totally, utterly disorientated. She put up a trembling hand to her mouth, her face twitching slightly and she felt the shivering begin inside her. It attacked her poor, bewildered heart, then her throat which would not work, moving at last to her legs which began to buckle.

"Sally . . . Dear God . . . Sally, my love, my love," Adam cried as he leaped forward and caught her in his arms. He held her like a drowning man holds to a piece of driftwood. They were both shaking and shuddering now, great spasms that bound them together, even their teeth chattering, for they were both deeply shocked by his words, even he who had spoken them.

"Dear God," he began to mumble, "dear God, did you think . . .? Sally, my lovely girl, you didn't believe . . . Jesus, don't you know by now how I feel about you? Don't you know?"

"No," she said through numbed lips. "I thought it was her . . ."

"Dear sweet Jesus," he whispered, holding her violently trembling body to his which was trembling just as badly. "I hold you more precious than life. You have *brought* me life and . . . everything I have of value, you have given me. Don't you realise?"

He began to shake her, as though she were an obtuse child, one he must make understand. His eyes pierced hers. His hands were on her shoulders and her head lolled and rolled with the force of his vehemence when suddenly, like a cat which has been lying suspended in the sun, then comes to shivering life when an intruder approaches, she sprang away from him. With all the force she could muster she raised her hand and hit him across the face, the blow so fierce it nearly knocked the pair of them off their feet.

"You bastard," she hissed and, as it usually did, her hair began its own lively dance. "You've let me believe all these months that you were pining for that bloody woman up there. That you still loved her though she was mouldering in her grave and all the while . . ."

He had his hand to his cheek and his eyes had begun to water. It was his turn to be disorientated now. He was shocked by her attack on him and bewildered by the ferocity of her anger. His own threatened, then escaped though he couldn't have said why. Emotions were high, charged with some power which captured them both and his reaction was instinctive.

"What the devil are you talking about, woman?" he roared. "Where in hell did you get that bloody idea from?'

"From you . . . from you. How many times have I found you gazing at her soulfully . . ."

"In the name of all that's sensible!" He began to laugh. "Soulfully . . . is that how you saw it?"

"How else was I to see it?" Her face was crimson and her eyes flashed with a danger which he chose to ignore.

"Don't be so bloody foolish," he said flatly. "Would I allow my wife to find me gazing . . . what was the word, *soulfully*, into the past if it meant anything to me? Would I?"

His voice was ragged with a rage that was hazardous but when he took a step towards her, as though he would return her blow, she did not flinch.

"You stupid bitch, you must have known . . . could you not see how I was, how it was with me, what you meant to me? What you have done for me, and the girls . . . this house . . ."

"Did you know how I felt about you?" Her voice was like acid and beyond the green baize door, in the frozen silence which filled the kitchen where every servant stood like stone, Clara began to cry.

"Well, I hoped you . . ."

"There were never words of love between us . . . never. You had me believe that I was no more than a good housekeeper."

"That's a bloody lie. Hell and damnation, we were . . . partners."

"In bed, yes, but whenever . . ." Her throat began to work and it was clear she was close to breaking. "Whenever I came downstairs, there you were . . . staring up at . . ."

"Don't exaggerate. I scarcely even notice . . ."

"Liar, liar." She was becoming hysterical and her hysteria suddenly brought him at last to the realisation of what was happening between them, the words they had thrown at each other, and their meaning.

"Sally, don't . . . don't, my dear love." His voice was high, anguished now in his horror of what they were doing to one another. "I love you. I love you. I thought you knew."

"I'm not a bloody mind-reader, Adam Cooper."

She was calming a little, still inclined to weep, she thought, and probably would before long but his words had begun to filter like the sweetest, purest honey, into her mind, into her soul, into her heart which eagerly soaked them up. All these months when she had told herself sternly that Adam's heart was buried with Oralie, that she must be grateful for what she had; that she must not hanker for what could never be hers and all the while it had been here for her. She had felt something in him, sensed a change but had not allowed herself the rapture of hope. She had been happy, happier than she had ever been in her life, even though she believed that Adam still loved Oralie, for she had found fulfilment in what she saw as his kindness, his generosity, his good-humoured tolerance, his patience and his trust.

Now the one gift she had never expected was hers. She had only to reach out and take it.

"Sally," he said huskily, "forgive me if I've hurt you." His wide mouth quivered and his blue eyes were as dark as a stormy blue sky but there was a depth to them that told her, without words, of his love. He spoke them just the same. "I love you, lovely girl. I love you. I have never truly loved before, never." He was speaking of Oralie now. "And I never will again. Will you . . . take my love?"

"I might." Being Sally Grimshaw she tossed her head, not yet ready to forgive him, but he swept her into his arms and began to kiss her and the next thing she knew she was in their bed, and so was he, and in the kitchen they all let out their breaths on a long collective sigh.

It was as though it were their wedding night which they consummated again and again and all around them in the house the servants crept about, avoiding one another's glance since they knew where the master and mistress were and what they were doing and on a sunny Sunday afternoon as well!

Later he took her for a walk across to Near Paddock where Flame whickered, recognising Sally, and Harry, unaware of the incongruity of it, flirted with the mowing pony whom he adored. The carriage horses kicked up their heels in the clover-studded grass and in the quiet beneath the trees away from the house in which children were happy, away from their home where they were happy, away from their bed in which they made love with one another, he told her about Oralie. She stood in his arms, her back to his chest, his chin resting on her tumbled hair which she had not bothered to tie up since her husband who loved her liked it that way.

"I'll be totally truthful, lovely girl, since, for God's sake, there must always be truth between us."

"Yes," but she knew she would not like it.

"I was besotted with her. She was beautiful." Sally did not like it but she did not let him see it. "I couldn't see anything . . . anyone but her. All the men were mad for her. She was full of fun, a wicked sort of a fun, that captivated you, dazzled you, baffled you. She had something in her that you could not get a hold of. A brilliance . . . a magical something that brought men to their knees. I wanted her badly. I didn't give a toss for her money. I'd have taken her in rags and let Coopers Edge crumble to dust for all I cared. There were dozens after her. She was always surrounded by men and when she said she'd marry me I couldn't believe my luck. I was . . . well, she wanted the wedding immediately so I gave in, without a fight, I might add. We were to sail for India which I thought explained the haste. I was glad of the haste because I couldn't wait to get my hands on her. In fact . . ." He bent his head until it rested on her shoulder. It was a gesture of deep penitence and Sally knew how badly he was affected.

"We did not wait until our wedding night. She was as eager as me . . . and . . . when Leila was born six months later, prematurely, I was told, I thought . . . I thought . . . I was ignorant of such things, you see and . . . we had anticipated our wedding night . . . so you see I thought nothing of it."

He sighed deeply. She felt his chest move against her back and she bent her head to kiss his hands which were clasped across her breast. His voice was toneless as he continued.

"She was popular . . . a great favourite with the officers and I have it on good authority that she was unfaithful to me with most of them. So you see, I am not even sure if I am the father of either of my . . . my daughters."

There was a long, painful silence broken only by the sound of the cropping of the animals in the paddock. Sally felt her heart begin to weep for this man, this good, brave man who had known nothing but pain and humiliation and betrayal, the adversity of scandal and vicious gossip but who, despite it all, had retained within him a sweetness and a courage which could not be measured. He could not have been blamed had he become bitter, disillusioned, cruel even, railing at a life which had flung more at him in a year or two than most people know in a lifetime. He had done his best for the two daughters of Oralie, daughters who it was obvious had nothing of him in them, at least in their looks. They were small replicas of the woman in the portrait above the fireplace in the hall, though it seemed they had none of her spirit.

"Why did you keep her portrait?" she asked him, her eyes focused on the small herd of fallow deer which was moving slowly across the park. She did not, as yet, feel she could look into her husband's eyes lest the suffering she might see there weaken her.

"It was my . . . hair shirt. A penance, I suppose."

"You have nothing to be penitent about, Adam. The wrong was all on her side."

She turned in his arms then and looked up into his face which was working with some deep emotion she could only guess at. He had regained his colour but there was a look of strain round his eyes and faint smudges of violet. He was looking over her head, probably at the same herd of deer and his eyes, reflecting the vivid arch of the sky, were the blue of azure. He closed them for a moment and the length of his dark lashes formed a shadow above his wide, flat cheekbones, the cheekbones of some Norse ancestor who had plundered these shores centuries ago. His long, soft mouth was curling at the corners as it usually did, as though he were on the verge of smiling, but he did not smile.

Sally reached up and brought him back to her by laying her mouth on his.

"Tell me, my darling." There was a deep tenderness in her voice. Her heart moved in a helpless, melting way then bucked in her breast at his next words.

"I killed her."

The words shook her to the core, though she knew he did not mean it literally and she hugged him to her fiercely, protectively.

"No . . . no, Adam."

"Yes. I knew the child she carried was not mine. We had not . . . been together for many months, you see . . ."

"Go on."

"I drove her out, as I was entitled to, as society applauded me for doing since it was known I was a wronged husband. I drove her into the arms of her lover who was known to be dissolute and not the kind of man who would care to be landed with another man's wife, even if she was carrying his child. Perhaps the child was not his, who knows? If I had allowed her to stay . . ."

"You told me she left to go to her lover . . . of her own accord."

"I lied. It made me feel better. I drove her out, made her go, though she begged to be allowed to stay but I could not bear it any longer. And so . . . she died. If . . ."

"No . . . no, Adam, don't go on. It was not your fault."

"If I had not made her go she might be alive today. When I heard she was dead I was glad but it was I who killed her."

Sally stepped away from him so abruptly he almost fell. She stood with her hands on her hips and he watched her impassively. On her face was that narrow-eyed, unyielding, God-give-me-patience look which was very familiar to her servants, and to Adam himself. She was scarlet with aggravation and her eyes were a vivid snapping gold, like those of a maddened cat caught in an alley.

"What utter nonsense, Adam Cooper, and if I hear one more word of this self-pitying rubbish you and I will have serious words. How can you blame yourself for the actions of a self-willed, self-centred, downright dishonest woman who does not deserve one moment of your remorse? God in heaven, man, she brought it on herself and I for one am glad she's dead. There, call me wicked but it seems to me everyone's life is better without her in it. Her daughters, you, and certainly me, since what she held so cheaply, I value more than my life. And I'll tell you this, my darling. That picture comes down this very afternoon and shall be burned before the day is out."

He was weeping as he stepped into her arms.

20

Sally was amazed at the way she was content just to drift through the days and weeks that followed, doing nothing that could even vaguely be called work, not as she had known work at the Grimshaw Arms. Once she could barely bring herself to sit down for longer than five minutes at a time. Now she left more and more in the capable hands of Mrs Trimble while she rode with Adam across the autumn parkland, glorious with the changing shades of the trees. Blue smoke from young Reuben's bonfire of raked leaves misted across the flame of the woods while calm and sweet peace brooded tranquilly in Sally's heart. She and Adam wandered in a white world of snow and frost, hand in hand through the pale winter sunshine, the dogs quiet at their side, their breath wreathed about their heads, the air windless, pink flushes on the snow, the woods quiet and silvery.

Spring came with its usual exuberant explosion of the first snowdrops, the rich spectrum of crocus and soldier tulips, the proud trumpeting of daffodils in a massed carpet beneath the greening trees. There were silver dews and scented evenings and the girls grew and began to shout across the gardens as they ran in circles about their stepmama and Papa who loved one another so dearly and so openly that it wrapped protectively about them who had known none and the babies crowed with the wonder of it all.

Evelyn Trimble had proved in more ways than one to be a saviour to her mistress and when the question of who was to take over the tenancy of the Grimshaw Arms was brought up it seemed she had the perfect answer.

"It's my sister, madam, and her husband, and, if I may be so bold and not seem to be blowing my own trumpet, the same woman, our mam, brought us both up in the same ways. If you understand my meaning."

Sally did, exactly.

"She hasn't had the training I had in the kitchen but she's a good plain cook which, meaning no disrespect, is all that's needed in a country inn. She doesn't mind hard work, in fact she thrives on it. She's even-tempered, cheerful you might say and she's a good head on her. Jack, that's her husband, well, he's not got the brains our Ruth has, but he's got the muscle needed in a public house though he's even-tempered with it and as willing as a plough horse. Pull together, they do, and they make a good team."

She and Sally were seated in the small sitting-room, and, the occasion being what it was, not the usual menu-discussion kind of occasion, Sally had ordered coffee.

"Fetch two cups, Maddy," she told the astonished housemaid, astonished because who ever heard of a cook sitting down to take coffee with her own mistress? Of course, their mistress was not the usual run-of-the-mill sort of a mistress, they had quickly found that out. She pleased herself what she did. And the captain let her do it since it seemed she could do no wrong in his eyes.

Take the matter of Mrs Richard Porter, for instance, who had called on the mistress a few weeks ago. It seemed Mrs Porter, as the older resident, not in age but in the number of years she had lived in the district, should be the one to call first on a newcomer. Strictly speaking as she was sure Mrs Cooper would know, Mrs Porter said, shaking out the full skirt of her fashionable gown and ignoring, or perhaps not noticing Sally's total bewilderment, they should have been introduced in the home of a mutual friend before calls were exchanged. But it seemed none of her friends was yet acquainted with the new Mrs Cooper so Mrs Porter had decided to ignore the rules of etiquette just this once and call anyway. She did hope Mrs Cooper would not be insulted. She did not add that her husband, who knew Adam Cooper for a wealthy, influential and potentially useful man, had been the one to urge her to call.

The cards had been brought in on a silver salver and Henton could not hide his satisfaction over this, their first proper caller. Naturally Mrs Cooper's sister visited her, bringing those brats of hers, preening and nodding like royalty as she was handed down from the carriage by Alec who had been sent to the landing stage to meet her off the ferry. Mrs Grimshaw, who was Mrs Cooper's sister-in-law, was a frequent visitor as well with her own infant daughter, often accompanied by Mrs Grimshaw's mother, Mrs Norton. They had thought themselves to be exceedingly grand, you could see it in their air of hauteur, at least until they crossed the threshold of Coopers Edge and saw the splendour of the home in which plain Sally Grimshaw was the improbable mistress. And you could tell these callers irritated Mrs Cooper no end since everyone in the house was aware that she wanted the company of no one but the captain, their twins and Miss Leila and Miss Aisha. Nevertheless she was forced to put up with them, since they were related to her brother Freddy.

"That woman will drive me to distraction," she told her

husband who had her on his lap, his mouth warm against the soft skin just below her jawline, his hand cupping her breast.

"Which woman is that, lovely girl?" he murmured, fingering her nipple until it hardened in his hand.

"You know who I mean," she answered somewhat breathlessly. "Freddy's dratted wife. I swear I'll personally throttle her if I have to listen to one more word of complaint about my brother. As if I don't already know his faults, chapter and verse, and could enlighten *her* as to some of his more colourful escapades and if you keep that up it will give Tipper a heart attack when he comes in to check on the fire."

"Don't you like it, my darling?"

"Adam . . ." Her breath was becoming ragged and his mouth curled in mischievous laughter against her throat. "I'm trying to tell you about Dorothy and Freddy."

"I'm listening, I really am. Just take no notice of what my hand is doing," he said, hand now inside her low-cut bodice.

"Well, she says he's gambling again. He and Jacky are going off to that casino. Oh God . . . Adam, how can I . . .?"

"What is it?"

"How can I concentrate when you're doing that?"

"I can stop if you want."

"No, you can't, and I don't want you to. Let's go upstairs."

"That's very forward of you, Mrs Cooper."

"I know," clutching his head to her now bare breast.

"What about Freddy and his gambling and you haven't brought me up to date on the progress of . . . what's it called?" His tongue and teeth teased her nipple.

"It's a she and her name is Angela."

"Of Angela."

"Damn Angela and her mother and her mother's mother. Take me upstairs," which he did, laying her on their bed and making love to her with the exact degree of roughness and tenderness which is the mark of the true lover.

Sally took a liking to Mrs Richard Porter, who, on the occasion of her first visit, had sent in not only her own card but two of her husband's as well which, Sally learned, was the correct thing to do when calling on a married lady.

The whole thing was an astonishment to Sally who had no idea that society ladies went to such rigorous lengths to maintain etiquette and, knowing no better, said so to the pretty Mrs Porter who sat opposite her in her drawing-room, drinking tea. Again, drinking tea was considered a serious breach of conduct since a visitor calling for the first time stayed for no longer than five minutes, Mrs Porter told her, begging her forgiveness. But, as Sally said to Adam later when she was describing the event, she would no more entertain a guest in her home without offering refreshments than she would fly to the moon on a broomstick. And Sally had found she couldn't really be irritated by her visitor and the web of punctilious convention in which she was enmeshed since it would be like showing impatience to a well-meaning child. Mrs Porter was harmlessly good-natured, you could see that, eager to be friendly, a bit giddy perhaps and inclined to chatter of inconsequentials, which was all she knew. She was twenty-three, she confided artlessly to Sally, and had four children herself. She was the wife of a gentleman in the business of shipping, as most gentlemen were in Liverpool or at least in some trade connected with the sea. They had a house just outside West Derby on the very same road as Coopers Edge. Coalgate House. Perhaps Mrs Cooper had passed it on her travels, Mrs Porter ventured.

"Oh, please, do call me Sally."

It was Mrs Porter's turn to be astonished. She had been brought up by a mama who had taught her that friendships should not be casually formed. There was a rhythm, a routine to the strict rules of "calling" and so far Mrs Cooper had broken every one.

"Then you'd best call me Helen," she said, breaking another herself, quite taken out of herself by the extraordinary frankness and plain down-to-earth common sense of Mrs Adam Cooper.

They spent a pleasant hour discussing their children, the local society families with whom Helen was acquainted, the merits of this or that dressmaker, though Sally confessed she only knew the Misses Yeoland. Did Sally like to hunt? Helen asked guilelessly and when she was told that her hostess had only recently climbed, for the first time, on to the back of a horse, declared herself to be amazed.

"You do know I was an innkeeper's daughter," Sally asked her bluntly, "before I was married?"

Yes, Helen had heard but was willing to overlook this fact, it seemed, since it was important to her husband, Richard, though she did not say so, to have as a guest in his house, a man whose fortune, come from his deceased first wife, might be diverted into his own growing concern. It never hurt to have friends with money who might be prevailed upon to invest some of it to Richard Porter's advantage, he had told her. She found she didn't mind at all since Sally Cooper's outspoken humour and refusal to conform to the social mores of the day were like a breath of fresh air let into a stuffy room in which all the windows had previously been closed.

Captain and Mrs Adam Cooper were invited to dine at Coalgate House the following week which was quite extraordinary, Mrs Trimble, who seemed to know about such things, confided to her mistress, since Mrs Cooper had not yet returned Mrs Porter's call, this being the rule in polite society. There were two other couples dining, a Mr and Mrs Frederick Page, Mr Page being in the business of cordage and canvas, and Mr and Mrs Samuel Patmore, who was "in" cotton. They were quite flabbergasted to find that the new Mrs Cooper was prepared, nay, eager, to talk about matters which had always been considered fit only for a gentleman and what seemed worse, that her husband didn't seem to mind. But then, she told them, smiling sweetly, she had been in business for herself for nearly fifteen years of her life so the ladies would understand, she was sure, why she found the gentlemen's conversation so fascinating. The ladies, and their husbands, didn't, but then as *she* was so fascinating, so completely out of the concept of any woman they had ever known, not only her brain, but in her looks, which were really nothing to write home about, they forgave her for it. After all, her husband was so wealthy.

Though Sally considered calling and dining out a complete waste of her own precious time, which might more pleasurably be spent with her own family, and in the evenings with her husband whose company was the only one she valued, she found herself, through Helen Porter, slowly being drawn into a round of hospitality that she could well do without.

"I know, lovely girl. Do you think I enjoy spending an evening discussing with Richard Porter the advantages or otherwise of importing cotton from Alexandria and exporting iron bars to God alone knows where, for I certainly don't, nor do I care. And I can make neither head nor tail of the shares he seems bent on selling me into an Admiralty contract for the carrying of mail, though no doubt it could prove profitable. He talks about immigrants as 'freight' or 'cargo' and how much of it can be crammed into one ship. But we must consider . . ." He paused.

"What?" Sally leaned towards him anxiously.

"There are the girls." His face was grave, sad somehow and as always she leaped in as though whoever had put that expression there hadn't reckoned on Sally Cooper and her fierce protective loyalty to those she loved.

"The girls? What have they to do with it?" She frowned.

"Well, I know they are young yet but one day they will be of marriageable age and it is up to me . . . and you, lovely girl, to see that they move in a society where they will meet young men of good family. I feel . . . I owe it to them."

Sally knew he was thinking of Oralie and with an ease which she had learned over the past few months she quickly closed the discussion simply by kissing him until he forgot about it. She made no more resistance on the matter of dining with the Porters. She even organised, with Mrs Trimble's help, a small dinner party of her own, inviting those ladies and gentlemen whose hospitality she had herself enjoyed.

The half-hour before dinner when it was Mrs Cooper's duty to make her guests feel happy, comfortable and at their ease and which, Mrs Trimble confided to her, could be the making or breaking of the most experienced hostess, went off without a hitch. But as Sally said cheerfully as she wriggled more comfortably against her husband's chest in their bed later that night, they all knew each other so well it needed no effort on her part to entertain them. All that was required of her was to drift about, smiling and nodding in agreement with whatever was said to her. Mrs Trimble's cooking was superb and more than made up for any deficiency in *her*. Henton's choice and serving of the wines, the unobtrusive efficiency of the servants, made Sally's part as hostess almost unnecessary. She could have gone off to bed and no one would have noticed, she told him blithely.

"I would," he answered. "In fact I could have come with you."

"Shall we, next time? Slip off and go to bed?"

Their shared sense of the ridiculous was a great joy to them, joining them even closer together though it was a constant source of bewilderment to their servants.

Sally became engrossed, though not too much since she knew Adam would not like it, in the refurbishing, restocking and reopening over the winter months of the Grimshaw Arms which had begun at the end of October. Mrs Trimble had proved to be as good as her word regarding her sister, Ruth Hodges. There was a similarity between them, not just in looks, which were plump, comely and grey-haired, but in temperament and talent.

As though in retaliation for what Sally had done to him, Richard Keene had left the inn in a state which could, with the best will in the world, only be described as run-down. You would have thought the place had been empty for a dozen years and not eighteen months, Mrs Hodges remarked in that brusque, "let me get at it" manner Sally was to come to know so well. She and Sally had left Jack rooting around in the stable, neither of them certain of his purpose but best leave him, Mrs Hodges wisely said, her manner implying that men were like that. Best left alone while the women got on with the serious business of life.

The flagged floors of all the downstairs rooms were an inch deep in filth which Mrs Hodges kicked at disapprovingly, and cobwebs were draped like fine lace from beam to beam. The windows were incredibly dirty and Sally swore they'd not been touched since she last polished them herself in August of 1855. The plaster on the bedroom walls was flaking and damp since several tiles had come off the roof the winter before last and, not being replaced, had let in the rain of eighteen months. There were field mice in the scullery and some roosting birds in the chimney but Mrs Cooper wasn't to worry, Mrs Hodges told her, her Jack would soon have the whole lot cleared up and as good as new. She'd already got her eye on two decent maidservants and a barmaid and her and Jack would manage nicely. Give them a week or two and the place would be ready to reopen for business. Mrs Cooper wasn't to be concerned about her rent, neither. It would be paid on the first of each month and . . .

Here her voice softened strangely as she continued. Mrs Cooper wasn't to bother her head over the Grimshaw Arms. It was in good hands with her and Jack and any time Mrs Cooper wanted to pop in for a cup of tea and a chat she was more than welcome.

"What! You said that to the captain's wife an' them gentry?" her husband gawped when she told him.

"Nay, though she might be a lady now, and I mean that in the proper sense of the word, Jack Hodges," as though her husband might give her an argument over it, "she's not one to refuse to sit down with the likes o' me an' you."

Sally did drink a cup of tea with Ruth Hodges on several occasions after the Grimshaw Arms was returned to its former glory, glorying herself in its restoration. If it hadn't been for Ruth Hodges behind the bar, majestic and good-humoured, and not Sally Grimshaw, the place might have been exactly as it was two years ago.

Even to Arnie Thwaites propping up the bar counter!

Sally and Adam passed their days in a state of quiet content, with Leila and Aisha, and the growing joy of Dominic and Naomi Cooper, who, as Sally had predicted, were on the verge of being absolutely ruined, not only by Adam, Leila and Aisha, who adored them, but by every servant in the house and every worker on the estate. They were both dark as night with the sapphire blue eyes of their father but otherwise not identical.

"I don't know where all those dark curls come from," Sally said musingly to Adam as the pair of them hung besottedly over the canework bassinet in those first weeks. "We've all been fair in the Grimshaw family."

"It did take two of us to make them, lovely girl."

"I know, darling. I remember it well."

"And I'd like to point out that my hair wasn't always grey. I wasn't born with it, you know. I believe I was as dark as these two in my younger days."

"Really?"

"Yes, really, and don't look at me as though I'm a venerable old greybeard whom you can't imagine without a toothless head and a crutch."

"I wasn't, Adam Cooper."

"You were," and, as Tilly remarked privately to Mrs Trimble, they were off again, the pair of them, giggling and holding hands and, when her back was turned, kissing one another as if it was the last day for it. Anyone less like a toothless gaffer with a stick than Captain Cooper couldn't be imagined.

It was late in April and the twins were walking, or rather tottering and falling down at every other step, much to the admiration and wonder of everyone who watched them, from their parents and sisters to young Reuben, Noah and Eppie who were that day turning over the soil in readiness for summer planting. Alice had been left behind in the nursery, glad to catch up on a bit of sewing, she said, watching from the window as the little procession made its snail-like progress round the corner of the house towards the stables. Trixie and Bess were prancing backwards in front of the two girls, begging them to throw sticks for them, grinning in that way dogs have when they are having fun and which is almost human. Adam though he might put Dominic and Naomi up on Bunty's patient back, he told Sally cautiously, knowing her views on it. They might be forward in walking at ten months just gone but that did not mean they could go galloping off across the park, she said sternly. They'd have to learn to ride before long, Adam pleaded or they'd be left behind by their mama and their two sisters who were all three making good progress in the paddocks and meadows at the back of the house. Sally, on Flame, was already cantering beside him across the gentle parkland to the Home Farm and back, and Leila and Aisha, on Dolly and Star, the ponies Adam had bought for them, were doing wonderfully well.

Sally pushed the double baby carriage which had been specially made for her by Charles Burton in Oxford Street, London. It was a large, high-backed, three-wheeled vehicle, designed only for toddlers who could sit up and take an interest in the world, which her two certainly did. It was pushed from behind, with a large hood to protect its occupants from inclement weather. The trouble was, Dominic and Naomi, now that they could walk, resisted fiercely all attempts to put them in it, particularly Dominic who was already showing early signs of his mother's intractable determination to do only what he wished to do. He was not quite eleven months old and was still relatively easy to pick up and restrain beneath the hood of the perambulator, roaring his displeasure which was ignored. What he would be like when he was older and stronger, his nurse shuddered to think, though his charm, when given his own way, was immense. Naomi was softer, more pliable, even-tempered like her papa, whose treasure she was.

The paddock where the horses cropped was shaded all along its perimeter by massive hawthorn trees which were in full and magnificent pink bloom. Harry and Flame, Dolly and Star, Wally and Piper, Jupiter and Mars and even little Bunty moved languidly in the spring sunshine, seeking the shade. Their visitors stood for a while, their arms on the top of the shoulder-high fence, the girls with their feet on its lowest bar. The babies' prattle caused the animals' heads to rise in curiosity. Sally had brought carrots and apples and the horses began to move towards them, nodding their heads and flicking their well-brushed tails, nosing against the shoulders of the humans, blowing through their wide nostrils as they took the titbits from the palms of Leila and Aisha's hands. The girls were identically dressed in plain gaberdine skirts in a warm brown shade, with ruffled shirts of cream cotton, and sturdy black boots. They wore no bonnets and their hair, thick and a shining colour as bright as a garnet, hung in a dishevelled tangle from the cream satin ribbons which had originally tied it up in a thick plait. They had been running and skipping, chasing the terriers, leaping over fallen logs in the wood, playing peek-a-boo from behind tree trunks with the stumbling babies, shrieking with laughter, as free and unrestrained as young colts. One of Mrs Trimble's wise adages was that it did not take children long to learn how to be children!

Sally watched them, smiling in remembrance of the two repressed little girls who, just over eighteen months ago, had barely dared to raise their eyes from their own laps, let alone speak, and laugh, run and jump and be, as Adam had wanted them to be, hoydens and tomboys. They had settled in at school and were happy there, learning not only the things young ladies of good family learned, but geography and history, mathematics and French. They were open and friendly with the servants and their teachers and friends at school, Sally had been told, though they were still shy with strangers which was no bad thing, for shyness in young girls was admired in the society of which they would be a part. Sally loved them now and knew her love was returned. She was wealthy in love, rich in its treasures, seeing it in her husband's eyes, knowing it with their shared passion in bed, feeling it surround and protect her every day that dawned. Her babies tumbled towards her in great delight whenever she appeared and her staff held her in great respect, even affection, she thought. She was being accepted by the local gentry, not that she cared for herself, only for Adam and the girls and, she supposed, for her and Adam's children now.

Always in the background was the gentle strength and patience of Job, who was to marry Tilly in June. He loved Tilly, he told Sally, during one of their meetings in the park, and Tilly loved him though he couldn't think why, he said wryly, but when he turned to Sally, his eyes crinkling, his eyebrows raised in rueful amusement, what he felt for Sally Grimshaw was still there softly shining. He and Tilly were to have one of the estate cottages which, according to Tilly, would, when Job had finished with it, be no less magnificent than the castle in Balmoral where their queen spent so much of her time. They were both to continue to work for Captain and Mrs Cooper, though for how long Tilly would do so remained to be seen, intimating that Job Hawthorne's virility would not be long in putting Tilly in the family way.

They put the babies in the carriage, strolling down the paddock fence, the dogs nosing ahead following rabbit trails, the horses trailing behind in a straggling line on the other side of the fence in hope of further titbits.

A fenced meadow, sometimes used as a paddock, lay beyond what was called Near Paddock. It was a delight to the eye and the heart and the nose with its sweet country fragrance and its full spring blooming of wild flowers, knee-deep in field mouse ear and campion, in buttercup and lady's smock, in shepherd's purse and meadow saxifrage and speedwell. A shimmering sea of colour, white and red and rosy pink, gold and lilac and blue, a beauty which was almost too painful to look at, an enchantment to the senses set in a pale sea of silvery grasses which brought them all to a bemused halt.

They stood for ten minutes or so, their silhouettes becoming smudged as the early twilight began to fall. Birds were settling for the night, squabbling and noisy but growing quieter as darkness drew near. Even the girls were still, crouched in the grass with the panting dogs.

"It's grand, isn't it, lovely girl?" Adam murmured to his beloved wife and the sigh which whispered from him was one of pure content.

A small flock of sheep were grazing a hundred yards away, moving slowly from sweet patch to sweet patch, ewes with their heads down and butting babies doing their best to get to the teats beneath their wandering mothers as they cropped.

A flicker of black and white rose from a clump of longer grass. A lapwing, scolding and fierce in its defence of its nest, made a run at one of the ewes and she took off in alarm, her two lambs frisking behind her.

"It will have eggs laid there," Adam told the girls, "or

perhaps even hatched chicks. A lapwing's been known to chase off dogs and even horses who get too close to her nest at this time of year." He looked at Sally as he spoke and in his eyes was the certainty that he would do the same.

They turned then, sauntering back up the slope, the perfection, the peace of this their home laying its kind hands on them all.

It frightened Sally now and again. This joy, this bounteous goodness which the fates had heaped on her, this brimming sea of happiness in which she swam so serenely. It frightened her lest she flounder in it and become washed up on the arid shore she had occupied before she married Adam. She was a different woman now, she was well aware, from the prickly, priggish Sally Grimshaw who had judged her sister Violet for her carelessness in producing one baby after another; from the opinionated arbitrator who had overlooked Freddy's sweetness of nature and saw only his weaknesses.

It was her turn to sigh. The babies had fallen asleep, their dark heads close together as they lolled in the confines of the baby carriage. Leila and Aisha walked ahead of them, soft laughter drifting back and the dogs padded quietly at Adam's heel. Her arm was linked in his as he pushed the perambulator and she held it tightly with both hands, her head resting on the strong curve of his shoulder. He dropped a kiss on her hair which smelled of sunshine and spring flowers and was like tangled silk beneath his lips.

"I love you, Sally," he said quietly and seriously. "You don't know what you have given me."

"I love you, Adam, and I do because I know what you have given me. We have exchanged hearts." She looked up at him and smiled.

They saw the strange carriage standing on the gravelled carriage circle as they turned the corner of the house and began to saunter across the wide stretch of lawn which lay before it. It was a handsome carriage, polished and gleaming, a dark green and pulled by two matched greys.

"Oh, bugger it," Adam said, ignoring his wife's rule on swearing. "Who in hell is this, and at this time of day? Not one of your new friends, I hope, because if it is they'll receive short shrift from me." Sally didn't know why, perhaps it was a presentiment of what was to come, but her heart felt like a small bird which had blundered into her throat and now fluttered there, trapped. She put a hand up to it, her left hand, for her right was holding Adam's forearm with a grip that made him wince.

The wide front door was standing open, the light from the lamps which Tipper had just lit streaming out in a golden flood across the steps. Sally, with that portion of her brain that was not numbed with dread, thought how welcoming it looked, but why was Henton standing at the top of the steps and why did his elderly body appear to be sagging? Henton, who always stood tall and straight despite his age. His grey hair, usually brushed back so neatly, was standing on end and even in the semi-light, his face was like a skull with no flesh on it.

"What the devil . . .?" Adam began and for reasons he couldn't understand he pulled his wife closer into the safety of his protective arm. The girls sidled over to him, one on his right the other on Sally's left. They huddled close, not knowing why, only knowing that they were afraid of the dreadful tension which had come to shatter the loveliness of their day. Only the sleeping babies were unconcerned.

Henton, or so it seemed, was incapable of speech, merely indicating with a trembling hand towards what the hallway held. Alice, for reasons best known to herself, slipped down the steps and without a word took the handle of the baby carriage from her master's hand and began to push it towards the side door where Dicky had made a ramp to accommodate it.

'Leila, Aisha, come with me," she ordered in the strangest voice and they went without arguing.

Adam and Sally moved woodenly up the steps and, passing the bowed figure of the butler, entered the hallway. A woman stood there before the leaping fire. A woman with a long, slender figure. A woman with wine dark hair coiled on a neck that had the drooping grace of a willow. She had velvet grey eyes with a sparkle of humour and a chip of ice in each one. Eyes that said she could be as deadly as a well-aimed knife if she was crossed. She was beautiful and she was smiling.

It was Oralie Cooper and behind her lounged a triumphantly grinning Richard Keene.

21

The house was like one in which someone was dead and not, as Tilly said hysterically, returned from it. Tilly, deep in shock, as they all were, couldn't seem to stop talking. What was to happen next? she implored Mrs Trimble to tell her. What was to become of them all, as though this dramatic turn of events was to throw them all out on the streets to a life of poverty and degradation. She couldn't make top nor tail of it, she cried, her voice anguished, and didn't want to really. Well, how could anyone? She'd never in her wildest dreams ever imagined that such a thing could happen. A good and decent man like Captain Cooper. A man with two wives at one and the same time and it wasn't right, particularly as one of them was her mistress, Mrs Cooper – Oh, dear God, was she still Mrs Cooper? – of whom Tilly was inordinately fond. And what about Job? Had they seen the effect it had had on her Job? Dear God, she thought he was about to go straight through to the front of the house and kill the man who had brought Mrs Cooper . . . Sweet Lord, was the stranger to be called that? And had it not been for Tipper and Dicky, Jimmy and Alec, yes, it took four of them to hold him, would have done so. They'd have hung him and poor Tilly would have been a widow before she was even a wife, she rambled. What was to happen to the mistress, *their* mistress, not the one who'd turned up on the doorstep as casual as though she'd been on a trip over the water to Wallasey and gone no more than an hour. Nearly eleven years had passed since the captain had brought the little girls home, babies they'd been, no more, hiring staff to look after them, though Tilly had not been here at the time, saying their mama was dead. Now, from the grave, so to speak, their mama was come back. So how was it going to affect those children? she begged Mrs Trimble to enlighten her. To be faced with their beautiful but surely heartless mama sitting down to breakfast with them tomorrow morning accompanied by her guest, who had turned out to be none other than the devil who had tried to put Tilly's Job in prison a while back. How? How? Why? What did it mean? Where would it all end? And on and on in a meandering discourse which was Tilly's way of displaying her great and sorrowing misery for the dead-eyed woman who was, or so it was said, packing her own suitcases at this very moment.

Mrs Trimble let her chip away at it, repeating herself again and again while the rest of the servants stood about like disturbed and homeless ghosts, or wandered from place to place as though they had no idea where they were. From the pantry to the stillroom, from the window to the open back door to gaze sightlessly into the dark and empty yard. Empty that is, except for the bulk of Job Hawthorne who squatted like an enormous and threatening demon against the far wall, waiting, Mrs Trimble knew, to see what Miss Sally, as he still called her, was to do.

What *was* Miss Sally to do? Mrs Trimble wondered sadly as she absently sipped the umpteenth cup of tea Clara had pressed into her hand. What does a second wife do when the first turns up smiling and saying she was back, come to claim her rightful position as Captain Cooper's legally wedded wife, which she undoubtedly was, and to take up the rearing of her own daughters?

What *could* she do? Upstairs, in the elegant warmth and tranquillity of the room which had been hers for such a short time, Sally Grimshaw asked herself the same question. This room which had been hers and . . . no! . . . NO! That was where madness lay and she must not let it get a grip on her, for she needed her wits about her at this moment of decision. She stood in the silent and ice-bound world where the woman called Oralie Cooper had catapulted her and felt nothing. They said a great sorrow was like that. When there is deep and racking grief some force of nature which is kind to sufferers takes over and plunges those who suffer into a state of death-like trance where there are no words, no feelings at first, nothing to be done but wait. There was an emptiness which she knew without question would become filled with an agony she would be unable to stand and the dread of it settled like heavy armour on her body. She was protected for the moment by the insensibility of shock.

Her expression when she looked at her reflection in the mirror to drag back her hair into a tight knot was haunted. Her memory had blanked out the horror of that moment when the figure of Adam's wife had stepped down from the portrait – had they not watched it burn together, her puzzled mind had asked – and become a real woman. Now, as Sally Grimshaw again, she had dressed herself in her plainest, severest gown. She would never see Adam again. She said it out loud, trying out the words but they were meaningless. Her brain knew he was no longer there but her heart even now was still listening hungrily for his footsteps outside their bedroom door. He had been torn from her life, ripping a great jagged hole in it and soon the pain would be unbearable, getting worse with every moment of realising that he was no longer hers.

Something dripped on to her hands which she had folded so tightly in front of her, the fingers were dead white and she was surprised to find she was crying. Downstairs, she supposed Oralie Cooper and Richard Keene were dining at the table where she and Adam had dined for the past nineteen months and where Oralie, as Adam's wife and mistress of this house, had a perfect right to be, but it did not seem to concern the reflection of the lifeless woman who stared back at her from the mirror.

She was not to know of the scene which had taken place between Oralie Cooper and the stout-hearted and loyal Mrs Trimble who had taken a shine to the woman she thought of as the "real" Mrs Cooper the minute she clapped eyes on her. In the drawing-room to where she had been summoned, Mrs Trimble, frozen-faced, had stared with gimlet eyes into those of the woman she was expected to call her mistress and said she would do her best to provide a meal, which might be difficult at such short notice. She had not expected . . . guests, she added grimly.

Oralie Cooper raised exquisitely shaped eyebrows. "Oh, come now, Mrs . . . er . . ."

"Trimble . . . madam."

"Trimble! What an unusual name, is it not, Richard?" Oralie laughed that throaty laugh which had once enchanted Adam Cooper.

Richard agreed, smirking, that it was and Evelyn Trimble vowed she would find herself a new position before the week's end. She was used to working for quality folk and by that she did not always mean those who had been born pedigreed. Sally Cooper was quality in Mrs Trimble's opinion, despite having started life in an inn, and this

. . . this woman was not, no matter what her rank in life might be.

"Very well then, Mrs Trimble, cannot Mr Keene and I dine on what you were to give my husband and his . . . er . . . Miss Grimshaw."

Mrs Trimble saw red then, she told Tilly later. For this harlot, she could be called no less, to cast a slur on Mrs Trimble's mistress was almost more than she could bear, but at that point there was still some confusion as to what the master and the mistress were to do so until it was decided best say nothing. She swallowed the acid taste of contempt which threatened to choke her.

"Very well, madam," she replied and for the first time in her life Evelyn Trimble deliberately cooked the kind of meal she would not have served to the pigs in the stye on the Home Farm.

Sally Grimshaw did not know this and it is doubtful she would have cared had she done so. She knew nothing, only that she must get out of this house as soon as she had packed what she and the twins would need for a night or two. That was all her senseless mind could manage for the moment. Suitcases, baby things, clean underwear, the carriage to be called to wait on the turning circle where Richard Keene's equipage still stood. Nothing else. She knew where she was going, of course, at least for the time being. Like a badly wounded, probably dying animal making its painful way to the safety of its lair, but beyond that, and what she and the children would need for the immediate future, there was nothing.

She could not think about the terrified, weeping girls in the nursery. They had Alice who loved them and was not Nanny Mottram. Whom Nanny had loved she had chastised but Alice was not like that and would hold them together and get them through, since it did not seem to Sally that their mother would take a great deal of interest in them.

But who would lead through to the other side of this the distraught man who lurked somewhere in the dark beyond the house, and who had, for eighteen precious months been her husband? She had been lacerated to the bone, the bones themselves hacked through with a rusty saw as she and Adam had fumbled their way through their last meeting.

"Don't go." His eyes were agonised, sunk in deep purple pits of hopelessness. He spoke jerkily and his body twitched in some strange way as though the shock of seeing Oralie Cooper had disconnected the messages his brain sent to his limbs.

It seemed they could only speak in monosyllables lest they break up and disintegrate completely.

"I must." Her voice was harsh, disembodied, nothing to do with the loving woman he had married a short eighteen months ago.

"You are my wife, not her."

"No . . . she . . ."

"You belong here . . ."

"No . . ."

"Yes, Sally. Don't leave me. Or I will come with you."

"No . . . please . . ." Her throat felt as though a snake was wrapped about it, drawing tighter and tighter.

"We'll take the children – all of them – she doesn't want the girls . . . find a house."

His desperation was punishing her, crucifying her. She knew she should be shrieking and fighting, for this man was truly hers, as she was his, but if she did the ice would crack and she would drown in the flood of its melting. She held a hairbrush in her hand which she had been about to put in her suitcase and she looked down at it as if wondering what its purpose could be.

"No." It was all she had to say to him.

"Sally, don't do this." His voice broke in agony and her heart did the same but she continued to look down at the hairbrush. He held out his arms to her but looking up she saw it and stepped away hastily. She was a cold thing now, capable of cruelty, for it was the only way.

"Christ, what am I to do without you? I can't . . . can't go on, not without you, lovely girl. Stay . . . or take me with you."

His face was skull-like, a skull in which the blue of his eyes was achingly vivid. He pushed a trembling brown hand through his hair and she wanted to go to him, smooth it down, comfort him, hold him in her arms until he was at peace as she had done a hundred times before, tell him she loved him and, quite simply, would die without him, but she did not. He was another woman's husband, not hers.

"How can I stay with . . . her here?"

"She must be made to leave. I'll give her money – and him, for that's what he wants – to go away."

"She is your wife and cannot be made to leave." Her face and voice were wooden and lifeless. "And it is her money you would give her."

"No, when a man marries what his wife has becomes his. I would not . . . deprive her—"

Sally interrupted him harshly. "So she is your wife then?"

"No, no . . . you are my wife. I love you."

"We are not legally married."

"You are my wife, legal or not." He was fighting for control. His face was bloodless and so were his lips as he spoke. "I was told she was dead."

"It doesn't matter now. She is here."

"But we must talk."

"There is nothing to talk about."

"Dear God, will you stop fiddling with that bloody hairbrush and listen to me. Sit down, please. It cannot all be decided in a moment. This is madness. We are a family, we have children . . . our children who must be considered. We *must* talk about it. Be calm and talk to me, Sally. Sit down and let us speak sensibly about what is to be done."

"There is nothing to be done. A man is not allowed two wives."

"Christ, I can't bear this. Where will you go? Wherever it is I shall come after you, you know that. You are my heart and I can't live without you. I can't bear this . . ." he said again.

"You can. You will."

"Jesus Christ, Sally, how can you be so calm?" He closed his eyes briefly and she thought he swayed. She wanted to beg him to leave. To say, "Adam, if you love me . . . go," but she couldn't. She was going to lose him for ever and could not speak of love.

"You're tearing me to shreds, Sally." He had begun to weep, the harsh, ragged tears of a man whose heart is breaking but she turned her face from him and when he stumbled from the room she continued with her packing. She had not seen him since.

She rang the bell and when Tilly came running, ordered the carriage to be brought round to the front door.

"Where are you going?" Tilly asked her suspiciously.

"That's no concern of yours, Tilly. Ask Alice to—"

"Oh, yes it is. You're goin' nowhere without me an' I know Job'll feel the same."

"Don't be foolish, Tilly. You and Job are—"

"Coming with you, madam, if you please, an' even if you don't please. Me an' Job have a lot of . . . fondness for one another but I'm not that daft that I don't know what he feels about you. You'd not get beyond the front door without him, an' where he goes, I go."

The solid casing of stone which had her in its claw-like grip cracked a little and pain sliced at her, a pain so deep it came from a part of her she had not known existed, but she stuffed something called gritty determination over it and it subsided, for the moment.

"No, Tilly."

"Yes, madam."

"I can't take you."

"Then the pair of us'll follow the carriage on foot."

"Oh, Tilly . . . Tilly."

For a second she almost gave in to the longing to fling herself into this maidservant's comforting arms and weep. Her eyes burned dry in their sockets. Her head ached and so did her throat and chest and in her was a bitterness, a hatred, a venom which, if let loose, could seriously wound someone, probably herself. She supposed that in her place – ha! *her* place – at the dining-room table lounged the woman who had, eleven years ago, almost destroyed Adam Cooper and seriously damaged her two daughters. She would be laughing, drinking the wine Henton poured for her, her beauty a living, glowing thing which nothing could kill. And now she was to destroy them all again, smash to pieces the warm and lovely world Sally Grimshaw and Adam Cooper had built together for their children, and for Oralie's.

"Very well, Tilly, go and pack and tell Alice to fetch the twins."

"Oh God, madam, this will kill the master, you know that."

"Do as I say, Tilly. I'm to leave at once."

Their laughter floated up the stairs to meet her as she and Tilly, a wailing baby each in their arms, came down them. Mrs Trimble stood beside Henton and to hell with protocol, and from the open kitchen door at the far end of the hallway, several pale, weeping faces peeped.

Mrs Trimble didn't weep and neither did Sally Grimshaw now, for were they not the same kind of woman? Strong in adversity.

"If you need me, madam," was all Mrs Trimble said.

"Thank you, Mrs Trimble."

"Thank *you*, madam." It was said as though Sally Grimshaw had given Evelyn Trimble something she valued and would treasure for the rest of her life.

Job held the door of the carriage open for her, taking Dominic for a second, then handing him in to her. He did the same for Tilly with Naomi, then followed the two women and the fretful babies into the carriage.

Mrs Trimble and Henton watched as the carriage drove off down the drive towards the gate. They looked despairingly at one another as a burst of laughter erupted from the dining-room, then moved back inside the house.

In the bit of woodland by the gate a tall man leaned dazedly against the trunk of an elm tree, watching as the carriage in which his life was held passed through the gateway. When it was gone, even the sound of it dying into the darkness, he turned away blindly. He began to walk slowly, like a man wounded who knows he must keep moving but feels his life ebbing away from beneath the hand he has placed over the wound.

For several hours he floundered, he didn't know where,

just putting one foot in front of the other in the pitchy dark of the night. He walked into the trunks of trees, grazing his face and fell over objects that the night had concealed, limping and bruised, bloody and broken. He wept and even screamed his pain into the heavy black skies above him, startling the small herd of deer in the park into a mad stampede of terror. It began to rain and still he blundered on and when at last dawn broke he made Flora cry out in terror as he crashed through the back door into the kitchen where she was seeing to the range.

"Hot water, girl, and at once," he snarled, making for the doorway which led into the hall. The girl cowered back, for he was an appalling apparition, covered in blood and bruises, mud and wet leaves. She barely recognised him as her master and when Mrs Trimble entered the kitchen – well, she couldn't sleep, could she? – Flora was vastly relieved.

"Hot water," he repeated to Mrs Trimble.

"Yes, sir. In your dressing-room?"

He turned on her then, the pain on his face like a mask through which his eyes glittered.

"Good God, woman, do you think I can bear to . . . to go in there . . . when she . . . have you no mercy?" he roared.

"In the spare bedroom at the end of the landing then, sir. Clara will light the fire." Mrs Trimble's voice was calm and compassionate.

Half an hour later Alec, driving the carriage which had taken his mistress away last night, was sent off to deliver a message to Mr Ernest Saunders, Captain Cooper's solicitor, demanding that Mr Saunders attend Captain Cooper at once.

It was no more than six thirty but Mr Saunders came at once.

It was vouchsafed to no one what the two men talked about, closeted in the master's study. Maddy was summoned several times and a great deal of coffee was drunk but the captain did not speak to her but sat with his face staring into the garden where Reuben and Noah and Eppie, not knowing what else to do, were busy getting on with life. They had all heard Flora's description of their master's face and the state he was in this morning: the bruises and the blood and the wild disorder of his clothes; but he was neatly dressed, bathed and shaved now, Maddy reported. Just as he always was, in fact, if you didn't look too closely into his eyes. Such a lovely vivid blue they had been, wasted really on a man, the maidservants had whispered among themselves, with those long black lashes framing them.

They didn't look so glorious now, with the brilliance of superb health, the happiness of a man who had loved and lost his wife and family and home, washed out of them. Mrs Trimble had seen them when she and Flora had carted up jugs of hot water for his bath and she didn't like the look of them, or him, not one little bit. Perhaps this solicitor chap might be able to help. Off his head the master had looked to her and could you wonder? Only God above would know what he would do next. They knew where the mistress had gone, of course, their *proper* mistress, and not that strumpet who, Henton had quietly divulged to her, had gone to her bed, the one she had once shared with the master, stumbling and laughing, flushed and triumphantly beautiful with the best part of two bottles of wine and a bottle of brandy inside her.

"Goodnight, Richard, sweet dreams," she had called out to her guest as he was about to climb into his carriage. "I'll let you know when the welcome home party is to be, though I'm sure we'll meet again before then. You must come and dine. I mean to become socially active again, you know, that is if there's anyone worth being socially active with. Still one can but try and I'm sure all my old friends will be only too delighted to renew our acquaintance if only to find out where Oralie Cooper has been for the past eleven years."

Wouldn't they all, Henton murmured to Mrs Trimble!

She had gone to her bed, ringing for another bottle of brandy and for one of the maids to come and help her undress. Hot water, she wanted and a plentiful supply of warm towels, if such things were available in this house, she said to Cissie who was the one chosen to wait on her. She'd have her hair brushed and the fire banked up and the window opened slightly and no one was to come near her in the morning until she rang her bell. Tomorrow she meant to do something about this room. It really was incredibly dull and old-fashioned, colourless, somehow, she told the frozen-faced maid as her hair was brushed. She was used to the brilliant hues of India, you see, from where she had come only a few months back. Where she had been since she didn't say. Her overnight bag had been unpacked and her things laid away neatly as she had ordered. Tomorrow the rest of her luggage would arrive, she informed Mrs Trimble. Maddy and Cissie, who had attended to the emergency preparation of this room for her, again on her orders, had been quite racked as to whether they had been doing the right thing. But in view of the lack of their master's interest and the absence of their mistress who should have had the ordering of it, what could they do but get on with it?

"Where has the woman gone?" Mrs Oralie Cooper lazily asked Cissie, not concerned really, giving the impression it was just idle curiosity.

"What woman is that, madam?" Cissie asked bravely, though she knew full well who the intruder – she could think of no other name to call her – meant.

"Don't be pert with me, girl," the woman who was called Mrs Cooper snapped. "I asked you a question and I expect it to be answered." Her eyes, such a soft and velvety grey a moment ago had sharpened to a dark gunmetal.

"I'm not sure . . . who . . ." Cissie had stammered. Cissie had been a housemaid for a long time, working her way steadily from kitchen skivvy to the position she now held which was that of upper housemaid. It was a long time since anyone had intimidated Cissie Newton but this woman did it now.

"Well?" Mrs Cooper tapped her fingers dangerously on the arm of her chair.

"She's gone back to where she came from, madam," Cissie mumbled.

"Oh, and where is that?"

"The . . . inn, Alec said. The Grimshaw Arms."

"Oh yes, now I come to think of it Mr Keene did mention she was a barmaid."

"She *owned* the place, madam," jumping in with both feet to defend the mistress whom she had once described as no better than she should be.

"Did she indeed?"

"And still does. The master bought it back for her." Cissie's voice rose in a crow of triumph and her eyes gleamed, but she knew she had made a mistake. The silver trinket box with which Oralie Cooper was idly toying crashed on to the dressing-table top and with such force Cissie recoiled and dropped the hairbrush. Mrs Cooper's face was twisted into something which could only be described as fury. Her eyes were funny, too, Cissie told the others later, not quite focused and then, just as suddenly, she was smiling, indolent, as she picked up the box again, just like a cat stretching in sinuous pleasure.

"I can see I will have to take a look at the servant situation in this house; er, what did you say your name was?" she asked smilingly.

"Newton, madam. Cissie Newton."

"Newton. I shall remember that. Well, off you go, Newton. I will require your services as a lady's maid until I find one of my own."

"Madam, I'm not trained . . ."

"You do like to argue, don't you, Newton?" The new mistress smiled lazily at the housemaid. Mrs Cooper was dressed in a silky, lacy bit of a thing the likes of which Cissie had never seen before. A lovely shade of pearly blue and so sheer you could see the peaked bobs of her nipples through it and the darkness at the division of her legs. Her skin was a pure driven white, so fine the pale blue veins in her half-exposed breasts were clearly visible. She was drinking brandy, sipping it with evident enjoyment and already half the bottle Cissie had brought her was gone. Cissie had never seen a woman drink brandy before and she was shocked.

"Tell me, Newton, what were those grizzling bundles the barmaid and the servant were carrying as they got into the carriage?"

Cissie's mouth tightened but she had the good sense not to let her resentment show. Grizzling bundles, indeed! The pride and joy of the whole damned house turned out like unwanted puppies, and madam with them. Dear God, for two pins . . .

"Yes, Newton, you have something to say?"

"No, madam."

"Good, now the bundles."

"Captain and Mrs Cooper's children, madam. Twins. A boy and a girl."

"Dear me. Mr Keene did not tell me my husband had fathered a couple of bastards."

"Madam!" Cissie gasped in horror but Oralie Cooper only smiled.

"Off you go, girl. I think I might sleep now. Oh, just pass me that box on the dresser before you go."

A faraway dreaming look of anticipation drifted on to Oralie Cooper's face. She took the box from Cissie's hand, clutching it to her almost naked breast as though it were a lover.

"Goodnight then, madam," Cissie said but madam didn't answer. She was rooting about in the drawer of the dressing-table and when she had found what she wanted, a key, she smiled and sighed as she fitted it into the lock of the box.

Oralie Cooper did not rise until almost noon the next day. She rang the bell to summon Cissie who returned to the kitchen with a face on her that would frighten the cat. Well, she said breathlessly, you could have knocked her over with a duck's feather, looking round the circle of fascinated servants. This included Evelyn Trimble who would not normally have allowed gossip in her kitchen but things were so . . . out of kilter, she didn't know whether she was on her head or her elbow, really she didn't. And anything she could find out about this woman who, having barely got her toe in the door had made it quite plain who she was and what she expected of them, might come in handy, though she didn't quite know what she meant by that. It caused Evelyn to become blinded to the rules she had carefully preserved in all her years as an upper servant and she listened as avidly as the rest to what Cissie had to tell them.

"She looked like death," Cissie said dramatically. "All . . . shrivelled, her eyes like . . . like black holes in her face, and – well, I dunno – not a bit like she was last night."

"What? Give over," Maddy gasped. "She's the bonniest woman I've ever seen in me life. She must be thirty if she's a day but you wouldn't put her past twenty . . . well, twenty-five perhaps."

"She doesn't look like no twenty-five this morning, take my word for it. More like a hundred and five. Not that I could see her clearly because she wouldn't let me draw back the curtains and she says Alec's to go at once to the Adelphi where Mr Keene's staying and fetch him over immediately."

"What for?"

"She doesn't confide in me, Maddy Fletcher, so you'd best send Tom over to the stables with a message for Alec. In the meanwhile she's asked for a pot of Angelica tea."

"Angelica tea? Where am I to get a pot of Angelica tea, whatever it is?" Mrs Trimble protested.

"I've not finished yet, Mrs Trimble. She'll have half a peeled apple, some seedless grapes, an apricot, and half a peach cut up with some figs done in syrup."

"God in heaven!"

"She'll have a bath then and I'm to get her dressed. When Mr Keene arrives he's to be shown up to her room at once."

"God in heaven," Mrs Trimble said again, weakly.

"Shall I tell her you'll go up and see her, Mrs Trimble? Likely she'll want to discuss the lunch and dinner menus." Cissie's voice was faint, the voice of a woman who was fast approaching the end of her tether. Mrs Cooper had frightened her last night but it was as nothing to the apparition which had greeted her out of the dimness of the shrouded bed this morning. She'd to go back in half an hour, Mrs Cooper had told her, and Cissie would have given ten years of her life to have their brisk, cheerful, bustling little mistress back in control of her.

Her brisk, cheerful, bustling little mistress was none of these things now as she lay like a laid-out corpse in the bed in the best bedroom in the inn known as the Grimshaw Arms. Mr and Mrs Hodges had been open-mouthed with amazement when the Cooper carriage had turned into their yard last night and a room demanded for Mrs Cooper. Mrs Cooper was, of course, the owner of the inn and could do as she liked in it but when she had walked into the packed bar parlour, her face like uncooked dough, her eyes looking at nothing, to say she and Jack were alarmed was to put it mildly. She'd had one of her babies in her arms and her maid trailed behind her with the other and at their back was the enormous chap many of the totally silent customers remembered. Several boxes and travelling bags followed, the coachman asking Mrs Cooper most solicitously where he should put them, but she didn't seem to know and Mrs Hodges was too flabbergasted at that moment to tell him.

A fire was lit in the room, the bed aired and her maid put her in it, taking the wailing infants off to the second-best bedroom, refusing curtly to answer any of the landlady's anxious questions.

Order was restored in the bar parlour which was in an uproar with avid speculation and it did not go unnoticed among the customers that the big man settled himself grimly at the foot of the stairs and when, the inn being closed at last, the landlord and his wife proclaimed they were off to bed, it took him all his time to let them go up to it.

22

Sally Grimshaw and her bastard twins! That's what they said about her but for the moment Sally Grimshaw couldn't summon up the strength to care. She was grieving badly. It was as though she were widowed and her mourning must somehow be got through and until it was, if it ever was, nothing mattered to her.

Mr Ernest Saunders visited her a few days later, shown into the small parlour by a somewhat disgruntled Mrs Hodges who had had her whole routine knocked for six by the untimely arrival of the owner of the inn. She was not best pleased to be deprived of her own parlour either, she told her Jack. Sally Grimshaw sat and rocked there for most of the day and sometimes far into the night and where was Ruth Hodges to put her bum down? she asked aggrievedly, but Jack had no answer.

"Your husband has sent me to—" Mr Saunders began but Sally interrupted him, her voice harsh and ragged with her pain.

"I have no husband, Mr Saunders."

Mr Saunders shrugged and sighed sorrowfully. "Well, no, perhaps you're right, Mrs Cooper—" Again she interrupted him.

"My name is Grimshaw. Miss!"

"Well, if you insist."

"I do, and please, Mr Saunders, nothing you can say will make me see him."

Which was true, for Adam had tried and had it not been for Job would have succeeded. For three days he had tried, coming to the inn, his face like that of a haunting spectre, his startling blue eyes on fire with some fever which gripped him, his hair a rough and tumble of silver grey curls, hammering on the door when it was shut, giving Ruth Hodges the screaming palpitations and how was it to affect trade? she asked Jack, and she didn't know how much more she could stand. Neither could her perplexed Jack who couldn't understand what a lady like Mrs Cooper was doing here in the first place. This was her place, they both admitted it, but could she be asked to leave? they asked one another, though it went against all the principles of Ruth Hodges' soft heart to turn out such a wounded little creature on to the streets, and them babies too. Not that she'd be here long, surely, what with him hanging about just waiting for her to come out. That big chap of hers kept him from her, though don't ask Ruth how he did it. Talked to him by the hour, he did, the pair of them slumped on the bench that stood at the front of the inn and when they'd done the captain would climb on to his horse and ride quietly away. But he always came back.

It seemed Sally Grimshaw had turned her face against him. Poor soul, it was all over Liverpool what had happened to her, those in the know coming down, some on one side, saying it served her right, some on the other arguing that she had married him in good faith and couldn't be blamed for her own sin. Ruth Hodges had a good heart but the inn was her and Jack's livelihood and though the astonishing return of Sally Grimshaw did not turn custom away, rather did it bring it in, for there were many customers who wanted nothing more than to get a good "scen" at "old iron knickers" in her defeat, in the long run it would do neither her, her Jack, nor the business any good.

"Miss Grimshaw," Mr Saunders said quietly, "will you let me speak?"

"If you must." It was said with total uninterest.

"Your . . . Captain Cooper is quite out of his mind over this and has asked me to look into the legalities of the matter. He needs to see you, in the meanwhile, talk to you, and if you refuse to see him I cannot vouch for what he may do."

"It doesn't concern me, Mr Saunders," the slowly rocking, frozen-faced, dead-eyed woman in the chair said. She was clean and tidy, her hair dragged savagely back from her bony face. It seemed to Mr Saunders that her hair had lost its glorious colour and he wondered where the curiously attractive, level-headed, sometimes tart, but always humorous woman with whom he had dined a time or two at Coopers Edge had gone. She would recover, there was no doubt in his mind of that. He remembered her vigorous defence the year before of the big man who hovered protectively just beyond the door of the parlour. She was a woman of guts, of spirit, of backbone, though it was hard to believe just now. Ernest Saunders was positive she would get through this but would the man who had sent him to her? Would Adam Cooper? He was strong with that touch of arrogance in him the upper middle classes had acquired over the centuries. He had survived the wretchedness of knowing the wife he had worshipped years ago was as faithless as an alley-cat. Of coming to the realisation that beautiful Oralie Cooper had some deep cankerous blight in her character, something missing that made her indifferent to the pain she inflicted on others. A sensualist with a flagrant disregard for truth, honesty, loyalty. Eleven years ago she had left him and her two daughters and had been obliterated in the heaving mass of humanity that made up the continent of India. Dead, it was said, in childbirth, delivering the premature child of a man who was not her husband.

Adam Cooper had survived the appalling scandal, protecting his children from the worst of it by bringing them home to Coopers Edge. He had taken up his shredded life and carefully sewn it together again. He had recovered from what must have been a difficult situation in the army circles of India, resumed his military career and weathered the storm.

They were both survivors, Adam and Sally, but would Adam manage it a second time? Ernest Saunders doubted it. That was why he was here. To see what he could do to help to bring them together again. Not as husband and wife since they could never be that again while Oralie Cooper lived, but in some way, Adam had begged him, that Sally might agree to.

"Why won't you talk to him, Mrs . . . Miss Grimshaw?" he asked persuasively. "He only wants to talk, for the moment at least. To make sure you and his children are provided for. He is willing to . . . to give you time to reconsider this . . . well, what he sees as a rash flight from your home. There are things that can be done . . . legally, I mean, to persuade . . . Mrs Cooper . . . to leave Coopers Edge. Under the law as it stands a woman's property becomes her husband's when she marries as you well know and so she is totally dependent on Adam Cooper. A way could be found . . . well, I won't bore you with the details," since it seemed to him she didn't care one way or the other. "A clever lawyer can always find a way, and I'm a clever lawyer." He smiled self-deprecatingly.

"Will it mean that I am his wife and she isn't? Will it mean that my children won't be illegitimate?"

"No . . . but . . ."

"Then there is no more to be said, Mr Saunders."

"Miss Grimshaw, please. You are being very harsh. Captain Cooper is not to blame for . . ."

"Is he not?" Her voice had the rigidity of ice in it. "I am yet to be convinced of that."

Mr Saunders looked surprised. "What does that mean?"

"It means that there was a certain lack of substance in my . . . in Captain Cooper's account of his wife's death. I had no reason to doubt him. I trusted him, naturally, and did not ask to see proof . . . documents. I supposed in that vast and teeming country there would be difficulty in . . . in obtaining such proof since no one, him included, had any idea where she had gone. She and her lover just vanished. So, where did Captain Cooper come by the information that his . . . his wife was dead? Did he even receive such information? Does the passage of time – ten years or so – allow it to be presumed she is dead, or did he marry me . . .?"

Ernest Saunders was shocked. "Good God above, Mrs Cooper! Are you implying he knowingly married you bigamously?"

"I don't know, Mr Saunders. And it doesn't matter now. It's done with . . . ended."

She continued to rock and stare sightlessly into the fire, the fire Mrs Hodges was longing to sit by herself.

Ernest Saunders sighed. Not once had Sally Grimshaw turned to look at him. There was silence for several minutes, broken only by the chiming of the splendid grandfather clock which stood against the wall.

Mr Saunders seemed to come to some decision.

"Miss Grimshaw, this is *me* speaking now and not Captain

Cooper who I'm sure would not dream of doing such a thing unless he was pushed into it. I am merely reminding you that those children of yours are his also."

Her head snapped round then and he had her full attention. "There is not a judge in the land who would deny them to him if he demanded them," he continued apologetically. "You are . . . unmarried, Miss Grimshaw, and the courts do not look kindly on unmarried mothers. They are sinners, you see, and will contaminate their own children with their sin. Captain Cooper—"

"You bastard . . ."

"No, it is your children who are bastards, Miss Grimshaw." Ernest Saunders was not a deliberately cruel man but something had to be done to slice through the outer shell of this woman and reach the essence of her, get to where the thinking essence of her lay.

Her face worked, losing its tight shape, the skin of it seeming to droop and become flaccid and hollowed. Her eyes had exploded back to life, changing colour as he watched from the blankness of brown glass to a flashing amber set in crystal. They were almost yellow in her fury, like the eyes of a big cat, a tiger, or a leopard he had seen in the Zoological Gardens. Her lips drew back and stretched over her teeth in a snarl and again he was reminded of that caged and furious animal at the zoo.

"He's threatening to take my children from me?" Her voice was no more than an appalled whisper and Ernest Saunders, who had been a solicitor for a long time and had seen many pitiable things in his long career, felt his heart constrict. He was earning his fee here, doing what he must do for his client who had begged him to bring this woman and her children back to him in any way he could. He had not meant with threats, Ernest Saunders knew that, but the devil drives where needs must and he was willing to try anything, anything that was not illegal, or even anything that was, if he could get away with it.

"No, he is not. You should know him better than that, Miss Grimshaw. It is I who am telling you that he could do it if he wanted. At the moment he is not himself. He will do, or say, anything you want if it means you will allow him to . . . to be a part of your life. To be a part of his. He wants you to return to Coopers Edge and be its mistress . . ."

"And his, presumably."

"You're very harsh, Miss Grimshaw."

"And honest, Mr Saunders. I cannot live a lie. He has a wife living in his home. What place is there for me and my children?"

"I have told you that she can be . . . persuaded to leave. If she was, would you . . .?"

"No."

Ernest Saunders sighed, leaning forward, his elbows on his knees, his hands dangling between them, his head down. After a moment or two he lifted it and studied her.

"Would you like to hear her story, Miss Grimshaw? I have spoken to Richard Keene and since I'm sure you know it was he who found her and brought her back, it might interest you."

Oh, yes, it had not taken a great deal of conjecture on Sally's part to make her aware that somehow this was all Richard Keene's doing. He was a man who never forgot a grievance. A man who would stop at nothing to avenge himself on anyone who he thought had wronged him. Insulted him. Got the better of him and Sally Grimshaw, in his opinion, had done all three. She had thwarted him almost two years ago when he had tried to get at her through Job but that had not been the end of it. Far from it. Going to lengths which were not only extraordinary but costly, he had eventually found Oralie Cooper and persuaded her to come back to ruin Sally Grimshaw's life.

How sweet that revenge must be to him. She let the wretchedness well to the surface of her mind, then, gripping it like a razor blade which would slice her to pieces, she nodded her head.

"She didn't die in childbirth as Captain Cooper was led to believe though the son born to her did. He doesn't even remember who it was who told him that story. You must realise that then, as now, he was stricken by what had happened. His mind was not sharp as it usually is, as it should be as a soldier. He believed her to be dead, or perhaps he chose to believe she was dead in order to free himself of her and begin a new life."

Yes, she remembered Adam's words . . . his feeling of haunted guilt – he had confessed them to her – of his gladness when he learned of her death. The picture in the hall. A hair shirt, he had called it. A penance because he had forced her to go. Had he truly believed her to be dead, or had he, as Mr Saunders said, chosen to believe it because it released him from her for ever? How would she ever know? How in the name of God would she ever know?

She made a small noise like an animal in a trap and lowered her chin to her chest.

"Go on."

"She simply disappeared, and her lover with her, and it was not until Richard Keene found her in a . . . a house of ill-repute in Delhi, that she reappeared. She was . . . with a man, not a white man, you understand, and I will not offend you with the exact circumstances, but he told me, not caring really since she was no more than a pawn in his game, that she would have lasted no more than a few months. She is a drug addict, you see, Miss Grimshaw. For years she has drifted from man to man, wealthy men to begin with, men who treated her like a queen. Not white men or it would have come to the attention of the white community. She has lived in palaces, Miss Grimshaw, been dressed in silk and diamonds, or so Keene told me, but, as she got older and the opium began to take its toll, those men became less, shall we say, elevated. It took him months and God knows why he set out on such a perverse hunt. The world believed her dead but . . . well, it seemed Keene did not. He is an enormously rich man, Miss Grimshaw, and he evidently considered it worth spending a lot of money in his quest. He began here, in Liverpool, he told me, questioning everyone who had known her, discreetly, of course, until he had a clear picture, a clearer picture than even her own husband had of her, and from that he deduced that she was not the sort of woman simply to lie down and die, which, of course, was the truth. He has travelled to many places in India, following rumours and trails and, if it had not been so insane, one could almost admire his tenacity.

"Anyway, to cut a long story short, he found her and took her to some quack in India who fixed her up enough to enable her to travel and brought her back to England. He told her about . . . about you and Captain Cooper and from what he tells me it was that more than any medical treatment that helped her to recover. He put her in a sanitorium down south somewhere where she remained for several months. When she was cured he brought her home."

For five long minutes there was silence. From somewhere above their heads a baby cried, one of hers, he presumed, but she did not stir. Just as Ernest Saunders was beginning to think she never would, she spoke and her voice was as dispassionate as that of a woman who is deciding on whether it shall be beef or mutton for lunch.

"Thank you, Mr Saunders. You have been kind but, really, whatever the health of Mrs Cooper it is nothing to do with me. Now then, if that is all, you really must excuse me. I have decisions to be made and plans to set in motion," which was a lie, for all Sally Grimshaw wanted to do was dig a hole, climb into it and bury herself in the dark of insensibility. To retreat into the haven of grey fog which was her consolation. Grief and loss and fear racked her but it was not visible to Ernest Saunders.

"Are you to speak to Captain Cooper then?"

"No."

"He will not let this be, Miss Grimshaw. You know that."

"Yes, I suppose I do. I will deal with it when, or if, it happens. Now then . . ." She stood up and shook out the plain grey barathea of her skirt. Her hands went to her hair and her eyes to the mirror in a gesture Freddy Grimshaw would have recognised and one which she had not used for many months. She smoothed back her hair into its rigid coil.

He had left and she had sunk down again into the rocking-chair when someone knocked on the door. She lifted her head and turned it slowly, amazed at the effort even the smallest movement took. It was as though her brain was so frozen in its agony it took a moment or two to register something and then to send the necessary message to the part of her which was to be involved.

"Come in." Even her voice was hollow, hesitant.

They came in together, Tilly and Job, awkward, not sure whether to smile at her or whether, in the circumstances, it would be inappropriate. Job almost filled the tiny sitting-room, his rough head brushing the ceiling. Sally, in her dazed and uncaring state, had no idea where he was sleeping and she felt a small spasm of shame move through her. These two had come from decent, comfortable, worthwhile employment, willing to follow her to God alone knew where, not knowing if they were to end up in the workhouse, or some similar establishment, and since then had guarded her and her children with dogged devotion. Her babies, thrust into Tilly's care, had been fed, bathed, watched over, she supposed, without a word of complaint, or even question and she had accepted their loyalty without a word of thanks or even recognition. Without even knowing or caring, if she was honest, that loyalty was being so unreservedly given.

They shuffled their feet and looked at her in embarrassment.

"The babes are with Polly, madam. She's the barmaid," Tilly added quickly. "She's a nice reliable lass and they've taken to her. They'll be all right with her for a couple of minutes."

The babies could have been left in the care of Arnie Thwaites for all the interest their mother had taken in them, Sally's heart whispered desolately, and really, this couldn't go on. She had been here for almost a week and she had done nothing but sit about in Mrs Hodges' parlour, or lie like one dead in Mrs Hodges' best bedroom. Her loneliness and need of Adam were so intense she was half mad with them; so deep and complete she had barely been aware of how badly she was suffering. How depleted her body and mind were becoming. It was so easy to sit here and drift into the trance-like state which kept the pain at bay. She realised she was in limbo, a waiting place that longed to have the hours, the days, the weeks and months over so that the pain would lessen. She was lost and terrified, sitting like a marble statue with her eyes on the hands of the clock, watching them tick on, and waiting, waiting, for the kinder time to come.

But it wouldn't do. Sally Grimshaw, who was buried deep inside this suffering woman, said it would not do.

"Sit down, please," she told Job and Tilly.

"Well . . ."

"Sit down, Tilly, and you, Job. Are we not friends?"

"Well . . ."

They sat.

"I'd ring for tea but I don't think Mrs Hodges would appreciate it." She smiled slightly and that tiny spark of humour seemed to reassure them and they smiled in return.

"Well . . ." Tilly said for the third time. Sally knew she would do the talking and Job would let her.

"Yes, Tilly, please say what you have to say and then it's my turn."

Tilly looked surprised but she drew in her breath and spoke. "Well, not knowing what your plans are, madam . . ."

"Before you go any further, Tilly, may I say that it would be more appropriate if you addressed me in future as Miss Grimshaw, or even Sally, if you could bring yourself to do it."

Tilly gawped and turned to look at Job. The idea of calling this lady by her christian name was too much for her, forgetting that not very long ago Sally Grimshaw had earned her living as Polly did every day behind the bar of the Grimshaw Arms.

"How about Miss Sally?" Job said and smiled that slow endearing smile that told Sally Grimshaw she'd always be his guiding star whatever he called her.

"Well," Tilly said, "if that's all right with you, madam . . . er . . . Miss Sally."

"It is, now what is it you want to say to me?"

"It's me and Job . . . er . . . Miss Sally. We were wondering if you'd mind if we got married, right away, like. As a married couple we'd be in a better position to . . . well, help you, if you see what I mean."

Sally showed her surprise.

"No . . . no I don't, I'm afraid."

"Well, Jack . . . Mr Hodges – not that it's up to him since this place belongs to you – has said he's no objection to Job and me fixing up that cottage at the back. There's no one lived in it for ages . . ."

An image of a droll Irish face drifted across Sally's vision and she heard again that soft Irish whimsey which had threaded through her life before this one. Tim-Pat who was as full as blarney as only the Irish can be, cheerfully and skilfully avoiding anything that smacked of hard work, good at nothing but getting his wife in the family way. Over a dozen of them had lived in that cottage and she wondered where Richard Keene's vindictiveness had scattered them to.

". . . and it'd suit me an' Job a treat," Tilly was saying. "It's as sound as a bell. Job's had a good look at it, haven't you, Job?"

Job nodded, his soft grey-green eyes concentrating on the drawn face of Sally Grimshaw.

"We'd always have a home then. We've a bit put by, me an' Job, an' if we were to find work and . . . well, the thing is if it was needed there'd be a place for you and the babies. Job could do it with a bit of help from Dicky—"

"Hush now, Tilly, that's enough," his patient voice commanded and the interruption was so unprecedented Tilly closed her mouth without another sound. Her face, which was as open and bonny as a daisy in a field, showed her astonishment though and she turned to look wonderingly at Job, her mouth opening again as though to rebuke him.

"Hush now, love," he went on. "Nobody's asked Miss Sally what she wants to do, have they?" For it seemed to Job Hawthorne, who knew Sally Grimshaw almost as well as her own husband, that her face had become even whiter and more drawn as Tilly enthused about the cottage. For some reason his Tilly had got it into her head that, this being Miss Sally's place, she would remain here, perhaps become an innkeeper again, take up her old life, for where else was she to go? But how could she? How could she remain here with Captain Cooper hanging about like a demented ghost, with reminders all about her of what she had lost, what she had treasured for nearly two years: with the carriage going past the door every day and them two little girls who would ride in it? With news coming down to her every day of what was happening at Coopers Edge. With that bitch taking her place alongside the man who would be Miss Sally's husband until the end of their days. A woman who could love only one man, was Miss Sally, and it seemed to him that the captain was made of the same fibre. With the return of the first Mrs Cooper it was an impossible situation and the only way to resolve it was for one of them to go away and who else could it be but Miss Sally? He didn't know how this was to work out, not at the moment, but it seemed pretty obvious that if she was to get herself back to the woman he had known and loved for all these years, she needed a quiet place and a quiet space of time in which to do it. She needed her strength and she could not win it back with her old life passing by her door every day of the week.

"Miss Sally?" he asked lovingly and it seemed Tilly did not mind that special note in his voice.

"You must be married, of course, if that is what you want, and the cottage is yours . . ."

Tilly turned to beam triumphantly at Job, for though she loved this woman who had been so good to them all, she was not as perceptive as the man she herself was to marry. There, her expression said, I knew it would be all right, but Job put a hand on her arm as though to calm her enthusiasm.

"Let Miss Sally finish, love."

"Thank you, Job, and you, Tilly, for what you have done for me, what you are still doing for me, what you are offering me but . . . but I can't stay here, you see. I must get away if I'm to . . . recover. Get away from all the memories, not only of Coopers Edge but of what I was once here at the inn. Though legally it is mine I can't take it over again. It wouldn't be fair to Mr and Mrs Hodges, even if I wanted to. No, I'll find a place where I can have the . . . the time and the quiet, the absence of distractions to work out what I am . . . am to do with . . ." She could not go on but it was obvious what she meant. With the rest of my life, her painfully contorted expression said. How I am to get through to a place which will give me, if not the joy I have known in these last months, then at least some fulfilment in the love of my children? Work, that was what she needed, though she did not say so and Job, at least, understood.

"You must do whatever you think best, lass." His voice was soft. "And you know you'll not be alone. Me an' Tilly'll go with you, wherever it is, won't we, Tilly?"

Though she was open-mouthed in astonishment and, if she was honest, a bit disappointed at the idea of leaving behind the nice little cottage she had envisaged herself and

Job settling into, Tilly knew full well that there would be no life for her without the two people she thought the most of in this upside-down world which was suddenly hers. She nodded.

"You'll need a bit o' help with them babies so you say where it's to be," Job continued, "an' we'll get packed up—"

The crash which interrupted what Job was saying shook the very structure of the inn and afterwards Jack swore he had seen the tankards on the bar jump an inch or two into the air.

They all three turned their heads and stared at the closed door of the parlour, a startled expression on their faces and Tilly put her hand to her mouth. It sounded as though some great weight had been dropped from a great height and really, what with one thing and another she didn't know whether she and the mistress, particularly the mistress, could stand another shock, not even with the strength of her Job to lean on.

Her Job stood up with that swift grace which was unusual in a man of his size and reached for the door handle. In a moment he had it open and was in the kitchen from which the small sitting-room was entered. Polly stood there, one baby in her arms, the other at her feet with a bit of rope tied about its waist, the end of which she clung to as if it were a life-line. On the floor surrounding her were spoons and pan lids with which the child was playing.

"What . . .?" Job asked, looking about him anxiously and when Polly pointed with a trembling finger towards the coffee-room, he turned in that direction. With Sally and Tilly at his heels he followed where she was pointing and from where, suddenly, the most piteous cries were coming. Jack's voice could be heard now, saying over and over again, "Eeh, lass . . . eeh, lass . . . eeh, lass," while all the time the moans increased and echoed about the place like a ghost in full throat.

They all three crashed into one another as they came to the stairs which led out of the coffee-room and up to the bedrooms. Lying at the bottom of them, with her husband jerking about like a landed fish which does not know how it got into such a predicament, was Ruth Hodges.

23

The tales which began to circulate about Captain Cooper's wife, his real wife, that is, made for uneasy listening. The people who heard them were uneasy because, being simple folk who were not used to such scandalous behaviour, they could scarce believe the captain would allow it, not with them girls of his close by. Perhaps he was part of it, some said, but then you'd only to see him hanging about the Grimshaw Arms for a sight of his children, or rampaging about the countryside on that there horse of his, as though Old Nick himself were after him, to realise that such things held no interest for him. Gone in on himself, they said, brooding and silent, a recluse now, the word was from Coopers Edge. He lived in a corner of the house, well apart from where his wife carried on with those strange, wild folk who seemed to gather about her, eating in his own rooms, keeping to himself except for his dogs, riding out on his bay across the parkland where only the deer wandered now, the sound of laughter, the excited yipping of the dogs, the shouts and laughter of children gone for ever.

Today we make tomorrow's memories, Mrs Trimble said before she left and it seemed that was all Captain Cooper had now. Memories. The only time he came to life, and that was only the once, since it appeared she wasn't unduly interested anyway, was when he came home one day to find his wife had come up to the nursery and removed her daughters from Alice's care.

Oralie Cooper was lounging on the sofa in the drawing-room, a thin black cigar in one hand, a glass of brandy in the other. The room was filled with what seemed to be dozens of men and women, drinking, laughing, chattering, flirting, wandering in and out of the conservatory in groups of two or three, with glasses in their hands, but her attention was not on them but on her daughters.

In that mysterious way that had flabbergasted Cissie when she had "maided" her for a week when Oralie first returned to Coopers Edge, she looked as young and as exquisitely beautiful as she had on the day Adam had first seen and wanted her. She wore an afternoon gown of emerald green poult de soie, a pure corded silk of rich quality. It had a jacket bodice shaped to her tiny waist, flaring out below it with basques. It had a deep "V" opening at the front of the bodice, plunging down between the valley of her smooth white breasts, and if she leaned forward, Tipper had confidentially told Jimmy in the stables, you could see the bobs of her bare nipples. And she *knew* you could see them! Her wide skirt was flounced and supported on what was known as a "cage" crinoline. When she moved she didn't walk, she kind of swayed, slowly, and in the sure knowledge a lovely woman has that every man within sight is watching her.

Adam knew he had paid for the gown, as he had paid for every item of clothing – and there were many – she had bought since she had come back six weeks ago. Lace-trimmed petticoats and chemises, a summer wardrobe of silk dresses of every colour imaginable, evening dresses of velvet and silk-mousseline and satin, gold chains and gold earrings, gloves and dainty kid boots. He didn't care. He didn't care if she sucked him dry and spat him out, but he did care about the two little girls who had been loved by Sally, who had been brought out of the darkness into the light by Sally and who never stopped pleading with him to bring her home.

Leila and Aisha, like two little puppets whose strings are being jerked by a cruel puppet-master, sat side by side on the opposite sofa to their mother, their young faces strained and awkward as they did their best to answer her questions. Yes, this lovely creature whose portrait had once smiled down at them from the wall in the hallway was their mama, and they were to call her so, though it did not seem right to them to do so.

"And what have you done at that dreadful school today, my darling?" Oralie asked Leila.

"We are learning French, Mama."

"French! Then do say something to us. Listen, everybody, my daughter is about to speak to us in French."

Everyone obediently stopped, their faces smiling expectantly as they waited for Oralie's daughter to speak to them in French. Oralie's daughter, only recently brought out of the repressed state Nanny Mottram had squeezed her into, and rapidly slipping back into it, could not even speak in her own language to these supercilious beings who were her mama's friends, let alone French.

A big, fat tear spilled from one eye, then the other, running slowly down her pale cheeks.

"Oh, you've made her cry, Oralie," someone sniggered.

"Not I. She is doing that all by herself. But will you look at them, Rupert?" Oralie begged a man of about forty who stood behind her and was fondling her neck. "Don't you think they are like me?"

"Not as beautiful, my sweet, but passable."

"There, you see, girls, Mr Moreton is of the opinion you are not as beautiful as your mama."

"You are the original, my darling, they are but pale copies, the beauty shared between them," Rupert answered, though it did not go unnoticed by more than a few that Rupert's eyes narrowed curiously as he studied the two distressed children, particularly Leila who was fourteen, with small ripening breasts and as fresh and untouched as a dewed rose-bud.

"Now then, you old lecher." Another man, slightly younger, laughed in a high, tittering voice.

"Paddy, now would I?" Rupert grimaced wolfishly.

"Given half the chance, old boy."

It was at that precise moment that Adam Cooper threw open the door. He was not quiet about it and every head in the room turned, including his daughters', Oralie's daughters, who were seen to gasp in relief.

"Go upstairs, girls," he told them, his mouth held in a kind of snarling smile, the smile for them, the snarl for the rest of the company.

"Darling," their mother drawled, "they have done nothing wrong. They were merely entertaining my guests."

"My daughters are not here to entertain your guests."

"*Your* daughters, Adam?" Oralie smiled silkily. She drew deeply on the thin cigar, blowing the smoke expertly into a perfect ring, watching it as it drifted to the ceiling, then took a long swallow from the brandy glass.

"Go upstairs, Leila. Take Aisha with you. It's all right, I'm not cross." He knew these daughters of Oralie fretted badly for Sally and soon he would have to do something about it. They must be protected from these people his wife – God, how foul that word tasted in his mouth – entertained and when – dear God, let it be soon – he had recovered, if only by a small degree, for he would never be wholly recovered from his serious injuries, he would tackle it.

The girls scampered from the room, looking at no one, only their papa who was the one rock they relied on to whom they could cling. There was Alice, of course, but Alice was a servant and easily overruled by their mama. She had done her best, arguing that they were tired and about to eat but their mama had spoken sharply to her and took them down to the drawing-room anyway.

Adam let the door close behind them, then, before they knew what he was about he stepped lightly across the carpet, raised his fist and knocked Rupert to the floor. His head hit it with a gratifying "thunk" and for the first time in six weeks Adam Cooper knew a moment's satisfaction.

"Goddammit, man," the one called Paddy shrilled, "there was no call for that." He backed away as Adam turned on him, his face a twisted mask of snarling menace.

"Perhaps you'd like to stop me," he hissed, his expression telling them there was nothing he'd like better than to take on the lot of them. "I overheard that last bit of conversation between you two and I'm telling you now that if you're not out of my house within five minutes I shall call my men to assist you."

"Adam, dearest, what a fuss about nothing. Rupert and Paddy were only teasing."

Adam turned on her, a terrible blankness in his eyes, his face dark with his loathing.

"I'm not your dearest and I never was. These . . . friends of yours may have been *teasing* my daughters," his mouth was hard and cruel, "but they'll not do it again. Get them out, all of them, and don't invite them back."

"I shall invite whom I please when I please. This

is my house as well as yours. It is my money that restored it and allowed you to live here like a prince with that . . ."

"Be careful, Oralie. Don't foul her name with your tongue or I swear I'll hit you."

"Hit me. Dear God, will you listen to him?" she begged no one in particular, watching with apparent unconcern the rapid departure of her friends, knowing they would be back, including Rupert who was muttering of assault, and the law. She made no move, however, to beg them to stay. She was bored with them, bored with this rural, backwater life which, after six weeks, was already beginning to pall, despite the assorted company of men and women who were her guests, and the little "something" with which Richard supplied her. She could not really call these people her friends, since she had met most of them through Richard during the past six weeks, though one or two were from her old life, the life she had led before she married Adam. Rupert Moreton, for instance. Rupert had a wife and several children whom he rarely visited, tucked away on his country estate somewhere between Liverpool and St Helens. Rupert had been her lover many years ago. In fact she had a strong feeling he could be the father of her elder daughter though she couldn't swear to it. There had been so many!

Marva Lowe had ridden over, dressed as always in her weary-looking riding habit and a man's top hat. Marva, who had been Oralie's girlhood friend and as wild as she was, which was why Oralie had taken up with her in the first place, had brought her husband, Andrew. Andy, as he liked to be called, owed money to nearly every man in Liverpool which was one of the reasons why he and Marva had dashed over to Coopers Edge to see Oralie, whose husband was known to be enormously rich. As soon as she had heard Oralie was home, said Marva, and what a shock it had been, for they had been told she was dead, but a delightful one, of course, she and Andy had saddled up their pedigreed thoroughbreds, which were as undisciplined as themselves, and come over.

They had been more or less permanent guests ever since. They were as hard up as ever, they told her carelessly, and ready to sponge on anyone who would let them, though they did not say so, naturally, as they helped themselves to the champagne and caviare which was all that seemed to be served at Coopers Edge and on which Oralie apparently lived. They were not to know that the cook in the kitchen, the new one Oralie had been forced to employ when Mrs Trimble gave her notice, since even she knew her servants must be fed, was capable only of preparing what she called "good, plain but nourishing food". The household's diet for the past six weeks had been nothing but plates heaped with dubious-looking meats and vegetables, smothered in unrecognisable sauces, followed by apple tart and thin, lumpy custard. Not that Oralie cared about that since she herself lived on fruit, champagne, herb teas which the cook ungraciously brewed for her and imported, exotic, already prepared delicacies such as the caviare. What her husband and daughters ate was of no interest to her.

Of the indoor servants who had served Sally Grimshaw, or Mrs Adam Cooper as she was then, only Henton, Tipper and Maddy remained. Henton said he was too old to start again at his age and Tipper, who was young and easily impressed by anything new, found the change to his liking. He was a good-looking young man and came in for a lot of attention from the ladies who filled Mrs Cooper's drawing-room, and not a few of the gentlemen. Tips were good and he'd be a fool to give it all up, he told Mr Henton, who cared neither whether Tipper stayed or went.

Maddy had been offered and had accepted the position of housekeeper, flattered by Mrs Cooper's proposal that she take over from Mrs Trimble in the running of the house. It was something she had not in her wildest dreams expected to gain for at least another ten years, if then. Her wages had been raised from twenty pounds to forty-five a year, an offer which took her breath away. Mrs Cooper had found a lady's maid of sorts and, with Alice Cartwright, the complement of staff was complete. Alice had told Captain Cooper she could not, in all conscience, not caring what he thought, leave the two girls totally to the mercy of their mama, her frigid tone implying that neither should he.

The rest had gone, Cissie to a decent job in Liverpool, easily found since Captain Cooper had written her such a glowing character reference. Clara had been taken with Mrs Trimble to Mrs Trimble's new position as cook to an old family friend of the Coopers, out at Rainhill, saying that as she had started Clara's training she might as well complete it. The remainder of the kitchen maids had been found decent employment, since they were all good girls, trained up by Mrs Trimble under the watchful eye of the woman Mrs Trimble still insisted on calling Mrs Cooper. None of them wanted to go since this house had been their home, Cissie for nearly ten years but how could they stay with the "goings on" which went on under its roof? You never knew what was to happen next. It was unnerving, to say the least, to come across a half-clothed gentleman pursuing a lady in the same state on the top landing and she for one was not used to such things, Cissie sobbed on Mrs Trimble's ample bosom in that first week, and as for Mrs Cooper, and the state she and her bedroom got into overnight, it was enough to frighten the wits out of the bravest. The stink up there caught at your throat and God knows what caused it. Though it grieved her to leave them two little girls and the sad and shambling figure of the man who was her master, she was off.

She eyed Maddy. "And I'll bet you're not far behind me, Maddy Fletcher, for all your grand new job."

It was the talk of the district, the mass exodus – well, almost – of the indoor staff of Coopers Edge. A cook of indifferent talent, a sluttish kitchen maid who she said was her niece, a butler, a footman and a young housemaid who was expected to be a housekeeper overnight were all that remained to serve the family which had been all but destroyed by the return of its rightful mistress.

But that was only the half of it! Arnie Thwaites thought he was seeing things, or that time had mysteriously run backwards two years, when he swung open the door to the taproom on that first evening and saw Sally Grimshaw, just as she had been then, looking at him over the bar.

"Good evening, Arnie," she said, bold as brass, just as though she had never been away. "What'll you have? The first drink's on the house . . . well, on me."

"But . . ."

"Now then, Arnie, it's not like you to hesitate when offered a free beer."

He could not say she smiled at him exactly. She was dressed as she had always been, neat, trim, plain, with her hair dragged back from her face which had not improved since last he saw her. In fact, it was thinner, bonier, with her cheekbones ready to come through her skin, he thought, and her colourless eyes sunk in deep, purple pits

"Well, I never," he gasped, "if it isn't Mrs Cooper."

The half smile dashed from her face and she folded her lips into a grim line. Leaning on the bar counter so that she and Arnie were almost nose to nose, she unfolded them again and hissed at him, like a snake that has been prodded to fury.

"Let's get one thing straight, Arnie Thwaites, before I pull you a pint, and that's the question of my name. Last time I stood here I was Miss Grimshaw to you and it's still the same. If you want to continue to drink here, you and the rest of the customers" – several having drifted in and who now stood slack-jawed at his back – "then you'd best remember who I am, who I have always been and who I shall continue to be to you. Sally Grimshaw. *Miss* Grimshaw. Now get that into your head and you and me'll get on a treat. You know how I run this place. Good beer, good food, good value. That's what I give and that's what you'll get and if you don't like it the Bull's just up the road."

Jack Hodges, just come down the stairs from the bedroom in which his wife, and "wire-puller" lay with a broken hip, hovered in the coffee-room doorway, wondering what his Ruth would say if she knew what had just passed between Miss Grimshaw and one of Ruth's most loyal customers. They had recovered most of the old trade from the days when Miss Grimshaw had been in charge and had built up a nice, profit-making little business. His Ruth was a good manager, a good landlady, a decent cook, knowing what men wanted in their drinking house, giving them what once Sally Grimshaw had given them. This was their livelihood, this inn, and Miss Grimshaw was only there until Ruth was back on her feet, she had promised them. But when would that be, he agonised, and when she had gone would they have any customers left?

She worked like a trojan that night, pulling pint after pint of ale alongside Polly, having lost none of her dexterity and speed, it seemed, serving the pickled eggs and onions, the cheddar cheese and crusty bread she herself had baked that afternoon. Pork pies, and pease pudding and faggots were instantly available and when two gentlemen stepped into the bar and asked had they two rooms for the night since they had just ridden in from Oldham, she had them settled, their fires lit, their beds made up and aired and a splendid meal of succulently thick slices of pink ham, mushrooms, eggs, tomatoes and thin fried potatoes in front of them before they barely had time to take off their coats.

Aye, she was a worker all right, but it was her tongue that frightened Jack Hodges though he daren't say a word to his Ruth who was fastened like a beetle on its back in the bed they shared.

Mind you, that maid of Miss Grimshaw's was worth her weight in gold. Once she'd settled them bairns to sleep she'd got down on her knees and scoured the kitchen floor to the high standard even his Ruth would have approved of, then started on the kitchen range. Of course she would have had plenty of practice up at Coopers Edge. Jack was not to know that Tilly had not performed such menial tasks since she had begun skivvying nearly ten years ago.

And the big fellow was just as helpful, taking over Jack's cellar duties without a word said to him, telling Jack to leave it all to him and to see to his wife who lay prostrate and worried out of her mind upstairs. What he and Ruth would have done without these three he didn't dare think since he and Polly couldn't have managed by themselves. A blessing, perhaps a bit mixed, if Sally Grimshaw's tongue was anything to go by, but a blessing all the same and if they could just keep the place going for him and Ruth until Ruth was back on her feet he'd be eternally grateful.

At the end of each day, with every muscle and bone and sinew in her body pulling every which way, since it was nearly two years since Sally Grimshaw had done any hard, physical work, she fell into her bed exhausted, praying for sleep. Only in work and sleep could she find any relief from the suffering which would not let her be. She longed for Adam with a savagery which brought her to her knees at night.

At first she wept silently, tears which slid from beneath her closed eyelids, leaking out from between her eyelashes, sliding down her hollow cheeks and dripping into the plain cotton pillowcase beneath her head. It was like the tide that comes, small, rippling waves that gently touch the shore, then, as the wind and moon catch it, bringing the rollers, bigger and bigger until they crashed in a white-crested explosion of grief on to the beach. A tearing, screaming grief that had her biting at the pillow, stuffing the blankets into her mouth lest she bring the rest of the sleepers to her bedroom door.

First thing, long before anyone was up she would be in the kitchen, scrubbing and deep scouring everything her eye fell on and even, on one occasion, out in the yard chopping wood until Job caught her at it and dragged the axe from her hands. He had folded her wordlessly into the strong circle of his arms and held her until she stopped shaking, then gently led her to the deserted kitchen where, still in silence, they drank a cup of tea together.

Once she said simply, "My heart is broken, Job."

"I know, my lass, I know," he answered.

Violet and Freddy came, their faces identical in their condemnation, not of Adam who had married her while he had a wife living, but of her for leaving all that wealth, that fine position she had had and which they had basked in. And to come back to this, they said, eyeing the small, cramped parlour with the contempt members of the landed gentry might show at being forced to sit down in a labouring man's kitchen. Surely that woman – what? – oh, yes, Adam's wife, he supposed he must call her, surely she could be persuaded to sling her hook, Freddy railed. The captain was a wealthy man and everyone knew that money could buy anything, even the silence of gossips who were fanning the scandal for all they were worth. Captain Cooper had power and influence in Liverpool. His family name was respected. What in the name of all that was sensible did Sal think she was doing, living and working at the Grimshaw Arms, she who had become accustomed to luxury and . . . on and on and on . . .

"It won't be for long, Freddy," she interrupted quietly. "Only until Mrs Hodges is back on her feet."

"Oh, thank the Lord." Both their faces lit up. They were well aware, as was everyone in the neighbourhood, that Adam Cooper spent hours each day patiently waiting for a sight, or even a word of his wife – or rather of their Sal – and his children, and that his lawyer had been a visitor at the inn. Why the captain didn't just go in and drag their Sal home where she belonged was a mystery to them both, but then they did not understand, nor were they even aware of the unusual quality and depth of the love which bound Adam and Sally together, and which now kept them apart.

"So you're to go back then?" Freddy declared triumphantly, since Freddy was in financial trouble again, due to his inability to keep away from the gaming table and was hoping to get Sal to bail him out. Jacky was no help and his father-in-law most abusive on the subject. Now, with this rift between Sal and her husband, things looked a bit dicky for Freddy Grimshaw again.

"No, I'm not to go back, Freddy. I don't know where I'll end up but it won't be at . . . back there. I intend moving on as soon as I can. I shall look for a house and work. I have a little money of my own . . ."

Freddy's jaw dropped and Violet put her hand to her bosom.

"You must be mad. Off your head. He'll not stand for it, or this, for much longer, you know that. We all know that."

"Who?"

"Your husband, you silly cow."

"I have no husband. When will you all see that? He has a wife already."

"Oh, Sal, come to your senses," Violet begged tearfully, for she had enjoyed enormously the kudos of being the sister of Mrs Adam Cooper and would miss the carriage ride from the landing stage up to Coopers Edge no end.

"This is none of your business, Violet."

"You're my sister," Violet wailed, but it did no good and they both left without achieving a thing. They'd be back again, they told her warningly, especially Freddy who was going to be in serious trouble if he didn't find the cash the moneylender was dunning him for. He was wondering if, on the way out, he might tap the captain, who was, after all, his brother-in-law. He had been leaning against the wall on the other side of the lane, nodding politely as Freddy and Violet came in but when they left he had gone.

Job and Tilly were married a week later. The wedding was short and simple. The Wesleyan Chapel just outside Old Swan. Tilly's mam came and a cousin or two, Mrs Trimble and the maidservants who had once worked at Coopers Edge, and Miss Grimshaw. Polly minded the babies and after the ceremony the guests tucked into the spread which Miss Grimshaw, as they were told to call her, had prepared for them.

Tilly and Job spent their wedding night in the spartan

room which had once been the attic bedroom of Bridie and Flo when Miss Grimshaw had been landlady. It would do for now, Job and Tilly said, at least until Mrs Hodges was on her feet and they would be on the move again. At least they all had a roof over their heads, Job said, and work to do, remembering perhaps those days of almost two years ago when he and Miss Sally had slept rough under the hedges until the captain rescued them.

Aye, it would do for now, Sally Grimshaw repeated to herself as she stared blindly at the ceiling of her bedroom, but she must get away soon before it was noticed that she was pregnant again with another bastard.

24

Sally supposed she should have expected it but when, at a leisurely pace as though he had all the time in the world and meant to enjoy every minute of it, Richard Keene rode into the yard, she felt the shock of it hit her like a sledgehammer.

She had not seen him since she left Coopers Edge. Then, as he lounged indolently behind Oralie Cooper, he had had the same self-satisfied smirk on his foxy face, the one repeated today. The same one, in fact, that he had worn over two years ago when he had strolled insolently into the inn and told her it belonged not to the Grimshaw family but to Richard Keene.

Her first instinct had been to gallop wildly into the yard and look for Job, not to protect her against Keene but to protect Keene from Job, for there was nothing more certain than the fact that if Job caught Keene up to no good on her premises, all sense would leave him and there would be a bloodbath.

Job had mentioned casually this morning that he was going to knock a nail or two into some shelves at the cottage where Tim-Pat and his family had once crowded and multiplied. She was aware that he and Tilly were somewhat cramped up in the attic where Bridie and Flo had once shared a bed. The bed, which was mid-way between a single and a double and perfectly adequate for two females, was a bit of a squash for the newly married couple. Not that they seemed to mind, at least Tilly didn't, she told Sally blushingly. There was no such admission on Job's part.

But the cottage, which was structurally sound, had a lot of potential, Tilly's wistful words which had probably come originally from Job and, as Job had some spare time on his hands during the day, it seemed a shame to let the cottage moulder away into an even worse state of disrepair. It could do no harm, he told Sally, to do it up a bit, and would certainly cost next to nothing to put right, which, it being Miss Sally's property, could only put value on it. It was really only a question of replacing crumbling woodwork, putting a new clay tile or two on the roof, replastering and painting the walls and putting in an odd new window frame here and there. He and Dicky could knock up what was needed. Dicky had become a good friend of Job's during Job's stay at Coopers Edge and though he didn't say so, missed him about the place. He wandered over whenever he could, his pipe in his mouth, to give Job a hand. He hadn't a lot to say for himself, like Job, and Sally wondered how they managed to communicate but it was very soothing being in their quiet company as they sawed and hammered and painted, their heads wreathed in identical clouds of fragrant blue tobacco smoke.

The cottage was sturdy, built of stone with a clay tiled roof. The fireplace, a bit knocked about by Tim-Pat's lot, was enormous with a dilapidated range set in it. There was no running water which had to be fetched from a pump in the stable yard. It was plain, basic, with a kitchen-cum-scullery, a tiny parlour and two bedrooms above and how Tim-Pat and his brood had ever fitted into it was a mystery, Sally said to Job.

Now it was looking very spick and span, the new wood

and paint giving it a fresh, pleasant fragrance which it had never had when Tim-Pat and his family had occupied it. Tilly, and Sally as well, since she was glad of anything which kept her busy, scrubbed floors and blackleaded the range, polished brass and windows and even the few sticks of furniture which Tim-Pat had left behind and which Job and Dicky had put in good order.

"We might as well put up a bit of decent curtaining while we're at it," Tilly said longingly, sighing deeply, "and that feather bed could do with a clean."

Before long, and almost without anyone being aware that they had done it the little cottage stood gleaming in the sunshine, as cosy and comfortable, and as ready to occupy as Tilly's yearning hands, which could not wait for their own hearth to tidy, could make it.

"Will you let it, Miss Sally?" she asked diffidently. "It'd bring you in a few bob which would come in handy."

"I suppose it would, Tilly."

"Job says he's going to knock up a decent table and them chairs, with new rush seats in them, have years of life yet."

"That's good of him. I'm grateful."

"And that old dresser only wants a few pots on it and it'd look right homely."

Sally knew exactly where this conversation was leading and she was well aware, and so was Tilly, that probably before the month of May was out, when Ruth Hodges would hopefully be on her feet again, the five of them would be on their way to some unknown destination.

She smiled and took Tilly's hand. "You want to . . . to move in, don't you, Tilly? No, don't pull away. Every woman wants her own place when she's married." A spasm rippled across her thin face but she kept her voice steady. "I know

I did even though I'd always had my own kitchen here . . . and well, why shouldn't you? But please" – as Tilly began to jump about with excitement, her rosy face wreathed in smiles – "please don't get too attached to it. You know I can't stay here, don't you? You do understand that, don't you, Tilly?"

Tilly nodded gravely, sadly, for she surely did love that sweet-smelling, lovingly renovated little home across the yard and could think of nothing more heavenly than to settle down in it. But she knew Miss Sally was eager to get away, probably up north somewhere where she hoped to find a little house, a job of some sort, though God knows what, and make a new life for herself and her children. This hanging about practically on the doorstep of Coopers Edge, with the captain for ever patiently waiting outside the inn and the carriage going by daily with the girls in it, was really getting her down, Tilly knew that. Job had done his best to persuade Captain Cooper to stay away, telling him that he was only causing Miss Sally fresh pain and, given time, who knows, perhaps she would agree to talk to him. She was very frail in spirit and Tilly knew she was afraid of the captain. Afraid that if she had him in the same room as herself he would further weaken her and she would allow herself to become what she could only ever be to him, and that was his mistress.

So on that day Job Hawthorne was at the back of what they still called Tim-Pat's cottage, hacking away at a tangle of honeysuckle which had brought down an ancient arbour on which it had climbed. Tilly was polishing, for the second time, what she called *her* windows, while she kept an eye on the babies, and when Richard Keene casually tied his glossy chestnut mare to a handy ring in the wall and sauntered across the yard, neither of them saw him. Sally was in the kitchen but Keene was not the sort of man to enter any establishment by the servants' entrance. Instead he strolled round to the front of the inn, opened the door and entered the taproom.

Sally was alone. She had just stripped Ruth's bed with Jack's help since it needed a strong man to lift the still inert figure of Ruth Hodges while the sheets were dragged from the bed. Both Jack and Ruth were sweating when it was done, since Ruth was no lightweight and the pain of being moved drenched her in a slick of perspiration. Sally had brought down the soiled bed linen to the kitchen where Polly was on her knees with a scrubbing brush in one hand and a bucket of hot water at her elbow.

At once Sally felt that familiar spurt of irritation she always felt, even now when nothing much mattered to her, when she came across one of her staff doing a job with less than thought, thoroughness and efficiency.

"What on earth do you think you're doing, Polly?" she snapped in a fair imitation of Sally Grimshaw of two years ago.

Polly, who was humming tunelessly to herself, stopped. Her mind had been dwelling on the moment last week when she had been kissed behind the cellar door by a certain underfootman from Abercromby House who spent his evenings off at the Grimshaw Arms and of whom Polly had high hopes. Miss Grimshaw's tart voice had brought her back to the present with a nasty clamour. She raised her head in surprise, pushing a damp strand of her hair from her forehead with the back of her hand.

"I'm doing't floor, Miss Grimshaw. There were mud traipsed . . ."

"You knew I was going to get the dolly tub out to soak these sheets, Polly, and you know there will be water and possibly soda spilled. Surely you could have thought ahead and done the floor after the sheets had been steeped."

"Well, I never thought . . ."

"That's the trouble, not enough thought. Now go and empty your bucket and fetch the tub from the yard."

"Yes, Miss Grimshaw." Polly got to her feet resentfully. Mrs Hodges was a demon for what she called a proper routine and Polly hadn't minded since Mrs Hodges employed her but Miss Grimshaw, who was nothing to do with Polly, was even worse. She bossed Polly around as if she were Polly's mistress and her only doing them a bit of a favour scrubbing the damn floor in the first place. She was a barmaid not a skivvy and Miss Grimshaw had no right to . . .

Polly was still chunnering under her breath as the gentleman rode in, fastened his horse to the ring and disappeared round the front of the building.

As Keene's shadow fell across the taproom floor, stretching almost to the counter, Sally drew in a deep, painful breath, doing her best to get some air into her lungs which felt as though a fist had punched them until they were empty. She put a hand to the kitchen table to steady herself, watching as Keene strolled across the taproom, took off his top hat, placed it on the counter and smiled that smile of his she so well remembered.

"Aah, Miss Grimshaw, there you are. I'll have a brandy, if you please," he told her through the open door at the back of the bar. "I'll take it at the table in the window."

Though he smiled he looked immensely threatening, tall, thin, cadaverous, his time in India turning his flesh to a dirty yellow colour as he waited, narrow-eyed, for Sally to react.

Her bitter hatred gave her strength and put the words in her mouth.

"You'll take it nowhere, you bastard. Get out of my inn before I call Job to throw you out." As she spoke she advanced slowly through the doorway from the kitchen into the area behind the bar, finding to her surprise that she had a kitchen knife in her hand.

Keene's smile deepened and he held up both his fleshless hands in mock surrender.

"Please, Miss Grimshaw, don't make things any worse for yourself by threatening me with that knife. Gladly though I would see you hang I would not care for it to be over my murder."

"Get out of my inn."

"*Your* inn, Miss Grimshaw? Oh, I realise that fellow who bigamously married you for some strange reason bought the place from my agents and, believe me, if I had not been out of the country" – his smile became a leer – "on a matter of some urgency, I would not have let it go to him. I suppose it is yours in that respect but it is let, I believe, to a Mr and Mrs Hodges, who are, in consequence, the landlord and landlady and surely the only ones who can say who is or who is not allowed to drink here."

"That's of no concern to me. This is my property and I want you off it at once or I won't be answerable for the consequences."

"I see your acid tongue is still working. I would have thought that having the position you struggled so hard to achieve taken from you by its rightful owner, the *real* Mrs Cooper, might have wrung some of the shrewishness from you but I see I was wrong. How that man could bring himself to live with you for two years is one of life's mysteries. To get into bed with you must have been a chore but he must have done so since you have two bastards to prove it. Well done."

He was staring at her intently, like a snake hoping to hypnotise a bird. Sally could feel the revulsion and dizziness race through her, one going to her stomach, the other her head, and she fought to stop herself from reeling back in pain. But with that revulsion and dizziness came something else. It was called loathing and it put a stiffener in her spine and lifted her head.

"You're a degenerate, a vile and filthy pervert. Yes, pervert, for the way you live is a perversion of all that's good in the human creature and if you have nothing better to do with your life than meddle in mine then I can only pity you."

"Is that so, miss? Well, let me say it was worth every penny I spent, and I spent a fair few, to find and bring back to her proper place the wife of the gallant captain. A beautiful creature, is she not, who, once I had got her back on her feet, has repaid me in a thousand ways, the most valued being, of course, your downfall. In return I provide her with . . . well, let us say she is grateful to me. Now, Miss Grimshaw, there are not many people who get the better of me but when they do I always make sure they pay for it. As you are paying, Miss Grimshaw. I went to a lot of trouble and considerable expense but by God that moment when you were kicked out of Coopers Edge was the most satisfying in my life."

"I was not kicked out, Keene, I chose to go and believe me when I say I could go back this afternoon if that was my wish. *She* would be the one who would be kicked out, as you so graciously put it, his wife, but . . . but . . ." She paused painfully.

"Yes, Miss Grimshaw?" he asked smoothly, his colourless eyes as flat and expressionless as those of a lizard. "You were saying?" His thin lips curled up at the corners in derision. He was watching her closely as though he could not bear to miss one moment of this pain he was inflicting on her already badly injured heart.

Dear sweet Lord, she didn't know what she was saying. The room was beginning to spin and the knife was heavy in her hand. She looked down at it dazedly, then dropped it with a clatter and she did not see Keene's eyes widen in apprehension. The thundering blur which went past her barely registered. A dark shape which made some noise she did not recognise, leaping across the chest-high counter as though it were no more than a foot from the floor.

A hand gripped her arm and she turned blindly and when Tilly began to scream she recoiled as if a red-hot wire had been thrust in her ear.

It was a repeat of that night upstairs in this very building almost two years ago, only this time it was in broad daylight and when Job's fist drove into Keene's stomach and the air exploded from Keene's lungs, not only could Sally hear it, she could see it. There was a dull crunching sound as Job's other fist splintered Keene's nose and a fine spray of blood spattered Job's clean shirt. Keene's eyes rolled up in his head and he dropped to the floor like a stone.

"Don't let him kill him. Stop him, Sally . . . he'll kill him. Job . . . Job . . . Job . . ." Tilly was screaming but it appeared as though Job, wrapped in a blind and soundless rage, could not hear.

"I'll teach you a lesson you'll not forget in a hurry, you bastard," he was muttering, leaning down, his hands under Keene's shoulders, doing his best to drag him upright so that he could knock him down again.

It took four of them to get him off. Jack, who had almost fallen down the stairs like his wife before him, and who had come to see what all the bloody noise was about, was a powerful man himself but he might have been a small child for all the impact he had on Job. It was really Polly, who confided afterwards that she had three brothers and a pa who liked nothing better than to beat each other up when they had the drink in them on pay day, who stopped it.

"Get him round the knees," she was shrieking, as she vaulted over the counter, not knowing what the hell was going on. "Bring him down," and when Sally and Tilly, not over the counter but under the flap which was safer if not as quick, followed she had Job's knees in a kind of rugby tackle, though, never having seen the game which was played on the fields of England's finest schools, she was not aware of it.

In the kitchen where Tilly had followed when she saw her husband going like a greyhound across the yard, the twins howled their displeasure in the wooden pen Job had made for them and into which she had flung them. Above their heads Ruth was pounding on the bedroom floor with the stick Jack had hopefully had Dicky make for her, crying at the top of her voice, "What is it, Jack? For God's sake, lad, whatever's up?" Her voice was shrill in her fear.

Their combined efforts, and Polly's strong young arms about his knees, had brought Job to the floor, his weight falling across the supine form of Richard Keene, who was beginning to move as though he was coming round. Job went down with considerable force, winded himself, and on top of him were Tilly, Sally and Jack.

Richard Keene opened his eyes and slowly lifted his hand to his damaged nose but continued to lie beside the others. He groaned, then with a loud snort turned his head to one side and was still. There was a suspension of all activity, a stillness filled with the laboured breathing of the tangled bodies on the floor. The increasingly shrill cries of Ruth rained from above and, deafening them all from the kitchen, roared the full-throated bellow of Dominic Cooper who was incensed at being shut up in his pen with only his sister for company and none of the doting adults who were always on hand to do his bidding.

"You'd best get up to Ruth, Jack," Sally said at last, slowly getting to her feet. She was shaking like a leaf on an aspen tree and she put her hand protectively to the small bulge beneath the fullness of her skirt. "And would you mind seeing to the twins, Polly, while Tilly and Job and I tend to this gentleman? Perhaps you could take them for a walk," since the baby carriage had been delivered to the inn by Alec soon after they had taken up residence there.

It took several minutes to sort out and arrange the babies, who did not want to go in the baby carriage either, Dominic told them vociferously in his baby prattle, and to get Polly, who seemed to hold no resentment against Miss Grimshaw for her earlier remarks, along the sunny lane towards Old Swan.

"Visit your mother, Polly," Miss Grimshaw told her graciously. "Take your time, there's no hurry," and Polly needed no second bidding, for it was not often she was given time off when it was not her day for it. Besides, her mam loved kids and, having no grandchildren of her own, would be only too pleased to take these two off her hands while they had a nice cup of tea without her pa and brothers filling the place with their demanding male presence.

But Jack hovered anxiously, eyeing the still figure of Richard Keene, reluctant to leave them even though he was increasingly pulled by the now hysterical moans of his Ruth who must be soothed.

"You'd best see to her, Jack," Sally told him calmly as though this sort of thing was a common occurrence in the bars she had served in. "You go up and stay with her for a while. She sounds dreadfully upset. We can manage here, can't we, Job?"

"Who is he, Miss Grimshaw?" Jack asked curiously. Even he, with his patient, plodding mind, was dumbfounded by the violence he had witnessed here and the chap on the floor, obviously a gentleman by the cut of his blood-spattered clothes, looked to be in a bad way.

"He's . . . an acquaintance of my brother's, Jack. He wanted . . . money and when I refused he became . . . abusive. I had to call for Job. But don't worry, I think he's coming round now. He'll have a right face on him in the morning but Job'll get him on his horse and away to . . . to his home."

"Well . . ." Jack scratched his head. He could see no sign of the fallen man coming round but Miss Sally knew what she was doing, he supposed, and, the habit of obedience being strong in him, he lumbered off in the direction of the stairs.

"I'm coming, queen, I'm coming," the three rigidly frozen figures who stood about Richard Keene heard him say.

Richard Keene was not only in a bad way, he was dead!

Sally had known it, don't ask her how, since she had only twice in her life seen a corpse. One had been her ma and the other her pa who had both died peacefully in their beds. Richard Keene had gone far from peacefully. There was an almost greenish cast to his face under the blood which masked it. It had stopped flowing but it lay in a bright scarlet flower in the middle of his face. His eyes were closed.

Sally stood for no longer than it took Jack to reach and begin to climb the stairs, then she sprang into life, dragging Job and Tilly with her.

"Come along, sir, Job will help you to stand," she

made sure Jack heard her say, aware that Job was staring, first at her then at the recumbent figure on the ground in some astonishment. Job and Tilly, though something told them there was no life in the man Job had knocked down, had not yet got to that stage of sharp, incisive thinking which Sally had passed through and it was doubtful Tilly ever would. Keene was dead where he should not have been dead. Some seizure of the brain, perhaps, or the heart. A broken nose and some smashed ribs did not kill a man, Job would know that since he had suffered both and if she could just get him on the move he would soon snap out of his temporary shock, the shock that had taken his mind, his senses, his ability to think clearly, which had not deserted Sally Grimshaw. Tilly simply stood in the same deeply shocked state, one that would be of no use to anyone.

"Quickly, Job, pick him up and take him to the back of the cottage," Sally snapped, her eyes brilliant and her voice urgent with her need to get these two into some positive action.

"Tilly, you put the kettle on and make us a cup of tea then sit in the chair by the fire until . . . until I come back." Anything to give Tilly something to do! Something familiar! Sally didn't care a damn about Keene, or the rights or wrongs of his death. All that concerned her was that Job should not be punished for it. As far as Jack and Polly were aware Keene was merely winded, beaten about the face by Job and the only ones who knew it to be false were here and they were not about to disclose it, not if Sally Grimshaw had anything to do with it, and Tilly would feel the same when she had pulled herself together.

"Miss Sally . . ." Job began dazedly but Sally pushed him to one side as though he were a troublesome child who had got in her way. She knelt down to check Keene's pulse to make sure he really was dead, though to be honest if Job buried him alive she'd lose no sleep over it.

"Job, come out of it, man. He's dead and believe me we three are not going to swing for it. He's done enough damage to my life . . . and yours too, and I'll not let him persecute us further. We must get him out of here, and quickly. Now pick him up and . . ."

"Miss Sally, I'm not sure we . . ."

"Hell and damnation, Job Hawthorne, will you get him out of this taproom before someone comes in or must I do it myself?" She took Keene's feet and attempted to drag his body across the flags towards the flap of the bar counter and at once, as she knew he would, Job leaped to stop her, picking up the still bonelessly flaccid body of the dead man.

"Where?" he asked helplessly.

"Behind the cottage."

"The cottage?"

"Dear God, if you don't get a move on I swear I might as well go for the police myself. Now, what were you doing before this?"

"Digging the honeysuckle. The arbour was . . ."

"Excellent. Take him there and cover him up with . . . with some . . . some branches or something. When it's dark you can dig a deep hole and bury him. I'll keep Jack and Polly occupied while you do it, then tomorrow, you can repair the arbour and . . . well, you'll know what to do."

"What about his horse?"

Her face whitened further and she clasped her hand to her head. Dear God, she'd forgotten the bloody horse. It could not be left where it was, telling the world Keene had been here, which didn't matter, but had not left, which did. They couldn't hide the animal. They couldn't sell it. The horse had come from somewhere and would have to be explained unless . . .

She felt the nausea tug at her and bile rose to her mouth. Her back ached all of a sudden and her head felt as though a flight of swallows was circling inside it. Tilly, not yet on the move, her eyes fixed unswervingly on the thing which hung limply in her husband's arms, stood as one poleaxed but soon, probably within the next few minutes, she would come out of her trance and begin to fall apart if Sally didn't get her on the move. Someone must be ready for her when she did. This must be all arranged, disposed of, put in order before Tilly Hawthorne settled into the screaming hysteria that was threatening.

"Tilly, I told you to put the kettle on," she said sharply and this time Tilly obeyed, moving off stiffly in the direction of the kitchen.

"There's a . . . a gypsy encampment on the bit of common at the corner of Green Lane," Job ventured hesitantly. He was beginning to think now. "He . . . must be seen leaving . . . Jack must see him leaving . . ."

Sally looked at him hopefully but already she could see what he meant. Leave a horse there in the dead of night and the travelling folk were not likely tamely to take the animal to the authorities with the tale that it was not theirs. They would see it as a gift from heaven and when they left the chestnut mare, probably black by then, would be hidden among their own stock. Job could hide the mare until nightfall, tether it down at the end of the orchard where no one was likely to go in the dark and which was hidden from the road. When it was the black of night, with Keene safely in his last resting place, Job could lead the animal across the fields at the back of the inn and tie it up stealthily where the gypsies would find it tomorrow.

"Can you ride a horse, Job?" she whispered, not wanting Tilly to be aware of what was afoot. The less she knew the less she could reveal.

"I can have a damn good try."

"Take his coat and hat before you . . . leave him behind the cottage. You'll have to . . . to set off for Old Swan, then double back behind the inn to the orchard."

"Aye. I know what to do, Miss Sally."

When Jack came downstairs to say Ruth fancied a drop of brandy to soothe her tattered nerves he was just in time to see Miss Grimshaw waving off the hunched figure of the injured man as he rode away on his mare. A bit awkward the poor sod looked, but then wouldn't any man who'd just had Job Hawthorne's big fist in his face and ribs.

"And I don't want to see you in the Grimshaw Arms again, d'you hear," she called out just before the horse lurched out of the yard and into Prescot Lane.

"He's gone then?" he asked anxiously.

"Oh, yes, I gave him a drop of brandy, Job got him on his horse and he left, as you saw."

"He was all right then?" for Jack wanted no trouble with the authorities.

Sally had got out her bowl and flour with the intention of making a few scones for their tea, she murmured, but she turned, surprise on her face.

"All right? What d'you mean, Jack?"

"He didn't say 'owt about . . . Job fetchin' him one?"

"Not a word, Jack. He knew he was in the wrong. No, don't worry, you'll hear no more from that customer."

Strangely, she had the best night's sleep she had had for weeks but when she woke she had begun to bleed and knew she was losing her child.

25

The carriage drew up at the front of the inn and Sally felt her heart lurch and buck in her chest. She was still inclined to jump and twitch whenever anyone strange came to the inn, her mind flying instantly to that piece of ground behind Tim-Pat's cottage where, saying he thought a bit of crazy paving would look grand, Job had repaired the arbour, pruned and tied up the honeysuckle and laid a path beneath which Richard Keene's body lay.

Tilly was a bag of nerves in the first couple of weeks after the incident, she said, which wasn't good for her in her condition . . . oh, yes, she said proudly, Job had already put her in the family way, but strangely, that very condition seemed to calm her so that she could put what had happened out of her mind. In fact Sally was inclined to think she really did believe that Richard Keene *had* ridden away on his mare that dreadful day. She became placid, as a breeding animal is placid, and once the initial shock had worn off she seemed to accept what had happened with surprising stoicism. She loved Job and she loved Sally and so long as they were not in any danger, little else seemed to matter.

Sally and Job, after the horse was slipped away in the night and the grave covered, their own state of shock dispelled, told one another they felt no guilt, for he'd been a bastard of the worst kind who deserved what he got, may he rot in hell, Job added grimly, but Sally knew he felt remorse. Not for the death of Keene himself but that he, Job, had taken the life of another human being. He hadn't meant to, Sally knew that and in the weeks following she told him so a dozen times.

The carriage which drew up was maroon, polished and gleaming. The horses that pulled it were black and just as polished and gleaming and the coachman who drove it looked as though he had been spring-cleaned.

For several moments Sally thought she was about to faint as the blood left her head and drained away to wherever blood goes to at times like this. It was not very often she even glanced out of the taproom window, for the sight of Adam quietly waiting for her to give him permission to speak to her was more than she could bear. When he was there Job would warn her with a nod of his head and she kept away from the front rooms of the inn, continuing the hard and punishing work she inflicted on herself in an effort to get through the day with her sanity still intact.

It was eight weeks now since she had fled to the Grimshaw Arms, seven since Ruth Hodges had fallen heavily and awkwardly down the narrow stairs and broken her hip and in all those weeks Sally had not once left the inn. Sometimes, of an afternoon, if the weather was fine and work permitted it, she and Tilly ventured out with Dominic and Naomi into the small, flower-studded paddock at the back of the inn, which was shielded from the road, not only by the inn itself but by a dense growth of trees and shrubs. The children were allowed to totter about, their unconcerned baby laughter not heard by their father who waited in the lane at the front. They would roll in the wild flowers, grabbing at buttercups and blue forget-me-nots, or daisies and cornflowers which were no bluer than the blue of their eyes that they had inherited from Adam Cooper, and Sally Grimshaw's heart, which showed no sign of healing, would beat grimly as though to tell her this was a heavy load it bore. They said little, she and Tilly, not even about the future. She was hoping, praying that Ruth Hodges would make some progress towards recovery and they could all five of them pack their bags and go, but Ruth's hip just did not seem to heal and as yet she could not even swing herself out of the bed, let alone put a foot to the floor. The doctor was of the opinion that the bone below the hip joint, the femur, as he called it, had also been fractured and that the ligaments which held the lot together – in laymen's terms – were torn in consequence. He could think of no other reason why it was taking so long to heal, he said, shaking his head and narrowing his eyes as though there was nothing he would like more than to get a look at what was going on beneath Mrs Hodges' skin. But he could see his patient was in good hands, he added, unaware of the despair which corroded Sally's heart.

"Sally," Ruth said to her one day. They were on first-name footing now. "Sally, I don't know what me and Jack would have done without you, lass. And I don't just mean down in the bar neither. You and that Tilly of yours have looked after me as if I was one of your own and I'll not forget it. I know things are . . . bad for you right now and that you're . . . not yourself just yet . . . nay, love, don't look like that," for it seemed the smallest thing these days set Sally off to weeping. Apart from the heart in her which ached and longed night and day for Adam, there was the sorrow at the loss of her child. Inconvenient it might have been to be pregnant now, but it had been hers and Adam's and it was an added grief for her to carry.

"What's to do, lass? Is it the bairn?" since her miscarriage could not be kept hidden. Ruth's kind voice was as soft as the hand she put out to stroke Sally's smoothly brushed hair but Sally shook her head wordlessly and ran from the room. Ruth looked down at her hands and sighed. Her hands had always been the hands of a working woman, rough and callused in places where her scrubbing brush rubbed but now, after lying here all these weeks, they were as smooth as any lady's and her own heart trembled whenever she looked at them. They, more than anything, told her what was to become of her, for this hip of hers was as painful and immovable as on the day she had fallen. She had lost weight, despite lying here doing nowt, and the well-stuffed flesh on her bones hung on her in soft white folds. It was the worry as much as anything that did it, since she knew that without her to see to things her Jack would fall apart and then what was to happen to this wonderful chance they had been given? She knew Sally longed to be away and when she did how were they to keep going without her in charge? She had said as much to their Evelyn last Sunday when she called, which she did every week on her day off, and though Evelyn did her best to chivvy her out of the despondency which had her in its grip she could tell her sister was as worried as she was. Sally must leave soon, there was no getting away from that, even if the inn did belong to her, and Ruth and Jack could not keep on paying her rent for ever if no business was done. Besides, Sally and her servants were doing all the work and should, by rights, be getting a wage. It was a terrible situation from which, at the moment, there seemed to be no escape.

From her bedroom she heard the sound of wheels and horses' hooves on the cobbles below and wondered, without a great deal of interest, who it was.

The coachman climbed down from his box. The carriage, since it looked like rain, had its top up and as Sally watched, trapped, frozen and appalled, unable to move away from behind the bar counter and escape to the kitchen, Alec, for it was he, opened the carriage door and held out his hand to its occupant.

Two occupants, stepping down hesitantly, looking about them with apprehension set in every line of their young bodies. Beautifully dressed, of course, in what Sally had scathingly called their "Nanny Mottram" clothes, bonnets and gloves and hair gleaming like polished garnets.

A great bursting explosion of joy bloomed inside her and for the first time in eight long weeks her face split into a rapturous smile.

"It's Leila and Aisha," she screamed to Tilly who was just about to go into the yard to speak to Job and at once Tilly whirled about, a similar expression of gladness lighting her rosy face.

"It's Leila and Aisha," she screamed in her turn to her husband, who had Naomi under one arm as he did his best to prevent Dominic attacking the back fence with Job's saw. It was Polly's day off and she was sorely missed, since the good-natured young woman was only too happy to mind the babies now that a pattern, fixed on the day of Keene's death, had been set where she was allowed to walk down to her mam's with the baby carriage.

Sally flung open the front door of the inn and held out her arms. With cries of delight and smiles that split their flushed faces from ear to ear the two sisters flew across the cobbles and into them, pressing themselves against her, clutching her in desperate, painful arms and the smiles and exclamations which were the manifestation of their rejoicing turned to tears, great gulping sobs which could not be held back.

"Sally . . . oh, Sally, please come home," were the first recognisable words they said.

"We can't bear it without you."

"Every day we pass here on the way to school."

"I said to Aisha . . ."

"And I agreed . . ."

"And we made Alec stop, didn't we, Alec?"

"Yes, miss."

"We couldn't go on, you see, without you and the babies."

"And Papa is so sad."

"And all those horrible people who . . ."

"Please, Sally, please . . . why are you here and not with us? Have we displeased you? Are you cross with us?"

They would not let her go, clinging to her as badly frightened young animals will cling to their protective mother, and her broken heart, which had thought it could stand no more pain, hurt her so badly she was ready to double up with it.

Job emerged from the yard and the babies, both of them hefted up against his chest, somewhat bewildered by all the commotion, began to babble, recognising their sisters, not as their sisters, but as people they remembered and with whom they had had fun. The trio who still clung together in the doorway suddenly became aware of them. The girls turned to look and at once their tear-streaked faces smiled. They dashed at their eyes with the sleeves of their pretty dresses and wiped their noses the same way.

"Dominic? Naomi? Is it . . . they've grown so, oh look, they remember us."

The babies, in that lovely trusting way young children have, held out their arms and crowed and each young girl took hold of a smiling, wriggling, magical armful of love.

"Oh, Lord," Tilly wailed, tears on her own face, "will you look at that?" then moved to take the infants' place in her husband's arms.

They did not go to school that day. Alec was sent with a message to Miss Davies to say they were indisposed, then given instructions to go home and return to the inn at the time he usually picked them up from school. He was not to breathe a word to anyone, not anyone, was that understood?

"Yes, Mrs Cooper," he answered, barely recognising this pale scarecrow dressed in plain colourless clothes which were too big for her as his golden, laughing mistress of only eight weeks ago.

For the first time Sally did not argue about her name and title. She was too tired, too elated by the visit of the girls, too worried, for the appearance of her stepdaughters was going to provide her with further troubles. She could not turn away from these young girls. She could not reject them out of hand. She could not even give them an explanation they could accept, for they were very young. They had been kept as infants by Nanny Mottram, not allowed to develop as children should and just as they were starting to emerge from Nanny's constriction, as they should, their "dead" mama had come back and Sally herself had been forced to leave them. It was too much for them to bear.

They took off their bonnets and gloves and even their boots, for the sun came out and shone on the paddock where for a couple of hours and in bare feet Oralie Cooper's daughters forgot their mama who frightened them, forgot the dreadful, laughing men who had once come into the nursery where they sat with Alice; forgot the sad man who was their papa, and played as children should.

The ghost of Richard Keene, as she walked with them

down the path over his grave, did not haunt Sally Grimshaw. It was two weeks since he had died and been dumped unceremoniously into the ground at the back of Tim-Pat's cottage and he might have been some stray cat run over by a farm waggon for all the thought she gave him.

The girls helped Sally to make some scones for afternoon tea. They watched in awed admiration as Job and Mr Hodges manhandled a barrel of beer up the cellar steps. What a wonderful place this was, they said to Sally, begging her to tell them about her life when she was as old as they were, which she did and she realised that though she was with his daughters she had managed to put Adam out of her mind for long minutes at a time.

They did not want to go home when Alec came for them, crying sharply, shuddering and hiccupping in Sally's arms, begging her to let them stay. They had been upstairs to pay their polite respects to poor Mrs Hodges and had taken her a vase filled with wild flowers which they had picked while Dominic and Naomi slept. They had peeped into some of the achingly clean and empty guest bedrooms, murmuring how lovely it would be to stay in one, marvelled over the pumps and all the paraphernalia of the taproom and now, as Alec patiently waited while Mrs Cooper did her best to put them back into the immaculate condition in which they had arrived, they sobbed and clung, first to her, then to Tilly and even to Job.

"It's no good, Sally," Tilly murmured to her. "How in God's name do you expect to get them home in this state and hope that no one will notice? Look at them, an' I don't just mean their dresses which look as though they've been dragged through a bramble bush, but the rest of 'em."

Sally had to agree. Their faces were blotched with crying,

their eyes haunted like two puppies who have been thrashed unjustly. Leila was the worst of the two, staring with horror out of the window at the carriage as though at the tumbril about to take her to the guillotine. There was something odd – Sally could not quite put a finger on it – about the lovely young girl, an inclination to cringe away from Jack whom she didn't know. She was polite and well mannered as she had been brought up to be, quieter than Aisha where once she had been the leader but now she hung back and only smiled but rarely.

Sally sighed. She looked better. There was some colour in her cheeks. She had rolled in the flowered paddock with the four children and raced Aisha under the fruit trees in the orchard. She had played pat-a-cake and made daisy chains and the laughter, for children do not restrain themselves in the presence of a grief they do not recognise, had lifted her grieving heart a little.

"What am I to do, Tilly?" she asked wretchedly. "I did not ask for this to happen but it has and I . . . must do something, but what?"

Tilly shook her head sadly. "I don't know, Sally." The "miss" had been dropped on the day Keene died. "Them girls is hurting badly, just like . . ." She dared not speak his name, the man who had become a familiar figure in the lane at the front of the inn but she nodded her head in its direction. "They're only children and don't understand. That . . . that bitch up there's no mother to them, but you are, and you can't ignore it. You've a responsibility which you took on when . . . well, when you wed their pa. Things is altered but them girls haven't. They love you as if you were their own mam and you can't deny it, or them."

"But what am I to do, Tilly?"

"Do what my mam always did when something was troubling her."

"What was that?"

"Sleep on it."

"You mean . . .?"

"Aye, send a note by Alec and tell the captain they're stopping with you, for tonight at least."

Sally was aghast. If possible her face became even more haunted and she put a hand to her mouth. Her eyes were an enormous and incredible golden flame in her face as she shook her head.

"I . . . I can't write to him. He might think it's . . . an invitation."

"Lass, lass, forget about yourself, and him, for a minute and look to them girls. They need your help badly, Sally. I'm not saying bring them here for good because we both know you can't, but give them something . . . something solid, dependable in their lives. Somewhere to go when they need it."

"And when we move away?"

Tilly shook her head. "I think we both know that's not going to happen, love, at least for a while."

"Tilly, I can't seem to think properly. How am I to . . ."

"I know, Sally, it's terrible hard but it must be done. What about that solicitor chap? Why don't you send Alec for him, urgent like? It don't seem to me that them girls will be missed up at Coopers Edge for a while. What was his name? Aye, that's right, Saunders. He could speak for you. Explain what's happened. Make some arrangement. Happen the girls could come and visit." And with a toe in the door in the shape of his daughters would the father be far behind? Tilly exulted since, married or not, Sally Grimshaw and Adam Cooper were meant to be together.

Sally was dying, inch by slow inch, before Tilly's eyes and if Tilly could get them together again she did not care what means she used to achieve it.

If Ernest Saunders was surprised to be summoned, post haste, to the inn on Prescot Lane, it did not show on his smooth lawyer's face when Sally Grimshaw explained why she had sent for him.

"I want you to impress on . . . on Captain Cooper most strongly that this in no way means I am changing my mind about . . . things. He is a married man whose wife lives under the same roof as him."

"Oh, come now, Miss Grimshaw, you must have heard the stories which circulate about what goes on at Coopers Edge. You make it sound as though Adam and Oralie Cooper are sharing a life as man and wife and I can assure you it is not so. There are . . . well, the mildest description of what takes place there is 'wild parties'. God knows where those people come from."

"It is no business of mine, Mr Saunders."

"It is the business of these children. Oralie Cooper's children whom you wish to shelter under your roof for one night."

"But their father . . . he would not let them be . . . involved . . . hurt?"

"He is badly hurt himself, Miss Grimshaw. He is not himself, Miss Grimshaw, and it worries me, who am a stranger really, to know that . . . well, I'm sorry. As you say it is not your business and it is certainly not mine, so I will deliver your message to Adam Cooper and tell him they will be returned, providing he agrees . . . when?"

Dear God, her head was spinning round in circles. For eight weeks she had been concerned with nothing but her own pain and the necessity to drag herself through one endless day after another. Her brain had become numbed, for even the work she did, hard and demanding, was done in the automatic way she had learned as a girl. She had no need to think so she had simply switched off, given herself to the thick, choking clouds of her sorrow, let Tilly and Job look after her children and sunk into the sea of senselessness that was her only refuge.

Two weeks ago the world, in the shape of Richard Keene, had come knocking at her door, but with an indifference, a callousness even, which failed to shock her, she had dealt with him, not by actually bringing about his death since she had no idea what had killed him but by disposing of his body and hiding all traces of him and his visit to the inn. Was that the action of a rational woman? She didn't know, nor could she bring herself to care. He was dead. Good riddance. It was one less problem to drag her from the silent world of grief in which she was mired.

But today she had been forced out of it again, made to think again, made to consider someone other than herself, and it hurt.

"I . . . don't know, Mr Saunders, but if he will allow it I will sleep on it and then tomorrow . . ."

"Yes, Miss Grimshaw?"

"I will let you know."

They were to come every other Saturday and stay overnight and if they wished it Alec was to drop them off on their way home from school for half an hour. The coachman was not at all inconvenienced as he sat in the sunshine and drank a foaming glass of beer with Job while he told him of the terrible goings-on up at Coopers Edge.

The change in Aisha was quite astonishing. With Sally to confide in she became again the blithe young girl Sally herself had made of her. It was as though the hours she spent with her stepmother, with Tilly and Job, with Dominic and Naomi and even Mrs Hodges who became increasingly fond of her, gave her a refuge, a place of peace and safety in which she could rearm herself against the turmoil of what went on at Coopers Edge. It seemed to give her an inner strength to carry her through, to give her the courage to pass by and ignore the growing ruination into which her home was falling and to allow her a small island of normal home life. She spent her days at school and a part of most evenings with Sally where she and Leila tucked into one of Sally's delicious meals, since, in her innocence, she had revealed the inadequacy of the food they ate at Coopers Edge.

Sally was content in their company and glad to see a lessening of their distress, but she could not help but brood on the anguish of the lonely man who was their father and who, even in the hell of his own loneliness, was willing, for the sake of his children, to give up many hours of the small joy of having them about him.

Inevitably he was talked about by the girls, their words lapped up by their stepmother despite the torment it caused her to listen to them. In their naïvety they told Sally and Tilly and Job, and even Mrs Hodges, how dreadful it was for their papa when Mama's friends made such a commotion about the house. Of course he stayed for the most part in his own rooms, Aisha confided to them guilelessly, unaware of the nightmare picture she was painting, unaware of the rigidity into which Sally and Tilly had fallen, the frozen smile which iced her stepmother's face. He goes for long rides on Harry, she added, but when we ask him if we can go too he says he goes too far and too fast. Alice wondered if he would care to eat with them in the nursery and again he refused, but often they found him in the night nursery, just sitting beside the empty bassinets of the twins, in the dark, so they said and once he had been weeping. Gentlemen weren't supposed to weep, were they?

He never came anywhere near the Grimshaw Arms when his daughters were there.

The days were long and unending and though the summer sun shone from a tranquil blue sky, they were grey and sunless days to Sally. At least she was in her right mind again, she told herself, painful as it was, brought back to it by the responsibility she had painfully shouldered regarding Leila and Aisha. She had begun to enjoy their company, looking forward to the end of the day when the carriage drew up, and to the weekends when the excited chatter of the babies and Aisha's laughter brought the place to life.

Yes, Aisha's laughter, Sally slowly began to realise, but not Leila's. The older girl was quiet, grave, inclined to stay close to Sally, helping her about the kitchen and coffee-room, in the changing of the beds, willing to perform the most menial of tasks if it meant she could be with Sally. Tilly and Job, with Aisha, before the inn opened its doors for business, would take Dominic and Naomi, who would be a year old soon, out into the paddock. Sometimes they went beyond to the orchard where apples, damsons, plums and cherries were ripening. Games were played which involved shrieks of laughter and sometimes howls of displeasure from young Dominic who must always be the most important. Ruth said it did her heart good to hear them and if this blasted hip of hers would just mend she'd be out there an' all.

Leila did not go with them.

"I'd rather stay and help you, Sally," she would say. "You have so much to do."

"I can manage, sweetheart, really I can. There's only the

bread to get into the oven and then I'm finished. Go on, go and join the fun."

"No, thank you, Sally. I'd rather stay with you." Her face had a strained look about it and for the first time Sally noticed the deep smudges beneath her eyes. She was almost fourteen and a half. On the verge of womanhood. Perhaps that was it. Perhaps she had begun her "monthlies" which Sally, last year, had explained to her. Alice would help her, she knew it, but if . . . if . . . if what? Why did she have this sense of unease whenever she looked at the exquisite little face, so pale and pointed and solemn? But could she be blamed for being solemn, poor kid, living as she did in the middle of that . . . that madhouse into which her mother had turned Coopers Edge? She was older than Aisha and had understood why Sally could no longer live at the home she had made for them. She knew a gentleman was allowed no more than one wife, the first one, who happened to be her mama and, unlike Aisha, who still believed that Sally would come back to them one day, she knew the woman she had come to love would never live with her papa again.

Sally took off her apron and sat down at the kitchen table. "Let's have a cup of tea, shall we, darling?"

"Can I make it, Sally?" Leila was already reaching for the big brown teapot, the one in which Sally and her ma had once brewed their tea ready for a right good gossip, as Sally's ma had called it, and which had survived the catastrophe which had blasted Sally Grimshaw's life when Richard Keene had come into it. It was a symbol somehow, of something good, she supposed, though what that would be for her, whose life was in shattered pieces about her, she didn't know. Something must be decided soon.

Elbows on the table, the sound of squealing joy coming from beyond the kitchen door where Job swung Dominic high over his head, they sipped their tea in companionable silence. They sat side by side on the bench, their arms touching and when Leila's head dropped and came to rest on Sally's shoulder, Sally knew she must speak.

She put her cup carefully into the saucer. "What is it, darling? I know something is troubling you. It can't be anything to do with . . . with your father and me because I know you understand that. So what is it, tell me? You know I love you as if you were my own daughter."

"I wish I was, Sally." Leila's voice was high and thin with pain. "I *hate* her and . . . and all those . . . those dreadful people. They're always there and sometimes . . ."

"What is it, sweetheart, tell me?"

"Papa says we must stay in the nursery but . . ."

"What?" Sally put her arms about the girl's shoulders and drew her to her own breast. Leila was as tall as Sally now but she burrowed her face into Sally's neck and clung to her for dear life.

"She . . . she made us go down to the drawing-room once and . . . he was there."

"Who? Who, darling?" but it seemed now she had begun Leila could not be interrupted.

"She asked me to speak in French and . . . when I couldn't, she laughed. I began to cry. I didn't mean to . . . but I was frightened, Sally. Then Papa came and told us to leave and he was so angry. Papa hit him – the man – I heard it from the hall, and made them all leave. She laughed and Papa shouted that they were not to come back . . . but they do. Sometimes we go into the garden with the dogs and to the stables and Jimmy says he's . . . going to smash his face in if he comes nosing about there again but . . . but he . . ."

"Who is it, darling?" Sally's heart had begun to beat with a force which made her whole body jump.

"I don't know his name. He's a . . . friend of Mama's. Alice and Aisha say I'm to ignore him when he meets us . . . but he looks at me . . . and I'm so afraid."

"Tell me what happened, sweetheart. Has he . . . hurt you?"

"Oh, no . . . he once jumped out from behind a tree. I'd stopped to pick up a stick for the dogs and he said . . ."

"What did he say, Leila?"

"He asked me . . . if I would let him . . . I didn't understand what he meant. I ran and caught up with Alice and Aisha, but he's always there, Sally."

"Have you told your father, love, or Alice?"

"No . . . no, I wouldn't know what to say."

Sally sprang to her feet, her nerves jangling, her breath ragged, her pulses beating at double their normal pace in outrage. Her face was on fire and Leila stared at her in alarm.

"Well, my darling," Sally proclaimed, "I know what to say and I'm going to say it. Oh, yes indeed." She lifted Leila from the bench, cupped her face and kissed her cheek. "Now you go and fetch Tilly and Job. Do as I say, Leila, please, darling. Now don't cry, don't cry, my love, for I tell you this and you can believe it because I never make promises I can't keep. You'll never be frightened of him again, or of anyone and that includes your mama. Not while Sally Grimshaw lives."

They stared at her in amazement, all six of them, for even the babies seemed to know there was something unusual happening here when she came downstairs in one of her lovely, Miss Yeoland-made gowns. It was of silk, far too big, of course, but she had tied a broad sash of velvet about her waist. The colour of old gold the dress was, and on her head was the jauntiest Dolly Varden hat, like a flat pancake tipped over her forehead and laden down with golden ribbon and yellow silk buttercups. Her cheeks were on fire with something they had not seen for a long time and her eyes flashed golden flames of rage.

"Call me a cab, Job, please," she said crisply.

"A cab?"

"Yes, I believe you know what a cab is."

"Aye, but where are you to go?"

"To Coopers Edge."

26

Henton stared in open-mouthed, pop-eyed consternation when he opened the door to her persistent ring. He didn't like folk who leaned on his front door bell and he had been ready, in his grand way, naturally, to give whoever it was the edge of his tongue, since he was getting old and dispirited and it took him a long while to reach the front door. He spent most of his day sitting in his pantry, sipping the captain's good claret. The captain didn't seem to notice, or care, if he did and, as Henton muttered to himself, what else was he to do in this house where decent society never called? There were plenty of the other sort, of course, but they found their way in, bold as you please, through the conservatory, the side door, or even through the kitchen if they rode over on their mettlesome horses which they left with the resentful stable lads. Not that Jimmy or John or Noah were averse to seeing to the animals, since that was their job, it was the high-handed way they were treated by these worthless nonentities "madam" entertained.

It was a Saturday, a mild, mid-July day and almost three months to the day since the woman on the doorstep had climbed into the carriage and driven away. She had been like some wandering spectre then, white-faced, blank-eyed, ready, so Henton believed, to take off in the carriage to the landing stage and throw herself into the heaving waters of the Mersey.

But would you look at her now? Thin, oh aye, her face almost skull-like but with a flag of scarlet on her cheekbones and a golden glow to her enormous eyes which said that though Sally Grimshaw might have gone down a time or two in the past three months and even been tempted to stay down, from what he heard, she was on her feet now and spoiling for the next round.

She had paid the cab driver and let the cab go since, now she was again in command of herself and her life, she meant to have the Cooper carriage brought round to the front of the house when she was good and ready and have Alec drive her back to the inn.

"Is *madam* in, Henton?" she asked him, wanting to laugh out loud at the sight of his bewhiskered face falling into lines of comic bewilderment. His frock coat and trousers looked as though he'd been to bed in them. His shirt front was soiled and he had not shaved this morning. His dignity was gone and Sally felt the pity move in her.

"Madam?" he quavered. "You mean Mrs Cooper?"

"I suppose I do, Henton. I'll wait in the drawing-room, I think, while you inform her she has a visitor, since I am told she is not an early riser. Perhaps Maddy could arrange some tea for me?"

It was just as it had been two years ago when this same woman had come bustling into their lives and turned them every which way with her absolute determination to have Coopers Edge exactly as she had decided it was to be. Rode roughshod over them all, she did, including himself, forcing them to her will, her routines, her standards, her way of doing things which was after all quite simply the best, her attitude had told them. How they'd resented her.

How they'd despised her for her working-class background and yet she had brought them all into a tranquil, well-run way of life that had been very pleasant.

And where had it all gone? he thought sadly, as he shuffled up the hallway in his carpet slippers to tell Cook they'd a visitor to whom tea was to be given and would Agnes, who was madam's personal maid, scoot upstairs and tell her mistress because he certainly wouldn't dare.

"Who is it, Mr Henton?" the new housekeeper asked, while the slatternly cook looked on indifferently. There was always some guest or other wandering in and out of this house, going where they pleased, doing what they pleased, requiring a meal sometimes which disturbed her easy-going day but it seemed this was not one of those.

"Girl, you'll never guess, not in a month of Sundays." Tipper, who was lounging by the kitchen table studying form in the racing section of the *Mercury* since there was an event at Aintree today and several next week, glanced up, his interest caught by the stunned note in the old man's voice.

"Go on then, who is it?"

"The mistress."

"The mistress?" They spoke together, Tipper and Maddy, then exchanged glances, for why would the mistress ring her own front door bell to summon her butler? Was Mr Henton going doolally in his old age? the glance asked but his next words said not.

"No, not that one, you fools. Not her upstairs since she's not mistress of this house. Never has been, even when she came here as a bride, and never will be. I mean the proper mistress."

There was a silence you could have cut with a pair of scissors for perhaps thirty seconds while the cook and her niece the kitchen maid stared with growing interest from one dumbfounded face to the other. Maddy put a hand to the bib of her none too clean apron, its condition pointing to her tendency to drift with the majority and which said that if you lie down with pigs you become as they are, and began to squeak her disbelief.

"Put the kettle on, girl," Henton snapped, "and make madam a pot of tea." He sat down in the rocking-chair opposite Cook, the action telling them plainly that he was washing his hands of the whole affair.

Maddy wasn't! "What about the master?" she asked him, the expression on her face revealing her alarm.

"What about him?"

"What if comes down and . . ."

Henton sighed. "He's not in, you should know that. He went off on that beast of his a couple of hours since and if his recent routine's anything to go by won't be back till dark."

It was an hour before Oralie Cooper, roused by her maid and brought to her senses with her usual glass of brandy, held by the maid since her own hand was so unsteady, washed, dressed and carefully put together by the maid who was used to the routine by now, came gracefully down the stairs. Without hesitation, since nothing frightened or surprised Oralie Cooper, she threw open the door of the drawing-room and came face to face with Sally Grimshaw.

"Well, well, well, what have we here?" she asked silkily, posing for a moment in the doorway. She knew she looked superb. She always did after she had fortified herself with a dose of the "little something" Richard provided her with. She had not seen him for several weeks now but he always left her well supplied. He had never let her down, not in all the months she had known him and though she was getting low on the "milk of paradise" as she had heard it described by some of the famous people who shared her partiality for it, she was not worried. She knew she meant too much to him and his little plans for the woman who sat on her sofa. Oralie Cooper was the linchpin, so to speak, the hub of his crafty spider's web of deceit and he would not risk it all by carelessly leaving her without what was a necessity in her life. She knew exactly how much it took to keep her from falling into the rhythm of wild mood swings, the high of dizzying elation, the low of dragging depression, the hopeless despair, the cramping pain, the sickness which occurred when she was careless. Taken properly it enabled her to keep up with, even to overtake the men and women who were entertained in her home. The drinking, the wild games, the antics they all got up to in each other's bedrooms and, as long as the indulgences did not reach the nursery floor, were ignored by Adam. Her husband, whom she thought of with the utmost contempt and who seemed to be slipping away more and more each day from the realities of life, would draw the line at that, she knew, even in his silent, rudderless state.

She had often wondered what kind of woman could reduce Adam Cooper to such depths. He had once been a strong and handsome man. Now he was a pale shell who wandered on the periphery of Oralie's life, but as long as that life did not impinge on the world of his daughters, *her* daughters, it seemed he was prepared to let her do as she pleased.

Now she'd seen the Grimshaw woman again she was quite astonished, for she had nothing that would attract any man Oralie had ever known.

"Good afternoon, Mrs Cooper," she said to Oralie, not

rising, continuing to sip the appalling cup of tea which had taken forty-five minutes to reach her.

Oralie sparkled with laughter and shook her elegant head in disbelief then drifted gracefully across the room to the fireplace. Taking a thin, black cigar from the silver box on the mantelpiece, she lit it, drew smoke into her lungs and blew it upwards, stretching the flawless column of her throat. Lord, she was beautiful, Sally thought, admiring the flowing, slender figure, the supple waist, the hair so rich a colour coiled on her neck. She was fine-boned, patrician, pale-skinned and blackhearted and Sally found she hated her with a passion she had never known before. She had ruined the lives of six people, not counting the servants who had left this house rather than work for her, and the men, and probably women too, whose hearts she had broken in her carelessly selfish travel through life.

"So," Oralie said, turning languidly, "to what do I owe this pleasure, Miss Grimshaw? I must admit to a certain surprise in finding you in my drawing-room but do go ahead and tell me how I can help you."

"*Your* drawing-room, Mrs Cooper? Hardly that, but I didn't come here to argue the finer points of possession. I came here to warn you . . ."

"Warn me?" Oralie threw back her head and laughed.

"Indeed, and if you don't heed my warning I shall have you turned out of this house and on to the streets where I'm sure you'll find just the sort of occupation that should suit you."

Oralie was delighted. At last she was face to face in this desert of boredom in which she found herself with an adversary with some guts and backbone, which Oralie admired enormously since she herself was well endowed with both. She had no idea what this plain, thin but beautifully dressed little woman was talking about but it was evident that it was to be entertaining.

"Do you know, Miss Grimshaw, I think I could like you in other circumstances? Now, why don't you tell me what this is all about, but take your time, since it will relieve the ennui until my next guest arrives."

"If he is the man who is intent on abusing your daughter then I shall send Alec at once for the police."

Oralie, for a moment, was open-mouthed in amazement, then she began to laugh, peal after peal of throaty, delighted laughter.

"The police! Really, Miss Grimshaw, what on earth can you be talking about? Rupert is a gentleman. He may have whispered a little nonsense in my daughter's ear but it meant nothing. He has an eye for a pretty woman, you see. He is a dear friend." She fluttered her lashes suggestively and Sally felt the nausea rise in her throat.

"A pretty woman! She's fourteen."

"Oh, come now, Miss Grimshaw, you're making far too much of what was nothing but . . ."

Sally was aghast. "You knew about it. You knew your . . . lover was making advances to your fourteen-year-old daughter?"

"I guessed but there was no harm done. Why, when I was fourteen I had a . . . fling with my father's stable—"

"Madam, you are a monster. You would allow your daughter – a child, no more – to be . . . to be . . ."

Oralie Cooper's smiling face became hard and her eyes flinty.

"Miss Grimshaw, you forget yourself."

"No, madam, *you* forget yourself. I am ashamed to be of the same gender."

Sally could barely speak. Jesus . . . sweet Jesus, it was

worse, far worse than she had expected and it was at that precise moment of speechlessness that it came to her, not in a flash but with a gentle acceptance, that she was the only one, the only person in the world who could have it stopped. Make it all right again. Restore peace and order to the lives of this woman's children, to this woman's husband. Oralie's lover was intent on interfering in some way with her child and Oralie was aware of it. Dear Lord – it made her sick – and she, Sally Grimshaw, must have it stopped at once. She wanted to spring up and reach for that lovely neck, squeeze and squeeze until Oralie Cooper's smoky grey eyes became suffused with the red of bursting blood vessels. She longed to let her own savagery carry her on to the final accounting but that, though it would be very satisfying, was not the way.

"Rupert, is it? Well, you can tell Rupert that he is not to set foot in this house or grounds again and if he does the men in the stables and garden, who are devoted to me and my family, Mrs Cooper, will hold him under lock and key until the police are called. A charge of child molesting will be brought against him – no, don't interrupt me – and you will be forcibly evicted from Captain Cooper's home. Oh, don't think I can't do it, Mrs Cooper. You have been living here only because I did nothing to prevent it. Adam Cooper loves me. I have two children who are also his and I believe if I told him to burn Coopers Edge to the ground he would do it. He owes you nothing."

"That's enough, by God, that's enough, you little bitch. I have no intention of turning away anyone I wish to be a guest in my house. Yes, *my* house, bought with my money."

"This house belongs to Adam Cooper. He is not . . ." She almost choked then, as the tears came to flood her throat but she strangled them with a great effort, making her voice cold, implacable and determined to be believed. "At the moment he is . . . not himself, I know that, and only I can restore him to health."

"God in heaven, Florence bloody Nightingale, is it?" Oralie sneered. She was losing control. Upstairs lay the antidote for it, the antidote she paid for with her body since it was the only currency she had. Oh, she could buy gowns, furs, even jewels, she supposed, and Adam would continue to pay the bills but she had no hard cash to purchase the drugs Richard obtained for her.

"Something like that, Mrs Cooper. Now, shall we come to some arrangement about your daughters?"

"You can go to hell, madam, and take your arrangements with you. This is my house and I shall do as I please in it. And as for Adam you can take him with you to that bloody public house of yours, since I'm told he hangs about there all day long like some love-sick schoolboy. He's no use to me, as a husband or a lover. Oh, yes, I went to his bedroom one night and, being at a loose end, offered . . . well, I thought it might be . . . piquant, but, saint that he is he refused, so do you know what I did, since I was alone?"

"I'm sure it was something no normal woman would dream of doing."

"Probably not, but it was very enjoyable just the same. I took the footman into my bed. I can't even remember his name but, by God, he's energetic."

Sally stood up then, letting the cup and saucer slip to the carpet with a soft thud. She could feel the dizziness and nausea close in on her, wrapping its cobweb shroud about her and she knew if she didn't get away from this evil she would faint right here on the hearthrug. Her head was filled with the echoing sound of Oralie Cooper's laughter, the chink of decanter on glass as brandy was spilled into it, the exploding chirrup of the caged birds in the conservatory. There was badness in this house, a badness which threatened to overcome even Sally Grimshaw's stalwart determination, and she must get away from it.

"And I'll thank you, madam, to stop interfering with my daughters," Oralie continued, raising the glass to her lips and draining it. "If I wish them to come down to my drawing-room and entertain my guests then . . ."

If she had actively thought about it and carefully planned it, Oralie could not have chosen the words most likely to fetch Sally Grimshaw out of the blackness which was threatening her. She felt as though someone had thrown a refreshing, reviving bucket of water over her. She even shook herself thankfully. The colour flooded back to her cheeks and her eyes became brilliant.

"Then I'll bid you good-day, Mrs Cooper," she said icily, "and take up no more of your time. I shall keep Leila and Aisha with me until something can be arranged, probably your removal from this house by Captain Cooper."

"You bitch . . . you impudent bitch."

"More than likely, Mrs Cooper. I hold all the cards, you see. You have nothing. There is nothing for you here so I dare say we will see the last of you soon. Now I shall walk through to the stables and ask Alec to take me back to the inn. I shall arrange with Alice to have the girls' clothes sent over immediately."

"My daughters will not spend another night under the roof of a woman who is no better than a barmaid."

"A barmaid has a decent trade, Mrs Cooper, which is more than can be said of a whore."

They were both startled when the door was flung open with such force it hit a table which stood behind it and split one of the panels. In the doorway stood Adam Cooper. He was dressed for riding, his boots splattered and muddy, for it had rained the previous day, the brown spots of it staining his breeches and jacket and even his face, as though he had galloped like some winged creature across a morass.

It was the first time in three months that Adam and Sally had come face to face. The width of the room separated them, no more, and they were both deeply shocked by the ruin they each saw in the other. In their eyes was an identical expression of rapturous disbelief, of joy they could not hide, the beginning perhaps of a smile, the naked longing to reach out, to hold, to move once more into the safe, strong protection they had provided for one another, but Oralie Cooper stood between them, as she had done from the start.

"Sally . . ." she heard him whisper then Oralie began to laugh derisively.

"Oh, she's not come here to take you into her arms, Adam dearest, so you can wipe that foolish look off your face. She's quite a tiger, isn't she, in defence of what she prizes and it seems she prizes my daughters. Scathing, she is, and very offensive about my qualities as a mother and—"

"Be quiet, Oralie," Adam said wearily, advancing further into the room. Like Sally, his clothes hung on his spare frame. His hair had not been cut, nor brushed by the look of the tangle of silvery white waves which fell to his collar. He seemed to stoop, as though with age. His face, which was an amber brown colour from the sun, had a sickly yellow tinge to it, only the deep blue of his eyes the same in the message of love they sent.

"What—? Have you—? Why have you come, Sally?" For a second hope made his face radiant and Sally felt herself pulled towards him, a file to a magnet, a moth to a candle flame, then the face of his daughter clouded over his, anguished and pitiful and Sally felt the rage of it, which had been directed at his wife, seemingly to no avail, surge on a new path straight at Adam Cooper.

"Why?" she challenged. "You have to ask me that when right under your nose your children are in danger of being corrupted by this woman and her loathsome friends? I am several miles away but I know of it and yet you, who live in this house, and more shame to you, Adam Cooper, seem to be unaware of what is happening. Or perhaps you don't care in your self-pitying state."

"Sally!" His voice broke in agony.

"Does it not matter to you that your wife sleeps with the footman and other men besides? That half-naked men and women chase one another up and down the stairs, so the rumour goes. That excesses which shock the countryside take place under your roof and you do nothing about it. You are weak and cowardly."

"Bravo," said Oralie and clapped her hands in huge delight.

"For God's sake, Sally, have you no mercy?"

"Mercy! Mercy, is it? You need horsewhipping, Adam Cooper, for letting this woman do this to you and your family. I readily admit to some of the blame since I left them unprotected" – *and you*, her strongly beating and loving heart told her – "but even with so much being talked about, the drinking, the wild parties, I believed they were safe with you. I was wrong. This woman is no better than a harlot. I'll go so far as to say a procurer since she is prepared to look the other way while her lover – no, not Tipper – interferes with your child."

"*What!*" Adam's roar of rage could be heard in the kitchen and Henton lifted his head and smiled at Maddy.

"That's better," he remarked, then went back to his newspaper.

"Do you mean to tell me you knew nothing of . . .?"

"Sally, for Christ's sake, you know me better than that. You can't believe – even as I am . . . without you – that I would turn a blind eye to some bastard defiling my child?"

"Not your child actually, Adam, darling. His, or so I believe, though he doesn't know, of course."

Their two heads turned as one to stare in bewilderment which slowly turned to stunned horror as the full impact and meaning of her words hit them.

"Oh, yes, it could be true," she went on, the smoky grey velvet of her eyes beginning to chip with ice. It was as though a diamond shone in each one, a diamond set in dark luxurious lashes. She licked her lips which were a bright poppy red to match the gown she had on and she smiled, cat-like, showing small, feral teeth. "There were several candidates, you see, but I'd say Rupert was the most likely."

"You crazy bitch," Adam said, almost conversationally, as though he were remarking on the colour of her gown or the state of the day. "I could have you put away, do you know that, and believe me the temptation is very great but I think I would be happy to settle for your leaving my house, my life, my children's lives. In fact I shall send for my lawyer in the morning and arrange it. As long as it's not in Lancashire I'll buy you a house wherever—"

"Don't talk rubbish, Adam." Oralie's voice was shrill and she reached for the decanter on the small table by the sofa. Splashing some of its contents into a glass she drank deeply, then refilled it. She tossed that back, then, lowering her chin, stared across at them defiantly. She looked brilliant, cold and beautiful, with nothing in her eyes now but emptiness, no emotion, not even hatred, for it had been burned out of her in India.

Adam sighed and, with a weariness which snagged at Sally's heart, did his best to straighten up his bowed frame.

"I'm sorry, Sally," he said simply. "I'll put it right. I'll . . . make a home for them, a proper home and we'll all three wait with as much patience as we are able for you to come back to us."

She felt better than she had for weeks, she decided, as she drove back in the carriage to the Grimshaw Arms. She could feel the return of her old fighting spirit and she gloried in it. The flush of it warmed her cheeks and brought the light to her eyes. Even her hair seemed to have recovered its normal wayward inclination to misbehave, escaping in curling tendrils to wisp about her ears and neck. She was not awfully sure why she felt so exhilarated, only that the encounter with Oralie and Adam had shown her that it was impossible for her to turn her back, not just on Leila and Aisha, but on Adam. How could she take his children away from him which was what would happen if she allowed this to go on? They would never want to live at Coopers Edge again and neither she nor Adam, she was certain, would force them. So much depended on her, on Sally Grimshaw. How could she turn away from that liability? So many people looking to her for guidance and support and she could not run away from it. Adam was married to Oralie. On a piece of paper somewhere it said so but he was Sally's husband. She and Adam had built and shared a life together and though she had no idea how she was to manage it she'd not abandon it for the sake of a woman who, so said the law, had more right to it than she did.

Damnation, it was *hers*. It belonged to Sally Grimshaw and when she had a moment to draw breath, consider the wonder of it, make that serious commitment which must be made, she'd every intention of claiming it back again. It would not be easy. God, when had anything ever been easy for Sally Grimshaw but had she let it beat her? Well, almost, she mused, considering the hopeless dread, the defeat she had suffered, the grief for the loss of her and Adam's child, the tearing sorrow she had known for months now but her strength was returning and she'd grasp it with both hands and make it bear her on to her future.

Today we make tomorrow's memories. Where had she heard that? She couldn't remember but it didn't matter, for Sally Grimshaw was about to make a few of her own.

27

The rumour that something dreadful had happened at Coopers Edge reached them late the following afternoon.

The girls had been taken home in the carriage just after lunch, not willingly it might be said, for usually they were allowed to remain with Sally until tea-time but their papa had sent word that he wished to see them on a matter of some urgency and he would be grateful if Leila and Aisha could come at once.

"What d'you think it could be, Sally?" Leila asked fearfully. Sally had sworn to her only yesterday that she would never be threatened again and she had believed her, trusted her, had implicit faith that Sally would not allow that man, or indeed anyone, to frighten her again. Sally had been to Coopers Edge to see Papa, Leila assumed, and had come back with something glowing about her, even Leila had recognised it. Sally had told Leila and Aisha that everything was all right, that they were not to worry, that from now on their mama would have no more guests, ladies or gentlemen to bother them and that their home would again be the tranquil place they had known.

"But what can he want to . . . to see us about, Sally?" Leila was not at all reassured. Why couldn't Papa come here to the Grimshaw Arms? she wanted to know. Whatever it was he had to say to them, couldn't he say it here in the bar parlour, or in the little sitting-room? Her face puckered in a nervous frown and Sally was reminded of that timid child she had known two years ago. She clung to Sally's hand with both of hers.

"Please, Sally . . ."

"Darling, it will be all right, really it will. I imagine he wants to talk to you . . . about certain things he and I discussed yesterday. There are to be . . . changes at Coopers Edge."

"What sort of changes?"

"Good changes, sweetheart. I can say no more than that. Your papa will want to tell you about them himself."

"I don't want to go." The expression on Leila's young face had turned sullen as though she would dearly like to strike at something that she still did not trust. Her bottom lip quivered and she bit it, then clamped her mouth into a thin line, a habit she had acquired in her Nanny Mottram days when control was needed. Aisha watched her nervously, ready to be alarmed too if Leila was.

Sally pushed a hand through her hair. Last night for the first time in months she had brushed it vigorously, as she always did, then instead of snatching it back tightly from her forehead and into a bun, had threaded it with a bit of bright ribbon at the crown of her head, allowing it to tumble in charming disarray to her shoulders. They had all been slack-jawed with astonishment, not only in the kitchen where food was being prepared for the evening custom, but in the taproom and bar parlour which were beginning to fill up. What did it mean? Job and Tilly exchanged glances in which there was a hint of hopeful excitement. She had said not a word on the matter of her visit to Coopers Edge that day, though they both understood that it was to do with Leila and what Leila had told Sally. It must have been something pretty horrendous to snap Sally out of the drifting greyness in which she had existed since she left Coopers Edge but at the same time it had lifted her spirits, put an unusual spring in her step and a light in her eye which they found to their liking. Could it mean . . .? Dare they hope . . .? Had what they prayed for, or at least Tilly had, come about at last?

The men who were clustered at the bar counter that evening couldn't believe their eyes, for none of them, even the ones who had drunk there in Sally Grimshaw's hey-day, had ever seen her with her hair in that spectacular fall of curling light before. Amber, dark gold, some shade of tawny red and streaks of pale gold glinted in the last of the dying rays of the sun which fell through the window and the lamplight which Jack Hodges had just lit.

"Good evening, gentlemen," she called, tossing her spectacular hair as she came out from the kitchen. "Now then, who's next?"

"Bloody hell," Percy Carswell said out loud. The tankard of foaming ale he was about to put to his lips tipped sideways and he had spilled a good quarter of a pint before he noticed it splashing on to his boots.

"That'll be enough of that, Mr Carswell, if you don't mind. You know I don't care for language in my bar and those particular words are not suited to mixed company," indicating with a graceful sweep of her hand the presence of herself, Tilly and Polly.

"She'll wash yer mouth out wi' soap an' water if yer not careful, Percy," Arnie Thwaites tittered, inadvisedly.

"And I don't care for impertinence, either, Mr Thwaites. You should know that by now."

"Sorry, Miss Grimshaw," both Arnie and Percy mumbled, then shuffled thankfully away from the bar counter.

She was certainly her old self again, Arnie remarked to his drinking companions, vigorous with her tongue and with her opinions, ready to discipline any man who became unruly or what she considered to be over-familiar. But there was something added to her tartness now which . . . softened it. An inclination to smile a bit when she rebuked you, more than a hint of tolerant good humour in her manner and once, when she caught Arnie gawping at her in confusion over something she said, she even winked at him. He found himself watching her, quite fascinated as she whisked about the taproom, collecting tankards, wiping over the tables with her old briskness. She wore what she had always worn ever since Arnie had started to drink at the Grimshaw Arms: a plain, dark skirt over black boots, with a crisp white blouse buttoned up tight beneath her chin, but that glorious hair, that bit of bright ribbon transformed her.

It was funny really, the regulars said in little asides to one another, but they'd always thought of Sally Grimshaw as a plain little woman with nothing much about her to draw any man's eye, but this evening, those who stepped out of her brisk way remarked, they were amazed at how bonny she looked. Say what you like about Sally Grimshaw, who had married a man who already had a wife and two legitimate children, and who had foisted a couple of bastards on Sally, she gave good value for money as far as gossip was concerned. But then she'd always given good value for money in everything she did.

The girls had gone, unwillingly, sitting straight-backed in the carriage, two exquisite little creatures with troubled faces, the noonday sun putting a bright red light in their gleaming hair. They went because they had confidence in her and because she had told them, believing it to be true, that there was nothing to fear now at Coopers Edge. They were to trust their papa. She did, and tomorrow, when they called in on their way home from school *she* had something to discuss with them as well. She had kissed them and hugged them and told them to put their faith in her, and in their papa. She had waved them off and then gone into the kitchen to put a batch of biscuits into the oven.

Still she said nothing to Tilly and Job, moving about the place with that air of having a secret, some private truth which made her sigh and smile when she thought no one was looking. She took her children down to the orchard, treading lightly, unthinkingly over Richard Keene's grave, chasing the twins' unsteady progress down the path until they squealed like two little piglets.

"What's up, d'you reckon?" Tilly whispered to Job as they watched her go from the scullery window of the cottage. Tilly was, as usual, performing some completely unnecessary task about the scullery, like a child with a new toy who cannot bear to leave it alone and Job was watching her indulgently. Now that she was to bear his child, which was a miracle to him who had known no family since he was a lad, his love for her grew with each day. She was a lovely woman, pretty in her face but lovely inside herself with that simple goodness mixed with a tendency towards laughter and common sense which drew folk to her. The death of Richard Keene and their involvement in it, though it had distressed her at the time, had been put resolutely from her mind. There was nothing she could do about it. It had happened and was done with so best not dwell on it. That was her maxim in life no matter what had occurred, big or little, and it had stood her in good stead. No use crying over spilt milk, her mam used to say and so she didn't!

Job was content with her, content with his work and this cottage which neither he nor Tilly could resist fussing over. As they sat together of an afternoon when they had a few minutes to spare, they were for ever planning this or that or the other, something to improve the place and the thought that they might have to leave it soon came hard to them. Neither one of them considered for a minute that if that time came they were quite entitled, should they wish to, to remain here and work for the Hodges.

A couple of weeks after Keene's death two gentlemen, who appeared to be some kind of investigators, had called at the inn, saying they were looking for a horseman who had been seen riding in this direction a while ago. The rider and his horse had, apparently, vanished off the face of the earth and his solicitors were anxious to trace him. The two men showed a great deal of interest when it was revealed to them by Jack who, as landlord, was chosen to speak to them, that the gentleman had indeed been here that day. Jack did not mention the "bit of trouble", though, and neither did Polly who was a bright girl, since it was nothing to do with anybody, especially as Jack and Polly, with Miss Grimshaw, whose reputation was unblemished – at least in this regard – described with evident truthfulness how the gentleman had ridden away from the inn, his horse beneath him. The investigators had gone away satisfied.

It was this that gave a sense of peaceful security to Job and Tilly Hawthorne. The knowledge that that part of Job's life was done with, that he was free now to get on with the rest of it which could only be better . . . if only . . . if only . . .

It was Mrs Trimble who brought the news. She was a bit later than usual, she apologised to her sister as she panted up the steep stairs and into Ruth's bedroom.

Sally and Tilly had just bathed Ruth's increasingly flaccid body, exchanging pitying glances across her back as they sat her up to put a clean nightgown on her. Nearly three months she had been in this bed and still no improvement and her increasingly lethargic attitude, her listless indifference to all that went on about her, was a clear indication that her hope of ever being what she once had been was rapidly draining away. Sally knew that if something positive wasn't done soon to help Ruth she would simply die as it is possible to do if there is nothing to live for. She had an idea in her head and she meant to put it to Jack before long and it had to do with the small parlour at the side of the kitchen. The idea was that a bed could be put up which, after a while might become a couch and then a deep chair from where, if Sally's gamble paid off, Ruth could take hold of her life again and direct it and her Jack and the running of the inn as she once had done. Soon it must be, for Sally Grimshaw would not be here for much longer.

"Oh, Mrs Cooper," Mrs Trimble exclaimed with her loyal determination to show the woman who she still insisted was the mistress of Coopers Edge the respect she deserved, "you're up here." Her usually open face was wary, her eyes shifting in a most unusual way from Sally to Ruth and back again.

"Indeed," Sally answered, ready to smile in that strange and secret way which had been with her for the past twenty-four hours. "Shouldn't I be?"

"No . . . I mean yes. But I thought . . . well . . ."

Sally straightened up slowly. She gave the sheet she had just tucked under the feather mattress an extra pat without looking at it, her eyes clinging to those of Evelyn Trimble.

"What is it, Mrs Trimble? You seem . . . nervous."

"No . . . well, it's just that . . . oh, glory, it's no use." Mrs Trimble sighed then sat down heavily in the chair beside the bed, watched intently by the three other women.

"I'm late because I got held up by . . . by . . . Doris, my scullery maid whose sister Mary is laundry maid at Coopers Edge. You'll remember Mary, Mrs Cooper."

"Yes, yes, go on . . ."

"It's Mary's afternoon off and as they've no family close enough to visit I let Mary come over and visit Doris. Well, I can't have two young girls wandering about . . ."

"Mrs Trimble, for God's sake, never mind Mary and Doris. What's happened at Coopers Edge?"

Sally's hands clenched in their need to reach out to Mrs Trimble and shake the words out of her. Her body felt as though it would snap in two she held it so rigidly and her face had drained of all colour. She had felt it go. In her eyes was the silent message which begged Mrs Trimble not to burden her with any more pain since she simply could not cope with it.

"Eeh, lass," said Mrs Trimble, forgetting her place in her compassion. She read the message in Sally's eyes and in her own was one that said she'd give a year's wages to spare her but it had to be told.

"What, for God's sake. What?"

"Well, Mary doesn't go into the house much, as you know, but she heard Alec tell Jimmy that . . . that madam had gone off her head." Mrs Trimble shrugged uneasily.

"Gone off her head?" Sally stared stupidly at Mrs Trimble.

"I don't know in what way, Mrs Cooper, only that she seems to . . . to have lost her mind, though if you want my opinion she's always . . ."

"The . . . girls?"

"Lass, that's all I know. There's trouble up there, it seems, and someone's got to see to it."

Someone's got to see to it! The words clattered in her head in time to the rhythm of her feet as she ran down the stairs, Tilly so close behind her they were both in danger of tripping. Someone's got to see to it. Mrs Trimble's voice kept on and on repeating the same words over and over again until there was nothing but them in Sally's demented mind. Others jostled to be heard, others which said that this was Sally Grimshaw's fault and so it was only right that Sally Grimshaw should put it right. It was she who had sent them back there. True, it was at Adam's request but between them they had once more put those two stricken children – stricken by who their mother was – into a position which was fraught with danger. She had done her best to protect them ever since that day when the carriage had deposited them on the doorstep of the inn. She'd provided them with a bolt-hole to which they might come at need, a sort of haven, a place of security which, quite simply, had not been enough. She'd promised Leila safety, protection, wrongly impressing on the child that Sally Grimshaw's promises were rock solid and therefore Leila had nothing further to worry about.

Dear God . . . oh, dear God, what had she done? How could she? How could she be so careless, not only with these children's lives, but with all the people she loved, the dearest, of course, being Adam. People mattered, not convention or what society might think. Good God, did she give a fig for what Mr and Mrs Richard Porter's opinion of her might be, the Mr and Mrs Richard Porter who had come nowhere near her since she left Coopers Edge? Did she give a damn what the code of conduct should be, what social mores must be adhered to? And the answer was of course she didn't. This was her family who needed her and she had deserted them, turned away in her pride . . . yes, *pride*, her arrogance, her belief that honour, righteousness, doing the right thing was more important than they were. May God forgive her.

It was time now to make that commitment!

"Run for a cab, Polly," she yelled at the barmaid who almost dropped the glass she was dreamily polishing. Jack popped his head out of the kitchen, the expression on his face one of consternation, for if Miss Grimshaw was off somewhere in a cab who was to prepare the pease pudding and faggots, the sausage dumplings she had promised him? Job, hearing her shout and recognising trouble when it rose up and bit him, came thundering up from the cellar, his battered face twisted in alarm.

"A cab," Polly repeated.

"Lord, give me patience," Sally snarled through gritted teeth. "You know what a bloody cab is, don't you?" and in the corner where he had just lifted his first pint to his lips Arnie Thwaites gasped out loud.

It barely registered that travelling in the cab with her were Job and Tilly, Tilly still wearing her apron. Job had been her support and protector for so long now, the staunch prop on whom she could always rely no matter what, and now there was Tilly who had taken on the same role.

If it occurred to her to wonder who at the Grimshaw Arms was to mind her babies she certainly did not voice it. She was aware of nothing but her desperate need to get to the rest of her family who needed her. She didn't know why, or how, she only knew that her every nerve was stretched to the dashing gallop of the horses' hooves, willing it to go faster. Her face was pressed, white and frightened, to the window and when the animal pulling the wildly swinging cab surged up the drive of Coopers Edge and drew to a violent halt she was halfway up the steps to the front door before it came to its final slithering stop.

The hallway seemed to be crowded with a multitude of people, silent and waiting, presumably for someone to tell them what to do. Servants, for that was who they were, clustered in a shifting knot at the bottom of the stairs and in the shadows at the back there were other figures whom Sally could not make out. The cook and her niece had sat down in two of the comfortable leather armchairs which were placed beside the empty fireplace as though to ensure that the pair of them had the best seats in the house. They did not get up when Sally flung herself through the front door, not knowing at that point who she was; indeed they were enchanted with this unexpected break in the monotonous routine of their day, telling one another that they'd certainly have something to entertain their Nelly with when next they saw her.

It looked as though Henton, who leaned wearily against the newel post of the banister, and Maddy were ready to weep by the dread expression on their faces. Maddy was perched forlornly on the bottom step of the staircase, her head in her hands. Sitting close to her was a maid Sally didn't know, a comforting arm about Maddy's shoulders. The figures hovering by the green baize door which led into the kitchen, looking awkward and out of place and smelling strongly of the stables, turned out to be Jimmy, Alec and John.

As though, at last, here was someone to be relied on to solve this dreadful dilemma that had them by the throat they all, bar the cook and her niece, turned thankfully to Mrs Cooper, *their* Mrs Cooper. Their faces sagged with relief and they all began to speak at once. For several moments she let them, too overwhelmed by the unreality of the moment to stop them.

"Oh, madam, what are we to do?"

"She just ran mad and we couldn't stop her."

"God knows what she had in them bottles."

"And when we saw that there knife we just ran for our lives, didn't we, Agnes?"

"Nearly died of fright, I can tell you."

"We 'eard the screamin' clear over in the stable block."

"I said to Jimmy we'd best get . . ."

"Lost her wits, madam."

"Like a banshee wailing. I tell you I never want . . ."

It was as though her appearance had uncorked whatever it was they had been holding inside them and they began to turn to one another, exchanging experiences.

"Did you see her face? It gave me the fright of me life."

"Aged twenty years, she had, with her hair . . . screaming she'd kill every last one who got in her way . . ."

"Poor Tipper got the worst."

"And the master."

The roar that emerged from Job's mouth shocked them all, even Sally. Maddy began to cry in earnest, shushed patiently by the unknown maid, but the silence which fell was a blessed relief.

"Now then," Job said more calmly, "let's have the story one by one, starting with you." He pointed at Henton who didn't seem to be offended at being spoken to like that by the man who had been odd-job "lad" at Coopers Edge. It was as though their roles were reversed.

"Well, I was in the kitchen and when . . ."

"Briefly, please, Job," Sally managed to say with a calm she did not feel. The remark about poor Tipper getting the worst of something terrified her but even more terrifying was her total ignorance about what had happened, or was happening to Adam, Leila and Aisha.

"Aye, lass, that's best," Job agreed.

It seemed that Mr Saunders the solicitor had called early that morning and had been closeted with the master in his study for an hour or so. They had then both gone upstairs to speak to Mrs Cooper. It had taken Maddy and Mrs Cooper's personal maid a long time to rouse her and get her into a condition in which the master and Mr Saunders could talk to her, which they did, Henton confirmed, for another hour. There was a lot of shouting, not on the master's or Mr Saunders's part, he hastened to add, leaving them in no doubt who had been the cause of the trouble, then Mr Saunders had left. They had served lunch to the master, and the young ladies had come home but upstairs it was as quiet as the grave. Maddy, with Agnes, who had sworn there was nothing in the world would get her up those stairs on her own, had knocked at madam's door to ask if she wanted lunch but there had been no answer and then, just as they were turning thankfully away, like some apparition from your worst nightmare, Maddy sobbed, interrupting Henton's recital since after all she had been there and he had not, the door had opened and there she was.

It was then she had run amok, as Maddy put it, and had, for over an hour, gone from room to room leaving a trail of destruction behind her that had to be seen to be believed. She never wanted to have to go through it again, Maddy told them all and if madam could see all them lovely things smashed to pieces it'd break her heart. The master had followed her, doing his best to calm her but it was like asking the waves not to crash on to the shore. And then that knife. God in heaven, that knife! She didn't know how the master had kept out of its way, really she didn't.

"Oh, madam . . ." Her sobs were verging on hysteria but the other maid shuffled her into her arms and they clung together for comfort and support.

"Where is she now?"

No one seemed prepared to tell her. Their eyes would not

meet hers and the heavy dread that had settled in her heart when Mrs Trimble had told her of the trouble at Coopers Edge hardened and weighed her down as though it was made of granite.

"Where is the captain?" Job asked for her since he knew she was unable to speak.

They all began to babble at once then. He was upstairs. Oh, yes – Henton almost called Job "sir" in his distress – the captain was unhurt, thank God, though young Tipper, who had for some reason thought he might be able to soothe her, had run up to help and had been stabbed in the hand when he attempted to lay it on madam's arm. Lunged at him, she did, and said . . . well, Henton could not bring himself to repeat it in front of decent females what Mrs Cooper had said to Tipper, but suffice it to say that he had been shocked to the core of his elderly heart. Tipper was in the kitchen being tended to by Annie, the dairymaid, he told them, who was a steady, sensible sort of lass. The doctor had been sent for and . . . well, he had had no instructions from the captain who had his hands full at the moment, but did madam think the police should be sent for? With Mrs Cooper so violent surely . . . He left the question unfinished.

"Where is the captain?" she asked him. There was another question going round and round in her head like a merry-go-round at a fairground, a question which she knew she must put to him, one it seemed she could not bring herself to ask. It was a simple question. It had four words in it, the most difficult words she would ever have to speak, but speak she must. The thing was, the answer might be more than she could bear.

"Where is . . . Mrs Cooper?"

Maddy turned her blotched face into the maid's shoulder and moaned.

It was the cook who answered since she cared nought for this woman who had once, so it was said, been mistress here.

"She's in't nursery an' them girls is with 'er."

28

She swayed and would have fallen had Job not put his arm round her, but this was no time for weakness, she told herself as she thrust him away from her. Pushing past Maddy and the other maidservant who still cowered together on the bottom step she picked up her skirts and flew up the stairs, watched by ten pairs of startled eyes.

Hesitating for a moment at the top as though she knew she were about to see something that would devastate her, she began to walk slowly along the corridor. Doors to the bedrooms stood open, the doors themselves slashed and scored and inside them as she went by she caught glimpses of the destruction, as though some demon had gained entrance and, once in, had run amok. Delicate porcelain ornaments, silver hand mirrors and hairbrushes, china candlesticks, crystal scent bottles, boxes and caskets of silver gilt, pot-pourri bowls, pictures from the walls, fans, dainty clocks and lamps had been swept by some demented hand into an appalling broken tangle of devastation, scattering carpets with shards of glass and porcelain. Slim-legged rosewood tables had been flung at the walls and bed and window curtains torn down. Lovely quilted bedspreads, generations old, hand-made by scores of Cooper women, had been slashed to ribbons and Sally brooded on the strength of one woman who had, unchecked, it seemed, done all this.

For the space of perhaps ten seconds she stood at the door of the lovely bedroom which she had shared with Adam. It was as though a shell had hit it, shattering every piece of furniture and well-loved object she and Adam had chosen together. Even the silk walls had been daubed with something she could not bring herself to investigate.

Inside her some small thing began to quiver and grow icy, like a ball of snow which gathers more to itself as it rolls downhill. It filled her so that there seemed to be no room for anything like heart or ribs or lungs, threatening to choke her and she recognised it for what it was. A bitter, corroding hatred for the woman who had done this. A scalding rage that was on the verge of an explosion and it was directed at Oralie Cooper. The blood in her veins was hot, driving to every part of her body so she felt that if anyone touched her she would burn them. The heat of it melted away the snowball inside her and she bared her teeth like a she wolf protecting her cubs. This was her home that had been desecrated, her life, her place, the place in which she had loved and been loved, cherished, valued, and now some foul thing was trying to destroy it. She shook her head as though to clear it and, still ready to snarl her defiance, she prepared to defend it.

Job was behind her. She felt his supportive strength at her back and heard his gasp of outrage as he saw the shambles of the bedrooms. He put a hand on her arm as though to restrain her but she shook it off as she had done in the hall and began to leap up the stairs to the nursery floor.

Adam was outside the closed door of the day nursery, his forehead pressed to the panels, one arm cradling the other as though to protect it. He was speaking soothingly through the wood to whoever was on the other side of it, his voice soft and repetitive as though he had been at this for a long time and he was becoming hypnotised by it himself.

It was dim in the narrow passage with no light beyond what fell from a high window in the sloping roof. All the doors were closed, including those which led into the servants quarters at the back of the house. Shadows seemed to fall, stretching threateningly along the landing, grey and drifting, like mist, and Adam seemed to be surrounded by them. It was her imagination, she knew it, brought on by a sense of foreboding, a brooding, silent feeling as if at impending danger. There was nothing there really, only the gloom of the darkened passage but she felt as though she had walked into the cold mists of hell.

"Open the door, Oralie," Adam was saying. His face was as white as freshly fallen snow and beads of sweat trickled down his cheeks like tears. "Please, Oralie, won't you let me in? No one's going to hurt you but you are . . . frightening the children. They need to come out . . . they are . . . they've hurt no one. Please, Oralie, unlock the door and let me talk to you."

Strain showed in the rigidity of his bent back and legs and he gulped on the words, his throat working. Sally could see the muscles in it quiver with tension and, as quietly as she could, since she did not want to alarm whoever was on the other side of the door, she moved towards him and gently placed a hand on his braced back. He jumped violently and drew in his breath with a hiss as she touched him. His haunted face turned towards her. His eyes were deep, black pits in his death-like face and he smelled of the sweat of his own fear.

The front of his shirt was dark with something that she recognised with a thrill of horror as blood.

For a moment, when he saw who it was, she could see

the relief in his eyes and he sagged as though he would fall but she put her arms about him and held him steady. His head sank to her shoulder and she felt the shuddering in him as though, having held himself together for so long he would dearly love to let go. He began to slip towards the floor then he straightened up again, remembering himself and his need not to be weakened by this beloved woman who, he was well aware, would willingly take the load he carried. He made a great effort to hold himself upright.

"She has a knife," he mouthed, his face flinching in a spasm of pain as he leaned towards Sally's ear. "The girls . . ."

"You must come with me, Adam, you're hurt." She tried to draw him away but he resisted as though, should he leave his post some dreadful thing was bound to happen. He was on guard here, doing his best to protect his family, his children, his very life from whatever lay beyond the door and Sally's pleading must be ignored.

"No," he mouthed again, "she has a knife."

"We know, darling." She held him to her, fighting him, since he was determined not to leave. "But you're bleeding. Job will stay."

"You don't understand, I must keep talking to her, distract her if I can from . . . God knows what she'll do if she hears a strange voice."

"I know, my love, but you're bleeding and it must be seen to."

"A scratch, no more."

"No . . . please come . . . just for a moment," and with gentle, insistent hands she began to pull him towards the head of the stairs where Job waited to help her. All this took place in almost total silence with no more than a whisper of sound, Sally's lips against Adam's ear, his against hers. God alone knew what was happening inside that silent room but whatever it was she did not want to make it worse by letting the mad woman who held her own children at knife-point know that there was anyone but Adam here. At the same time Adam might be bleeding to death of whatever injury she had inflicted on him and it must be staunched.

They got him to the bottom of the nursery floor stairs and because he was frantic to get back to his post at the door, his soldier's training gave him the decisiveness to tell her and Job briefly what had happened. Not that they needed much explanation really since the evidence of it was before their eyes but there were details only Adam could supply.

"It's laudanum. She's been taking it, and sometimes, so she told me, opium itself from which the laudanum comes. Keene supplied her, apparently." His breathing was becoming laboured and when she put a hand to his shoulder, he groaned out loud. "He's . . . well, God only knows where he's got to . . ."

"He's dead."

"What?" For a second he was distracted from his own story.

"Never mind, I'll tell you about it later but won't you let me look at your wound?"

He took no notice. "She'd come to the end of it and . . . this" – indicating his shoulder – "is the result, though what Saunders and I discussed with her didn't help. She was told she was to go . . . leave Coopers Edge. Saunders spoke of finances and, knowing her addiction, said she would not be . . . that there would be money enough to supply it. He threatened her, if she would not go peaceably, with the asylum."

Bowing his head he slid slowly down the wall until he rested on his haunches, his hands on his knees. His whole body trembled and shook but making a tremendous effort he dragged it under control.

"She went berserk . . . it tipped her over the edge and without the drug she could not . . . she took a knife to Tipper when he came up to help me, then, on a mad spree of destruction began to smash . . . well, you saw. I was afraid to take my eyes off her . . . she had the knife, you see. Something she must have picked up in India, an enormous, long-bladed thing with a jewelled hilt. I was afraid to shout for the men for fear of making her worse, if such a thing was possible," he said bitterly. "I thought I could catch her when she tired but . . . but when I tried, she gave me this. Oh, Jesus God, before I could get a proper hold on her she was up the stairs and into the . . . the nursery. The girls were screaming . . . she locked both the doors and . . . Oh, God, Sally, if she kills them . . ." He rocked back and forth in his despair.

"Hush, hush, she's not going to kill them, I promise you that."

There you go again, her astonished mind said to her, making pledges you don't know you can keep. They might already be dead, her mind went on, dispassionately this time, but what else was she to say to this demented man who was on the edge of insanity himself? It was a woman's instinct to calm and soothe and comfort, in any way she could, and there might be more needed of her later than she could comprehend right now. But she must get them through this, this moment, this catastrophe and it did no good bogging herself down with possibilities which might not happen.

"Let me see what she did to . . ."

"I must get back."

"You must have your wound seen to. Job, run for Tilly. Tell her to fetch bandages."

"I must get back, Sally. Who knows what . . ."

"Be quiet and stop being the bloody hero. If you faint you'll be no good to anyone so sit still and do as you're told." With fingers which were remarkably steady she quickly undid the buttons of his blood-soaked shirt, doing her best not to gasp at what it revealed. The knife had slashed his shoulder. There was a deep ragged furrow across the top to the front and blood was running freely down his chest.

Adam was still rambling incoherently and she thought he was ready to lapse into an almost unconscious state so deep was his shock.

There was a rustle of skirts and a white apron appeared beside them. It squatted down and before Sally had time to register who it was, Tilly's voice hissed in her ear.

"Aye up," she said astonishingly, "let the dog see the rabbit." Adam had slipped away into darkness for a moment and while he slumped against Job who held him steady they mopped his wound and pressed a thick wad of clean lint against it. Tying it up as best they could with strips of linen, Sally was pleased with the results. It would stop the bleeding and would do until the doctor came to stitch it.

"I've fetched the brandy, Miss Sally," Job breathed in her ear.

"Good lad," blessing the forthright comfort of these two people who gave her so much and yet asked so little.

Adam had come round, blinking and wincing with pain, but with almost a full glass of brandy inside him he was able to stand up. The whole exercise had taken no more than five minutes.

Job took over now. "Is Alice with the girls?" he asked crisply.

"Yes."

"Good, she'll steady them."

"I must get back."

"Yes, talk to her, sir, keep her attention." Though there was no fear that Oralie Cooper could hear them down here, Job's voice was quiet but its very quietness and certainty seemed to put a stiffener in Adam's spine and he straightened up. "Try and get her to the door, if you can. Make her speak so that you know where she is."

"Christ, man, I'm afraid to tip her over." Adam was in an agony of fear, but just the knowledge that he was no longer alone had brought some colour to his face.

"I know, sir, but there's no hope of us getting in that way, not without a diversion. Who knows what she might do if we broke the door down and . . ."

"It's so bloody silent. You don't think she's . . .?"

"No, sir. There would have been . . . cries."

Sally's terror, which had been pushed into the background as she dealt with Adam, flooded over her again. Her mouth was so dry she could not have answered if someone had asked a question of her but her mind was clear and sharp as an icicle. The rage continued to simmer somewhere inside her and her teeth had a tendency to break into a mild and sporadic chattering, but she was calm, steady, prepared for that moment when she meant to get her hands on the woman who had caused so much devastation to so many lives. A trail of broken people gathered behind her, people she had shattered with her casual indifference to the suffering she had caused them and if there was one certainty in Sally Grimshaw's cold mind it was that she would never do it again. If she had a gun she would shoot her. Adam's guns were locked up in the gun cupboard in his study and God knew where he kept the key but if there had been a chance for her to get hold of it she would have made sure that, like Keene, Oralie Cooper would never trouble her daughters again. A sword would do, that one Adam had hung up on the study wall but she had no time now to fetch it. She couldn't leave Adam. She must go with him, stand by him outside the nursery door, defend him with her own life if she must, for her life was worth nothing if he was not in it.

"Go now, both of you," Job whispered. "Keep her . . . well, talk to her . . . keep her attention." He smiled encouragingly, that rare, sweet smile that gave his damaged face a strange beauty, then, turning on his heel, he ran lightly along the corridor and down the stairs, Tilly's hand in his.

Sally stood beside Adam and kept her arm about him as he talked and talked through the door into the total silence beyond, saying nothing much beyond the repetitive plea to the woman on the other side to unlock it and talk to him. Hours passed, days, or so it seemed in the misted dislocation of time that she and Adam dwelled in. Adam's hoarse voice droned on and on and she felt him begin to sway as shock and fear, exhaustion and loss of blood laid claim to him. Her arms tightened about him and it appeared to strengthen him as he continued to talk to the unseen mad woman who was his wife.

Once Sally thought she heard the sound of a whimper from somewhere and later a noise which might have been the almost silent snarl of a cat, but there were no cats at Coopers Edge, only those in the stable to keep the mice down. From far off in the deep recesses of the house came the faint echo of a crash, not loud and not recognisable and she wondered what it could be, but she was not unduly concerned with it since it was not happening here.

She was considerably startled when, on feet as light as the feathers on a bird's wing, several figures crept up the stairs and gathered on the landing. Adam had his forehead still pressed to the door, his voice murmuring through it and did not appear to notice. One of the figures was Alec and another was Jimmy, another John and the fourth Noah from the stables. They were carrying between them a couple of heavy objects and when Sally looked more closely she recognised them as hefty sawn-off logs about three feet long. The rest of the men, three or four, it was difficult to see how many on the darkened landing, gathered beside them. They appeared to be wearing a uniform of sorts. They were authoritative, motioning to the stable lads to position themselves before the two doors, one into the day nursery, the other the night nursery. Briskly and wordlessly they moved herself and Adam to one side as they themselves slid silently into place. They seemed to be waiting for a signal, poised and motionless and when it came she and Adam flinched, for it was as though someone had put a match to a barrel of gunpowder inside the nursery. She could hear thin screams of terror, recognising Aisha's voice and had time to breathe a silent prayer of thanks that she at least was still alive. The noise reverberated under the roof of the house as though trying to find a way out and instantly the stable men rammed the logs they carried against the two doors, smashing them open. With a great shouting surge all the men heaved and jostled to get through the day nursery door which hung on its hinges. A similar drama was taking place at the door to the night nursery further along the corridor but it seemed that none of these men, even those from the stable who were their own men, concerned Sally Grimshaw or Adam Cooper. It was as though, having been subjected to more than human minds and bodies could be expected to bear, some power inside them both had been released, giving them the strength to push aside the men in the doorway and be first into the room.

Sally didn't know she was snarling like some animal which

is being baited by a pack of dogs. Her lip had lifted back over her teeth and her narrowed eyes were slits of pure venom and on the far side of the room where the door which connected the two nurseries stood open, another woman with the exact same expression on her face began to scream. At the window where he was outlined against the softly pink fading of the evening sky, Job put his shoulder to the window and with scarcely any effort smashed it inwards. He leaped through the ruined window frame, still holding the smoking rifle, the shot from which had been the signal for the attack.

He began to yell, a diversion, Sally was aware in some cool corner of her mind, a full-throated yell which filled the room so that the thunder of it confused them all for a moment, turning even Oralie Cooper towards him and away from her purpose. The knife in her upraised hand faltered and with the presence of mind and swiftness of the experienced soldier he was, Adam Cooper was upon her.

The screams lifted the hairs on Sally's arms and neck, wild, high screams. One of the men in uniform was shouting, presumably to Adam to "stand back, sir, if you please, we'll deal with this," but he might just as well have broken into a chorus of "Rule Britannia" for all the good it did.

In the corner Alice Cartwright, who was willing to give her own life to protect those of her charges, looked like a woman who had just been crucified, her arms outstretched, her feet braced, her face contorted into an expression which was strangely similar to the one Sally Grimshaw bore. Behind her, crouched against one another, their eyes dark with shock, were Leila and Aisha Cooper.

It all seemed to happen so slowly, Sally was to say to herself afterwards as she brooded on that terrible moment, and yet Job moved with the speed of a panther as he gathered the three of them up and flung them through the now empty doorway of the night nursery into the waiting arms of Tilly and the stable lads. Sally could hear his voice as it always was, gentle, patient, comforting as he handed the girls to his wife, then he turned in readiness to take on Oralie Cooper who was doing her utmost to kill her own husband. The sight of her was enough to chill the blood of the most courageous, Sally had to admit and perhaps it was this which held the men bolted to the floor. Oralie's long, wine red hair was loose and drifting about her ravaged face and from beneath it her eyes glared, colourless and transparent in her bone-white face. Her mouth was stretched back over her teeth which seemed to be long and pointed and from between them hung strings of saliva.

Sally's whole attention was concentrated on the dreadful battle that was taking place. Adam was a soldier, trained to defend himself, but he was injured and had lost a lot of blood. Sally could see it bursting through the fold of his shirt, beginning to drip and spray about the room. Oralie, who, in her madness, had the strength of ten, was beginning to bear him down to his knees. The knife was above her head in her right hand and Adam held her right wrist with both of his as he did his best to stop that slashing blade from being plunged into his neck, but he was rapidly weakening.

'Stand back, sir, please," the uniformed man entreated, evidently waiting for an appropriate moment in which to take over. He had a revolver which he was directing at the panting, struggling couple, intending, Sally presumed with that part of her mind which appeared to be functioning on another level, to take a shot at Oralie, perhaps wound her so that she might be disarmed but her damn fool husband, the man's expression was saying, who'd been told to leave this to them, was in the way.

There was a hearth tidy standing by the coal scuttle in

the fireplace. It contained a brush to sweep the ashes from the grate, tongs to lift the coals and a poker, heavy with brass. The men were hopping from foot to foot, ready, the moment they had a chance without injuring Captain Cooper, to move in and grab the demented woman who was doing her best to knife him, but Sally Grimshaw's husband, as she knew him truly to be, was not going to survive Oralie's murderous attack unless someone was willing to risk their life to stop her.

They did not see her reach for the poker, nor hear the faint tinkle its removal from the stand made but they heard the sound a solid object makes when it connects with bone. They watched with horrified disbelief as Oralie Cooper dropped silently to the floor, followed by the massive poker Sally Grimshaw had hit her with.

They did not see Oralie go. They did not see the horse-drawn police waggon drive away nor the closed carriage in which the doctor and a woman attendant had charge of the unconscious patient. Alice, God bless and keep her, was in a state of nervous shock now that it was all over, and needed attention, and Maddy was not much better though she had barely been involved.

"It was that knife . . ." she kept on telling them again and again but Agnes, who had been Oralie Cooper's personal maid and who, it seemed to Sally, had a bit of spunk in her and might make a halfway decent maid with a bit of training, drew her away to the kitchen. Tipper was there with his hand in a neat bandage, already beginning to preen a bit over his part in the melodrama.

He was considerably startled, and voluble in his protestation of innocence, when Mr Henton told him he was sacked.

"What, after all I done . . ."

"That just it, lad, you've done a sight too much I'm thinking, and we won't stand for anything like that at Coopers Edge."

"Like what, Mr Henton?"

"You know what I mean. Go and pack your bags and be off with you. And I'm sure Mrs Cooper won't want to be bothered speaking to you before you go either."

"Mrs Cooper?" Tipper's jaw dropped.

"Yes, she's in residence again and things'll be very different now."

They stood side by side in the drawing-room, their arms about one another looking down at the feather mattress on which the sleeping young girls lay. Adam had been stitched and bound up and ordered most strenuously by the doctor to stay on that damned sofa until a bed could be found for him. A fine state of affairs, he'd declared, when a bed was not available to a man in his own home and it seemed Adam Cooper was of the same opinion.

"It's been three months, lovely girl and I'm starved for you." His mouth was warm in the tumble of her hair and his hand reached to caress the back of her neck.

"The doctor didn't mean that, Adam Cooper," she said tartly, though her own flesh was on fire at his touch. That secret tender place only Adam knew shivered with delight and her nipples rose as if in anticipation.

"Bugger the doctor," he said rudely. "My love . . ." His voice sank to a whisper though both the girls were deeply asleep. "Oh my love, I need you so."

"Darling, you have me. I am here and will not go away ever again. Besides, you have stitches. You have lost a lot of blood and are as weak as a kitten. If I wasn't here you'd fall over."

"Exactly, you're strong enough for both of us. I could lie down as the doctor instructed and you could do the rest. I promise I won't struggle."

"Adam Cooper . . ." She began to giggle. "You really are . . ."

"I know, but you must admit it holds a certain . . . attraction."

"You really believe you could?"

"I *know* I could, with a bit of help."

"Adam . . ."

"Sally, lovely girl . . ."

"Well . . ."

The servants in the kitchen, those that were left since Mrs Cooper had sent the cook and her niece packing, exchanged glances, not at all surprised when their mistress put her head round the kitchen door and asked would one of them keep an eye on her daughters. *Her* daughters, mind! She gave no explanation and they needed none.

She was home. It was enough.